More
Than Beauty
#1
10-26-24

MORE THAN PARADISE

WATCHDOG SECURITY SERIES: BOOK 4

OLIVIA MICHAELS

FALCON IN HAND PUBLISHING

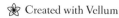

ONE

He's in the garden again. Paradise. The warm night air caresses his bare skin while a cool breeze teases him. He's searching for her like he always does, acutely aware that this time it's real, it's not the dream he's had a thousand times since reaching his twenties.

Impossible.

He feels the soft grass under his feet as he pads silently down a path through lush vegetation, the tangy green smell of crushed leaves rising around him with each step. He smells jasmine too—her scent—sweet and clean but undeniably sexy. It stirs him until he groans.

He must find her. Find her and make her his own. Though she's always belonged to him, as he belongs to her.

In his dreams, she's searching for him as ardently as he pursues her jasmine-and-salt smell. He waits to hear his name among the sound of crickets chirping and night birds singing. Will she call him this time, now that she's real, now that this is happening? Does she still love him, as she claimed to when they first kissed as young teenagers?

Impossible. She's only a dream.

And then he hears it—her soft voice saying his name. The breeze picks up and he can smell her skin. *Real this time,* he thinks. *Finally real, finally mine.*

He steps out from under the rhododendrons and she stands naked like him. Her back is to him, her body silhouetted in the moonlight—the cello-shaped curves so familiar. She turns and reaches out when she sees him. In a moment they are in each other's arms and he's kissing her. His erection pushes against her belly and she presses back, stands on her tiptoes slowly so that her skin glides against his shaft. He moans into her mouth, tasting her sweetness, his senses lost in her presence. His hands slide down until he's cupping her bottom. He lifts her and she wraps her legs tightly around his waist. He slips effortlessly inside her as she sighs.

His paradise. His home. So real, at last.

She whispers how much she loves him, how she's missed him all this time and he wants to tell her he's dreamed of her so many times but the tight warmth surrounding him takes away his breath until he's pushing deeper. So close to ecstasy, he begins to say her name...

...and realizes when he can't remember it, that this is yet another dream. Another fantasy. Unreal.

The garden fades even as he tries to grip her tighter. The moonlight becomes morning light seeping around his curtains. The hum of crickets is an oscillating fan, her salt-and-jasmine smell his own sweat soaking into the bedsheets mingling with a potted jasmine on the windowsill. Before the dream fades completely, he pulls his head back to look at her face, to remember her. The lost look on her face tears at his heart.

Costello woke with a pillow pressed hard against his cock and a curse on his lips. This wasn't the first time and it wouldn't be the last. He growled, punched the pillow, and headed for the shower to do something about his hard-on. He turned the cold tap on full blast and rested his forehead against the cool white tiles. *This time felt so real*, he thought.

For as long as he could remember, he'd dreamed of her in the garden. When he was a child so was she and they played in the shade of a citrus grove, climbing the trees, making up stories and games where he was a prince defending her against fierce monsters. And the fiercest, most frightening one came from a fountain in the center of the garden. It slithered from the impossibly deep water and crept through the garden, a dark shadow always watching them. Watching her and waiting for its chance to steal her away.

They grew up together in his dreams. As he became aware of girls, so she became more beautiful, more alluring. And she returned his interest. Long before he kissed a real girl in high school, they'd kissed under a full moon at the edge of the garden where a low wall protected the grounds at the edge of a cliff falling away into the Pacific.

The garden felt as real as the girl but every time he tried to remember visiting it as a child he came up with a cold, blank feeling. He could have visited it with his mom as a kid, no more than four or five, maybe six years old. But every time he'd asked his mother about the garden or the girl, she claimed she had no idea what he was talking about. *Maybe your old noggin is fooling you again, Baby Owl*, she'd say as she messed his hair up and he'd have to adjust his glasses. *We've worked in a lot of houses. Sounds like you've got them all jumbled up.* 'Work' was what she called their schemes, and what finally got him taken away from her and placed in a foster home.

He had no memories of the garden, or the girl who came to life so vividly in his dreams, who aged as he did. Over time, he came to accept it as pure fantasy.

Costello wasn't given to fantasy in his waking hours, despite his call name, Psychic. He'd earned the moniker because of his uncanny ability to know when he and his men were about to be attacked, and from where the bullets would come, or the explosion that would have taken them all out. He was the first person to tell you he didn't believe in the paranormal, or psychic abilities, or any other woo-woo New Age bullshit. He just had a near-photographic memory and incredible powers of perception. That's all. There was nothing psychic about seeing movement from the corner of his eye or remembering a face he'd seen in the market, one that shouldn't have been there ten miles away near the base.

He never told anyone about his dreams because he couldn't explain how real they were. How real *she* was. Her touch, her smell, the sound of her voice. Always consistent, detailed, down to the same mole on her shoulder dream after dream. His teammates would probably laugh, tell him that's why he couldn't stay in a relationship beyond a week. And that joke was too close to the truth. The second he dreamed of her and happened to awaken beside a different woman, he couldn't get out of there fast enough.

Showered and dressed, Costello watered the numerous plants throughout his condo's rooms and lanai. He paused at the newest ones. It wasn't the plants' fault they'd belonged to his mom—no, his *biological mother*—and he'd just inherited them, but watering them made him uneasy.

His buddies didn't know why he kept so many plants and he wasn't about to let them know that either. Anubis watched him do his rounds and if the dog judged him, he had no way of knowing. The dark-furred Malinois was as mysterious as his name. Truth be told, Costello was still trying to get used to his canine partner.

"Let's go, buddy," he told the dog, who fell into step next to him, a consummate professional. Downstairs, Costello loaded him into the SUV and chugged a protein shake on his way to work, trying not to let the dream seep into his thoughts. He was meeting a new client first thing and didn't need to be fuzzy-brained and distracted, let alone pop a boner in the middle of things.

When they got to Watchdog, Costello dropped Anubis off with Kyle, sad that his teammate was only back temporarily before moving permanently to Colorado to open a new branch of the security company.

He headed into the conference room where Lachlan already waited with the new client. A primadonna from what Costello had heard, a spoiled socialite from a high-class family. She and her mother had contacted Lachlan from Italy saying they needed a security team for their estate outside of Malibu. Apparently, she'd received threatening letters, which prompted their return Stateside and this meeting. Costello, familiar with this type of client, had already prepared his luggage, expecting to go straight to the property afterward.

"Sorry I'm late..." he started to say, when his gaze fixed on cello-shaped curves as his nostrils filled with the unmistakable perfume of salt and jasmine.

"Glad you could finally join us," Lachlan said with his usual sarcasm. "I'd like you to meet the woman you'll be guarding, Ms. Jordan Summers."

She turned from the window where she watched Kyle put the dogs through their paces in the courtyard. The fixed smile on her face froze and wonder crept into her eyes.

She looked like she recognized him. But of course, she would—he'd dreamed of her for years.

Impossible.

TWO

Costello vaguely heard Lachlan clear his throat as he stared at Jordan Summers and she stared back at him.

"Let me try again," Lachlan said, one eyebrow raised as he absently reached for the cut-down pen he used as a substitute cigarette, the one that wasn't in his mouth, that was probably hidden away in a drawer because *client*. "Jordan Summers, this is Elliot Costello...though it appears you already know each other?"

The woman looked startled, her eyes darting from Costello to Lachlan and back again.

"No, we don't," Costello said quickly. *Because how can you already know someone who doesn't exist, even if she's standing right in front of you?*

She composed herself. Pale green eyes looked away from him as Jordan turned her head to Lachlan. "If he says we haven't, we haven't."

Jesus. Even down to her voice. Costello's mind raced, looking for a logical explanation. Maybe there were just enough similarities between Ms. Summers and his dream woman that his mind was tricking him, telling him that their features matched when they didn't. But if that were the case, why hadn't it happened with other women before?

And then her words themselves hit him. Her answer wasn't exactly a no. Or a yes.

Lachlan was catching the same vibe, judging by his puzzled expression. He shrugged and gestured for them to take a seat at the conference table. Jordan walked away from the window and circled the table toward Costello. For a moment, he had the uncanny feeling that she was going to embrace him. Then he realized that she was coming around to that side so that she could keep her view out the window. He pulled out her chair and she looked up at him with eyes full of puzzlement. Well, that made two of them. She quickly looked away, back out the window, and he sat down beside her across from Lachlan. Her familiar scent teased him, bringing on a feeling like a cross between vertigo and déjà vu.

How the hell am I going to focus on anything in this meeting? He damn near pinched himself just to make sure he wasn't still dreaming. But if this were a dream, he'd take Jordan by the hand and lead her the hell out of here and back to their garden.

Jesus, Costello. Your dreams aren't real. Now listen to your boss while he tells you more about why the real-person-not-dream-girl needs your services and try not to embarrass yourself any further.

Four blue folders lay on the white-topped table. Right before Costello could ask who would be joining them, the conference room door opened and a wave of rose perfume drowned out Jordan's delicate jasmine. Costello turned to see a woman who could have been Jordan in another twenty years standing in the doorway and staring back at him, her expression unreadable. She flicked her gaze to Lachlan as the corner of her mouth turned up. "Say that you haven't started without me."

"Of course not, Mrs. Summers. We were waiting for you to rejoin us," Lach said. Costello detected a note of appeasement in his boss's voice. Nothing unusual there. Many of their high-profile clients needed some handholding, especially at first.

She closed the door behind her. "Lachlan, please, it's Daphne." She smiled at Lachlan as if they were on a date instead of a meeting and rounded the table to sit beside him. When she met Costello's gaze, she added, "I'm Jordan's mother." Once she'd taken a seat across from Jordan, the younger woman's gaze dropped to the blue folder in front of her. Daphne tilted her head and studied her face. "Have you said anything to the men, sweetheart?" Her tone sounded more appropriate for addressing a five-year-old than a grown woman. Jordan shook her head once. Her cheeks hollowed as she sucked them in. Costello could practically feel her biting them.

"Jordan has autism—"

"High-functioning Asperger's. I'm an Aspie."

Daphne frowned. "And, she's very tired and stressed from our flight," Daphne offered as an explanation no one asked for. "As am I, honestly." She rubbed her temples as if to demonstrate. "I had hoped we could conduct this meeting at the house instead of here." She looked at her daughter. "Jordan gets overwhelmed in new places and situations and she tends to shut down, which is why—"

"I'm all right," Jordan said without looking up. Costello noticed her hands clasped tightly in her lap.

Daphne raised an eyebrow. "Good, sweetheart. That's very good." The patronizing tone came back. "You're doing so well." Jordan's eyes snapped up to her mother then back down as she made the tiniest of sighs. Costello was suddenly holding back an uncomfortable laugh at their little battle of wills. He couldn't blame Jordan—with that tone, her mother was the definition of a helicopter mom.

Lachlan picked up his folder and opened it. "Ms. Summers is recently back from working in Europe, isn't that correct?"

"Please call me Jordan," she said at the same time Daphne said, "Italy, specifically." Again, Jordan met her mother's eyes, her expression flat where another daughter might show annoyance or even anger. Daphne smiled back. "You *are* doing well, aren't you?"

Costello jumped in. "Quite well considering you had a scare. It sounds like you have a possible stalker?"

Jordan glanced up at Costello. "Not yet."

"What my daughter means is that her half-brother, my stepson, is out of prison now and we're worried that he's the one responsible for the threats and that he may come after Jordan. He's unstable, to say the least. He—" Daphne took a deep breath as her eyelids fluttered—"he went to jail for murdering his father...my husband...in a drunken rage when Jordan was very young."

Something dark and heavy turned in Costello's stomach. His palms felt sweaty and his heart decided to run a sprint. He hadn't had a panic attack in years, not one that felt like this since he was taken away from his mom and put into child protective services when he was ten.

Lachlan took over. "Almost twenty-five years ago, Daniel Summers was arrested for murdering his father, Leo Summers, at their estate. Daniel was twenty-nine at the time and had a considerable drinking problem, as Mrs. Summers has indicated."

"Daphne." She smiled again at Lachlan.

Lach continued. "They were arguing, which was not unusual. Daniel was drunk—also not unusual—and assaulted his father. Daniel later confessed to the crime. He was advised to plead down from murder to voluntary manslaughter but refused." Lach's gaze flickered to Daphne, who looked increasingly upset, then back to his open folder. "His lawyers still dragged the proceedings out but eventually he was sentenced to thirty years. He's out now on good behavior, five years early."

So, Daphne's stepson is her age or even older? The woman didn't look a day over forty-five, which meant she was probably fifty. This was getting interesting.

Lachlan fixed his full gaze on Daphne. "Jordan was working on a project in Italy when she began to receive threats against her life along with photographs taken of her on-site, from an unknown source."

"Unknown source," Jordan echoed softly.

"You're rocking, sweetheart," Daphne admonished. Jordan had started the tiny movement when Lachlan began his speech and had gradually increased the more he spoke. She stopped cold at her mother's words. "Jordan can't help herself when she's nervous. Go on, Lachlan."

"Jordan has a point." He switched his attention to the younger woman. "Your stalker remains unidentified and there is no specific reason to suspect that it's Daniel Summers."

Jordan nodded and started to speak when her mother interrupted. "I beg to differ." Daphne sat up as straight and tall as she could. "While my daughter does have her admirers for her work and occasionally they get out of hand, this is completely different." She opened her Gucci purse and rummaged inside. "I have the originals with me. I'll be tossing this purse. Just keeping them in here give me hives." Daphne threw several sheets of paper and photos onto the conference table. They scattered across the surface as Jordan jumped in her chair.

Costello flinched too. She was just carrying evidence around willy-nilly? "Were these dusted for prints before you shoved them in your purse?"

Daphne waved him off as she rolled her neck. "God knows. Italians."

Is she for real? "You filed a report with the *polizia di stato*, though, right?"

"Of course. But I don't speak Italian, I speak French. I have no idea what they actually did, how seriously they took us."

"*La polizia ci ha presi sul serio,*" Jordan mumbled, and this time Costello couldn't hold his laughter in completely.

"So the police *did* take you seriously," he said, covering the last of his chuckle.

He won an appreciative glance from Jordan. God, those pale green eyes captivated him. *Straight out of my dreams.*

Stop it. Not real.

He did not receive the same appreciation from Daphne. "They weren't convinced it was necessarily Daniel, either." The slightly musical lilt had left her voice, flattening it out. "So, no, actually, they did not take the threat seriously."

Costello reached for one of the letters, skipping over the photocopies in his folder. The heavier paper was high-quality, not copier stock from an office store. Stationary. *Odd.* The letters were cut from a newspaper and pasted on with rubber cement. "Classic," he said. The message read:

I'M WATCHING YOU. YOU CANNOT ESCAPE ME.

. . .

"Pretty generic threat." Costello passed the letter to Lachlan, who examined it and nodded.

"'You cannot escape me' is hardly generic, Mr. Costello. My stepson means to kill my daughter for her inheritance, which he believes should have all gone to him. It's why he killed Leo." The name came out on a stifled sob. "Now he wants my precious daughter. I'm sure if John Charles had not heard his brother and father fighting and run to intervene, Daniel would have found and killed her, too. He always resented us."

Jordan started rocking, caught herself quickly, and stopped.

"John Charles?" Costello asked.

"Leo Summer's other son by his first marriage," Lachlan said. Costello caught him patting his shirt pocket for his chewed-down pen and the frustration in his clenched jaw at remembering it wasn't there.

Daphne sniffed. "John Charles and I don't always see eye to eye, but I'll forever be thankful to him for stopping his brother from going after Jordan."

"Was she in the house at the time?" Lachlan asked.

"No, she was in the garden. Where she always is, aren't you darling?"

Costello's vision practically blurred. He swallowed down bile. *A coincidence, that's all. Man up, for Chrissakes.*

Jordan took that opportunity to look at him again. Puzzlement was back in her eyes.

"That's right. You're a gardener, aren't you, Jordan?" Lachlan said.

Daphne snorted. "Hardly something so pedestrian."

"I'm a landscape architect," Jordan said.

"She means she's an artist whose medium is the outdoors.

Jordan creates installations that people and museums pay millions for. Here, let me show you."

Jordan's cheeks colored while Daphne rummaged through her purse again. She was obviously not comfortable with her mother's praise. Daphne took out her phone and pulled up an Instagram account before handing it to Lachlan. His eyebrows raised and he whistled as he scrolled through. "Damn, these are incredible. No wonder you have so many followers." He stopped on one, tapped the screen, and stared. "Wow. How did you do that?"

Dread filled Costello. *What if the photos are straight out of my dreams?* He shook his head. *They can't be. Dreams aren't real. Psychics aren't real. This is real. You're just reacting to having such an intense dream this morning. Now get over yourself.*

Lachlan handed him the phone. Costello's hand trembled as he took it and looked at the screen.

It was a video of a solidly packed field of white flowers, probably taken by a drone. At the bottom edge was a patio set with several tables. He tapped on the play button at the center and watched a time-lapsed video of a party taking place on the patio—as some of the flowers in the center of the field gradually turned blue in the form of a name in fancy script —*Henri.*

"How did you...?" In utter amazement, he looked from the screen to Jordan. His amazement doubled at her smile, which took her face from beautiful to breathtaking.

Her smile turned impish. "Guess. Hint, those are carnations."

"Oh," Daphne interjected as she clapped her hands once. "The gender and baby name reveal. That was a good one. That was commissioned at a nice price by the royal family of

—" her voice faded into Costello's peripheral as he continued to gaze at Jordan.

He chuckled. "You used water that was dyed dark blue and the flowers changed color as they drank it up. But how did you do it with that level of precision? Are they all in pots, or planters?"

She shook her head and leaned in closer as if bestowing an ancient secret. Her jasmine perfume cut through Daphne's roses to tease his nose. "They're all planted in the ground. I used IV start kits, one for each flower. I stuck the little needle under the base of the flower and connected the tubing to test tubes of blue water."

"But, how did you get the timing right? Otherwise, you and a crew would have been out there in the field jabbing needles into carnations while the party was going on and some of the flowers would already be blue while you were still working."

Jordan's smile widened and her eyes crinkled. "I insisted the party take place in the mountains where the air stayed cool until the sun rose high enough. We set up before dawn. The dyed water was frozen and it melted as the day got warmer. It was still a risk that it would be uneven, but I got lucky."

"Brilliant. You. Are. *Brilliant*."

"No, that's just a little party trick. Now, scroll back three screens and take a look at that garden. Nice, huh? For that one, I spent two months prepping the soil with a mix of..."

Costello was dismayed as the weight of Daphne's stare stopped her words. "Darling, I know you could go on all day about your work, but we need to focus, okay?" The talking-to-a-five-year-old tone was back.

Like a switch had been thrown, Jordan's smile disappeared and she looked back down at her blue folder. Costello wanted to leap across the table and throttle the woman for shutting her daughter down like that.

"Back to business," Lachlan said, now fidgeting with the corner of his folder, "have there ever been any threats like these before?"

"From time to time, Jordan has received inappropriate letters, but nothing quite so threatening as these." Daphne shivered. "As soon as I heard that Daniel was out of prison, I put two and two together and knew it was him."

"So you weren't aware he was out?"

"No, no one informed me."

"Why would you come back to the States?" Costello asked. "Wouldn't it be safer to keep Jordan in Italy, or at least out of the US?"

Daphne blanched. "Can't you see that he was already there watching her? The photographs." She tapped on one with a long nail lacquered in red. "We needed to leave immediately, and since Jordan refused her next commission, we had no choice but to return to California."

Jordan stiffened at her mother's words, her scolding tone. "I didn't like it and I needed a break."

Lachlan gave Costello a look that said *more here than meets the eye.* Costello couldn't agree more.

"Look," Daphne said as she rubbed the spot above her nose with two fingers, "I'm not hiring a detective agency, I just want some extra security around my daughter. Can you manage that?"

Costello kept his calm, but inside he'd had just about enough. "Ma'am." By the look of her sudden frown, that hit the target. "We need to access the threat level in order to execute the most appropriate response. I need to know the likelihood that it's Daniel Summers, or if I'm chasing a ghost. What if it isn't and I miss the true target because I'm going off your assumptions? I need to keep Jordan safe and to do that, we have to look at all angles."

"He's right," Lachlan added. "I'll be working with local authorities behind the scenes to get a handle on this. In the meantime, I'd advise upping your initial protection detail from one man to two, round the clock, in addition to other security measures we still need to discuss. Sound good?"

Daphne gave a curt nod.

"Fantastic. We'll assess from there as the situation warrants. Hang on." He reached for the phone in the center of the conference table and punched in an office extension then hit speaker.

"This is Nashville," the man drawled.

"Nash. I need you in Conference Two. New assignment."

"Be right there, Boss." Some of his accent dried up, as it did when he wasn't chatting up a prospective date. It only took him a minute to go from his office to the conference room. He took a seat beside Costello. Lachlan in the meantime pulled out an extra folder and pushed it across the table as he made introductions.

Jordan barely glanced up. Costello fought back the need to put his arm around her. Like a snail, she'd tucked herself up into an impenetrable shell.

"Now, if we can move on and look at the property," Lachlan said. "Page nine."

They all turned to their folders and flipped past the contract to a builder's plan of the gigantic house outside of Malibu. Costello seriously doubted two men would be enough. The place had to have at least ten bedrooms and it sat on several acres on a peninsula jutting out into the Pacific.

"We got enough coverage?" Nash voiced Costello's doubts.

"Most of Eden House is closed up," Daphne said. "We

haven't lived there for years. We won't be using much of the house beyond a few bedrooms, the kitchen, and dining, one of the living rooms."

"And the garden," Jordan whispered. Her leg brushed against Costello's. Was that by accident, or...?

Get yourself under control.

For the next hour, they went over the details of the house, the contract, and other specifics, but Costello's head was barely in the game. Partly because of Jordan's touch—on purpose or inadvertent, he didn't know—but either way, it threw him.

And partly because at the sight of the mansion, memories of his childhood with his birth mother, a woman he wished he could forget, came roaring back to haunt him.

Liar. Thief. Traitor.

THREE

Driving up to Malibu and the estate took over an hour. Costello and Nashville took separate SUVs and kept in touch via phone. Costello already had his things packed in anticipation of the job, but Nashville would return home after getting a tour of the place, and he and Reggie would come back the next morning. One of the Watchdogs, Reggie was a black Lab with a sniffer that wouldn't quit and a sweet nature. He was a complementary companion to Anubis, who was all-business when it came to guarding clients—the Malinois was the tall, dark, and handsome silent-type.

"Can you believe how that woman went on and on about dog shit? I was fixing to bring some in from the courtyard seeing as she was so hyped up about it." Nash said. Despite his words, his voice could have sent a baby off to sleep or charmed the panties off any supermodel.

Costello laughed. "Yeah, we're lucky we talked her into the dogs at all. I think she was sold on the idea that they could sniff out and attack someone before they got near the house."

"She is charming that way. It makes me wonder why she'd

go with Watchdog, it's that big of a problem for her. The dogs are kinda baked into the name," Nash said.

Costello wondered that too. He had his suspicions about it but kept them to himself. "Who knows? But Jordan seems to like dogs."

"You gonna be all right tonight, brother? You want me to come on back with my gear and start the job with you tonight?"

"No, I've got this. Saves you the drive time back and forth in traffic today. Besides, I don't think they're in immediate danger from a stalker. Those notes were on Italian stationery and the photos were current and undoctored. Whoever it was, was already there. The Summers left under the cover of night. If it was a random stalker, they gave him or her the slip."

"If it was a *random* stalker? What do you think are the chances it is her brother after all?"

Costello shrugged as if Nash could see him from the SUV and smiled at himself for the dumb move. "Can't rule it out. But, what are the chances Daniel would give himself away like that? Who gets out of prison after twenty-five years for good behavior, then immediately gets on a plane and flies to Italy for revenge against a woman who was a little girl the last time he saw her, and *then* telegraphs it once he's there with a threatening note? It makes no sense. Does the man even have a passport?"

"Truth, truth. Y'all see how agitated Lach was? He wasn't buying it either, was he?"

"I don't think so. But, our boss loves a good mystery. He can't help himself. It's why he's assigned two of us. More eyes, more recon."

"So what are your psychic powers telling you?"

Costello cringed, and this time he was glad Nash couldn't see the gesture. He knew his brother was just yanking his chain, and usually, he could brush it off, but not today. Maybe never again.

Just your mind playing tricks.

The problem was, Costello's mind never played tricks. He depended on it not to. His near-photographic memory and attention to the smallest events going on around him had kept him alive all his life, from his birth mother's schemes, through his tours in Afghanistan, to quickly identifying threats against his clients.

"My *powers of observation* are telling me I don't have enough information yet. Chances are, we'll have this job a week before Daphne gets bored and decides her daughter isn't in any danger since nothing's happened, and she'll have them on the next flight to Paris. It's happened with other clients before, especially if they were trying to drum up media attention."

Though his gut was telling him this wasn't the case. Not quite. "But who knows? If it's Daniel Summers, we know what he looks like. Lach is already sniffing him out and ready to put a tail on him. And if it's someone else who's followed them all the way back here from Italy, they'll mess up and we'll get them."

A third scenario prickled at the back of his neck and he did his best to ignore it. Because to give that any credence was madness.

"GPS says we're almost there," Nash said. "I don't remember any damn turnoff up ahead. I've been up and down this highway a hundred times, I've never seen one."

Costello had been to Malibu on assignments before. The houses tended to be built practically on top of each other, but Eden House was different. *Drive slowly once you get a mile past or you'll miss the road* Daphne had said before they left. From this direction, it required crossing the two-lane highway that skirted the ocean. At least the traffic wasn't bad.

"It's a private road and unmarked. When we go around this bend, you'll see the peninsula. There it is."

Eden House was just past Malibu on a narrow peninsula jutting out into the Pacific like an accusing finger. Costello kept catching glimpses of the tree-covered cliffs between branches as they drove along the highway.

"I see the peninsula but I can't see a house," Nash said. "*Any* house. Just trees and rocks."

"It's the only house out there." If Eden House had as much land around it as Daphne said, it had to be worth somewhere north of sixty-million dollars.

The day was uncharacteristically cloudy, foggy, and cool —more like San Francisco than hot and sunny Los Angeles— and muggy, the air clinging like a damp blanket to the skin. Or maybe it was just his nerves. The closer they got to the house, the more his skin crawled with...something. Premonition?

What if I recognize the gardens? What if there's a fountain?

Costello pushed down a memory from his dreams. The dark part, the part that was more nightmare than dream.

"Woulda been nice if they hadn't sped off like a bat outta hell when we hit the highway," Nash groused.

"Now who's psychic? I was thinking the very same thing," Costello answered. Daphne told them to try and keep up as she slid behind the wheel of a little black convertible and peeled out of the parking lot before Costello could turn the ignition.

He clicked on his windshield wipers against the mist and slowed down in order not to miss the turn in the fog. There—a break in the trees ahead gave the barest hint of a road. The GPS didn't even alert him. Costello put on his signal and watched Nash in his rearview mirror do the same, following his lead.

"Fuck, there it is. Glad I drove up here with y'all or I'd never find it tomorrow. Good eyes, Psychic."

"Thanks." Costello made the turn onto the private drive with Nash directly behind him. The road wound through a forest of bishop pines, their branches and foliage thick like oaks. Mist crisscrossed the way like torn bridal veils. The estate was hidden somewhere ahead. Costello turned off his GPS which was now telling him to make a U-turn like it was a goddammed oracle. Over the phone, he could hear Nash's doing the same.

A black shape showed itself ahead between wisps of fog. Daphne's car sat idling, now with the top up against the weather.

Nash scoffed. "Oh, thanks for waitin', sugar. Coulda never found the place without you."

Red taillights lit as the black convertible sped forward, disappearing into the mist and trees.

"Guess we're playing hide and seek with the ladies," Nash said. He followed with another wisecrack but Costello was stuck on the words *hide and seek*.

Let's play hide and seek.

He was a little kid again as his brain flashed to how his mom used him in her schemes whenever there were kids in the mark's family. *Let's play hide and seek.* A perfect excuse to snoop around a house and pick up all the bright and shiny things lying around.

Costello shook his head to rid himself of the sudden flashback. If only his clients knew what he'd done as a kid, they'd never trust him now.

Liar. Thief. Traitor.

This was not the time to remember his childhood and it

was never a good time to think about his mother. He needed to focus on the present. Costello gritted his teeth. Unfortunately, his present included dealing with a storage unit full of his birth mother's junk now that she'd passed. He'd put off going to the storage facility and opening the unit to see what he could sell and what he had to dispose of. Instead, he paid the next six months' rent three months ago when he'd learned that not only had she died but she'd left it to him.

The red taillights appeared again. Daphne had stopped. As he drove closer, he saw the reason and shuddered.

A giant wrought-iron gate blocked the drive. Walls made of dark brick stretched off into the trees on either side. But that's not what caught his attention and made every fiber of his body want to turn around and run.

It was the two stone angels kneeling on pedestals flanking the gate. Their carved heads were bowed and their hands folded in prayer.

The angels at the gate pray for us, but they keep their eyes shut tightly.

The words floated up from his old dreams. He hadn't dreamed of the angels for so long, not since he was a boy. There were angels guarding the garden but they never saw the danger. They never saw the fountain...

Hide and seek. Run.

His head hurt. Seeing the angels made it hurt more.

Coincidence. Just a coincidence, Costello. Get a fucking grip ASAP. Dreams aren't real.

Daphne stuck her arm out the window and presumably punched in a code on a keypad mounted on a pole. The gates swung inward and she motioned for them to follow. As he pulled forward, Costello had a crazy moment where he thought the angels' eyes might open as he passed between them.

Judging him or finally bearing witness, he did not know.

And now the house loomed ahead. Built in the Twenties, it was in the style of an Old World mansion with some Mediterranean villa elements. A cobblestone drive took over for the road. Many of the cobblestones needed replacing. The trees and bushes looked unkempt and overgrown. The place reeked of neglect. And still, something stirred in Costello's mind. He knew he'd never been there, but maybe his mom had targeted the place once and changed her mind. He had no other explanation for the déjà vu. His memory simply didn't play tricks on him, especially when he was a kid and his mom needed him to remember small details. *Stay sharp, kiddo, you're the eyes and ears on this team.*

Again, he pushed his birth mother out of his head.

Daphne drove her car around the side to a large free-standing garage and the two SUVs followed. All three parked on the wide span of cobblestones in front of the garage—a space broad enough to park five cars comfortably. The mist had become a drizzle so Costello grabbed his big black umbrella, opened it, and almost started to walk over to the convertible with the intent of offering its shelter to one of the women when he remembered Anubis in the back of the SUV.

It wasn't that he didn't like the dog...exactly. Hell, Anubis was more professional than some of the human bodyguards at Watchdog. He was obedient to a fault, silent unless he needed to bark, calm and self-contained. Scary-smart. But maybe that's what unnerved Costello. In his birth mother's old line of 'work', she'd never do a job where there was a dog present because they could be unpredictable, and she'd drilled that into her son. He'd never quite shaken off his distrust for dogs, even though he'd chosen Watchdog almost out of spite for his mother. One more way to show he was nothing like her.

Costello opened the door for Anubis and the dog calmly

jumped down and waited for his leash. Not a tail-wag, not a look in his eye that said *I'll obey you if I get a treat*. Professional. Which made him deadly, perfect for his job. Costello hooked his leash onto his collar and gave the dog a quick head scratch as if to convince both of them that everything was normal. In contrast, Nash was sweet-talking Reggie and had already given him two treats as he snapped his leash into place. The dog was all wagging tail and greedy stomach, *but that's a Lab for you* Costello thought.

He turned his attention to the car and the women waiting inside it. He started walking, trying to decide which one he should escort into the house. His natural choice was Jordan. *But that may be the wrong choice*, he thought. How would he feel with her practically tucked up next to him?

Nash followed suit behind him with his umbrella so Costello aimed for the driver's side—that was safer and made sense since he was the lead on this team, and even though Jordan was the principal, Daphne was signing the checks.

She smiled up at him through the driver's side window when he reached the car. Daphne opened the door and made a show of slowly getting out. She eyed Anubis and stood on the other side of Costello. "Thank you. So courteous."

"Part of the job, ma'am. You do not exit or enter a vehicle without one of us right there."

"Please, it's Daphne," she said as she slipped her arm through his. Definitely not part of the job, but it paid to humor the client at times, especially when the danger level was low. And it was low right now—Costello had scanned the area for any sounds or movements. The trees creaked and sighed in the breeze off the ocean and water pattered onto the undergrowth, but there was no sign of any human activity. Costello sensed no one but the four of them. The house itself looked abandoned as they made their way across the drive to a side door, much closer and convenient than the front entry.

Costello forced himself not to look back at Nash and Jordan. He could hear Nash trying to engage her in light conversation—something about music would be his guess—and Jordan giving one-word responses. He imagined she was walking with her head down and her eyes on the ground, much as she had through the hallways at Watchdog. He couldn't gauge her level of concern over the threats. He'd try and talk to her later, alone. As dangerous as that felt.

In the meantime, Daphne kept up a patter of conversation in his ear. "I'm sure the house is going to smell dank and musty. We really should have had it aired out regularly, but who can think about those things on a sunny day in Tuscany? You'll forgive us, won't you?"

"Of course," he mumbled back. "I'm going to need the code to the front gate. Are there any other gates? On the floorplan, I saw only one oceanside gate leading to a patio. If it's coded too, I'll need that code as well. Also, if you aren't already, we'll be changing the code every three days—"

"Every three days? I'll never remember that!" she chuckled lightly. "But you're the boss. Here we are." She pulled out a key to open the door.

"How many keys to outdoor locks do you have? I'll need to know and I'll need two extra sets to start, and you'll want to change all the locks ASAP."

Daphne appraised him. "Mr. All-Business. Do you really think that's necessary?"

"If the house has stood empty as long as you say it has, someone may have been here and taken an impression of the lock and made a key. We'll be doing a thorough sweep as soon as we get in. I want you and Ms. Summers to stay just inside the door with your phones ready until that's complete."

Daphne huffed. "Well, that'll take an hour at least. I don't want to just stand here. And I really don't like the idea of you going through my house unaccompanied." Costello tried not to flinch at that. She had no way of knowing his past, did she?

Daphne pushed the door open and glanced down at Anubis as they walked in. "You're sure he's housebroken?"

The woman was getting on every last nerve. And *Jordan* was the one with the spoiled heiress reputation? "I can assure you, we are complete professionals. We're just checking to make sure the house is actually empty of unexpected occupants, that there hasn't been any vandalism, no nasty surprises. If we did encounter a hostile, we want you as close to an exit as possible."

They stepped into a large mudroom, the walls lined with benches and pegs. *Wait. Something's wrong.* Costello tensed.

"I really doubt anyone has taken up residency in our absence. We do have a property manager who looks in from time to ti—" Daphne stopped as Costello grabbed her arm. Was that the sound of footsteps farther inside the house?

Anubis went on high alert. He stayed silent but his hackles rose and his leash went tight as he strained forward. Costello turned to Nash and put his finger to his lips then pointed ahead. Nash gave a curt nod and motioned for the women to stop and stand behind them. Reggie whined and Nash signaled for him to be quiet.

The footsteps came closer. Costello and Nash were both armed but shooting a possible intruder was the last resort. Whoever was walking toward them was not rushing or trying to hide their presence. Maybe it was the property manager on an unscheduled visit. "Did you tell anyone we were coming?" Costello whispered.

Wide-eyed, Daphne shook her head no and clutched his arm again. He gently shook her off.

"Identify yourself," Costello called.

"Identify *yourself*," a man called back. He sounded more puzzled than threatening.

"That's my brother," Jordan said, her voice neutral behind him.

Must not be the brother freshly out of prison. Costello glanced at Daphne for confirmation. Instead of looking relieved, she bristled at the sound of her stepson's voice. "It's him."

"Daniel?"

"No. John Charles." She sighed as the man walked through the door on the opposite side of the mudroom. He looked Daphne's age, which made sense but still threw Costello off. Her marriage really was a May-December match.

John Charles smiled. He was handsome and Costello could see the resemblance between him and Jordan around the eyes and mouth. "Daphne, what a surprise. Jordan." He nodded to his little sister.

Daphne frowned. "What are you doing here? You have your own place."

"I was feeling nostalgic. Decided I wanted to come home for a while. Besides," He swung an arm around, "The place needed airing out."

"Mother was just saying that," Jordan said.

It sure does need airing out, but not from stale air. Costello could smell the bourbon on the man's breath from halfway across the room as he approached them. He'd enunciated his words deliberately the way some drunks do when they're trying to overcompensate for slurring.

"Day drinking alone in a creepy old house. Nothing to see here," Nash mumbled under his breath. Costello's lips twitched as he tried not to smile. Leave it to Nash to lighten any situation.

"So." John Charles stopped a few feet away and crossed his arms. He swayed ever so slightly. "What are you doing here? Don't you have gardens to plant and celebrities to seduce in Italy or France or wherever?"

Daphne's nostrils flared. "Don't you ever speak that way about my daughter again."

"What? I was talking about both of you. You both have your specialties."

'Get out." Daphne snapped her fingers and pointed at the door like she was talking to a badly behaved dog.

John Charles smiled, then broke into a chuckle. "It's good to see you again, Daphne. I've missed you."

"Why are you here?" she snapped.

Costello stepped in. "I have to ask the same question, Mr. Summers. We weren't expecting anyone to be at the house. What are you doing here?" Had he received warnings the way Jordan had? Was Daniel threatening the entire family?

John Charles shrugged and looked around. "What, now I need permission to visit the house I grew up in?" He looked at Jordan, who regarded him warily. "Do I have your permission to be here, Jordan? How old are you again?"

"I think you need to answer Elliot's question," she said.

John Charles' eyes narrowed, then he broke into another smile, his lips pressed tightly together. "Well, it's a little personal and a lot embarrassing. My, uh, fiancée needed some time to herself after we had a disagreement, so I'm obliging her by staying here for the duration."

Daphne raised her eyebrows. "She moved in with you? And you left her in your house?"

"Yes and yes. I'm nothing if not a gentleman."

"I'll go with nothing," Nash breathed. Costello held back a chuckle.

"Enough with asking *me* twenty questions, Daph. What are *you* doing here and who are the dudes and the mutts?" He rubbed his temples and Costello wondered if he was already developing a hangover. Or maybe recovering from one with the help of a little hair of the dog.

She tilted her head. "Did you know that Daniel is out of prison?"

"Did you catch that I don't want to answer any more questions?"

This was going nowhere fast and Costello had a job to do. He pulled himself up to his full height which was several inches taller than John Charles but he added a smile. It usually paid to be friendly, especially with drunks. "Excuse me, friend. I'm Elliot Costello and this is my associate, Nashville Jones. We're with Watchdog Security. Our clients received some threatening letters in Italy and were concerned about their immediate safety so they came back Stateside and hired us. Mr. Jones and I weren't expecting anyone at the house and we don't really like surprises in our line of work."

"And why should I care?"

Okay, so friendly wasn't going to work. Costello put his smile away. "Until I get a full picture of what's going on here, I will be asking more questions whether you like it or not. Now, question one, are you here alone, or do you have a drinking buddy?"

John Charles' demeanor changed to sulky. "I'm here alone. Have been for the past three days. I didn't feel like seeing anyone."

"And what are your plans for staying or leaving?"

He sighed and for the first time looked genuinely remorseful. He looked past Costello to Jordan. "Sis, I'd really like to hang out here for a while longer if you don't mind. It's a big house, I can keep to myself. You'll never know I'm here. I just need a few more days to regroup. And if Daniel is out of prison as you say, you might want me here anyway. For moral support if nothing else." His last words actually sounded tender. His gaze flicked to Daphne. "Can't believe you'd come back *here* of all places, knowing that."

"I didn't have much of a choice. I'm hoping this will be a brief stay."

Costello thought that was odd—they were made of money and could have gone anywhere.

"You can stay, John Charles," Jordan said. Again, that flat affect, so unlike the vibrant woman who loved talking about her work. Costello glanced back at her. She was looking at the slate tiles that made up the floor, obviously not happy about the situation. He wanted to lift her chin and tell her she was in charge, that she could kick her brother out if she wanted. Instead, she was shut down, folded into herself like a flower at night.

"As your security consultant, I'd advise having as few people here as possible." He looked back at John Charles, "And swearing them to secrecy."

Daphne stepped back and put an arm around her daughter. Jordan stiffened. "Darling, I don't like this either, but I think you made the right decision letting him stay." She looked at her stepson—no love lost there. "As long as he keeps to himself and doesn't tell anyone we're here."

John Charles gave her a smile that didn't come anywhere near his eyes. "Of course. I want everyone, including myself, to stay safe." He dipped his head. "Now, if you'll excuse me, I have a bottle to crawl back into." He spun on his heel and Costello was surprised he didn't end up on the floor.

Daphne blew out her breath as she shook her head after

he left. She dropped her arm from around Jordan and the younger woman visibly relaxed. "Well. That was both unexpected and unpleasant." She ran a hand down her tailored jacket as if it needed smoothing. "Let's get on with the tour. We'll just skip whichever room he's made into his den." Daphne took ten steps before she looked back, glancing down at the dogs. "And you're sure they're housebroken?"

FOUR

J ordan breathed a sigh of relief after her mother's house tour. She'd dodged a bullet with the last potential client in Italy, but her plan had worked and they were back in California, back home. Walking through the house, she wanted to retreat to the only place that meant anything to her. The gardens.

Back to where it all began. Back where I left my heart. Maybe my soul.

Her mother had packed their things when Jordan turned sixteen and off they went to Europe until now. Jordan had often wanted to come home, to the first gardens she ever fell in love with, but time and again, her mother came up with one excuse or another. And then when Jo Jordan's career took off, she barely had time to even think of her home and its gardens unless she was dreaming.

Nearing the French doors leading to the back patio, her hands opened and closed repeatedly with anticipation as she pictured the gardens as they were when she was a little girl and her father not only did some of the gardening but had an entire staff taking care of them. That was how her mother had met her father; she was on one of the landscaping crews, they worked side by side a few times, fell in love, and had Jordan.

Mama hates that I'm different she remembered telling her father while they walked through the garden.

He'd gotten down on his knees and hugged her. *Mama loves you just as much as I do* he'd said. *But you should try talking to her, to anyone, not just to me.* Jordan's hands had opened and closed back then against her father's back at the mere thought of trying to talk to anyone but him. She'd had even less control over them than now. She clasped her hands in front of her, which helped.

Jordan stepped through the French doors on the ocean-facing side of Eden House and onto the patio overlooking the garden that haunted her dreams, now overgrown and fallen to ruin. She walked to the edge of the stairs and stopped. The last time she'd stood here she'd been a teenager on the brink of leaving for Europe with no idea that it would be years before she came back home.

So much deadwood in the rhododendrons and oaks that needed trimming. Scattered leaves that needed to be swept up and composted so they could feed new life. Cracked and broken pavers that needed replacing in the shaggy lawn. Planters full of weeds and overgrown perennials.

She lifted her eyes from the courtyard just outside the doors. There ahead was the vast blue expanse of the Pacific, the perfect backdrop to the gardens, at least once she'd restored them. The clouds had broken and the sun was peeking through in places and shining on the water. The ground sloped gently to the dark brick wall overgrown with ivy and bougainvillea separating the gardens from the wild rocky cliffs that in some places plunged straight down to the water at high tide or to a beach at low. Off to the left, an iron-work gate broke the monotony of the wall. Beyond the gate was a patio overlooking the ocean, with a set of stairs cut into the cliff all the way down to the beach.

She could bring the garden back to what it was. She *would* bring it back. And the garden would be just for herself, no one else paying her to do what they wanted.

A garden just for her—and for Elliot.

She could hardly believe he was finally here with her.

She had scripted in her head what she'd wanted to say to him at Watchdog, but as soon as he walked into the conference room, all the words dissolved. One look at his gorgeous face, at the look he gave her, and she was left speechless.

She thought about his initial shock at seeing her in the conference room and then his immediate cover-up, saying they'd never met, that they didn't know each other. He was acting strangely, but what else could she expect? So she would follow his lead, keep his secrets for him until he was ready to reveal them.

It's a game of hide and seek with us.

But then he'd taken an interest in her gardens as she'd hoped he would, and the words flowed easily, naturally. If only her mother hadn't been there interrupting, they could have talked all day.

She had researched him thoroughly and knew his life's story—the good and the bad—and she had her dreams of him. Jordan was eager to see how well her dreams would match up to reality. So far, she was not disappointed. God, he was so damn handsome in person. The pictures she'd seen didn't do him justice, even though he looked so handsome in his uniform as a SEAL. It took everything she had not to just blurt out *We know each other down to our souls*. She had so much to tell him, so much to catch him up on. And she wanted to hear his stories about growing up. All the details she couldn't research.

He just needed to trust her.

That was a scary thought though. She needed to tell him what was really going on and hope she wasn't in too much trouble. So long as they could dodge her mother.

Jordan's plan had worked so far and her mother didn't have the faintest idea.

But how much did Elliot suspect? What would he think of her once she told him the truth? Or was he too preoccupied with his own past? Was he inside right now thinking about her, hoping that she'd keep his secret? Was he angry that he was here, that he was potentially compromised because of her?

"No, no, no," she said out loud to chase away the thoughts. Elliot angry with her was too hurtful to think about. She thought instead about his face when she told him about the party trick with the carnations back in the conference room. His smile, the light in his eyes—that was how she'd always imagined him looking at her. That expression filled her with warmth like sunshine on a field of lavender. She'd dreamed about him so many times and every time he was happy to see her. More than happy. In her dreams—both the daydreams and the ones she had at night—they'd grown up together and shared, well, everything.

Jordan felt his presence right before he stepped out onto the patio behind her. Anubis was with him. The dog's toenails clicked differently from Reggie's—more precise and deliberate. Much like Elliot compared to Nashville. Thankfully, her mother wasn't with Elliot. Jordan hated the way Daphne was already starting to cling to him.

Elliot paused just outside the doors. Maybe he didn't want to disturb her. God help her if he was hesitating because he was angry at being here and blamed her for it. She clasped her hands together tightly.

She turned to look at him. He was completely distracted, looking at the garden like it was about to bite him. Her heart sank. Well, what did she expect? *Get your head out of your dreams. This is real now.*

"Is something wrong, Elliot?"

Her words seemed to startle him but not enough to bring his full attention back to her. *Please don't be afraid of me.* She couldn't read his expression but he seemed to be looking for something, as if trying to find—

Oh, of course. Everything is different from what he was expecting. "It needs a lot of work, doesn't it?" she asked him. "Elliot?"

That brought his attention to her. She looked at his familiar, handsome face. *Perfection.* The sun finally broke through the haze as if to emphasize the point. It lit his hair, turning it almost golden. The sunlight on his skin picked up his scent and carried it to her. She could stand and just stare at him for the rest of the day.

He blinked rapidly as if awakening and looked at her as if she'd stepped out of the dream he'd just had. Then he walked up to her. "Nothing's wrong. Not a thing that I can see."

Her cheeks turned hot as all the things she'd planned to tell him went right out of her head. *Garden. We were talking about the garden. The thing you know best. Talk about that.* "But it needs a lot of work, don't you think?" she repeated.

"Nothing you can't handle."

She relaxed as warmth spread in her chest. She unclasped her hands absently. "Thank you. Would you like to see the rest? Such as it is?"

He looked away, back to the circle of lavender in the middle of the courtyard, and his eyes became unfocused again. "Sure."

They started down the steps and Elliot stumbled on the

first one. She caught him before he could slip, Anubis on the other side as if he could help balance his partner.

Elliot's cheeks reddened. "Thanks, I can't believe I did that." He ran a hand through his hair.

"It's okay. I do that when I'm distracted, too." She smiled and hoped it would reassure him. She knew exactly why he was distracted but wouldn't for the love of God bring it up now.

Jordan walked down the steps to the courtyard and approached the first planter. It used to overflow with trailing vines but now only supported a few sickly ones; nothing she couldn't restore. She touched the soil and smiled at its familiar feel and rich scent. It had been a couple of days since she'd been able to dig her fingers into the dirt, between the sudden preparations to return to the States and then the long plane ride home. She felt calmer instantly. Behind her, she could still sense everyone else's presence in the house as if they were all walking along the threads of a spider's web, but being outside in her garden took away some of her tension.

Once the dog was assured Elliot was all right, Anubis lay down at the top of the stairs. Elliot followed Jordan into the garden. His footsteps released the sharp smell of the creeping thyme growing between the pavers under his feet. Jordan tried her best to determine what he was feeling. She didn't want to guess and get it wrong and she also didn't want him to think she was stupid or uncaring. But as he stood next to her, a smile spread across his face that was easy to read, giving her hope.

Jordan brought her attention back to the courtyard. "I'll start here and work my way out to the rest of the grounds. I want to bring this tomb of a house back to life, starting of course with the gardens."

"If anyone can restore this garden, it's you," he said softly.

"I scrolled through your feed some more. I couldn't help myself. Your gardens are breathtaking. Otherworldly."

Her heart sped up and her hands opened and closed until she noticed them and stopped. She tried to keep the tic under control when anyone else was around because it brought attention to her differences and at times unnerved people. Her mother constantly pointed it out—teasing when she was a child that gradually turned to scolding when she didn't grow out of it.

"It all started here," she said. "My father was an avid gardener though he left most of the heavy lifting to his staff. That's how he met my mother. She worked in the gardens and they became friends. And then more than friends, obviously."

Elliot surprised her with a laugh. "Lucky for the world."

Not understanding, she deliberately tilted her head and blinked. That usually got a response when she needed clarification. Elliot studied her and she thought of how he used to wear glasses as a little boy, thick round lenses that made him look owlish. She knew he'd been teased for them. For a lot of things.

"If your parents hadn't fallen in love, you wouldn't be here and the world wouldn't have your beautiful gardens."

Jordan smiled without thinking about it. He made her want to burst out of her skin. She didn't know what to say back, so she sent as much warmth as she could into her eyes, hoping he'd understand how he'd made her feel. She felt her hands opening and closing again a little too late and clasped them tightly. They drew his attention from her face to her hands. *Dammit.*

He quickly looked up again. "Did I embarrass you? I'm sorry."

"No. Oh, no. I just. My hands get...restless." Jordan laughed and bobbed the way some of the girls did in boarding school when they got caught out. *Stop. You don't have to do this, not with him.* "If I had my way, I'd work in the soil from sunup to sundown every day. Keep them busy."

"You don't do that already?" Then Elliot shook his head a little. "No, of course, you wouldn't. You probably spend most of your time directing an entire staff."

"I mostly do now, yes. That's why it's so good to be home." She looked around the garden. "I can do a lot of the work myself here, right beside the crew. My mother won't let me do that when I'm working for a commission. She says it's not good for my image." She glanced at the house, double-checking that her mother wasn't listening from somewhere. "Sometimes I imagine walking away from my life and starting over anonymously in a greenhouse or on a farm. I've already made enough money that I don't have to worry about things. I mean, I think I've made that much."

"You don't know?"

Crap. He thinks I'm dumb. Or spoiled. "I mean, I have an idea. But my mother handles the finances so that I can focus on my work. I'm not good at that sort of thing. Math is hard." She repeated the joke in a funny tone she'd heard hundreds of times and hoped he'd laugh.

He didn't laugh. He studied her instead. She clasped her hands tighter. This was harder than she thought it would be, standing this close to him and still a world away. God, he was perfect, just like she knew he'd be. She decided to try one of the speeches she'd scripted ahead of time, refining her words and trying to predict all his responses. "Thank you for being here, I wasn't sure you'd—"

"There you are," her mother practically shouted from the patio. She glanced at Anubis as if he were a bug and descended the stairs. She appraised the two of them as she approached. "Jordan, do you need to rest? You've had a busy day already." Her eyes flicked to Elliot then back again.

"I'm not tired. I need to work out here," Jordan answered, looking down at the pavers. But her mother's attention was already back to Elliot.

"We were just discussing the garden," Elliot said. "I want to get an idea of the grounds, see about installing cameras."

Jordan's head snapped up. *How could he want that?* The garden was her only real safe place because there were so many places to hide.

Too late. Daphne was nodding in agreement. "A good idea. Long overdue. But I refuse to have any installed inside the house. I like my privacy." She snapped a smile at Jordan, a dismissive one she knew well. "I think it's time to go in, Jordan. Resting will do you wonders."

Are we really doing this in front of Elliot? "I'm fine, I promise." She gave her mother a warm smile that she hoped Elliot would read as *I really am fine.*

Daphne's eyebrow went up. "You know how you get when you're overly tired. I'm just trying to head off any...unpleasantness."

God, she wanted to die. She never knew quite what to say back that Daphne wouldn't somehow turn into just the opposite of what she'd meant. And yet, she knew her mother did this out of love, like her father had told her. She was just trying to protect her daughter.

Only, it hadn't felt that way for a while. Especially with the last potential client. Jordan suppressed a shiver at the memory of him staring at her as if she belonged to him.

"Daphne, you must be worried about Jordan, and understandably so with the threats and now with her brother being out of prison. But, I'm right here and I'll make sure nothing happens to her."

Her mother laughed lightly as if Elliot had just told a great joke. "Mr. Costello, you will come to learn that more often than not, Jordan happens to Jordan."

That hurt. Not that her mother hadn't said similar things to clients and even friends about Jordan, but to say it to Elliot? She felt the tears spring to her eyes before she could stop them. No one ever listened to her when her mother was around. The ball of fury built in her stomach. *No. I'm in control. This is not going to happen.* She swallowed hard. *Stick to your plan. Enough is enough.* She tried to remember the words she'd rehearsed the next time this situation arose while her mother went on.

"...with her autism, she can sometimes overdo it and act out if she's been overstimulated, and considering recent events—"

"I am perfectly in control, Mother, thank you for your concern." There. She'd said it and she did it while making perfect eye contact with both her mother and Elliot. It felt odd to stand up for herself, but having Elliot there somehow made it easier than she'd imagined. The next words flowed freely. "I think I'll finish looking over what needs to be done in the garden, then I'll come in for something to eat. Elliot is here with me and I'm not afraid."

She smiled up at him and caught a warm look in his eye that she hoped she wasn't misreading.

FIVE

The entire day was one of the strangest of Costello's life. And that was saying a lot considering all the things he'd seen and done in his life. All the things his birth mom had put him up to until he was taken away from her and went to live with his adopted family. He'd taken their last name in gratitude and love. On his twelfth birthday, Elliot Lewis had become Elliot Costello, adopted son of Peter and Rhea Costello, brother of Michael, Patrick, and Megan. His life of constantly moving to new apartments had calmed down after they'd taken him in at ten. Then it picked back up when he'd joined the military.

But today? Start to finish, today was just...strange.

Calling Eden House a *house* was not doing it justice. The place went on forever and touring it had taken an hour, Daphne leading them around while Jordan followed as silently as a ghost. Every step Costello took felt like walking on his own grave. The house had ten bedrooms, various sitting rooms, studies, bathrooms, some rooms that seemed to have no use now beyond storage, and much of the furniture was covered in white sheets from when Daphne decided to take

Jordan overseas in her early twenties. They skipped the bedroom John Charles had holed up in.

The house had given both Costello and Nash the creeps—even the dogs seemed off, picking up the vibe from the men—and Daphne acted as though she hated the place, which made sense considering her husband had been murdered there. Also, some of the rooms felt eerily familiar to Costello, a continuation of the déjà vu he'd had when he saw the gates. He avoided glancing out the windows overlooking the gardens in the back—he wasn't ready to 'recognize' them from his dreams.

He didn't want to know if there was a fountain.

Most of his dreams of the garden were good ones, especially now that he was an adult. But every now and then, he'd dream of being a child again, alone in the night garden, unable to find the girl. And he'd see the shadow of a man, tall and menacing. Chasing him to a fountain in the center of the courtyard.

He'd wake up in a cold sweat, heart pounding, knowing that his own shouts had awakened him.

So while Costello assessed the house for security risks, a part of his brain went back to being a little boy who watched the world through a pair of thick round glasses, waiting for danger to strike.

Daphne brought them downstairs to the back of the house. Her steps had slowed from their efficient clip. "I saved the office for last," she murmured.

Of course. The office where Leo Summers was murdered by his son, Daniel.

Costello's heart sped up, his mouth dried out, and his palms started to sweat. *Why?* He'd seen combat, watched brothers die right in front of him. Why would a decades-old crime scene fill him with unreasonable dread?

It looks out onto the courtyard and the fountain. The thought drifted up out of nowhere. Daphne turned the knob and opened the door.

Darkness.

"Hang on." Daphne fumbled for the light switch beside the door. A couple of overhead lights flickered on and then immediately went back out. Daphne tsked. "Old lightbulbs."

The back wall was entirely covered by heavy velvet drapes. She crossed the room and pulled a cord. The curtains swung to one side of the room with an ear-piercing squealing sound as they moved along the old runners. Behind the curtains was a wall of windows and a door leading outside. The glass was foggy with condensation, obscuring the view, which was fine with Costello. His dread turned to tentative relief. If there was a fountain just outside he couldn't see it.

Why would there be? Just because you dreamed it? Stop it.

In front of the windows was a large mahogany desk with yellowing stacks of papers on it. The tiled floor was bare of any rugs, unlike the rest of the house. Costello imagined a rug covered in blood, a man lying there bleeding out after being bludgeoned to death by his own son. His heart pounded again.

"I hardly ever came in here after..." Daphne said almost to herself. She shook her head.

"We can get someone in to clean it up." Jordan spoke for the first time on the entire tour.

Daphne raised an eyebrow at her daughter. "Do you think?"

Nash broke the tension. "The windows and the door are weak spots in the home's defense. We'll have to do a ton of wiring in here."

Costello shook his head to clear it of the fog. "Exactly. Are there any lights just outside? That's our first deterrent."

"Well, let me think. I don't really remember," Daphne said. Thank goodness Nash took the initiative to check the door and go outside so Costello didn't have to. He was seriously thinking of recusing himself from this job and letting Nash lead. But what would he tell Lach? *Yeah, I can't do this one, Boss, because I have these dreams...* No way. Totally unacceptable.

"No lights out here," Nash said as he came back in.

"We'll get them installed," Costello said.

"More expenses." Daphne pursed her lips and clucked. Her eyes darted to Jordan. "But anything to keep my little girl safe."

That made Costello cringe. He didn't miss Jordan cringing too.

They wrapped up the tour in the kitchen. "That's it for the house," Daphne said.

Jordan glanced at Costello. "I'm going outside," she announced. She didn't wait for a response, just turned on her heel and practically jogged out of the kitchen.

"Don't wander off. Stay by the house," Daphne ordered as if she were speaking to a small child. She shook her head as she watched her daughter retreat. She turned back to Costello and Nash. "Give me an estimate for any alarm systems or whatever before you install them," she said. "I want to keep the budget from getting out of hand." She gazed around the kitchen, which looked like it hadn't been updated in decades. "This place is a money pit." She rubbed her temples. "I'm going upstairs to gather myself before the rest of our belongings and luggage is delivered. It was on the flight behind us. Excuse me." She left the kitchen, presumably for one of the bedrooms upstairs.

"Wonder if her budget allowed for first-class tickets for her luggage," Nash said.

Costello smiled ruefully. "You don't really think she'd fly her suitcases coach, do you?"

Nash grinned, then went serious. "You gonna be okay by yourself here today and tonight, brother?"

Sure, as long as I can get my suddenly overactive imagination back in line. "Yeah. I'll walk you and Reg back to the car."

Nash nodded and they headed for the mudroom and side door. Anubis stopped just inside and sat down to wait right before Costello gave him the command to do so. Costello found he wanted to walk his brother out as quickly as possible so that he could find Jordan in the gardens and have a chance to talk to her alone. He was haunted by the first look she'd given him back at Watchdog, as if she knew him. Or was that just more of his imagination? *Don't act the fool* he told himself. *Don't embarrass yourself by asking her stupid questions. When would you have ever met?*

As children, of course, his mind told him. *In the garden.*

Those are dreams, not memories he argued back. True, as a child he'd met his share of rich kids on Jordan's level, but he remembered every one of them. He made himself remember them out of guilt—and he had to admit, out of self-preservation in case one ever tracked him down and came after him—because he'd had a hand in swindling their parents. Jordan had not been one of them, he was positive.

"Where y'at?" Nash asked.

Costello shook his head. "Just thinking about the job."

"I'll write up the estimate for the security system, run it past Lach this afternoon, and bring it out tomorrow," Nash said. They'd reached his SUV and he opened the door for Reggie.

"Thanks. I appreciate it."

"This old place already has you in its teeth, don't it?" Nash asked.

That's the understatement of the year. But he wasn't about to say that out loud. He looked up at the sky, which was beginning to lighten as the clouds broke at least. Maybe in the sunlight, everything would look different and he could get his head on straight. "Just beginning-of-the-job jitters. You know how it is."

"I know how *you* are, Psychic. You don't get beginning-of-the-job jitters, golden boy. Y'all be careful tonight, y' hear?" Nash tagged him on the arm and got into the vehicle. Costello raised a hand in goodbye, then went to his SUV and took out his duffel. He carried it up to his designated bedroom, Anubis at his heels. He left the duffel on the bed, deciding to unpack it later so that he wouldn't miss his chance to talk to Jordan alone. He even skipped his habit of checking all the drawers for left-behind belongings. But he felt his feet drag on his way to the garden. Though the bedroom window looked out onto the courtyard below, he only glanced at the Pacific in the distance where sunlight broke through the clouds and turned the water into a shining sheet of glass.

He did not want to see the courtyard. The fountain.

Anubis let out an uncharacteristic whine as he looked up at his human partner. Costello scratched his head and they went downstairs to the French doors leading out to the garden. He braced himself while mentally beating himself up for being an idiot, then stopped dead on the patio.

No fountain. Where it should have been in his mind's eye, right in the middle of the rectangle of pavers and planters, was a circular bed of overgrown lavender.

Of course there's no fountain because this is a real garden, not a dream one. Now, will you finally put this delusion to rest?

Jordan was standing at the edge of the patio. She said something but he couldn't pull his attention away from the courtyard as he tried to get his racing heart under control before he embarrassed himself with a panic attack.

She called his name and his gaze drifted to her. The sun broke through the clouds and touched the garden with warm fingers. It backlit her hair, turning it into a halo worthy of the most beautiful angel. *Gorgeous.* His heart flipped in his chest and his breath caught for a different reason as the panic seeped away. Looking at Jordan, he felt as if he'd stepped out of a nightmare and into the best dream ever. He needed to talk to her, *now.*

He took one last look at the circle of lavender and walked toward the woman of his dreams.

That night, Costello tossed and turned in bed, dreaming. He was small again, no more than five years old. He was running, looking for something, no *someone.* His thick glasses slid down his nose and he pushed them back up as he ran through the long halls of Eden House. Every door was locked; his mom would be mad that he couldn't get into them. That was his job on their team. Hide and seek. But he needed to get out to the garden. Jordan was hiding and he had to find her before—

Elliot stood outside in the night garden and called her name. How could he have ever forgotten it? But calling her name was a mistake. *He* would hear and there would be blood. Elliot needed to hide, but he also needed to make sure Jordan was safe, that she didn't see the blood...

...In the fountain. The fountain was full of blood. As Elliot watched helplessly, it poured down the sides and stained the rug over the pavers. His head hurt like it was about to split open—

And Costello awoke sitting up in a cold sweat, his head pounding with one of his migraines. He used to get them as a kid all the time, but they had decreased once he was an adult. They came back from time to time after he was out of the service, and this one was a killer.

"Fuck," he whispered as he pressed the heels of his hands into his eyes, creating stars. The migraine sloshed around in his skull. He crawled out of bed and found his duffel on a chair. He searched blindly in a side pocket for the migraine pills he sometimes used, trying to remember how old they were and if the prescription had expired. It really had been a while since he'd needed them but he always took the prescription bottle along on a job just in case.

His hand closed around the bottle and he twisted off the top, the mere pressure of pushing down on the lid sending more pain into his head. He pulled out the little blister pack inside and realized he only had one dose left. "Fuck, fuck, fuck." It would have to be enough. He didn't have time to pick up a new bottle tomorrow and no way in hell would he admit to Daphne that he was in any way compromised. He'd call it in and grab it later, or maybe text Nash and have him grab it on his way, though that was a last-resort choice that would make him look weak.

Costello dry-swallowed the pills and hoped they'd kick in soon and that his headache would be gone by morning. Without opening his eyes—even the dimmest light could make it worse—he stumbled back to bed and lay down.

Where the memory of his dream waited for him. It had been so long since he'd dreamed of being a kid again in the garden. He pressed his hands against his eyelids again as if to force the dream out of his head.

There is no fountain. There is no fountain...

SIX

In the morning, Jordan came downstairs, her sketchbook tucked under her arm and a handful of drafting pencils in a little case in one hand. She headed to the dining room for breakfast, or rather, what was supposed to be breakfast. The room was empty, the table bare. She shrugged and headed for the kitchen and found the cook her mother had hired the day before preparing eggs to order, bacon, sausage, and pancakes. The cook had laid out plates and silverware on the kitchen island and was in the middle of telling Daphne that she wasn't a maid and wouldn't be setting the table in the dining room but was happy to serve buffet-style or plate up as requested.

Jordan felt her mother's displeasure—she was used to being treated like royalty. Daphne sniffed and grabbed a spoon and a container of yogurt from a selection of high-end brands the cook had brought, set it on her plate, and strode into the dining room without another word.

Nash, whose SUV Jordan had heard drive up somewhere near dawn, watched Daphne walk away and then looked at Elliot, his eyebrows raised. Nash had a face that was easier to read than most people's and it wasn't difficult for Jordan to tell he was amused. Besides, she'd seen people look at her mother like that before. And she knew that if Daphne ever caught them at it they weren't long for their jobs.

John Charles wandered into the kitchen. Jordan was used to seeing her older brother's face clean-shaven, his hair neat, and his clothes crisp and clean. She almost didn't recognize him with his scraggly stubble, his hair uncombed, in a robe over pajamas that smelled like it had been a while since they'd seen the inside of a washing machine. He even walked differently, with a bit of a shuffle instead of his usual shoulders-thrown-back stride. Elliot and Nash eyed him and only nodded when he looked their way. *No love lost there* Jordan thought.

He turned to her and smiled. "Good morning, sis."

"You look different," she said.

"Well, I'm not feeling my usual self either, Jordan. Heartbreak'll do that." He grabbed a plate and then noticed her hands were empty and handed it to her. "Ladies first." He gestured for her to go ahead of him. He looked at the scrambled eggs the cook had just plated and crinkled his nose. "Think I'll be starting with some black coffee anyway."

Nash opened his mouth and Elliot elbowed him. He cleared his throat instead.

John Charles held out a mug and the cook filled it while he studied Elliot and Nash. "So, you goons going to just hover around this place and keep my sister safe?"

"Our services extend to all members of the household," Elliot answered in a tight voice.

"Fantastic. I feel safer already."

One nice thing about dealing with her brother, his sarcasm had stopped flying over Jordan's head years ago. It didn't mean she wanted to hear it non-stop though. It looked like he was going to stay in the kitchen so she decided that she'd grab her food and eat in the study off the garden. Jordan set her pencil case and sketchpad on the counter and added some pineapple slices and strawberries to her plate alongside the eggs and a strip of bacon the cook had plated for her.

"What's your name?" she asked the cook.

"Carol, miss."

"Nice to meet you, Carol, I'm Jordan." She stuck her hand out to shake, then realized Carol had her hands full. "Sorry," she said. She fumbled with her plate, silverware, coffee mug, pencil case, and sketchpad. Her cheeks heated and her jaw clenched as she thought about what to pick up first without looking like an idiot, hating that this didn't always come naturally like it did for other people. At least her mother wasn't here to make it worse with her 'helpful' instructions. John Charles watched as he sipped his coffee. Elliot was watching too which made it that much worse.

She stopped, took a deep breath, then stuffed her sketchpad under her arm, and tried to decide if she should pick up the flatware next and put it on her plate, or if it would fall off while she walked, making everything worse. The only way to do it would mean the handles touched the eggs, and ew, gross.

"Can I help you?" Elliot asked as he started toward her.

"No, no, I'm fine, I can manage something as stupid as this." God, she felt like she was barking at him. "Thank you," she remembered to add.

John Charles chuckled. "Jordan likes to maintain her independence," he said, which was his standard line for whenever she felt awkward. She had not missed him much since she'd last seen him.

"There's nothing stupid about trying to do something that takes eight hands when you only have two," Elliot said. She braved a glance at his face. He was smiling with soft eyes. He wasn't teasing or being mean. Even his voice was gentle, but the tone didn't make her cringe like her mom's did. It felt...nice.

She smiled at him, putting plenty of warmth in her eyes. "Too bad I'm not an octopus."

"It would make gardening faster, wouldn't it?"

She laughed at the sudden image of an octopus with a trowel in each tentacle. "It sure would."

Without having to think about it, she added the pencil case to the sketchbook under her arm, picked up the silverware with a napkin in one hand, looping two fingers through the mug's handle, and carried the plate in the other. Done. She headed for the kitchen door while John Charles said, "Knew you could do it, sis," behind her as he golf-clapped.

She didn't want to see Elliot's expression after that.

Jordan and Daphne sat at the long, carved wooden table in front of the giant picture window overlooking the southwest corner of the property. Jordan had wanted to be alone after her fun little conversation with her brother in the kitchen, so she'd brought her breakfast there instead of the dining room. But Daphne came in shortly after, coffee cup in hand, and sat down at the other end. She pretended to be interested in the view outside, but it was obvious to Jordan that her mother was more interested in watching Jordan sketching in her notebook as she nibbled on her bacon and sipped her coffee.

"What are you working on?" she finally asked.

Jordan ignored her as she drew a line down the plastic ruler that snapped into the spiral spine.

"Jordan. Speak when you're spoken to, please." Not the first time she'd heard that from her mother.

Jordan didn't look up but kept sketching. "A new bed for the heirloom tomatoes I ordered. I'm adding an entire vegetable and herb garden to the grounds just outside the kitchen."

Daphne frowned and took a sip of her coffee. "I mean, what are you working on for your next installation?"

"Told you. I need a break." She drew another line.

"Why on earth does this place need a vegetable garden? We won't even be here that long."

"Break." How many times did she need to say it? "Break, break, break."

Daphne gave her coffee cup a tight-lipped smile. "You don't need breaks. You can't even put that notebook down for more than five minutes unless you're actually out working in the dirt."

Jordan didn't bother to answer.

"I wish you could carry on a conversation like a normal person."

Jordan inhaled slowly through her nose and out through her mouth, her hand never stopping as she moved on to a keyhole garden design. "If I were a normal person, you wouldn't have the chance to travel and live like we do nearly as much, would you?" *Yes!* She'd been saving *that* one up for a while now.

All of Jordan's accomplishments became her mother's bragging rights. Her dreams, her desires were twisted and stunted until they served what Daphne wanted, which was always more of everything faster. And it took Jordan so long to realize it that it made her feel stupid, which fed into what her mother always told her—she was incapable of functioning on her own in the real world and needed her mother's guidance so that no one would take advantage of her. There was an irony to being set free behind what amounted to a walled garden—free to create, to focus on the one thing that made her happy and do it surrounded by luxury, while Daphne took care of the day-to-day to keep things rolling.

But Jordan wasn't free at all, and the more her mother wanted, the more she became a prisoner.

But then came the day Jordan realized that the door to her walled garden was open just a tiny bit, so she pushed at it. Now she was home.

Daphne's eyes widened momentarily before narrowing to slits. "Well, that lifestyle's going to end, isn't it, if you decide to extend this 'break, break, break' much longer."

"It's been one single day, Mother. Hardly a break." *Careful. Keep your voice even. Don't give her a chance to twist your words into something they aren't.*

Daphne ran her finger around the edge of her coffee mug. "I can't stop thinking about the commission you turned down. He's an impatient man despite seeming laid-back. I know you don't get that, but if we don't give him an answer soon. We'll lose a *very* lucrative opportunity."

"I already gave you my answer, you just don't like it." She'd scripted that, too, over and over on the plane, along with all her mother's possible responses. Jordan shuddered at the memory of their meeting with Mr. Porter. He was rumored to bring young girls to his secluded island retreat in the Caribbean and 'loan' them out to his influential friends. She knew the moment Marcus Porter's gaze landed on her like a mat of stinging nettles that the rumors were true. All she wanted to do was brush at her skin as if he'd touched her physically and left her covered in filth. And when he did actually touch her bare arm, it took everything she had not to scream at his slimy touch.

She'd stayed mute during the negotiations as was expected while Daphne talked prices with him up until it was time to sign the contract. Then Jordan had stood up from the table and shouted *no*. There was no way she was going to this monster's island for a year to design and build a labyrinth for his entertainment. She could only imagine what would happen there and it made her sick to her stomach to think she'd have any part of that.

"You didn't give me an *answer*, Jordan. You threw a tantrum. It was very embarrassing."

"He's a terrible person."

Daphne rolled her eyes. "He was perfectly charming. You can't believe everything you read. Just think about what they say about *you*." Daphne went on. "They call you spoiled and demanding and when you act like you did it just feeds the gossip mill. Imagine where you'd be if you didn't have me here to offset your tantrums. You couldn't make it in the world. You can't negotiate when you're emotional and unpredictable."

She scooted closer as if Jordan couldn't hear her already. "You have no idea how much I go through to protect you. How much energy I spend shielding you from people who would take advantage of you if they knew you were autistic. How hard I work to cultivate your persona." Daphne's voice changed to the tone she used when talking about Jordan in public. "She has an artistic temperament, and you know how artists can be sensitive. She's not rude, she's always thinking about her work because she's so driven. Well, her father, God rest his soul, spoiled her at an early age—"

"Don't talk about Daddy." *Dammit.* She'd told herself never to let her mother know when she'd gotten to her. Jordan started rocking. The page in front of her stopped making sense.

Daphne grinned. "Spoiled her *rotten* at an early age. Now she expects the same treatment from the rest of the world."

"That's so not true."

Daphne took another sip. "Oh, I know it isn't. I don't actually *think* that, darling, why would you assume that?" Her voice dripped with sweetness. Jordan pictured each word shaped like a thick drop of syrup. "See, this is why you need me. You can't lie worth a damn and you have zero guile. They'd eat you alive out there otherwise. But the Jordan I've created makes them tiptoe around us. That's how we get our way." She tipped the mug against her lips and finished her coffee. "I worry about what's going to happen to you after your next birthday."

No, not this conversation again. Jordan didn't remember when she'd stopped sketching. She gripped her pencil and tried to stay calm. "That's why I needed a break. I have to take some time to think."

Her mother's titter felt like a series of pinches along Jordan's spine. "Darling, I'm trying to *help* you! You wouldn't need to waste your time thinking about what to do if you would just agree to the conservatorship. You could go on designing gardens to your heart's content. Nothing would have to change. When you come into your inheritance, it's only going to bring you more headaches. I can help you with that."

Jordan was ashamed by how tempting her mother's suggestion sounded. She still held the power—the more she worked, the more money came in. If she stopped, so did the income. It was a blunt weapon, but it had gotten her out of working with Mr. Porter, at least temporarily.

Then there was the secret weapon that had gotten her back home.

"I need to think." Jordan looked down and resumed her

sketching. She kept her mother in her peripheral vision—it was never a good idea to look away from her completely.

Daphne stared into the depths of her coffee mug. "If you want to say no to that commission, you can say no."

Jordan finally looked up. Was her mother really giving in for once?

"I simply didn't approve of your childish way of doing it," Daphne sniffed.

Jordan looked back down. "Thank you. Please call and tell him no."

"I'll do that later today. See how easy that was? You can get so much more accomplished when you use your manners." Her mother started to take another sip and remembered her mug was empty. She stood up. "Can I get you more coffee, darling?"

"No."

"Anything?" Her appeasing tone was back, the one she used to get her way. Now Jordan couldn't be sure if her mother would actually go through with canceling the commission. Her heart clenched.

"Call and tell him no. Please. For me."

Daphne blew a short, hard breath out her nose but kept smiling. "Of course." She stood and started to reach out to run a hand down Jordan's hair. No way did she want her mother touching her right now so she jerked away. Daphne's hand hung in the air a moment before she left the room through the door closest to the kitchen.

Jordan glanced up from her sketching and looked at the other door that led to the rest of the house. "I know you're there," she called out. She'd felt Elliot's presence the moment he'd stopped outside the door in the hall not long after her mother had come in.

Elliot stepped into the room. Was there a little color in his cheeks? "Sorry. You must think I'm spying."

"That's your job though, isn't it? To keep an eye on me?"

He walked to the table and took one seat closer to her than the one her mother had used. "It is. It's also my job to be as unobtrusive as possible. But you caught me."

"Hide and seek," Jordan said with an easy smile.

The color left his cheeks and drained away. *So, he still doesn't want to talk about it.* That was okay. They had time. Jordan planned on staying home as long as she could. Until the place grew and bloomed into something beautiful instead of something dark and tragic.

SEVEN

Hide and seek. Just like my dreams.

Costello fought back the urge to believe Jordan and his dream woman were one and the same and that he'd somehow known her without ever meeting her.

There are no psychics. Nothing but frauds.

He changed the subject to the reason he'd come in after overhearing Jordan and Daphne's conversation. He wanted to be clear he hadn't misunderstood what he thought he heard. "So, you and your mother work together?"

Jordan nodded. "We do. I'm the right brain, she's the left brain."

Costello smiled. "You're the artist and she's the numbers cruncher."

"Exactly. She makes sure I don't have to worry about that side of things so that I can do my best work. We're a team."

Costello nodded. *Go carefully.* "But, would you say she's the leader of the team? It sounds like you sometimes disagree on commissions."

Jordan covered a wince. "It's...it's changing." She started rocking then quickly stopped herself and Costello vowed to look up Asperger's and autism online. "Feels like she's looking more at the numbers and less at me these days."

Which is the same impression I got. The woman didn't hesitate to undermine her daughter's choices and autonomy. And if she was seriously contemplating a conservatorship...

Jordan asked point-blank, "You still don't like my mother, do you?"

Whoops. Am I that obvious? "It's not my place to like or dislike my clients. You'll get the same level of service from me either way." He didn't add that liking a client made the job that much easier and a lot more pleasant.

She surprised him with a laugh. Then she looked down and peered up at him through her lashes. "But you still like me, don't you?" Her voice had gone soft and tentative. This was not just flirting. She was asking something bigger. And he had to bite his tongue to keep from speaking the truth—that he'd been waiting for her all his life.

"I do like you, Jordan." The words sounded so small, almost empty compared to what he wanted to say. What he wanted to do, which was sweep her up and carry her off some-place where they could be alone and he could show her just how much he liked her. Just a whiff of her jasmine-and-salt fragrance was enough to send his heart racing and his cock begging. And the smile she gave him at his answer melted his core.

She lowered her voice. "I need you to know you can trust me. Just like I trust you." That surprised him even more. Trust her? What was she getting at?

They both looked up at the door when they heard a sound. A moment later, Anubis trotted in and they exhaled simultaneously as the dog walked under the table and sat beside Jordan. *She heard him at the same time I did.* Costello wasn't used to civilians matching his level of hyper-vigilance.

But he imagined a lifetime of growing up under Daphne's thumb would put anyone on guard, not to mention that she'd lost her father in a horrific way at an early age. Trauma had a tendency to sharpen the senses and put one on permanent high alert.

"Jordan, if you need to talk about anything, I'm here. Whatever you need."

"I know. And the same goes for you."

For me? "I don't understand."

She reached out and covered his hand. "I know that *your* mother died recently."

Costello practically jumped out of his skin. "How...how could you know that? *Why* would you know that?"

Had Daphne dug that deeply into his background when hiring Watchdog and shared it with Jordan? It seemed unlikely she'd confide in her daughter about, well, anything. And to dig that deep would have taken time and a great hacker or PI. He hadn't gone by his birth name in decades with the sole purpose of putting his mother as far behind him as he could. As far as he was concerned, he was a Costello. *They* were his family.

He fought to keep himself from reacting too strongly. He gave himself away though and Jordan took her hand away quickly. Her pale green eyes darkened. "I'm sorry. I understand why you don't want to talk about it. Please, we can go back to pretending that I don't know a thing about your mother."

Costello's stomach churned like the ocean outside. Now he knew why other people were quick to call him Psychic and how they felt when he pointed things out about them that he'd observed, or the times he saw a suspicious person and acted moments before anyone else even noticed anything was amiss.

Which is exactly what's going on here. Jordan didn't have

any mysterious psychic powers any more than he did. "So...
did *you* research me?"

Jordan nodded enthusiastically. "Yes! I found you." She
lowered her voice. "I nudged her into hiring Watchdog over
another company. She thinks she picked you guys out but it
was me. Don't tell her." She leaned over and petted Anubis
who had plopped down at her feet. "I like dogs."

Costello laughed. Mystery solved. She'd hired a top-notch
private investigator and done her research before hiring
Watchdog. More proof Jordan was quite capable of taking
care of herself without a conservatorship. "Well, considering
you know about my birth-mom, I'm surprised you still went
with us. With me."

Jordan straightened up from petting Anubis and looked at
him with such warmth and tenderness in her eyes his heart
stuttered. "Of course, I did," she said in a tone that implied
anything else would have been ridiculous. The tenderness in
her gaze turned to hurt. "You don't think I'd hold her crimes
against you, do you?" She blinked rapidly. "You were so young
when she made you her accomplice. Since then, you've made
so much of your life, Elliot. You should be proud, not embarrassed. You aren't her. You never were and you never will be."

Costello exhaled sharply as if he'd been gut-punched.
Hell, her words were more than a gut punch—they were a
direct hit to his heart. How could a complete stranger know
him so well and both hurt and heal him so completely with
only a few words?

*I need to pull back. I can't let this get personal. I'm already
feeling things I shouldn't.*

"I appreciate your vote of confidence," Costello said as he
stood up to leave.

And damn, if she didn't look even more hurt. Her eyes
went wide. She bit her lower lip and looked away. "It's why

you changed your name, so you wouldn't be found. I'll keep your secret," she said. "We won't talk about it anymore, I promise." She rocked slowly a couple of times then stopped.

"I...thank you." He ran his hand through his hair as another migraine loomed. "I'll let you finish your work." Costello nodded at her sketchpad. "I'll be just outside the door." And he turned before he could see any more hurt in her eyes.

———

Two days later, Costello watched the landscapers hard at work spreading compost and getting ready to add rich black soil to a raised bed. But mostly, he watched Jordan in her element. Gone was the woman who kept her head down and her soul tucked in out of sight like a snail. She was replaced by a vibrant and beautiful young woman who was absolutely the queen of all she surveyed. Or more like a commander overseeing her crew—make that two crews, one for the new garden and one sprucing up the established one. She knew exactly what she wanted and directed the men with a shout and a smile, in English, Spanish, and a smattering of French.

God, she was stunning. Everything he'd dreamed of and more. And she was in more trouble than perhaps she realized.

Costello's thoughts drifted back to the conversation they'd had. His migraine refused to go away for most of the day, leaving him exhausted, but not out of it enough to miss just how manipulative Daphne Summers really was. A conservatorship for Jordan? For this obviously capable woman who, granted, interacted with the world a little differently, but was by no stretch of the imagination helpless.

"Pedro!" She yelled. "*Por favor, más suciedad por aquí.*

Gracias!" She pointed to where she wanted the next load of dirt dumped. Then she picked up a rake and helped spread it, smiling and chatting about all things gardening as they worked.

He couldn't believe Jordan was actually entertaining the idea of letting her mother take complete control of her life after her birthday and the granting of her full inheritance. But then again, her confidence when it came to running her life outside of her artistic endeavors was practically non-existent. Probably because she hadn't been given the chance to run it—smothered by Daphne all her life, told she was incapable, spoiled, helpless.

Despite wanting to talk to Jordan, Costello went back to keeping a polite, professional distance, never taking his eyes off her while on duty but keeping conversations to the minimum required pleasantries as he'd done on so many assignments—the way he was *supposed* to do his job. This assignment should have been fine, easy, given that they were staying in the lap of luxury—even if it was faded—and there was no sign of any outside danger, no additional threatening letters, and Lachlan had located Daniel Summers in Los Angeles and had eyes on him. Yes, an easy, straightforward assignment.

But that was all on paper. The reality was that this assignment might fucking well kill him. His nightmares had only gotten worse. Every night the same thing—Costello as a terrified boy searching for Jordan, trying to keep her safe from the shadowy figure from the fountain. And the migraine that started the first night never quite went away; it ebbed and flowed throughout the day and hit him like a thug after every bad dream. Nash had picked up his prescription migraine medication on his way back to Eden House but the pills were barely better than aspirin, which Costello was eating like

M&Ms along with enough strong black coffee to keep a dormful of college kids cramming for finals awake for a week.

As he stood watching Jordan from the patio, the bright sun beaming down felt like its sole purpose was to remind him to embrace the suck. He was grateful for his extra-dark sunglasses and the wide overhang providing merciful shade. But guarding Jordan either provided the most relief—allowing Costello to lose himself in watching her every move—or it was going to be what ultimately killed him. All he wanted was to talk with her again about more than the weather or her plans for the day so he could adjust her level of protection. *Oh, hell, why deny it?* He wanted to do much more than that. Thoughts of running his hands over her smooth cello curves, of slipping her shirt off her shoulders and dipping down to lick the valley between her breasts filled his mind. While he may not have been dreaming of her—*no, not her, you've never dreamed about Jordan*—at night since he'd gotten to Eden House, his daydreams about her were near-constant.

Anubis stood guard beside him along with Reggie. Nash was inside taking a quick bathroom break. He'd do a tour of the house and make sure Daphne was fine. And John Charles, who had decided to extend his staycation after a long, loud 'conversation' with his fiancée.

Costello heard the door open behind him and Reggie thumped his tail three times, letting him know Nash was back. His partner came up beside him and apropos of nothing said, "You ever notice how killers always go by their full names? John Wayne Gacy. John Wilkes Booth." His lips barely moved, his voice reserved only for Costello.

"Not Ted Bundy. Or Jeffrey Dahmer."

"You're missing my point." With the slightest head tilt, he indicated the house behind them. "Old boy insists on using both names at all times. John Charles."

Costello held back a grin. "You're saying he's a serial killer or an assassin?"

"I'm saying he's an ass. Like, a total ass."

"Hadn't noticed."

Nash side-eyed him. "Oh. Y'all are pulling my leg. Got it." Full-on Southern sarcasm voice. "Bless your heart."

"I agree he's a complete ass, but he's our ass to watch."

"See, now I'm not sure that's true. He wasn't part of the original deal. I say we throw him over the cliffs."

Costello's eyes widened behind his dark glasses. Nash was the most laid-back guy on the team but that didn't mean he wasn't one-hundred percent professional. He usually let the little annoyances that went along with protecting 'difficult' principals slide right off his back. "What'd he do just now, piss up your leg?"

"Not up *my* leg, up his fiancée's leg, then up Daphne's right after. That man is a mean old snake."

"Don't know about the fiancée but I think Daphne can handle herself."

Nash shifted his weight. "Don't make it right. You don't talk to ladies like that."

"Like how?"

"Something about money. It's always something about money, isn't it? Or sex. Sex and money, yes sir. Root of all fun. I mean, evil."

Costello snorted, then covered it with a cough when Jordan looked up. "Did you catch what they were arguing about?"

"Just a bit. I think old Two-Name is having some financial troubles with the family business."

That was interesting. "Really? It was started by his great-grandpa. One of the first big shipping companies on the West coast. It should be doing well. It's not like people aren't buying stuff from China."

"Yeah, well, a guy like him could probably fuck up a wet dream. Who the hell goes on an extended drunkcation when he's got a multi-billion-dollar business to run?"

"Someone with a broken heart?" Costello said, returning as much sarcasm as Nash had given him.

This time, Nash had to cover a snort. "Yeah, right. You think he gives two shits about his fiancée? The way he talks to her, I bet she's a year outta high school, got a budding modeling career"—Costello could hear the air quotes around that—"with tits and ass that don't quit and she calls him daddy because it makes him feel like a big man."

"Jesus, Nash. Respect."

"Just sayin', I think she's in it for the money and that money tit dried right the fuck up. Heard him ask her if she's got everything packed yet, then got all pissy because she apparently doesn't. That don't sound like a man who's giving a lady time to think and reflect, but a weasel who's skippin' out on the mortgage and left her to sweep up."

Costello didn't like the sound of that one bit. "So what'd he say to Daphne?"

"Oh, he caught her eavesdropping and accused her of gloating. And truth be told, she kinda was. Told him that's what you get when you date a child, and he said she outta know being as she was a child bride. He called her a spoilt bitch and a leech and I'll be damned if she didn't lap it up like cream, knowing that she'd gotten to him."

"Told you she can handle herself. What else did he say?"

Nash grimaced. "About that time, they realized I was there and they broke up the fight. Went their separate ways."

"Damn."

"Whatcha thinking, brother?"

"I'm thinking if John Charles is driving the business into the ground, it would make sense he'd retreat to the family estate. What if he's here seeing what he could sell, and Daphne and Jordan disturbed his plans with their arrival?"

"So maybe the house isn't his? I wonder what the will looks like."

Costello smiled. "I know what the will looks like. I had Lach dig it up and he emailed it to me yesterday."

He'd sent out that request right after his morning conversation with Jordan. Even though the request was way out of bounds for a normal security job, the assignments Watchdog took on often became more than that.

"Leo Summers set all three of his kids and his wife up with hefty trust funds and put Daphne in charge of the house so she and Jordan would have a guaranteed place to live. But, she can't sell it without permission from John Charles, Daniel, and Jordan once she comes into her whole inheritance, which is on her next birthday. That doesn't mean John Charles wasn't here poking around and seeing if there was anything of value inside the house that he could sell. No one's lived here for years. He probably figured he could get away with it."

"So old Leo left the family business to that loser?"

"John Charles was named chairman while Daniel was CEO. Makes sense—the chairman is sometimes just the public face of the business while the real work gets done at the CEO level. Before Daniel went off the rails, Leo had been grooming him to take over while John Charles was basically off fucking around. Daniel's the eldest son and seems to have taken the responsibility seriously. At least when he wasn't blackout drunk."

"Or murdering his father. Small detail."

"That too." Costello allowed himself a whip-quick smile, but damn if his head didn't suddenly throb. "John Charles sued to have Daniel completely removed from the company and succeeded. But things get interesting now that Daniel is out of jail. The will says that if John Charles, Daphne, and finally Jordan pass away, it all goes to Daniel. Same deal for any of them."

"Damn. Winner takes it all. Loser's gotta fall."

"Jake, is that you?" Costello joked. Their teammate, Jake Collins aka Crooner, was a human jukebox who could pull up just about any song lyrics on command. And more often, *not* on command, driving everyone around him nuts. Luckily, he'd found a woman who could do the same trick and loved music as much as he did. Rachael Collins was even now climbing the music charts with her latest hit.

"Heh. Yeah, you're right. Now Jake's got me misquoting lyrics that ain't even country." Nash shifted his weight again as he studied Jordan, who had moved on to a different part of the garden and was directing a small crew of three that was planting a row of oleanders. "Having read the will, you think Daniel's out to get her? Get *them*? Daphne says her stepson is still well-connected."

"If that's true, then Daniel's got some assholes for friends because our man is living in a run-down hotel room." Costello adjusted his sunglasses, hoping to magically block out more light. "He's eating gas station food from down the street and he doesn't go out for much else. Easiest tail ever."

"Any visitors?"

"Not that they've seen so far. Gina's going inside for a day or two in case someone is being sneaky about seeing Daniel. Wouldn't be hard to slip through our net with rent-by-the-hour going on in some of the rooms."

"Wait, Gina?" Nash asked. "Lach's putting a defenseless woman into a situation like that?"

They grinned at each other over the joke. Spooky knew how to handle herself just fine.

Nash got quiet for a moment. "I hear she's watering your plants."

"Gina? Yeah, I asked her to keep an eye on them." His head throbbed again. He thought of the new plants he'd inherited from his mom after she died in hospice and the peace lily from her neighbor sent for the funeral—such as it was. He'd always kept plants, told himself that if he ever bought a house he'd turn the entire yard into a lush garden to rival his dreams. Ultimately an empty garden though without his dream woman there with him.

Costello inadvertently sighed as he watched Jordan. Distracted, he belatedly caught the change in Nash's posture. "She, uh, been watering your plants very long?"

What is he...? Oh! No way. "Gina's just doing me a solid from when I rescued her amaryllis from the office at Christmas."

Nash nodded.

"Really. Just a favor."

"Didn't say a thing."

"Right, that's the problem."

"Doing you a *solid*." Nash rocked almost imperceptibly on his heels.

"Don't go there. There's nowhere to go."

"Mmm."

A couple minutes passed.

"It's just, I've never seen you with a girlfri—"

"Drop it, Nash, or I'm kicking you off this assignment." Costello's migraine punched the side of his head, made worse by Nash's chuckle.

Daphne joined them on the patio. She'd put on a wide-brimmed straw hat and sunglasses but she still shaded her eyes with her hand as she looked out at Jordan. "My daughter is costing us. What a folly." Costello detected a snuffling to her voice as if she'd been crying. She looked the two men over. "Then there's you two."

"Do you wish to terminate the contract early, ma'am?"

She sniffed. "Daphne, not ma'am. I realize I'm old enough to be your mother, but you don't have to rub it in." She smoothed her hands down her skinny thighs. "No, I don't wish to terminate the contract early. But I do wonder what good you're doing. I could stand out here and watch her for free."

Costello let a moment pass. "Close your eyes."

She turned to him and he imagined her eyes must have widened behind her glasses. "Excuse me?"

"Close your eyes."

She huffed but did as he said. "Okay. Now what?"

"Tell me how many men are in the yard."

"What?"

"How many men?"

"I don't...I don't know."

"Fifteen. How many are wearing blue shirts?"

"Um. Three?"

"None. Ten white shirts, three off-white, one light green, and one joker in red. How many are Spanish-speaking and how many speak French?"

"This is ridiculous. You've been standing out here for hours. I've been here thirty seconds."

"Eight minutes, actually. And yes, we have been standing here for hours. That's what we do. And we watch, and we notice things, and we keep any bad things we notice from turning into tragic things. And while the two of us are standing here, there are others on the team in the second and third rings who are watching elsewhere, either through their own eyes or on a divided-up screen now that the cameras are installed."

"Your point?"

Maybe it was the headache pushing him, but Costello couldn't resist. "There is more going on here than meets the eye."

Daphne crossed her arms. "Like what?" Her tone had gone casual as if he were offering her selections off a menu.

"We've located your stepson and he doesn't seem to be a threat to you or your daughter."

Daphne's mouth opened in shock. "Where is he? I want to be sure. As I've said, he has friends. I'm sure he's made more in prison."

"He's at the Barr Inn in Los Angeles."

"Never heard of it."

"Not surprised at all," Nash said.

Daphne actually laughed. "One of *those* places, huh?"

Nash gave her the grin and head tip he'd stolen from Brad Pitt in *Legends of the Fall* that he bragged melted panties. Daphne grinned back.

She looked back at Costello. "You could learn a thing or two about manners from your friend here." Then she turned and they watched her saunter back into the house, Nash grinning. Costello thought about telling him to keep it professional, but at this point, that might make him a hypocrite.

When Costello turned back, Jordan had stopped working and was watching them. He felt a rush of shame despite the fact he'd done nothing. Jordan went back to work, her voice a little less enthusiastic.

EIGHT

For three days, Jordan avoided talking to Elliot, which was difficult since he almost never let her out of his sight, including now—he stood silently at the door as she walked around the table she liked to use for her sketching. Anubis lay under the table watching her every move. His tail thumped when she'd bend down to pet him but his eyes stayed alert to any danger.

Her heart felt knotted up like the roots of an old tree. Every time her mother came into the same room, it only squeezed tighter. Jordan was used to seeing Daphne flirt with all sorts of men, from their clients to the doorman, and it never really bothered her before. It seemed harmless, and the few times Jordan had called her on it her mother told her it didn't mean anything, that it was just a way of 'greasing the wheels' and getting her way.

But Elliot was different. Watching Daphne smile and preen in front of Elliot and Nashville turned Jordan's stomach sour and sent her outside where she could breathe again. Today it didn't help that the clouds had rolled back in and the wind was gusting hard enough to bend the trees and shake the house, that it was terrible gardening weather and Jordan was forced back indoors with nowhere to hide.

She busied herself with arranging flowers she'd cut from the wild-gone gardens the day before knowing the weather was about to turn. Vases lined up on the table in front of her between mounds of flowers, like early rosebuds, eucalyptus stems, lavender and larkspur, various greenery, and of course poppies. The poppies had seemed cheery the day before but now they felt garish against the gray day. Jordan tried not to compare them to her mom, but there it was.

She was putting together several vases for around the house including a vase for each person's bedroom, one for the kitchen, and one for her father's old study in honor of his memory. Jordan couldn't help but style each arrangement to fit everyone's personality. She smiled to herself as she added a peacock feather to her mother's vase of poppies and daffodils.

Did Elliot just laugh? Jordan looked up from her work and saw the hint of a smile just disappearing from his lips. Her heart immediately sped up as anxiety filled her. Was he laughing at her? With her? His expression had gone unreadable but she liked the way his eyes looked, the light shining in them.

"Sorry," he said as the smile returned. "Quite unprofessional of me."

"I don't mind," Jordan lied. "But can I ask, were you laughing *at* me?"

He chuckled again. "Never." He indicated the vase with a chin lift.

"You were laughing at this?"

Elliot left his post by the door. He stood across from her with the table between them. "I was laughing at that, and it was very unprofessional of me."

Jordan grinned. "Why were you laughing?"

"Because I know a thing or two about flowers. I know their secret language. I read a book once on how people used to send flowers to each other, as messages." He gave an exaggerated glance over his shoulder. "Don't tell Nash I told you that or I'll never hear the end of it."

Jordan laughed. "I wouldn't dream of it. And yes, I've read about that too."

"I'm not surprised." Elliot gestured at the table. "Which is your favorite flower?"

"That's not a fair question," Jordan said. "Each is different. Every flower has its good qualities, and my favorite varies by the day."

"What about today then?"

Jordan looked over the table. She finally pointed to one of the piles.

"Tulips. They are one of the only flowers that keep growing even after you've cut them. Like they're saying, fuck you, I'm still alive."

Elliot smiled again. "I always liked that about tulips as well. I usually got them for my mom for Mother's Day. Even though they tended to outgrow their vase I never wanted her to trim them so that they would fit again. I wanted to see how much they would grow."

"I need to fill the house with tulips then. This place needs new life. It's haunted by tragedy. Growing up, this house was quiet as a tomb, soundproofed by all sorts of secrets."

Elliot looked around the room. "Yeah, I can see that. But it's different today. You're bringing life back to this place." He looked over her shoulder, out the window at the new vegetable garden. "That alone gives life to this old house. All the vegetables you're growing. I can't wait to try them. I know they're going to be amazing."

Carol says the same thing, that she can't wait to cook with

them. We'll see. Do you know I've never had a vegetable garden before? I've always focused on flowers and landscapes."

Elliot tilted his head. "Is that by choice? I mean is that by *your* choice or by Daphne's choice?"

"Oh, it's my mom's choice, of course."

Elliot looked again at the flower arrangement Jordan was making for Daphne. He shook his head and smiled.

"Okay, Elliot, tell me. Why did it make you laugh?"

"That vase is for your mother, isn't it?"

Jordan grinned. "Why yes, yes it is. You really are psychic."

"There's nothing psychic about me. I pick up on things sooner than other people. Put the pieces together a little faster."

"Has there ever been a puzzle you couldn't solve?"

"Sure." Costello swallowed hard. "I'm looking at her."

Jordan's heart fluttered. "I'm not a puzzle. I'm just a woman. I like plants, like to garden."

"You do more than garden. You create these perfect little worlds for people that reflect them. How do you do it?"

"I don't know. I just do." She paused to think. "Maybe it's the same as you. Maybe I see things that other people don't, or see them in a different way. Plants have their own language. They tell me when they don't like the soil or they're getting too much water or not enough sun. The bushes that I shape for the bigger installations already have their forms inside them, I just go in and find them and bring them out with my shears." She touched one of the daffodil petals, turning it over to study its underside. "I know which plants and bushes and trees are going to get along once they're in a garden together, and which ones are going to try and choke each other out so I chose carefully. That's why people think my gardens are so peaceful."

She shook her head. "I wish I was that skilled with people." She gave him a wan smile. "But people don't always show you who they are. They hide things, and I'm not very good at finding the shapes of their intentions underneath."

"I think you might be better at that than you know. You've just been told to ignore your gut feelings. To let others make those decisions for you. But that's changing, isn't it?"

Jordan bit her lower lip, weighing what she could say and what she couldn't. Hypocrite that she was, she hid more of herself than she showed the world, like a tree with beautifully patterned wood under rough gray bark, or a rose waiting to bloom, still in its protective green calyx covering. She had to hide things or else her mother would take them and make them her own.

"So how did you know this vase was for my mother? You never told me."

"Well, it's like you said. Plants have their own language. And I happen to know it. At least for some flowers. Poppies can mean extravagance and wealth. They also put people to sleep." Elliott ran his finger along the frilly trumpet edge of the daffodil Jordan had just examined. "Most people call these daffodils. But they have another name. Narcissus." He tapped his nose. "For Daphne, that one is right on the nose. And if that wasn't a dead giveaway, the peacock feather is. A proud bird, and the symbol of Hera, queen of the gods."

"It really is obvious, isn't it?" Jordan asked.

"Well, I just hope your mother doesn't speak the same language that we do." His voice had gone soft. Jordan liked the way her skin felt when he spoke in that tone.

Elliot looked at the vase next to her mother's. "I take it that you're making one for everyone."

"I am. I wonder if you can figure out the others." *No, Jordan, you idiot. Why did you say that?* Her heart sped up again. Would he be able to read the flowers she put in *his* vase?

Elliot looked at the next vase. "Well, here we have a vase with rosebuds in it. And eucalyptus." He rubbed one of the waxy leaves between his fingers and leaned forward to smell it. "There's lavender. A little sprig of juniper. And nasturtiums. If I had to guess, I would say this one's going into the kitchen for Carol."

"It is! You're really good at this. Break it down for me though."

"All of these are edible except the eucalyptus. And rosebuds can signify new beginnings. She's newly hired. The eucalyptus is actually medicinal; you can steam it in a pot of boiling water to clear the sinuses. Or freshen a room, maybe clear it of cooking smells."

Jordan practically clapped her hands together. "Excellent. And yes, the cook we had when I was growing up used to steam eucalyptus when she chopped onions because she knew the onion smell could make my eyes burn even if I was in the next room. It still does. But the eucalyptus took care of it."

Elliot raised his eyebrows. "You could smell them from the next room?"

Jordan's cheeks heated with embarrassment. "I have very sharp senses. Hyper-alertness. Not uncommon with people like me. And when I was little-little, I used to throw a fit when I'd smell the onions. Her cheeks heated further. "Also not uncommon for people like me."

"I'm not like you, but I have the same thing. The same hyper alertness. It's kept me alive. I've had it ever since I was a little kid. My mom developed that in me." His eyes darkened. "She found it useful."

"And it saved you and your team later, I'm sure."

Elliot squeezed his eyes shut as if he were fighting off a headache. "You don't need to hear about me." His voice had gone flat. Even she could hear that. He took a step back as if to return to his post by the door.

Dammit. She'd brought him down without meaning to. *Typical me, always misreading things.* She struggled to think of the right thing to say to make him feel better and to keep him close. Now that they were talking again, she didn't want to stop.

"I *like* hearing about you. You've done so many amazing things, made so much of your life. I know you're a SEAL but I don't know how you must have felt about it while you were on active duty. If you were proud or scared or excited, maybe sad."

Elliot stepped forward again. He gave her a small smile. "All of the above, depending."

She thought of telling him she'd asked the angels at the gate to watch over him, even though they kept their eyes closed. "I could only guess how you felt when I read the stories about you. I mean, you weren't mentioned by name in any of the military ones of course, but I was assured they were about you and your team."

Elliot's eyes went wide and he took a step back. "You... must have hired the best to look into me."

Oh, God. This was going downhill fast. *I should just shut up, let him get back to his duties.* Instead, she said, "I did hire the best. I'm sorry. I've upset you. I only wanted—"

He raised a hand, stopping her. "I know why. I understand."

"Do you?" Their eyes met with an intensity that normally

would have made her look away, maybe even leave the room. She saw her own gaze reflected back at her, full of frustration at not being able to say what she wanted to say. No matter what she did, it came out wrong. But...did she see that same frustration in his eyes? Or was she just projecting how she felt and what she wanted? Hoping that he'd finally open up to her about the past.

Elliot looked away first. He shifted his attention to the vase next to Daphne's. "Alstroemeria, clematis. Daffodil again." He smiled at that. "The alstroemeria is for wealth and business. Clematis is cleverness. And we went over narcissus already."

"But in this case, I went with the daffodil's meaning. Unrequited love."

"Ah, yes. A double-meaning for this flower." He pursed his lips. "What about the dried lotus pod? That wasn't in the book I read on flower language or I'd remember it."

"Estranged love."

"I sense a theme." He winked. "Obviously, this is for John Charles since he's still on the outs with his fiancée." He moved on to the next one. "Three left." He studied the next vase of flowers. "Juniper is in all three of the remaining vases, I see. Juniper means protection. This one has dried reeds. Music. Not hard to say whose it is just from that." He touched one of the yellow daisy-like flowers. "Coreopsis has two meanings—always cheerful and...love at first sight."

Jordan's cheeks reddened. "In this case, it means always cheerful. At least from what I've seen of Nash," she said quickly. "And you're right. That one's for Nashville."

He moved on to the next vase. Jordan's palms broke out in a light sweat. *Elliot's vase.* He said nothing as he read the arrangement. Jordan had used juniper, lilac, white rosebuds from her favorite part of the garden, with ivy trained around the roses and trailing down the side of the vase. And jasmine she'd harvested that morning despite the wind.

Elliot's eyes widened, then fell almost to half-mast as he touched the closed white jasmine buds tenderly, giving each one a tiny stroke that sent lightning through Jordan's body wondering how that same touch would feel on her skin. *I shouldn't have included the jasmine. I shouldn't have made a vase for him at all.* She felt exposed, as if she'd just shouted her feelings for him.

Mercifully, he said nothing and looked at the last vase meant for her father's study. "More juniper for protection," he said. "And white roses, like this one has," he pointed to his vase then went back to the other, "but in fuller bloom. A more mature, but still pure love. But this arrangement has rosemary for remembrance. Pinks for a child's love." He touched the cypress branch. "This is for mourning a death." He looked at Jordan, his features soft. "You're so eloquent, Jordan. I know exactly who this is for. I'm sorry about your father."

She couldn't help the sudden tears. "He was a good, strong, loving dad. I miss him every day. He taught me to love gardening." She touched one of the white roses. "These were his favorites."

"I haven't seen any white roses in the garden. Did you order them?"

"You haven't seen...but of course you have. They're—" She stopped. They were treading on his secrets again. Or, he was protecting hers. *Of course.* "I guess you haven't. They aren't close to the house so you wouldn't have seen them."

"I'm lax in walking the entire grounds. I've let the cameras do the work."

"I'd love to show you everything. Though later, I guess." She looked out the window at the damned weather; for once she didn't welcome a much-needed storm, if the clouds ever decided to actually rain. When she looked back, Elliot's attention had returned to his vase. His cheeks looked flushed.

"Last one." His voice sounded rough. "Juniper for protection. Rosebuds for a brand new relationship. White means innocent." He grinned. "A friendship."

She nodded, a lump in her throat at that word.

"Lilac, now that's an interesting choice. Lots of different meanings. Youth, humility. But also the first signs of love."

Jordan bit her lip.

"But to be safe, I'm going to go with its last meaning in this case. Confidence."

You're wrong. It's all of the above Jordan thought. She only nodded.

"Ivy around the roses." He worked one of the leaves between his fingers. "Also an interesting choice. Often found at weddings."

"Ivy is for fidelity," Jordan said.

"Fidelity, yes." Elliot nodded. "So. Protection, confidence, fidelity." He brushed a rose. "New *friendship*." A funny smile took over his lips. "Thank you for your confidence in my abilities to protect you."

Jordan would have given anything to read between the lines. If there were even lines to read between.

Elliot wasn't done. "But that leaves the jasmine." He touched the tightly closed buds again the way that she'd always wanted to be touched—with gentleness and reverence, his entire attention focused on the erotic little buds. She would have given anything to be those flowers. He bent forward and closed his eyes, bringing his face close to them, and inhaled. "No scent, sadly."

"They're night-blooming. So tonight when you're in bed they'll open and fill your room with their perfume." Her voice sounded deeper and quiet to her ears.

His breath came out long and slow between his lips, his eyes still closed. "I won't be sleeping tonight. Nash and I rotate night shifts." He opened his eyes and looked at her. His voice sounded as rough as the cliffs.

She swallowed. "Then I'll refresh them for tomorrow night." Her words caught for a moment. "I don't want you to miss that."

He straightened up then caught her gaze again. So intense her entire body throbbed. "Well. These shouldn't go to waste." He pulled the jasmine from the arrangement and came around to her side of the table. Jordan held her breath until he stood inches from her. He reached out and she thought he was going to put his arm around her until he picked up an empty vase. He put the jasmine into it and poured in some water from a pitcher. He searched the table and added tulips, the last of the white roses, and cedar. "I've made a vase for you now."

Jordan translated the language of flowers in her head. White roses for friendship. Tulips—traditionally a declaration of love. But, they'd just talked about how tulips continued to grow against the odds, and he'd compared her to them in that way. Jasmine—sensuality, but also *separation*. Her heart skipped a beat.

But it was his last choice for the vase that stole her breath. Cedar, for strength. But also, *I live for you.*

He remembers she thought to herself.

NINE

The wind eventually blew itself out by the following evening and Jordan wanted nothing more than to get outside. After her conversation with Elliot the day before, Nash took over guarding her while Elliot got some rest since he'd be up all night. Reggie replaced Anubis on the watch. The two dogs were like night and day. Both were alert and professional, but Reggie was also playful with a streak of mischief. Jordan wondered if it was a difference in the breeds —Anubis being Malinois and Reggie a Lab. Their human partners were so different from each other in the same way, it might just be the dogs themselves who were different.

Dinner went as awkwardly as ever. At least John Charles seemed to be pulling himself together. He'd shaved and smelled like he was back to showering daily. At some point, he'd left the house and come back with fresh clothes. Jordan wondered if he'd talked to his fiancée and if she still wasn't letting him come home. Jordan had told John Charles she was sorry he was going through a hard time with his fiancée and he'd waved her off, saying it didn't matter. He was unwilling to talk beyond that. Nothing new there.

He was also getting along with Daphne better than Jordan had ever seen. Not that they were buddy-buddy, but at least they didn't spew venom at each other across the table.

"Tell me, Mr. Costello, is it common for bodyguards to dine with the family they're serving?" Daphne asked casually.

Jordan's body stiffened and went on alert; her body had become accustomed to doing that whenever she heard her mother speak in that tone, even before Jordan understood what was happening. It took her a moment to realize Daphne's question was both a jab at Elliot as well as Jordan since she was the one who had offered, then insisted, they all eat together. She could have crawled under the table out of embarrassment.

"It's not usual, no," Elliot responded, smiling politely. "But it's very welcome. And it's good practice for when we dine in public. We'll need to go over—"

Daphne twittered. "Oh, we won't need to go over anything since Jordan won't *be* dining in public."

"Excuse me?" Jordan asked. She loved being home again, but she didn't intend to spend every moment at the house. She wanted to explore Los Angeles, preferably with Elliot at her side.

Daphne set her cutlery down and gave her daughter what Jordan had learned was her mother's disapproving frown. "You have a *stalker* after you, Jordan. Do you really think it's wise for you to go out in such a public place like that right now? Besides, on the best of days, you can be difficult in a restaurant." She glanced at Elliot. "Poor dear. She just can't help her autism."

"Asperger's." Jordan felt her hands start to open and close and stopped them. "That's my preferred term, please."

"Well, it's all called autism now, so get used to it. It doesn't change your limitations, whatever you wish to call yourself.

Whenever we go out, I have to watch you like a hawk to make sure you don't overload and go into a tantrum—"

"That's not true!" Jordan bit her lower lip. The deafening silence told her she'd said that way too loudly. Her face filled with heat. What did Elliot and Nash think of her now?

Daphne folded her arms and made that little *hhm* sound Jordan hated. "All you do is prove my point, do you see that? I want you to apologize for your outburst like grownups do." Her voice had gone sing-songy like Jordan was five years old.

I'm not going to cry. I will not cry. Jordan clenched her hands together in her lap and forced herself not to rock in her seat. That would only make things worse. "I'm—"

Elliot set his knife down. "An apology isn't necessary, Ms. Summers. I don't think your behavior is out of line at all." Did he put the subtlest emphasis on *your*? Was he digging at her mom? "Without naming names, Mr. Jones and I have had clients do far worse under far less pressure. This was nothing."

He turned to her mother. "Mrs. Summers, I can understand your worries about everyone's safety, but I can also assure you that any of you would be safe with us in public. If you allow a threat to stop you from enjoying life, then the stalker has won. Our job is to keep you safe physically, but also mentally. If you're still living in fear with us around, then we aren't succeeding with our objective."

Daphne smiled. "I think we all feel perfectly safe here and that you're doing a wonderful job."

Jordan's heart did a little flip. Her mother was actually pandering to Elliot now, which from past actions meant she thought he was the strongest person in the room. *Amazing.*

Her mother turned to John Charles, who had been smirking the entire time. "Don't you? Don't you feel safer with these two here?"

He snorted. "I had no reason to feel like I was in danger from a stalker in the first place."

Daphne's eyes widened. She covered her heart, fingers splayed across her chest. "But, John Charles, Daniel is out of prison! Who knows what he might do? He's completely unstable and I can imagine he's very bitter towards all of us. Especially my daughter." She threw Jordan an unreadable smile, but her voice had gone sweet and light. "I know *I* feel better knowing that Watchdog is keeping an eye on Daniel's every move."

This was news to Jordan. "You're watching him?" she asked Elliot, her stomach sinking.

He nodded. "As a precaution."

"But that's all? Just...watching?" She hoped they hadn't threatened, or God forbid, hurt Daniel on her behalf.

He tilted his head. "Yes. Are you worried about him? I can tell you he hasn't made any unexpected or threatening moves."

Of course he hasn't. "No, I'm not worried," she was quick to say. "I don't even think it's necessary to watch him."

Daphne leaned forward. "Darling, he hasn't made any threatening moves that they've *caught*, Costello is trying to say. But I wouldn't want them to stop watching him. Out of anyone, he's the most likely person to have threatened you."

"No, he isn't." *Careful, your voice is rising.* Jordan took a quick breath. "I mean, the paper the note was sent on was expensive Italian stationary and the pasted-on letters came from Italian magazines and newspapers, right? And the photos, those were taken while we were there. Daniel couldn't have done it."

"He most certainly could have." Daphne straightened in her chair. "He could have easily tracked us down, flown over there, and threatened you."

"Personally, I don't see how," Elliot said. "He's dead broke, living in a terrible neighborhood, and hardly goes out. He seems too down on his luck and broken to get a job, let alone pull off a scheme like that."

"Then why are you watching him at all if you know he couldn't have done it?" Jordan asked. Could she ask them to stop?

"Because even though the odds are long, he's the best lead we have."

"He's the only lead you have because he did it. You don't know him. He has powerful friends—"

"So you've said, Mrs. Summers, but I think—"

"There's a better lead," Jordan interrupted.

"Jordan," Daphne said.

"No. There is." She looked from face to face. She knew her mother's warning expression, but John Charles looked... amused? Nashville's face was impossible to read because she barely knew him, but he didn't have his usual easygoing smile. Elliot looked intense, but not in the same way that had heated her up earlier. He looked intense because he was *listening* to her. Taking what she had to say seriously.

She liked it.

"There *is* someone else," she continued. "The last commission that I turned down."

Daphne's eyes briefly widened, then she waved her hand. "He's not a threat and we aren't going to talk about him. Client confidentiality."

Nashville snorted. "What? Y'all lawyers or doctors?"

Elliot shot him a look that didn't seem too friendly, which was strange because Jordan thought the two were friends. "Who is the client?"

"As I said, it's unimportant because he's gone and he likes his privacy. Believe me, it's a dead-end and you'd actually be stirring up unnecessary trouble if you did pursue him." She picked up her knife and fork which meant the conversation was over every time she'd done that to Jordan. Normally, Jordan would have followed suit. But not this time. It was too important to lead Elliot and Nashville away from Daniel.

"His name is Marcus Porter. He's a hedge fund manager and I don't like him."

"Jordan!" Daphne's knife and fork clattered against her plate. "What did I just say?"

John Charles lifted his eyebrows and sat back, studying Jordan. Elliot and Nashville exchanged an unhappy look.

I should just be quiet now. But she couldn't let things stand as they were. She kept her head down, gaze fixed on her lap. No eye contact. "I...don't know...but doesn't it seem more likely? He was there and he doesn't like hearing no. It's why I wanted to come home." *There. Good enough.*

Elliot spoke first. "I'll let Lachlan know." His voice sounded as steady and sure as granite but Jordan didn't dare look up from her lap to see his eyes. Was he angry? That would kill her.

Her mother gave off her nervous laugh. "Oh, honestly. A man like him is above that sort of thing. I haven't heard a peep from him since we said no."

"Since *I* said no," Jordan corrected. "And thank goodness my skin finally stopped crawling." She shivered.

Daphne let out an exasperated little breath through her nose. "It would have been life-changing money, even for us. But I let you have your way, didn't I? You are much too small a fish for him to care enough about to stalk you over turning down a commission."

Or too big a fish. More accurately, too old *a fish from what I've heard* Jordan thought. She couldn't help but smile though. "Is that supposed to be an insult, that I'm not good enough for a multi-billionaire to stalk? Especially *that* one?"

"He's done a lot for charity," Daphne sniffed.

Nashville snorted. "Excuse me. Spicy food." Jordan looked up when he coughed into his linen napkin.

John Charles snickered. "Spicy, all right." He downed his wine and stood up. "Honestly? I think this is all overblown. From what you've said my brother is incapable of tying his shoe the right way let alone finding out where Jordan was, securing a passport, flying across the ocean, taking pictures and sending threatening notes, then flying back here and lying low while he's watched. You make him sound like some sort of supervillain or spy when in reality he's a drunk and a fuck-up and a loser who has zero friends outside of prison. He knows that if he comes anywhere near here, he's going straight back in. He's number one on the suspect list if anything happens to any of us since he still stands to inherit everything. But he's not once tried to contact any of us, even while in prison, and I don't see him starting that now."

He pointed at Elliot. "I'm not the one who can tell you how to do your job, but as a businessman, I can tell you that you're wasting precious resources watching that pathetic fuck."

He tugged on his cuffs and turned to leave. "I have some business to conduct and it's morning in Beijing. Good night."

Jordan needed to get away from her mother. She pushed her chair back from the table. "I'm going out to the garden to see if anything needs watering. The wind probably dried everything out the past couple of days."

"I'll go with you," Elliot said as he stood up beside her. She ignored her mother's harsh look as Elliot accompanied her out of the dining room and to the French doors.

He stopped her on the patio just outside while he scanned the grounds, even more alert than he normally was.

"What's the matter?" she asked.

"Marcus Porter."

"He isn't here."

"I'll be the judge of that."

Damn. This was not what she'd intended, either. Elliot finally nodded and she walked down the steps to the court-yard and picked up the hose with the nozzle attachment. The breeze coming off the Pacific felt warm after the cloudy day. Jordan went along the row of planters and touched the dirt in each one, gauging the dampness of the soil and whether or not the plant needed a spray from the hose. Some drank faster than others, the greedy things. Overall the garden was doing well considering its long neglect.

"You're bringing it back to life," Elliot said as he pinched a lemon tree leaf and ran his fingers along its surface.

"You read my mind." She grinned up at him.

"Told you I'm not a mind reader, I'm just looking around and marveling at the new life that's here now, all because of you."

Jordan's heart sped up. He was right—the garden of her dreams was beginning to bloom around them. "All because of *you.*"

He stopped, then moved closer to her. That intense gaze was back, the one that heated her from the inside. "Why me?"

How was she supposed to answer that? Didn't he know what he meant to her? How long would they keep their secrets? Maybe she could still make him understand.

Jordan started walking again as she talked. "My mother criticizes me because she thinks I'm unaware of time passing. That I don't understand deadlines, that I simply get lost in what I'm doing, and she thinks it's a terrible flaw in me for which she has to compensate. But it's not like that at all. I understand time, just not in the way she does. She sees time-lines—this event, then this one, then the next, all leading from the cradle to the grave. For me, time goes around and around in cycles. You plant the seeds you have, they germinate. They grow and you nurture them, sometimes feeding, sometimes pruning the parts you don't want to keep. They bloom or bear fruit if you've done your part well, and you harvest what they give you. From that harvest, you take and keep the seeds through winter, then plant them again in the spring."

She laid a hand on his arm. "The past is never gone. It only lies buried, waiting to bloom again."

Elliot drew in a breath. He glanced at the house then covered her hand with his. "I feel like I know you, Jordan. Like I've known you all my life."

"Because you have. You've always known me, and I've always known you. But that's *your* secret, isn't it?"

His lips parted. "Jordan—"

She touched her fingertips to his lips and whispered, "I'll keep it a secret until you're ready to tell the truth. I know how scared you were as a boy. So scared."

"I—"

"Jordan? Are you out here?" Daphne called from the patio. "It's getting dark and you should come in."

"I need to check on the night-blooming jasmine and the moonflowers, Mother, and I can't very well do that in the daytime." She winked up at Elliot and whispered, "Of course I can but she has no idea."

Daphne put a hand on her hip. "Well, hurry up." She turned and went inside.

"Come on," Jordan whispered. "I have to tell you some-thing important." Then she turned and headed for a mass of white moonflowers across the open courtyard.

TEN

How can Jordan know about my dreams of her and the garden? That's impossible.

Or was that even what she was getting at?

No. I'm imagining things. Get your head back in the game, Costello.

Starting with dinner, the whole evening had thrown Costello off. He wasn't ready to take the surveillance off Daniel Summers quite yet, but now he had to think about a whole new possibility. A dark and dangerous one. Knowing that Marcus Porter of all godforsaken monsters had been in the same room as Jordan made Costello's skin crawl. He would have to change his focus and let Lach know about this new wrinkle. The bastard was already on Watchdog's radar. He was a money machine for the Capitoline Group, turning their millions into billions with his hedge fund. They had immense power and reach and often abused it. Porter traded in all their secrets, too, using the knowledge as a secondary currency worth more than dollars, as well as an instrument of blackmail that kept him untouchable. It allowed him to get away with the most depraved of crimes—human trafficking.

Most of what was known publicly were only rumors in tabloids and on conspiracy websites but that should have been enough to scare Daphne and Jordan. Costello couldn't believe Daphne would entertain the scumbag for even a moment. He went back over the way Jordan had acted at dinner. She wasn't worried about her brother at all it seemed and wasn't nearly worried enough about the possibility that Marcus Porter had her in his sights.

Or was there something else going on? He brought up a mental image of the letters and the photos and studied them. *Of course. I should have seen it before. Oh, Jordan, if it's what it looks like, you do know how to take care of yourself, don't you?*

Costello followed Jordan across the courtyard, hoping to get answers. The sweet, almost cloying smell of moonflowers filled the evening air. Jordan cupped one of the white trumpet-shaped flowers in her hand before looking up at him.

"I have to confess something," Jordan started. "I'm not in as much danger as you think."

Okay. Something else is going on. "What do you mean?"

Jordan looked away. "I have to tell you something but you might be angry with me or think I'm a bad person."

Now that she'd hinted at it, he had a feeling he knew what she was about to say, and it had to do with the threatening letters and photos, not his secrets. But he needed her to spell it out. "First, I could never be angry with you. Second, I know you aren't a bad person. If you had to do something wrong, you did it for the right reason. Tell me."

By now, Jordan was trembling in her short-sleeved shirt. Costello took off his jacket and put it around her shoulders as she slipped her arms through the sleeves. She gripped the front of the jacket without buttoning it up.

"Tell me so I can help you, Jordan."

She looked straight into his eyes. "That's *why* I did it. I needed your help." She took a deep breath. "No one is stalking me. I pasted those letters together and took the photographs myself." She looked down as if she were about to be scolded.

I knew it. "You used a drone for the photos, didn't you?" He broke into a smile when she nodded. She braved a glance through her eyelashes and saw his smile. He chuckled and that made her smile too. She nodded.

"I did use the drone. How did you guess?"

"I knew you had one since you had aerial photos of the gender reveal party. In each photo the alleged stalker took, you're looking down and your hands are blocked by a hedge or some other garden feature. At first glance, you look like you're preoccupied with the garden, but you're really looking at the controllers, aren't you? You're looking at the screen, making sure you're getting a good shot."

"Busted." This time she laughed softly.

Costello gently lifted her chin so she was looking at him again. She looked so vulnerable, his heart sped up. "You must have had a good reason to do that, to want to get out of Italy and come home. Jordan, you may think you'll be in more danger if you tell me what happened, but you can trust me." Her pale green eyes shone in the fading light. "Let me protect you. Help me by talking to me."

As Jordan told Costello about her encounter with Marcus Porter, his blood simmered with anger. Not at Jordan, who was only trying to protect herself, but at Daphne for putting her own daughter at the mercy of a predator and pedophile. Costello could only imagine what would have happened if Jordan had been forced to go to his island, isolated for months and at his mercy. When she mentioned the labyrinth Porter wanted her to create, he couldn't help but be reminded of the

Greek myth about the Minotaur and how King Minos who commissioned the labyrinth kept its creator trapped inside so no one would learn its secrets. Porter was a powerful man with secrets more dangerous than any mythological king.

"I don't blame you one bit for doing everything you could to get away from him, Jordan." He stroked her hair before he could stop himself. "You're afraid he's going to come here after you so you called us."

She shook her head, surprising him. "No, not at all. My mother said she would tell him I wasn't available. That we're saying no to the contract. He has no reason to come after me."

Costello's senses went on high alert. "You don't know him like I do. You knew the rumors and could see the man for what he is. Your instincts are good, Jordan, no matter what Daphne tells you, and you did a smart, brave thing by getting the hell away from him. Watchdog has done a full profile on Marcus Porter. Actually, we've had one for a long time. The fact that he let you meet him face to face concerns me. He does most of his work through intermediaries."

She looked off toward the Pacific. "That may be true, and I did want to get away from him. But he's not who I'm ultimately worried about, Elliot."

"Then who? Are you afraid of Daniel and just not letting on?"

"No. Not him, either. Daniel is a broken man, he's harmless now. I'm afraid of..." She looked down at the moonflowers. "I'm afraid of my mother. She's changed lately. She's pushing me to work faster and for the highest bidder. I used to only take on commissions I wanted to do, things that helped others, too. I didn't care what I was getting paid, or even if I was getting paid at all. I'm not exactly in the poorhouse." She jutted her chin back toward Eden House. "But the fact that she pushed me to work for that monster." Jordan shuddered.

"She always used to ask if I wanted to do a project and listened when I said yes or no. Not this time." Jordan met Costello's eyes again. "We'd discussed a long time ago the possibility of a conservatorship, back when I was younger, when I really didn't understand what it was. But now that I do, I don't think I want it."

"Of course you don't," Costello said. "You don't need it, not from what I've seen. You are more than capable of making your own decisions." Jordan started shaking her head again. "What? You don't think you are?"

"It's...I get confused sometimes, especially when I get overloaded. Just the thought of handling my own finances makes me shut down inside. I need someone, someone I can trust, and I thought that someone was my mom, but now... I feel like she's been lying to me. Maybe all my life. She's always said she's the only one who would never betray me. Who wouldn't try to use me for my money or for who I am. Because she's my mother." A tear slid down her cheek and Costello caught it, brushing it away. "I can't tell you how scared I was that I was going to be trapped with that man, and it didn't seem to bother her one bit. She wasn't even paying attention to me. She was just smiling and nodding along with him. She tried to tell me later that I was overreacting, that I was the one with the problem." She sniffled. "That doesn't feel right, Elliot."

Oh, mercy. "It shouldn't feel right, Jordan, because it isn't."

He glanced back the way they'd come. "We need to be getting back. We're off-camera—thank God—but if we don't show up soon, Nash at the very least will come looking for us."

Jordan grabbed Costello's arm. "What are you going to tell your boss? Will I get in trouble, like shouting fire in a theater?"

The way I want to pick you up and carry you off to a safe place and show you how I feel, I'm in way more trouble than you are. He didn't dare share his thoughts. He covered her hand instead, running his thumb over the top. Even this innocent touch was too much, was completely out of line.

"No, of course you won't get in trouble. We're not law enforcement, and like I said, I think you do need protection. You're not crying wolf. I just need to give the team a FRAGO."

"A what?" She gave him back his jacket. He wanted her to keep it but it wouldn't do for her to be seen in it.

"Fragmentation order. A change in plans." He finished putting his jacket on. "Now that I know who the dangerous stalker is who sent the letters," he winked and resisted the urge to brush his lips across her forehead, "I can focus on the real threat, the one you actually hired me for." *As well as figure out how to get you out from under the threat of a conservatorship.*

As if she'd read his mind, Jordan said, "If she tries to force the conservatorship, I need witnesses to fight for me. I need you to tell them I'm not incompetent. That I'm not stupid or crazy."

He tilted her chin up. "You're not incompetent. And in no way, shape, or form are you stupid or crazy. I think everyone around you is crazy. He looked around the garden and shook his head. And if he told her about his dreams, she'd know he was crazy too.

ELEVEN

Costello spent the rest of the evening thinking about ways to help Jordan now that he knew the truth. He sent off a secured email to Lachlan and Gina notifying them of the new developments and his suggested FRAGO. He didn't want to tip his hand and let Daphne suspect Jordan had faked her own stalker but there were still things he could do that she wouldn't be aware of. They could ease off their surveillance of Daniel Summers; Costello was of the mind that the man had nothing to gain by threatening Jordan and had shown neither the means nor the opportunity to do so.

The cameras around Eden House could stay because that was basic security. And it made sense for him and Nash to stay at the house to keep an eye on Daphne now that she was their biggest threat to Jordan's autonomy. Once Jordan's birthday came and went and she inherited the rest of her money and Daphne's guardianship ended, Jordan was safe to do whatever she wanted. But until then, Daphne could pull all sorts of strings to get her daughter into a conservatorship. Besides, he wasn't about to leave Jordan now.

He added a request for a deeper dive into Summers Shipping Company, particularly SSC's finances. It was reported to be worth two billion dollars the previous year, but there had been a longshoreman strike that went on for months, and there was that idiot who'd clogged up the Suez canal and sent the entire industry into a temporary tailspin.

Then there's Marcus Porter. Costello was tremendously relieved knowing that there was no stalker, but that didn't mean Porter was entirely out of the picture. The fact that he'd left his island—fortified by roaming speedboats full of armed guards, not to mention more muscle patrolling the beaches—to meet Jordan and Daphne face-to-face concerned the fuck out of him. More was going on there than met the eye; he could feel it. In the email, he told Gina to ask her 'friends' at the CIA about Porter's movements over the past month. He thought they would be interested to know what he'd been up to in Italy—maybe that would be enough of a trade for them to continue keeping an eye on Porter and let Watchdog in on the intel.

Once he got recommendations from Lach and Gina, he'd inform the rest of the team including Nash. Hell, maybe Nash would enjoy turning on his Southern charm full blast to distract Daphne, so long as lines weren't crossed.

Which makes me the biggest hypocrite to ever walk the earth. He glanced at the vase of fresh flowers on his nightstand. His bedroom was filled with the intoxicating scent of night-blooming jasmine, making him half-hard.

Costello closed the laptop, checked to make sure his gun was at the ready just poking out between the mattresses, and gave his pillow a solid punch before turning out the light. In the darkness, the jasmine became almost tangible and the caress of a salty ocean breeze slipping in through the open window raised goosebumps on his bare skin.

He could imagine Jordan in the room standing beside the bed and watching him, deciding if she wanted to slip between the sheets. His cock hardened further at the thought of her naked curves outlined in the moonlight as she placed one knee then the other on the mattress. The image of her swinging one leg over his body and straddling him, only a thin sheet between his stiff cock and her soft pussy, made him groan. Would she be wet, soaked for him before he even touched her? God, her hair had been soft as silk between his fingers earlier. He wanted to wrap a lock of it around his fist and pull her face to his, crush his lips against hers. He pulled off his briefs and fisted his cock—no way to get past his desire except to go straight through it.

She could be both as strong and as fragile as a tulip. He imagined touching her swollen clit the way he'd stroked the closed jasmine buds, willing them to open at his command. He'd make her give in to him and beg for more while barely touching her clit, flicking his tongue across her nipples, blowing over her belly, teasing her as softly and stealthy as she was teasing him. And she *was* teasing him, wasn't she, with the flowers? With her secrets and claiming to know him?

He fisted his cock tighter and rubbed hard. That was one side of her, but then there was the other, stronger side. He wanted to see just how strong she was, wanted to push her body to its limits until she screamed out his name begging for mercy, for another release, for both. He briefly wondered if she'd ever been with another man and a red hot poker of jealousy ran through his core and fired up his desire even further. He knew he could make her forget every other touch. He *would* make her forget every man but him. He wanted to take her roughly and yet let her know she was safe with him, safe to let go until she came hard for him, then cradle her in his arms until she came down from that space and found him waiting to send her right back there.

"That's it, Jordan. That's it, beloved," he whispered into the jasmine-laden air as he stroked himself harder and faster. "Come for me." He ran a dribble of precum around his tip and down his shaft. "Come around my cock." He grabbed his briefs and got ready as he imagined her tightening around him. He moaned out her name as he jetted into his briefs. He caught his breath then cleaned himself up.

God, he wanted her. He'd barely taken the edge off his desire and he knew it would never be enough until he'd claimed her. Right now he had to be careful—so careful—not to let his feelings show. He needed to bury them deep as if they were seeds waiting to grow when the season was right. Because when this was all over, nothing would stop him from...

From what? He punched his pillow again and growled into it. What could he possibly have to offer a woman of Jordan's standing? She was wealthy beyond belief for starters. Beautiful, talented, a world traveler. Sure, Costello had been to some exotic places, but there was a world of difference between room service in a boutique hotel and a hot and dusty tent in the middle of a hellscape. She'd been raised surrounded by luxury while Costello had been raised to grift off that same luxury.

Liar. Thief. Traitor.

At least until he'd been placed with the Costello family, who made him one of their own and showed him what a normal life looked like. One where he didn't have to lie and sneak and hide and steal. A life where he had his own room that didn't change every few months, where he went to school regularly. Where he had a good man for a dad and a loving woman for a mom. Siblings his age he didn't have to con out of their belongings. His birth mom had taught him exemplary manners but that was so that he could charm his way into the lives of the next marks. Once he was with the Costellos, he put his manners and charm to use for real, with genuine feeling behind them.

He'd done everything he could to make his new family proud, including taking their name. National Honors Society, community work, baseball in the spring, and football in the fall. Graduated high school early with enough AP credits to enter college as a junior at seventeen. And then his crowning achievement—entering the BUD/S program and becoming a SEAL just before his twentieth birthday. The older guys in the class had told 'the kid' he'd wash out but he proved them wrong and earned their respect.

Would that respect translate to anything in Jordan's world?

Did it matter to him as long as it meant something to Jordan?

Costello turned over. Here he was in one of the most expensive houses along the Malibu coast, the place that reminded him of his dreams of paradise, and instead of casing it he was protecting a woman his mother would have done everything she could to con out of a bit of jewelry or whatever shiny things were lying around for the quick snatching.

Thinking about his past reminded him that he still hadn't gone through his birth mom's storage unit. She'd been gone three months now, having spent her last days alone in hospice care. He'd lost all contact with her after the arrest and was surprised by the woman knocking on his door that morning three months ago with a couple crates full of plants and the keys to the storage unit. He couldn't believe his mother had kept tabs on him after almost twenty-five years and knew where he lived.

I was your mom's neighbor for five years the woman told him. He was skeptical—that would be the longest his mom had ever stayed in one place by at least four years. *She loved you, was really proud of what you'd become.* He was skeptical of that, too. All those years, and she'd never bothered to reach out.

Never tried to get him back.

That first month away from her, crying himself to sleep every night hoping he'd wake up to her saying *All right kiddo, we're outta here.* But she'd never even tried and signed away her parental rights without a word.

So what? He'd been better off without her. She'd promised him the moon, hell, she'd promised to get him eye surgery that would get rid of the Coke-bottle glasses the other kids teased him mercilessly about when he did go to school for however long until the next move. *They only tease you because they're jealous you're so smart, Baby Owl* she'd say and he'd do everything he could to prove her right, to show he was smarter than all the rest. He finally got his eye surgery before enlisting courtesy of the Costellos. His *real* family.

Costello drifted into an uneasy sleep. He tossed and turned, the rest of his night blanketed with fantasies of Jordan between unsettling dreams of casing Eden House for hidden treasure and wandering in the night garden calling out her name, trying to find her before the Shadow Man could drown him in blood.

At one point after he knew he'd cried out waking up from a nightmare, a cold black nose nuzzled his hand at the edge of the bed. Costello scratched his partner's furry head between the ears. Maybe he could get used to having a dog around all the time.

TWELVE

The next morning, Costello was ready to begin his new plans for protecting Jordan. He'd informed the rest of the team of the FRAGO after Lach and Gina assured him that yes, Gina's friends were quite interested in Marcus Porter's dealings in Italy. Anything that they could learn about the man and his island was much appreciated and her friends would reward Watchdog.

As friends do Gina had typed. *BTW your plants are thriving.*

Costello grinned and shook his head. He was as fond of Gina almost as much as she sometimes scared him. He chuckled thinking that maybe his plants were thriving because they were afraid of what she'd do to them if they didn't.

Now, to carry out his own new objective: boost Jordan's confidence and give her every reason and opportunity to show she was capable of anything, especially living independently and in charge of her own life. He headed downstairs to the kitchen for breakfast and his first mini-mission. Operation *Auto*-nomy.

Costello downed his second cup of coffee. Nash checked in and gave his overnight report—all was five-by-five, no intruders, nothing that would indicate Jordan was in any immediate danger from the outside, which made perfect sense now. Nash indicated that he'd already read the FRAGO and agreed with the new plan. No one but Carol the chef was around, but they still used code just in case.

"Reg and I are gonna go for a run, then I'm getting some shuteye," Nash said. The Lab wagged his entire butt at the mention of his name.

"Sounds good, brother." Costello bit into a red apple.

"Think we'll take the stairs from the patio out back down to the beach."

"Let me know how the beach is. I haven't been down there yet."

"Copy." He caught Carol's eye and did his best Brad Pit hat tip and smile. "Ma'am." The older woman's face flushed. He winked and she waved him off.

When he was out of the kitchen, Carol shook her head and said, "Heartbreaker, that one." Costello laughed and toasted her. And he realized he was...happy. How could that be after the night he'd had? But there it was. He was happy because Jordan was not in any immediate danger and he was about to spend the day with her.

The smell of rose perfume preceded Daphne into the kitchen and almost spoiled his mood. Almost. He noticed she was dressed up more than usual.

"Good morning." She smiled at Costello, a little crinkle around her eyes. Almost cheery.

"Good morning. You look nice today."

She did a flirty little eyebrow lift and drop. "Why, thank you for noticing. I'm going into L.A. today to take care of some business."

"What time? Nash should be back soon, or I can make a call and arrange for an escort." Costello pulled out his cell.

"Oh, no, no, that's okay. John Charles is coming along. We'll be fine."

Really? "I'd advise that you have one security person with you. He can meet up with you in L.A. if you'll give me the address."

She waved him off. "John Charles has assured me that my other stepson is not much of a threat. And as for the stalker, he's after Jordan, isn't he? And she has you to protect her." She smiled and her gaze flicked quickly up and down his body. "She's in capable hands."

Costello resisted clenching his jaw at her attitude and her perusal. "We will be going into Malibu to run a couple errands today. I can assure you, Jordan will be perfectly safe."

"Oh, I know it. Ta." She lifted a hand and left with a coffee mug and a container of yogurt.

Carol smirked. "Another heartbreaker." There was decidedly more sarcasm in her voice.

After letting Gina know Daphne and John Charles' plans—no way would he let those two make a move without his knowledge—Costello found Jordan working in the vegetable garden. When Anubis spotted her, he trotted ahead of Costello and—*was that a tail wag?*—nosed her hand as she knelt and staked a tomato plant. Completely absorbed, she yelped and jumped, then laughed when she realized it was only Anubis. She wrapped her arms around him and nuzzled into the top of his head and kissed him. And there it was again —that tail-wag.

"Sorry, I completely lost track of time and we have things

to do." She stood and wiped her hands off on her overalls. Costello loved seeing her this way—completely carefree, a creature of her environment and without anyone nagging her, she radiated confidence. "Give me a minute to get out of my grubbies and we'll be on our way. I'm excited to get out of the house for a bit."

"So am I." *And on to the next part of my plan.*

Costello exercised Anubis on the lawn while Jordan got ready. He threw a red Kong across the yard and Anubis ran after it. Kyle had told him that when he was training the dog, Anubis never really played but treated everything as a job. *Dog's serious as a heart attack* he'd said. *Whoever named him named him right.* Costello couldn't agree more as he watched the dog run back and forth as if he were duty-bound.

"Okay, I'm ready," Jordan said from behind him. He'd heard her come outside and down the steps. He turned and was stunned. Simply beautiful, head to toe. She wore a white sundress with capped sleeves patterned with branches from a lemon tree that just screamed happy. This was the first time he'd seen her in heels since they'd met at Watchdog. She'd put on makeup—also new—just enough to highlight her eyes and the apples of her cheeks.

Simply breathtaking. And when the scent of jasmine hit him, he needed to turn his body away before he embarrassed himself.

"Hang on," he said. "I'll come up to you." He signaled to Anubis that playtime—such as it was—was over. The dog heeled without complaint. They climbed the stairs and Jordan knelt to pet Anubis.

"Careful, he'll get dark fur on your light dress."

She laughed. "Like I care." She lifted her hand. "Just look at my nails. Permanently short and usually dirty. My mother finds them embarrassing."

"They aren't hers so it shouldn't matter."

"Shouldn't matter," she repeated to herself and got quiet for a moment. "These clothes are like a costume. They're just not me. They're a shell I put on."

"Well, you look lovely. But that's true for your overalls as well." *Cool it, Costello.* "Ready to go?" He offered his hand and she took it. After she stood up, they both looked at their joined hands. He held on just a little longer than necessary and she let him. He savored the feel of her soft skin and the calluses across her palm. Touching her was like touching a dream made real. Just before he let go, she gave his hand a little squeeze. Her pale green eyes met his and he had to look away. No way could the desire he saw there be anything more than a reflection of his own. His imagination, which he was no longer going to entertain. Not until this was over.

Nash and Reggie were back from their run. Costello left Anubis in Nash's care on their way to the garage. Costello stopped and waited by the garage door's keypad for Jordan to enter the code. She stopped too and casually looked around.

"Jordan?"

"Yes?" She looked back at him.

"Are you going to put the code in?"

"Oh. Um." She bit her lip. "I don't have it."

Costello frowned. "I gave everyone the new code yesterday."

"I know." She looked at the cobblestones. "I'm...not used to remembering things like that. So I didn't."

"Hey," he said softly. He lifted her chin. "I'm not scolding you, I promise."

"But I'm stupid." She opened and closed her hands.

"Jordan, love. You are nowhere near stupid. Don't ever, *ever*, say that about yourself again."

Doubt filled her eyes.

"Nope. I'm not going to let you think that about yourself. I *know* stupid. I went to school with stupid. I served alongside stupid before I was a team guy. I have zero patience for stupid and let me tell you, all I want to do today is spend the entirety of it with you, so therefore you cannot be stupid."

And there it was, the thing he wanted most—a genuine grin.

"Thank you. So, what's the code?"

Costello beamed. "Now that's a sure sign you aren't stupid. You recognize your behavior needs to change and you're willing to do it, no hesitation, no questions." He gave her the code and she punched it in.

Costello let out an involuntary low whistle when the garage door opened. God, now there was a gorgeous sight. And she was all his for the day. He admired her classic curves, her polish, her leather.

"You like her, don't you?" Jordan said next to him. "Her name's Bonnie." She grinned when he looked down at her. "Bonnie, meet Costello. He'll be your driver today." She took the keys out of her purse and held them out for him.

"Pleasure's mine," Costello said to the 1957 baby-blue Corvette convertible. "But listen, Jordan. As your security, I would normally drive you. That keeps you safe in case we're followed and need to make evasive maneuvers. But now that I know what the potential threats are and aren't, and that you aren't being actively stalked, I've modified the plan." He closed her fingers over the keys. "Today, *you're* driving."

Jordan gave him a tight-lipped, sad-eyed smile. "I can't drive her."

"Wait, what?" He glanced into the soft-brown leather interior. "Ah. Four-speed stick shift. Is that it?"

She bit her lower lip. "Yes."

Costello grinned. "Don't be embarrassed. A lot of women

—and men—don't know how to drive a stick. Not your fault, it's the fault of those who never thought to teach you." *And hardly surprising* he thought. Well, he'd modify the plan a little bit more. In fact, this was even better than he could have hoped. He took the keys.

Jordan walked toward the passenger side and Costello jogged the few steps to pass her. He opened the door and took her hand to balance her as she eased into the seat. Again, he was struck with the uncanny sensation of touching a dream as her fingers rested momentarily in his palm. He watched her slide her right leg in, the shape of her calf accentuated by her high heels, before shutting the door. She beamed up at him, looking straight into his eyes. Trusting. Happy. Clear-headed.

Costello rounded the car and got in. The leather seat welcomed him with comfort, its scent mingling with Jordan's jasmine. They buckled up and Costello took out his cell to find what he wanted. *There, that'll do.*

He turned the key. The car purred to life and Jordan closed her eyes, smiled, and leaned her head back against the headrest. Costello took a moment just to look at her before he shifted into reverse and backed out over the concrete floor that shone like smooth glass. The cobblestones made a satisfying popping sound under the white-walled wheels as they rolled down the long driveway toward the highway. The ocean breeze carried away the muggy humidity even before they reached the edge of the property.

Jordan sat back up and reached into her purse, Then, like a classic movie star, she pulled out a peach-colored silk scarf and tied it over her head. Oversized, white-framed sunglasses completed her look. If someone had snapped a picture of her just then, you would think she really was an unapproachable heiress. But after what she'd said to Costello, she looked to him like a girl playing dress-up, tongue firmly in cheek. It was a game, sometimes a game she won, and sometimes one she lost. It all depended on who was calling the shots. When Jordan was in the driver's seat, she won. But Daphne made it her life's work to keep Jordan on the passenger side.

We'll see about that. Starting right now.

THIRTEEN

Costello pulled out onto the highway—going north, away from Malibu.

Jordan sat up in alarm. "What are you doing?" she asked over the wind.

"We're taking a detour. It's a surprise, but I think you'll like it."

She studied him before her lips curled into a smile that made his heart beat double-time. "I trust you." Then she sat back and watched the road ahead, unaware of how those words gripped his chest in a vice. She was the definition of someone his mom had taught him to betray. He'd worked hard the rest of his life to earn the trust people put in him.

Costello took them up CA-1 to Highway 101 in Oxnard. Once they had the Pacific in view to their left again, he shifted up and let the car run like a wild beast. Something fast and sleek and confident. Jordan reveled in the speed, one hand covering her scarf, the other out the window and riding the breeze. Heads turned as cars drove past in the opposite direction. Sun sparkled on the water like a million wave-tossed diamonds. And Costello reveled in the reality of it all.

He took them an hour up the road before pulling off into a strip mall parking lot just before Santa Barbara. Yup, it was exactly what they needed. On either side of a nail salon were a hole-in-the-wall pizza place and a sushi restaurant. The rest of the mall was empty, dying, which left the parking lot pretty empty.

"Hungry?" he asked.

"Very," Jordan answered as she took off the scarf.

"Take your pick." He gestured to their two selections.

Jordan hesitated. "Whichever one you suggest."

"I've never been to either one of them so I have no idea."

Jordan looked at him, her head tilted. "Then what are we here for?"

"For the parking lot. But I didn't see you eat any breakfast, it's coming up on lunchtime, and I figured if you were hungry we could eat."

Her eyebrows knitted as she smiled and shook her head. She looked back at her choices. "How about pizza?" Her suggestion surprised him. Through the windows, the sushi place looked sparse and neat in a high-end way. The pizza joint suggested plastic, checkered tablecloths, and menus spattered with red sauce.

"Pizza it is, milady."

And that's where he made his mistake. Jordan's happy expression closed in on itself. "What did I say?"

"You don't need to call me that."

"Lady?"

"It's too...it's not who I am. Don't let the dress fool you." She looked out through the windshield. "It's who I'm supposed to be out there," she gestured to the world outside the car, "but not who I am with you. I'm just Jordan."

You'll never be 'just Jordan' with me. He didn't dare say that out loud. "All right, Jordan, let's get a slice." By the time he came around to her side of the car to open her door, her smile had returned. He held out his hand and there it was again, that throbbing current of energy with its epicenter where her fingers touched his palm. He placed his hand on the small of her back and his eyes roamed their surroundings for any hint of a threat as they crossed the mostly empty parking lot to the pizza place.

Just as Costello had predicted, the place had vinyl tablecloths, plastic utensils, and gallons of red gravy. Garlic-flavored heaven with a sprinkle of parm.

They took their seats in a booth and made their order. While they waited for their food, Jordan looked around the restaurant with an unreadable expression. Curiosity was there, yes, but Costello had no idea if she was thinking she'd made a mistake, or if she'd ever even been in a pizza joint and was taking in the new-to-her environment. Then he remembered her talking about her sensitivity to onions. Did the smell of garlic do the same to her?

"Everything all right?" he asked.

Her attention snapped back to him. Her eyes met his without hesitation and she smiled. "Yes, fine."

"The smell isn't getting to you?"

She lost her smile as puzzlement filled her gaze. "The smell? Oh!" Her smile returned along with wonder in her eyes. "You remembered about the onions."

"Of course I did."

Her cheeks reddened and her gaze fell to her lap, but her smile stayed in place. "No, it smells wonderful in here. Roasted garlic doesn't bother me at all. I'm excited about lunch."

"Then is anything bothering you? You looked like you had a lot on your mind."

She looked back up at him. "I'm...I feel like I'm at a crossroads. I love what I do, but lately, with back-to-back commissions and all the traveling, I'm getting...tired. Not of the work —never of the work—but of everything else that comes with it. The schmoozing. The deadlines that just keep getting tighter so that I can squeeze in one more project before the end of the year. Now that I'm home, I feel like I'm taking the first deep breaths that I've had in a long time. Maybe since I left. My mother thinks I don't need a break, but she's wrong, I do. Maybe even something bigger than a break."

The waiter brought their food. Jordan glanced up and thanked him, and Costello noticed how she didn't quite make eye contact. Their conversation ended as he watched Jordan savor every bite of her sausage and pepperoni pizza after they'd consumed an appetizer of fried mozzarella sticks drowned in marinara sauce. If there was one thing he loved to see, it was a woman shamelessly enjoying herself.

"Promise you won't ever tell my mother we ate here and what I had," she implored as she indelicately licked the grease off her fingers.

"Never. It's none of her business."

"She'd be mad if she found out I didn't just eat a salad. She says I'm bulking out."

Costello set his napkin down on the table and tried not to swear his head off. "You're a grown woman. You can eat whatever you want." *And you're beautiful. I can't take my eyes off you. You're fucking gorgeous like a blooming rose or a ripe peach is gorgeous* he added silently.

"It's not that simple," Jordan breathed.

"How can it not be that simple?"

Jordan picked up her paper napkin and used it to finish cleaning between her fingers. "It all goes back to what I was talking about. First, I'm not just a 'grown woman.' I'm an entire business and a business has to look good for its social media. Second," she hesitated, "a grown woman must always make responsible decisions."

She studied the tablecloth, her eyes downcast. And just like that, the unselfconscious woman who was so full of life a moment before was a snail in her shell again. When the waiter came to clear the table, she smiled vaguely up at him, her gaze touching only briefly on the spot between his eyes before looking down again.

Costello let the weight of her unsaid words settle before asking, "What happens if you make an irresponsible decision?"

"Then my judgment is called into question. I could become a danger to myself, couldn't I?"

Costello pressed his lips together and blew a hard breath out of his nose. "I have watched you closely from the moment you hired us and not for one second did I think you made any bad judgment calls. You got yourself to safety, Jordan, and I don't think you understand the odds were against you. Your mother on the other hand..."

She grinned. "Really?"

"Pardon my French, but, fucking really."

She giggled.

"So, yes, let's go back to what you were talking about before. The crossroads."

"Yes. I...don't know what I want."

"So talk it out with me. Daphne isn't here to correct you or tell you what she thinks you really want." He hesitated. "Or what *she* really wants."

Jordan picked up the napkin from her lap and wound and unwound it around her index finger while she talked. "I like being home. I know that much. There's so much to do in the garden and I'm the only person who cares about the place. I know my family would sell it if they could but I don't want to give over my share. John Charles even approached me about it—"

Costello held up his hand. "Wait. When did that happen?"

"The other day when you were asleep and Nash was on duty. John Charles waited for him to go on patrol."

Sneaky asshole.

Jordan went on. "He and my mother both want to sell. I know they have for a while. I was thinking about letting them, but now that I'm back, I want to stay. It's home." She met his eyes. "I know you understand what it is to finally have a home."

That cut him to the quick. "Don't think about me, think about you. You want to stay home instead of going from place to place. Yeah, I do get it. So, what are you going to do to ensure that?"

She took a deep breath. "That's where things get fuzzy. I've always left these matters up to my mother and until now it's been fine. But she's not listening to me anymore. So...I have to take control."

Costello closed his eyes. *Yes.* He opened them. "What can I do to help?"

"What you're already doing." She suddenly dropped the napkin, reached across the table, and grabbed his forearm. "You're listening to me. You're...I can talk to you. Without scripting things in my head ahead of time. I mean, I still do, because I've done it all my life; I try to think of all the ways a conversation can go and all my responses so that I look normal, but then I go off-script and...I can mostly still talk to you." She shook her head. "It's hard to explain."

He placed his hand over hers. "It sounds exhausting."

"It is." She blinked rapidly as her eyes grew shiny from held-back tears.

"No wonder you're tired."

She rolled her bottom lip into her mouth and nodded.

Costello patted her hand and lifted his away. He hated to break their connection, but if he didn't, he was liable to come around the booth and take her in his arms. He also broke their eye contact, realizing she might need a break. He'd done some research on Asperger's and read that eye contact could be difficult at times or with the wrong person.

"But it's hard to think of myself alone in such a huge house. It's a waste."

Alone. Costello rolled the word around in his mind and it stung like a ball of thorns. But he had no right to think she might consider being with him.

"So, what are you thinking?"

"I'm thinking I want to open the house up somehow. Not a museum exactly. That's almost as bad as living in a mausoleum. Did you ever notice how much those words sound alike? Museum, mausoleum. Museum, mausoleum." She shook her head. "Sorry. Getting off-topic. I want to open it to the public, but in a way that it does some good."

Costello liked the sound of that. "Like a community center of some sort?"

Jordan blinked rapidly again, but this time, there were no tears, only excitement. "Yes! Like that. Something that can help people somehow." She looked away and tilted her head. "I designed some play gardens for Ronald McDonald House, for kids whose brothers and sisters were sick. I know they have to spend hours cooped up in hospitals while their siblings get treatments, so I thought maybe if they had a place to play with lots of fresh air they would feel better too. It might take off some of the stress on them and their parents. I liked doing that. I want to do more things like that. I want to show people who've never gardened how great it is. I want to share what I know, but on *my* terms for once. And I want the house to help do that."

She looked back at him. "How crazy do I sound right now?"

Costello gave her his biggest, warmest smile. "Not crazy at all. You sound like a woman who knows what she wants, and what she wants is beautiful."

Jordan touched her fingers to her lips as she smiled and Costello's heart melted. "Thank you," she whispered.

"When I was little, I was in the hospital for, well, I don't know how long." He wasn't sure why he was telling her this; he never shared stories with anyone from before the Costellos adopted him. "I had the flu and it turned into pneumonia. Most of the time I didn't know what was going on. I was on a ventilator for a few days, in and out of consciousness. I had the strangest dreams." He paused. He was getting too close to telling her about his dream garden. His dream girl. Would she think he was delusional and trying to turn her into his fantasy?

She looked at him with anticipation-filled eyes, as if she could read his mind and was waiting for him to confess.

"Anyway. I think what you did for those kids is great, and I'd love to see what else you could do. You just need a plan, that's all."

"That's all, you say. Planning is not one of my strengths like it is yours."

"So, let me help you plan. If you want to involve the community, you need to reach out to community leaders and see what they need and tell them what you have to offer. And, I have a friend of a friend who could help you too."

"Really? Who?"

"She's the fiancée of one of my teammates. He's Kyle and she's Arden. She lives in Colorado but she's coming out to meet everyone. She runs an animal therapy program on her family's ranch. Sounds close to what you want to do, doesn't it?"

"It does." Jordan's voice was full of sunshine. She opened her mouth in a tantalizing O. "I could host a...a party. For Kyle and Arden. For your friends. All of them. And...and, the community. The leaders, like you said. Oh." She covered her mouth again and looked into the middle distance, thinking. "I...could do this." She looked back at him. "And, you would help?"

"Of course I would. Anything you need." *Brilliant.* An event like that would definitely build her confidence, and it would show a lot of people all at once how competent she was. The specter of Daphne managing to secure a conservatorship never left his mind. *Only a few weeks until Jordan's birthday and Daphne's guardianship will end. She'll have a harder time after that trying to control Jordan.* This would help guard against that.

"And I want to meet your friends. All of them. And your family. The Costellos, I mean." She rapid-fired her words. "I've been so curious about them. I want to know what they're like in real life."

In real life? Costello's stomach fluttered and his brain rebelled. She talked as if she were fiction. As if *he* were fiction. *Stop it.* His headache panged and he rubbed his temples. *She means instead of just reading about them in a dossier, that's all.*

"We should probably get going. I want to run my errands and then get back to the house. to start planning. And figure out if I even want to tell my mom." As she stood up in the booth, Jordan reached into her purse and took out her wallet. *Oh, hell no.* Costello snagged the bill the waiter left.

"This is on me." He glanced at the total and pulled out enough bills to pay and leave a generous tip.

Jordan's eyebrows shot up. "I'm not paying you to buy me lunch."

Wow, that stung, until Jordan sucked in her lower lip and turned crimson. "That did not come out the way I wanted it to. Give me a second." She closed her eyes and her face went blank. When she opened her eyes again she said, "You don't need to spend your money on me. You wouldn't even be here if I hadn't hired you, so...you...don't." She sighed. "Still not right. See how I am?"

Costello chuckled. "Hey, I'm learning to 'speak Jordan' so I think I get it."

That earned him a soft smile. "Glad someone can."

"Look, I'd feel like a complete jerk if I didn't pay. It was my idea to bring you out this way anyhow, so consider me off the clock for those thirty seconds it took to throw down some money. And believe me, I can totally afford it."

Jordan's expression relaxed into the unguarded smile he loved. "Okay. Thank you. For getting it. Me. Getting me. Oh, and the bill. Thanks for getting that too."

He grinned. "You're welcome. Now," he stepped out of the booth, "let's get to the real reason I brought you here."

She furrowed her brow as she scooted out of the booth. "The parking lot?"

"Yes. It's perfect."

"For what?"

Costello grinned. "Do you trust me?" His stomach flip-flopped at the words.

Jordan's eyes sparkled. "Of course."

"Good. Now it's time you learned to trust yourself."

FOURTEEN

With that, Costello turned and led her through the restaurant. He opened the door and surveyed the lot before he let her step past him. Everything felt five by five—no one watching them, no suspicious activity, and the parking lot was still clear.

Jordan walked toward the car and started to circle to the passenger side when Costello stopped her. "Wrong side."

She turned and gave him a look that said *are you kidding?* "I told you I can't drive."

"That's changing right now. I'm going to teach you to drive stick."

Jordan shook her head. "Nope. I said I can't drive."

"Actually, you said you can't drive *her*." He gestured to the car.

"Right. I can't drive Bonnie. Or any other car. You assumed I just meant stick."

Seriously? "And you led me to believe it."

"Because I'm embarrassed. Driving is a basic life skill and I don't have it."

"You're telling me you don't even have a license?"

MORE THAN PARADISE 127

MORE THAN PARADISE 127

MORE THAN PARADISE 127

"That's exactly what I'm telling you."

Unbelievable. Daphne kept her that helpless. Unless there was some other reason. "Why?"

Jordan looked at her feet. "They tried, and I couldn't get it."

"Who tried?"

"My mother and John Charles both. They tried to teach me when I was a teenager just on the driveway and I couldn't get it."

That stinks to high heaven. Costello leaned against the car. "Did they start with automatic?"

"No. They tried to teach me in Bonnie because she's my favorite and I couldn't get it. I'm clumsy and uncoordinated. They said I nearly destroyed her transmission and that I was impossible to teach. That I'd end up killing myself and probably someone else."

Costello gritted his teeth. "How many lessons did they give you?"

"Just one each. So two. But I sucked."

"Did it ever occur to you that maybe it was teacher error and not student error?"

Jordan glanced up at him. "I'm clumsy and uncoordinated by nature and I'll never get it. It's part of having Asperger's—"

"It's bullshit, is what it is. Pardon my French again."

Her eyes widened. God, he hated seeing the self-doubt clawing its way back into her and struggling to win. He had his work cut out for him.

"Jordan. I'm going to teach you to drive today. I don't believe that you are clumsy and uncoordinated by any stretch of the imagination. What I do believe is that you haven't been given an adequate chance to try." He stood up straight and put his arm out. "Get in the driver's seat. I'll talk you through how the stick shift and the pedals work, and then you're going to try it."

"What if I mess up Bonnie's transmission?"

"What if you don't and you learn to drive instead?"

The tiniest flicker of hope flared in her eyes and then it was gone. "But I'm more likely to—"

"You're more likely to learn how to drive when you have a patient teacher who doesn't tell you you're going to kill someone. Because you aren't, Jordan."

She took a deep breath. "You really think I can do this."

"I know you can do anything you put your mind to. So get in."

Jordan slipped behind the wheel. She squared her shoulders and looked him dead in the eye. "I'm ready."

Of course you are. "All right. The first thing I'm going to show you is the gear shift. Put your hand on the knob."

Jordan placed her hand over the rounded stick shift and Costello covered her hand with his. He tried to ignore his heart shifting up before they even started.

"You'll put her into neutral first. That's where you start. Move it to this position," He squeezed her hand gently as they shifted into neutral. "Now, see that pedal just beside your foot? That's the clutch. You're going to want to press down on that, all the way. Good. Next, is to start the car." He lifted his hand off hers, immediately missing her fingers under his.

"Forgive me, Bonnie," Jordan said, whisper-soft as she turned the key.

"She'll have nothing to forgive. Now, see where first gear is?" He waited for her to nod. "You're going to put her into first gear, and when you do, you'll lift up on the clutch slowly with one foot and give her a little gas with the other. Got it?"

"Here's where the tricky dance starts." Jordan swallowed.

"I'm right here. I've got you, but you're going to do fine."

He smiled and she reflected it back distorted—not quite real. "Put your hand back on the gear shift and we'll move her into first. All you have to do is take that first step off the clutch and onto the accelerator. Easy." He placed his hand over hers again and they shifted into first.

Jordan did exactly as he said. She lifted her foot slowly, slowly on the clutch, and gave Bonnie the tiniest amount of gas.

"A little more, keep it smooth," Costello coaxed as the car started to engage. "Add a little more throttle...good. You've got this."

Jordan grinned for real as the car started to creep forward. Costello let her hand up so she could grip the wheel with both.

"We're going to steer around the parking lot for a while until you get the feel for that. Then, we'll head out onto the street and turn left away from the highway and drive around for a bit."

She nodded, all her concentration on the car and the parking lot. She made several loops, practicing her braking and steering, and then he directed her to drive around the building to the back. She had to maneuver around a delivery truck but she did it without hesitation, a grin spreading across her face into a full-blown smile.

"I think you're ready to hit the streets," Costello said as they came back around into the parking lot. "Go straight ahead to the entrance and take a left."

"Are you sure?"

"Positive. It's just residential. We can drive around slowly, no problem. Let's go."

He expected her to hesitate or stop, but she actually gave Bonnie a little more gas and they took the turn a little fast.

They went up a gentle incline and headed for a neighborhood up ahead.

"Okay, next lesson. We're going to shift up. Listen to your engine and she'll tell you when to shift up and down. Watch the speed, too. Give her a little more gas."

Jordan gently pressed down on the accelerator until Bonnie started to whine.

"Hear that? She wants to move up. Put your hand back on the gear shift and we're going to move her to second."

"I didn't even get this far last time," Jordan said.

"Then you weren't given a decent chance."

She gave him the briefest glance before putting her hand on the gear shift. He covered her hand. "Take your foot off the accelerator and press smoothly down on the clutch. When we shift up, you're going to take your foot back off the clutch and add gas. Got it?"

"I think so."

"You've got this, I'm telling you."

And she did. Bonnie shifted up without a hitch. Jordan actually laughed. "I did it!"

"Of course you did. I never doubted you."

They continued up the straight road and Costello spotted a stop sign ahead. "Last lesson and you're a pro. We're going to shift back down and stop. You're going to let up on the accelerator and press down on the clutch, slow and easy like before. When it's to the floor, you're going to shift down to first. Let's go."

Once again, Jordan carefully followed Costello's instructions until they slowed a few feet from the stop sign. "Now, to keep from stalling—"

Too late. The car jerked and stalled. Jordan yelped and said, "I killed her!"

Costello laughed as he put on the parking brake. "No, you

didn't kill Bonnie. You just stalled her. Happens with everyone when they're learning. Hey." When he realized how rapidly she was breathing, how upset she really was, he reached out and gently took her chin in his hand and turned her to face him. "You're doing great, love. It doesn't have to be perfect, Jordan. You get to mess up."

"But what if I hurt someone?"

"You didn't hurt anyone. Not even Bonnie, I promise." Those tears she blinked back seemed way out of proportion to the situation. "What's wrong?"

She quickly bit her lip then stopped. "I never want to hurt anyone."

God, the things she's been through. "You're not going to. Whoever told you that was wrong, okay?" He brushed his thumb across her cheekbone. "I can't imagine you ever hurting anything bigger than an aphid, and they're just asking for it, the little sap-sucking dicks."

Jordan giggled. "Actually, it's not sap. It's..." She shook her head and stopped. She gave him a smile. "Off-topic. How do I get her to go again?"

That's my girl. "You tell me. How'd we start her the first time?"

Jordan remembered and repeated all the moves. They took a right into the nearest neighborhood and drove around for the next hour until she was comfortable shifting up and down between first and second and stopping the car. When she stalled a second time, she didn't let it intimidate her but got Bonnie running again immediately. She even got used to sharing the road with other drivers.

"Pull over to the curb here and park," Costello said. Jordan did as he asked. "I would love to let you drive back on the highway. I have every confidence that you could, honestly, but until you have a permit at least, let's stick to residential and parking lots." He pulled out his phone.

"A permit?" she asked, her voice full of hesitation.

"Of course. That's the next step." Costello scrolled through until he found the California DMV website. "Fill out this application, and thirty-three bucks later, you're ready to go in for a vision test and your permit." He handed her his phone. She took it and looked at the screen, then back at him.

"You don't need Daphne's permission, Jordan. This is your choice and yours alone."

She clenched her jaw. "You're right. It's not in place yet," she mumbled, then she started typing.

And if you're talking about the conservatorship, it won't ever be. I'll see to that.

Jordan stayed silent until she finished typing. "Um. If I put the application fee on the credit card, she'll know. Can I pay with cash in person?"

Costello plucked the phone out of her hand and typed in his card number. "Done."

Jordan frowned at him. "I thought we talked about this, that you shouldn't pay for my stuff."

"So reimburse me in cash. Why is it a problem?" He was ready for her answer.

"My mother has an alert on her phone whenever I use the card."

Costello's stomach plummeted. "Of course she does."

"I know, I know, but." She sighed out her breath in a frustrated huff. "She loves me, she's always protected me from the world for my own good."

"Jordan, she never taught you to drive. That doesn't keep you safe, that makes you vulnerable. There's a point where protecting becomes detrimental. And this is from a guy who protects people for a living."

"I really didn't need to drive. We've always had a driver."

And that's been your whole problem. "And now you don't need one." He shook his head. *Fuck it.* "You're driving back."

"Wait, what? On the highway? But you just said—"

"Forget what I said. We're doing this. *You're* doing this."

"It's against the rules. We can't."

"Jordan, normally I am an extreme rule-follower and this would be so un-Kosher it's not even funny. But, I also calculate my risks. In this case, I think the risk of not showing you how amazing you are right when you're at your crossroads outweighs the slim possibility that we'll get pulled over, and there's an even slimmer possibility we'll be confronted by a stalker. Unless you decide to attack yourself."

She grinned. "Not today."

"So. Stay in the right lane, don't speed, don't go too slow, we'll be golden."

She hesitated.

"Come on. Time to break some rules for the greater good." Costello froze inside. His own mother's words from so long ago rolled smooth as silver right off his tongue. Sometimes the memories jumped him when he least expected them. He did his best to hide his reaction.

It worked. "Okay. You're right," Jordan said. "Let's do this before I lose my nerve. Tell me what the difference is between highway driving and what we've been doing."

Costello covered with a smile. "In some ways, highway driving is way easier because you aren't starting and stopping all the time. You just shift up and listen to the engine tell you what to do. In the military, we have a saying, *watch one, do one, teach one.* You've already watched and done, now I want you to pretend I'm the student. I want you to tell me all the steps for starting, shifting up, shifting down, and stopping. When I know you've got that—and you do, Jordan—we're going to take Bonnie out of gear and just practice the hand movements for shifting up into third and fourth."

———

The drive back south to Malibu couldn't have gone better. The traffic gods smiled upon them and kept other cars—and assholes—to a minimum. Jordan did as Costello said and stayed to the right, letting faster vehicles pass while staying just above the speed limit. He kept his hand over hers when it was time to shift and felt her relax after the first time. God, the top of her hand was so soft compared to the hard-earned calluses adorning her palms. He tried not to think about how her hands would feel running across his chest and down his abdomen—but then again he didn't have to imagine it, did he? He knew from his dreams exactly how her hands felt doing all sorts of things—

Stop it, stop it. Shut that down right now before you pop a boner and embarrass yourself. You don't know how it feels because Jordan is real, not a dream. You're not going to find out right now because she's your principal. And that's the hard and fast rule you will not *break.*

But every time Jordan needed to shift, she glanced at him, at his hand, willing him to put it over hers. She acted like she wanted his touch even though she was past needing him to show her how to move the stick.

Stop it, I mean it. You do not need this.

But, God, her carefree smile, her little *whoop* of pleasure once she knew she got it and was in control. The golden, late-afternoon sunlight on her face. Her hair whipping out from under her scarf like a proud flag waving. Her spontaneous laugh every now and then, so joyful.

So damn *free.*

He had to convince himself that this was real, that he wasn't in some variation on his dreams that never left the garden. That there truly was nothing lurking in the shadows, ready to attack. At least not on his watch.

As they approached the next town, Jordan looked to him to help her.

"You've got this. We've been driving residential half the day. This is no different."

She nodded. "But...I'd still like your help with the gear shift. Just until I get my permit." And was that a mischievous smile? No, it had to be his overactive imagination.

He helped her though, without hesitation.

They drove past the turnoff to the house and Costello could swear he felt a chill from that direction. Jordan must have sensed it too. She stiffened up and gripped the wheel tighter. She even hit the gas just a little harder, as if to escape the house's gravity. They drove into Malibu and did their original errands with one addition—they went to the DMV where Jordan took a quick eye exam and signed up for a timeslot to take her written exam and driver's test. she walked out with her head held high and her shiny new permit tucked safely in her wallet.

"And now you can legally drive when this morning you couldn't. How does that feel?"

Jordan considered. "That feels...wonderful, actually." And God, there was that carefree smile beaming right at him again. "Thank you. I never would have dreamed of doing this if you hadn't pushed me."

"Now you can drive home legally." Costello chuckled.

She hesitated again. He watched her hands open and close rapidly, the first sign she'd shown that afternoon that she was really nervous. "Maybe you should drive home instead."

"Why? It's your car, and chances are Daphne won't be back yet. And even if she were, Jordan...again, it's. Your. Car."

"It's your car," she echoed without looking at him. "It is, but, I think it's best she doesn't know about the permit yet." She looked up at him, her eyes pleading behind her sunglasses. "You've got to trust me, too. Please."

Costello slowly nodded. "I'll always trust you, Jordan. But, I'm going to keep pushing you to trust yourself."

"This time, just this time, let's do it like this."

He considered her. She'd taken more than baby steps today in the self-trust department. He didn't want to push too hard. Like overfertilizing a plant trying to get it to grow faster. Sometimes, the fertilizer could burn a tender shoot and all the good turned to harm.

Then again, she knew her mother better than anyone. Maybe he was the one who needed the lessons in trust.

"All right. We'll play it your way."

She immediately relaxed, her hands stopped opening and closing. "Thank you." Jordan stepped around to the passenger side and he opened her door. When he got in and reached for the stick shift, she surprised him by placing her hand over his.

She grinned impishly at him. "Teach one."

Oh, mercy. He grinned right back at her, feeling like a mischievous kid himself. All the way back to Eden House, she kept her hand on his, right up until the house—and Daphne's car—came into sight.

FIFTEEN

Jordan knew it was too good to be true, that her mother would be home and waiting before them. They'd spent all day out and it was the best day she'd ever had. Europe couldn't touch it. Spending all day alone among her favorite plants couldn't even compare, and that was saying a lot. She loved being away from both home and her mother without a chaperone.

Because she didn't think of Elliot as a chaperone even though he was her bodyguard. It was different. *He* was different from anyone else. But she'd always known that about him. He *knew* her. He just needed to remember. Remember that he was hers and she was his, always.

Which was why she'd made sure her mother would choose Watchdog Security. It was true that Daphne exerted almost total control over Jordan, but that didn't mean Jordan didn't occasionally—and always subtly—*nudge* her mother toward what she wanted, especially since Jordan wasn't ever the loudest voice in the room. But lately, she was worried that her mother increasingly sensed those nudges—and was nudging back.

Like today, the fact that Daphne was back before dark. Had she lied, hoping to catch them at something? At least she wasn't waiting for them on the driveway, tapping her foot as if they were two delinquent teenagers who'd been caught sneaking back in. But so what if they spent the day out? She'd been perfectly safe the entire time. She'd had fun. She'd been...happy. Yeah, that was how she'd felt. That was happy. And she wanted more of it. With Elliot.

Jordan walked a tightrope. If Daphne knew she'd been driving without a permit, she could use it as grounds to move her case for a conservancy forward. Jordan sighed. Had there actually been a time when Jordan thought allowing her mother to rule her entire life was a good idea? That seemed so far away now, literally in another country. Now all Jordan wanted was the freedom to make her own choices, good or bad. After talking to Costello today about opening up the house, she wanted it even more. She could start to see her new future and she liked it.

"Are you all right?" Of course, Elliot had caught her sigh.

"I am. Actually, I'm better than I've been in a long time." She smiled at him, despite her nervousness.

Elliot parked the car in the garage. Yes, her mother's car was definitely a warning—she had plenty of room for it in the garage but chose to leave it outside. A heavy feeling of dread lowered over Jordan like a wet wool blanket, smothering the good feelings from the day. Would she accuse Jordan of showing bad judgment? What if she had photographs that she could show a judge? *That's my daughter driving without a license. She's obviously incapable of caring for herself...*

"Hey." Elliot took her hand, which she realized she'd been opening and closing in her lap. He ran his warm thumb over the back of her hand, instantly calming her. All the bad racing thoughts faded. "You're acting like you've done something wrong and you haven't."

"We broke rules." She started rocking in her seat.

"Yeah, we did. So what? We calculated the risks and we were right. Nobody got hurt."

"What if she saw?"

"She didn't see, Jordan. Your mother isn't omnipresent."

"Maybe she had someone follow us."

"She didn't do that either. I would have known."

"Psychic."

"That's me." He squeezed her hand. "Come on. Let's go inside."

"And you promise you won't tell her I have a permit? Or John Charles?"

Elliot frowned. What did that frown mean? Was he angry at her? Angry at her mother? Sad? There was nothing worse than not understanding how Elliot felt. With other people, that was just the water she swam in and she'd learned to fake it. Her silence helped, even if it meant people thought she was cold. As long as they didn't think she was stupid, she didn't care. But she never wanted Elliot to think she was stupid, or cold.

"What are you feeling right now?" The words blurted out of her as he opened her car door. She quickly looked away. God, she *was* stupid. *Never let anyone know you don't know what's going on.* That had been drilled into her. She'd drilled it into herself.

He gave her another look she couldn't understand. Was he puzzled? Still angry? "You really can't tell, can you?"

Don't cry. Don't cry. "I don't know if you're mad at me. When I get like...like *this*...it's hard."

"Like what?"

"Like...how I'm feeling right now. And I can't even tell

you what that is. I don't know the name for it. It's not scared, but it is. It's not sad, but it is. It's definitely overwhelmed." Jordan closed her eyes as everything became too much and she started to close down. She waited for Elliot to yell or to shake her; or worse, tell her she was stupid and walk away. All the things that normally happened when everything got to be too much.

All the reasons why it might be a good idea to let her mother take over her life. There was too much to lose otherwise.

Jordan felt Elliot clasp her hands. When she opened her eyes, he was kneeling down in front of her. The frown was gone and there was something else in his eyes, something she liked. He was trying to *see* her. "Jordan. You don't need to give your feelings a name for them to be real and true. As for how I'm feeling, I'm not mad at you, not at all. I'm annoyed that we've had a wonderful day spoiled by..." He paused. Maybe he was thinking hard about *his* words, like she had to when she hadn't scripted anything ahead of time. "...by having to worry about how Daphne will react. It's not right, Jordan. She treats you like a helpless child and you aren't. You're a beautiful, sophisticated, smart, talented woman. You should be treated as such. By everyone."

That gave her all-over body chills. It was so different from what she was used to hearing and feeling. She wasn't sure how to react. "I will always be her little girl and she will always have my best interests at heart." The words rolled automatically off her tongue.

"That sounds scripted."

Jordan's heart thumped. *Am I that obvious?*

"Hey, no, I didn't mean to upset you." He tucked a lock of her hair that had come loose from the scarf behind her ear. "What I mean is, it sounds like someone scripted that *for* you."

"It's what she's always told me. She makes me repeat it back to her when I get confused."

"Confused about what?"

"About anything. About what I'm supposed to do, or when I'm not sure what to say to someone. Like right now, when I'm upset, everything gets harder and I get over-whelmed and I don't know what to do about it."

"Like in the office at Watchdog, when you were so quiet."

Jordan nodded. "Right. It's just times like those. It's not always like that. When I'm calm. When there's more context. When I know someone better; all of that makes it easier to interpret what someone is feeling. And it's not that I don't have feelings, Elliot. You have to know that, please. It's just that I don't always understand them. Sometimes I don't understand what other people are feeling, and sometimes I can't put a name to what I'm feeling. The labels are too simple. Happy. Sad. Scared. Sometimes they mix together for me. Happy but scared. Sad but angry."

Elliot smiled and stroked her cheek. God, it felt so good. She loved his smallest touches and could only imagine what more would feel like. "Jordan, emotions do that for everyone."

That came as a surprise. She was used to being told she was different. Defective. "Then why is it different for me?"

"Maybe it isn't so much different as..." His eyes bright-ened. "Different types of roses have different colors, right? But they're all still roses, all still beautiful. You have feelings, I know that. And they can be complex. I've never thought of you as cold. If anything, I think you feel things stronger than most people do. I've seen your empathy, too. You care about the people around you and the plants you nurture. And just look at what you want to do next with the house. No, Jordan, you are the very last person I'd accuse of being cold and emotionless."

And that's all it took for her to calm down. Of course, this was her Elliot. He'd always have that effect on her.

"Ready to go in?" She nodded and he stood, pulling her up with him.

The house was quiet except for Anubis' claws clicking on the tiles as he came to greet them at the mudroom door. No sign of Nashville or Reggie—or of her mother, thank goodness. Jordan didn't sense her downstairs at all. Was she outside or upstairs in her room? Maybe she wasn't feeling well and that's why she came home early. But if that wasn't the case, she might be waiting in Jordan's room to talk to her. The house suddenly felt too small and close, but then again, Daphne could make the entire American continent feel that way when she wanted something.

Jordan went to her knees and buried her face in Anubis' dark fur. "Hi, Nubie."

"That dog adores you." Elliot bent to ruffle Anubis' ears.

"He's still your dog though. I'm glad I insisted on having him here. I've never had a dog before."

"No? You're a natural with them."

"Well, as long as they don't dig up my garden." She smiled up at Elliot, who laughed.

"This guy would never do that, would you?" Anubis cocked his head as if to say *are you joking? You think I'm that dumb?*

"Oh, I know he wouldn't. He's too much like you. Conscientious."

Elliot paused. "You think Anubis and I are alike?"

"You don't? It's obvious. You couldn't be better-matched."

He made a thoughtful sound but didn't say anything while they petted the dog, who was being uncharacteristically dog-like and enjoying the attention.

As they left the mudroom, Jordan felt like a teenager

sneaking into the house after curfew, which was ridiculous. Elliot was right; she was a grown woman in charge of her own life and her own decisions. She'd had an amazing day and she'd done nothing to be ashamed of.

Now that part is too bad she thought. All she'd had was the feel of his hands over hers as he taught her to drive, but that was enough to stir the embers in her belly into a blaze. She looked at Elliot out of the corner of her eye as they made their way through the house. So tall and handsome, and the way he filled out his suit hinted at the muscles underneath. In all the photos she'd seen of him, there was only one where he was shirtless, and that had spurred more than one fantasy. With him under the same roof, she couldn't help but think continually about how it would feel to run her hands over his body like a rugged landscape, to explore every ridge and hard plain with the tips of her fingers. To dig into his back as he arched over her, stroking his way to orgasm inside her.

"Are you hungry?" he asked as they neared the kitchen.

Yes, but not for food. "No, I'm still full from lunch, thank you."

He stopped walking and she automatically stopped too. "Anything else you need?" His voice had gone low, like a secret between them. Was it possible he wasn't ready for their day to end, either? That he didn't want to go back to watching her from afar, a silent sentinel. Could he want more?

The house was too risky since she didn't know where everyone was. But that didn't matter. There were other places. "I need to check on the garden."

"Do you want me to come with you?"

Yes, she did. Very much so.

Now that she was calmer and it didn't look like her mother was going to jump out of the shadows and demand her driver's permit, Jordan wanted to spend the next hour or two with Elliot watching the sun set over the Pacific. Anything to extend this wonderful day. Even the harder parts were better with Elliot there. He was so patient with her.

She gave him her warmest smile, making sure the warmth shone in her eyes. Then she realized she didn't have to think about it, not with him. "I would love that."

The smile he gave back to her was clear enough that she didn't have to wonder about his mood. She'd seen it several times that day. "So would I," he said.

She remembered her driver's permit. "Let me run upstairs for a second." She lifted her purse. "I'll meet you at the French doors."

Jordan went as quickly as she could, praying she wouldn't run into her mother. But there was no sign of her, just her closed bedroom door. John Charles was nowhere to be seen, either. *No time to think about it.* She entered her bedroom, took out her permit and hid it between the mattresses, and traded her heels for slip-on sneakers.

When she got back to Elliot, he offered her his arm and they strolled through the open French doors to the patio.

"Did you see anyone?" Jordan asked him.

"I talked to Nash. He's taking the dogs for a walk now since we're back. He said Daphne and John Charles came back a couple of hours ago and went straight upstairs."

Jordan nodded. They were at the far end of the garden now near the cliffs. Jordan looked back at the house, at her mother's balcony. The setting sun reflected on the glass, turning it a blazing orange. Impossible to tell if she stood there watching them. She could be at any window looking out and they wouldn't know. They did have the advantage of the long dark shadows to hide in. *Yes, I can take the chance.*

"Have you seen the white roses yet?" she asked.

"No. I haven't had a chance to explore."

"Do you trust me?" she whispered.

His breathing sped up and he swallowed. "Yes. Always."

Her chest tightened as her heart sped up in response. She wanted to be alone with him this minute.

Jordan clasped his hand briefly. "Wait a moment, then follow me through the trees. You'll see the white roses by the ivy-covered wall." She shook her head and dropped the hose as if she and Elliot just had a disagreement and then strode away, putting on a performance for anyone who might be watching. She didn't walk directly toward the roses, which were hidden from the view of the house, but she meandered back and forth, pretending to examine everything. She was playing a game of hide and seek not knowing if she was playing alone or if her mother was watching, same as always.

Elliot played along. He may have denied reading her mind, but he knew exactly what she wanted. But hadn't they played hide and seek for a long time now too? He'd taken a step after her as if to follow, then changed his mind and hung back. He kept looking her way as if to show anyone at the house that he was keeping an eye on her but from a distance. A perfect act.

He disappeared from her view as she approached the rose garden. Her father had planted it himself out here away from the house. He'd carried her to it one night on his shoulder not long before his death. *My secret garden* he'd told her. *Everyone needs a secret garden to escape to.* It was one of the finest bits of landscaping on the entire property and he took care of it himself. Not even her mother came all the way out here, preferring instead to cling to the gardens immediately surrounding the house.

Jordan's father gave her a lesson on caring for roses and told her that he loved her and he'd let her take care of them too, that this could be *her* secret garden if she ever needed it.

It's all yours, my little love he'd said, his eyes wet. *I want you to know that. This will always be your home, no matter what.* He'd kissed her cheek, then he gave her free rein to explore the roses and the ivy-covered wall.

And that's how she'd found her own secret garden within the secret garden.

A rustling behind her told Jordan that Elliot had made his way to her, but she'd already known. She'd felt his every step, knew exactly where he was at all times by the tingling of her skin. She turned to face him. He looked so handsome with the dappled light from the rhododendrons falling on his golden hair. It used to be white-blond but she liked this new color, appreciated its richness. His eyes were locked on hers like a man swimming for shore. She didn't need to look away despite their intensity. She never needed to break her gaze with him as she did with everyone else.

"This way," she whispered needlessly. No one could hear them this far from the house. The ocean crashed below them past the dark brick wall. She took his hand and shivered at the contact. She carefully picked her way through the roses that had become overgrown with neglect, until she found the buried stone path between them. "Watch out for thorns," she warned. One had already scratched her arm.

When they got to the wall, she thrust her hands into the ivy, searching. Elliot surprised her when he did the same. "You do remember," she said.

"I...don't know. But we've done this before." He seemed lost in a dream, like when he'd first arrived and looked around the garden.

She nodded. Then she found the wood beside the brick. It had grown rougher and more ivy-covered in the intervening years. She pushed it and it barely budged. Elliot moved behind her and placed his hands on either side of her body, penning her in. But instead of feeling panicked, she felt safe. Protected, with Elliot's body between hers and the house.

With a groan that made her stomach flip, Elliot pushed against the wood until it broke free of the clinging ivy and opened just enough to let them through. The door to her secret garden was open. She turned in his arms and looked up at him. He still had that dreamy wide-eyed look, like he couldn't quite believe what he was seeing.

"It's real," he breathed.

"Come on," she coaxed. "Hopefully, the path is still intact." Ivy vines grabbed at her hair as she squeezed through the opening. She was thankful for the light from the setting sun to guide them down the steep and twisty path on the cliffside. She had no idea if any of it would still be there, but at least they would have perfect privacy. The path led them between rocks and scraggly pines partway down the cliff until it widened out to a sandy-bottomed grotto that was still ringed with jasmine. She realized now her father must have planted it long ago, created this entire getaway; there was no other explanation.

"I know this place. It's all real," Elliot said as he looked around.

"Of course it is." She crossed the small grotto to see if the switchback path still led all the way down to the beach. Impossible to tell, but from what she could see, she thought it might. It didn't matter right now. She didn't bring him here to walk along the beach.

Jordan walked back to Elliot. He was looking between the rocks at the ocean. She smiled as he turned his head to look at her. Without hesitation, she spread her arms and he mirrored her movements until she walked into his embrace. She wrapped her arms around him, stood on her tiptoes, and kissed him, long and lingering.

He hesitated at first, his body stiffening. Then he pulled back and said, "I can't take advantage of you like this."

And there it was. Always the presumption that because she thought differently that she was somehow ignorant of the world, of her body, her own wants and desires. "There are things that I don't always catch right away, but that doesn't mean I'm innocent or naïve or have to be treated like a child. You said so yourself—I'm not a child. I know what I want and what I don't want. And what I want right now is the man I've been dreaming of all my life."

He searched her face before he pulled her in tight against his body. He tipped her chin up. "I can't believe it's you," he whispered as his lips brushed hers.

"Believe, Elliot. You're here with me now. I found you." Whatever game of hide and seek he was playing, she didn't care right now. He kissed her like they'd never been apart. She felt him grow hard against her and she welcomed it. All she wanted was to make love to the only man she'd ever loved her entire life.

Her Elliot. The boy in the fountain.

SIXTEEN

My God. Real, so real.

The shock of feeling like he was two people at once—his dream self and his real self—reverberated through Costello's body the moment Jordan kissed him. He'd followed her through the garden knowing what he'd find yet unable to believe it when he saw the roses. They were a wild and overgrown tangle compared to the carefully cultivated bushes in his dreams, as if they'd been cursed and twisted by some fairy tale witch. But there they were, blooming in all their glory, and he knew what lay behind them.

Their secret place through the ivy door.

Like the roses, the ivy had taken over and sealed the door shut. But with a solid push, Costello opened the wooden gate and the brisk ocean air caressed his face like it always did. From there, he moved into a waking dream. Of all the surprises Eden House offered up to him, this was the biggest. There was simply no explanation for it. The secret door did not exist in the maps and floorplans he'd gone over in preparation for this assignment. The brick wall was supposed to be solid except for the angel gate at the front and the smaller iron gate that opened onto the stone patio and its stairs down to the beach hundreds of feet below. So how could he possibly have known about the little wooden gate?

I couldn't have. It's impossible. This is all absolutely impossible.

But he knew exactly where he was going—to a little grotto sheltered by rocks and overgrown with jasmine, with a breathtaking view of the ocean between the boulders. Exactly as he remembered.

Not remembered. Dreamed. Not dreamed. Remembered.

His head spun with the conflicting thoughts. He had a photographic memory, never forgot a thing. But he didn't remember meeting Jordan as a child. He never knew her name.

Dreams aren't real. And there are no psychics.

But Jordan's kiss was real. The realest, truest thing he'd ever felt. He never wanted it to end.

And this time there was no waking up alone in his bed because there was no dream to wake up from. Jordan was the reality in his arms. Just kissing her like this was enough to shut off the unending questions in his brain.

Who cares if she's the same woman from my dreams? I want this *reality. I want Jordan.*

She was such a mystery to him still. The more he got to know her, the more he needed to learn. The more she surprised him. He needed to let go of his dream version of Jordan and take a long, honest look at the real woman in front of him.

But for now, it was enough to hold her. To feel her soft body against his, her silky hair under his fingers, smell her skin mingling with jasmine blossoms and salt air, a smell he'd known all his life. But she tasted so much better than anything he'd dreamed. When she started to pull him down he didn't resist her. This was how it always was with the two of them, as if no barriers existed between them and they were in perfect tune. He ran his hands up and down her back as he tasted her lips. His tongue explored her mouth and she let out the most delicious moan. After their knees hit the sand, he laid back and pulled her on top of him. She hiked up her skirt and straddled his hips, grinding against his hard-on until he was ready to burst.

A moment of clarity stole over him. What was he doing? This wasn't his dream. "Can't, love," he gasped. "It's not real. You're my client. Can't do this."

"It is real. We can do anything, Elliot. Right here, anything can happen. It's our little world right here and now." She kissed his throat and started unbuttoning his shirt. He found the zipper on the back of her dress and eased it down her spine then unclasped her bra. He ran his fingers over every ridged vertebra. She felt amazing. He had to stop this.

"Wait. I don't have protection on me," he said.

"My mom put me on birth control as a teenager because if I ever got pregnant it would get in the way of my work. Not that she ever let me be alone around guys, but," a sly grin stole across her face, "where there's a will there's a way. I haven't been with anyone for over a year. I've always been careful, never gone without a condom, but I want to with you. I want to feel you inside me with no barriers."

Jesus. He didn't know what to say to that. Costello had wondered if she was a virgin, if he'd have to go slow and gentle with her, fight his urges to go faster and rougher. This was a relief. He shook his head, angry with himself that he'd made that assumption. She was beautiful and worldly despite her seeming innocence. Of course she'd slept with men. But he imagined she'd had to sneak around behind Daphne's back to do it.

"Elliot? Are we? Do you...?" Frustration filled her eyes. "I need to know I'm reading you right. What are you feeling right now?"

Love. Pure, simple love.

Costello took Jordan's face in his hands. "I'm thinking that I am holding the most amazing woman in my arms right now and it feels incredible. You, Jordan, are the woman of my dreams. I can't expect you to understand that," he touched her lips before she could protest, "because I can't understand it myself. I've known you forever. I've wanted you forever. And now that I have you in my arms, I'm having the damndest time grasping that it's real."

She shook her head. "That's both of us. I've dreamed of this night with you so many times. Of bringing you here and kissing you in our secret place. And now my dream is real."

"Mine, too. I don't understand how, but it is. I'm done questioning it in case it disappears."

"Then kiss me again before it's too late."

He pulled her head down to his and took her lips in a bruising kiss. She gave him everything he wanted in that moment. Passion, fulfillment, the end of longing.

A dream come true.

As the grotto filled with shadows, Costello slipped her dress and bra off her shoulders. Jordan sat up to let the top of her dress slide down her torso. Her breasts were full and round. Her nipples puckered tightly as a sea breeze blew between the rocks. She tilted her head back and let the breeze play with her hair. Costello watched mesmerized as long strands danced across her shoulders and breasts. He reached up to touch her and she opened her eyes and looked down at him. He caressed each nipple with his thumbs as she bit her lower lip and watched him. He slid his hands down her sides to the flare of her hips, loving her curves, her warm skin, the jasmine scent that was all hers mingling with the night-blooming jasmine opening all around them.

"Better than any dream," he whispered. "Better than any wish or hope or fantasy."

Jordan took one of his hands and placed it against her heated cheek and closed her eyes. She turned her head into his hand and kissed his palm. Then she lifted up and shimmied out of her dress one leg at a time. Barely-there lace covered the last of her and Costello had to fight himself not to rip away the thong. She straddled him again and he propped himself up on his elbows. His gaze drank her in—her beautiful face, hair blowing in the breeze, the perfect swell of her breasts, her tapering waist and the gentle curve of her belly, her rounded thighs, the delicious secret still undiscovered behind the lace. *Truly an earth goddess.*

"I could stare at you all night," he said. "Just drink in your beauty. But I want to worship you completely." He sat up quickly and took her in his arms. He kissed her while she unbuttoned his shirt. She pushed his shirt off his shoulders and ran her hands down his chest, murmuring her approval straight into his mouth.

She pulled back from his kiss and looked at him as she ran her fingers over his body. She flattened her palms against his pecs until he could feel the ridge of hard, smooth calluses just below her fingers. She looked so delicate to him but she had built so much beauty with those hands through hard work. She brought places to life with those hands.

Costello cradled her as he laid Jordan down in the soft sand. He started with her throat and laid kiss after kiss on her warm salty skin. He grazed his teeth over her throat as she sighed and clutched at his back. He tried not to think about her with any other man. She was his and he wanted her completely. He licked the valley between her breasts. "Forget them," he whispered over her skin and watched the gooseflesh rise.

"Who?"

"Every man you've ever been with. Any man who's ever touched you. I'm going to wipe away their marks, their touches, their words. They don't exist anymore. I'm going to replace them by kissing every inch of your body. By making love to you so thoroughly and completely you'll never think of them again. You'll only feel me on your skin as if we've never been apart."

He looked up to see her languid smile. "You're fighting ghosts that aren't there, Elliot. They disappeared the moment I found you, if they even existed for me at all. Every year has been a circle leading me back to you and only you. I love you, Elliot. I always have, in every season of my life, I've loved you."

Costello pulled Jordan against him and claimed her mouth. She met him with equal hunger. His tongue explored her mouth as she welcomed him in. She tasted divine, sweet and ripe and he couldn't get enough of her. When he finally pulled away, he said, "Let me show you how much I love you."

He laid her down again and began exploring the landscape of her body in earnest. Where his fingers led his tongue trailed, circling her nipples until she cried out. He dipped into the valley between them, licking and blowing on her skin, bringing all her senses right to the surface. The sound of his name on her lips spurred him on. Despite what she said, he whispered against her skin for her to forget every other lover. Her body trembled under him as her hands roamed over his body, bringing up his own goosebumps. Her touch felt so familiar and so new at the same time. His cock grew harder, straining against the cloth that separated them. When Jordan started to undo his belt he wrapped his hand around her wrists and pulled them away.

"Not yet. If I let you do that this will all be over much too soon. Let me pleasure you first. I want to hear you screaming my name, Jordan." He gripped her wrist with one hand while he ran his finger over the meager lace and cupped her with the other. God, she was soaking wet for him. She moaned and squirmed under his touch. Impatient, he tugged the lace aside, then tore it off. Her lips were swollen, dark pink and glistening. He leaned down and breathed her in. Her desire smelled so good, so deep and warm. He blew across her skin and she lifted her pelvis. He ran his tongue between her folds, lapping her up. He flattened it hard against her clit before flicking it over the tip. "Has anyone ever made you come, Jordan?"

"Never." Her voice sounded ragged.

"Then no one's ever truly made love to you. I'll be your first."

"Let me touch you, too." She struggled against his hold but he didn't let go of her wrists.

"Oh, I will. But not until I've had my fill of you. Not until I've made you mine." He kissed her belly. "Do you want that? Do you want to be mine?"

"I'm already yours."

His heart pounded in his chest at her words. "Good." He nuzzled between her legs. "Because once I claim you, I'll be lost in you. I'll be yours, Jordan. Heart and soul, yours."

She whimpered beautifully under him as he made her writhe. He kissed the insides of her thighs until she shook. He parted her dark pink lips and ran his tongue around their edges as her body tightened and her breathing turned fast until she was panting. Then he backed off and blew against her swollen clit as she moaned.

"I'm going to keep taking you right up to the edge, Jordan, but I'm not letting you go over, not yet. I want it to be so good for you, beloved. So damn good." He watched her every move, listened to her every breath, studying and memorizing her like he'd never done with any other woman. As he licked and touched and blew across her skin, he counted her heartbeats and measured the spaces between, waiting for just the right moment to ease off, making sure she stayed close but never quite peaked. He needed to pause for himself, too. He'd always been a generous lover, but he'd never been so aroused by what he was doing to a woman. Her pleasure was his.

"So...good..." she moaned. "I can't..." Her fingers curled and she lifted her waist trying to press harder against him.

One flick of his tongue. Costello gripped her wrists while he rubbed her clit fast and hard. He brought her to the edge one last time. "Now, Jordan. Now I want you to come for me."

She bucked her hips rhythmically against his hand. He watched her face as she went from biting her lip to crying out his name. Her eyes flew open and she stared up at the sky. Tears slid down her face. When she finally met his gaze her eyes were glossy, her lashes wet.

He released her wrists, sat up, and took her in his arms, cradling her as she came down from the stars. He kissed her forehead along her hairline and stroked her cheek with his thumb. He nuzzled *I love yous* into her hair. When she came back to herself fully she wrapped her arms around him and pressed her lips against the hollow of his throat.

"That was the most amazing thing that's ever happened to me," she whispered into his ear. She flicked her tongue against his earlobe, sending pleasurable shivers down his spine. "Now, I'm going to do that to you."

"Jordan. You don't have to."

She pulled away until she was looking him straight in the

eyes. A very naughty, almost wicked smile crossed her lips. "You say that like I don't want to make you come. Like I don't want to hear you helplessly calling *my* name." She licked her lips. "I want to give you back everything you've given me, Elliot. I want to make *you* forget that I'm not your first."

Her hands snaked between them and she went back to undoing his belt. His cock straining against his boxer briefs did not escape her notice and she ran her hand over his length before she pulled his belt through the loops. Her smile definitely turned wicked as she looked at the belt, then looked at his hands.

Costello chuckled and took the strip of leather away. "Not tonight. Which isn't to say I won't let you play with that another time. Maybe when I can afford to be incapacitated because I'm not your bodyguard anymore." *Did I just say that? That we have a future together after this assignment?* He wanted that more than anything. And once Jordan was safe, nothing would stand between them.

But in the meantime, he'd done the second-worst thing you could do with a principal, just shy of actually getting them wounded or, God forbid, killed.

He'd made love to her. Fallen *in* love with her.

He wasn't ashamed of that. Hell, he'd fallen for her the minute he'd seen her in the conference room.

Before that. You know it was before that.

If anyone found out, he'd be off the assignment and away from her. Daphne would have a reason to get rid of Watchdog completely and where would that leave Jordan?

No, he wasn't ashamed. He didn't regret what they just did, but he already regretted what he was about to do.

Liar. Thief. Traitor.

He took her face in his hands. "I don't want to do this but I have to ask you not to tell anyone what happened here. For obvious reasons." His gut filled with cement. He was no better than the rest of them, using her and then asking her to lie.

Jordan smiled softly. "So many secrets between us. Of course, I'll protect you. I always will."

He ran his hand through her hair one last time and cupped her cheek. "When this is over. When you're safe, Jordan, I want... I want us to have a chance. If you'll have me."

Jordan placed her hands on his shoulders and leaned forward to kiss him. "I love you, Elliot. Always."

"And I love you, Jordan. Always."

SEVENTEEN

Costello led Jordan back up the path and through the secret door in the wall. They'd been off-camera for thirty-five minutes—not an impossible amount of time to explain away—but if they didn't get back in sight soon, they might raise suspicions. Costello could not afford to be taken off this assignment, especially not now.

He'd made the number one worst mistake by becoming emotionally close to a principal. He worried about being distracted, his attention compromised. *I mean, look at tonight* he thought. Anyone could have sneaked up on them while all his attention had been laser-focused on pleasing her. That made his cock jump. *Fuck, even now I'm not fully in the game.*

As he was pulling the wooden door back into place, the hairs on the back of his neck stood up. Rustling footsteps behind them grew louder. Jordan was busy brushing sand off her dress and shaking out her hair. He placed a hand on her shoulder to still her and she heard the steps too. "It could be Nash checking on us," he whispered.

He was correct. Nash, accompanied by Reggie, came through the trees. He looked back and forth between the two of them. "Ms. Summers, your mother is looking for you. I didn't see y'all on any of the cameras."

"I'd asked about the white roses in the vases and Jordan offered to show me where they grew," Costello covered. He caught Nash looking at the remaining dirt on Jordan's dress. "And you know me, I asked what her secret was to growing them so beautifully."

Jordan looked at him and blinked, looking confused for a moment. *Please, beloved, follow my lead.* Then she smiled. "And I'll use any excuse to go digging. So like I said, Elliot, bone meal, eggshells, and coffee grounds. You saw how well they break down just a couple inches under the soil."

Good, smart, amazing woman. "Right. Excellent compost. Now I was wondering..." He tried to ask the most mundane questions he could come up with and Jordan happily responded.

Nash's eyes practically rolled back in his head a few minutes later from boredom. "Well, I'm just the messenger, but Mrs. Summers is worried." He turned to head back to the house and Costello and Jordan followed. She looked up at him with uncertainty in her eyes and he stole a quick hand-squeeze to reassure her.

Daphne was waiting for them on the patio. She looked her daughter up and down and Costello's stomach knotted in worry that she'd read her daughter and know exactly what they'd just done. Her brows knitted in disapproval.

Oh, God, here we go.

"Jordan, I know money means nothing to *you*, but do you really have to dig holes in Oscar de la Renta?"

She looked down as if seeing the dress for the first time. "Oh." Then she shrugged and moved past her mother "Going to bed now."

Daphne rolled her eyes behind her daughter's back. She gave Costello a smile that said *what can I do?*

"I'm sorry about her dress," he said, feeling like he was absolutely betraying Jordan, talking about her as if she were no more than a naughty five-year-old. But he thought it was best to play along with Daphne, humor her.

She waved him off. "Can't be helped. She's like a child, a spoiled one with no sense of the value of things. Everything is a toy." She smiled smugly at him. "Walk me in?"

"Yes, ma'am."

She rolled her eyes again as they strolled into the house. She stopped him halfway into the study.

"Speaking of, I see *you* enjoy playing with Jordan's toys," Daphne half-scolded, half-teased. His heart stopped for a moment—did she know? No, not with that voice. Was she trying to shame him or seduce him with that purring tone? Either attitude would get her nowhere with him.

She took a step closer to him and he fought the urge to back up. Her rose perfume pressed itself against his nose. She stood entirely too close. "Tell me, Mr. Costello, are you a native of California?"

Keep it pleasant but distant. If you're a dick she'll just try and draw closer. "I grew up all over the place, ma'am."

Daphne smirked and shook her head slowly, her eyes never leaving his. "Still with the *ma'am*. Do I look *that* ancient?"

"No, you don't," Costello answered truthfully. "I'm simply being respectful." He added a smile.

Daphne smiled back. "You thought I looked like her sister, didn't you, when you first saw me." She walked in a circle around him, making Costello turn to keep facing her as she did. "Her older sister, but not old enough to be her mother."

"I might have, for a moment."

Daphne tossed her head back in triumph and barked out a laugh. "I knew it. Granted, I was young when Leo and I had Jordan, but I've done a lot to keep myself looking and feeling young." Her eyes danced over his body. "But, now I have the benefit of wisdom that comes with age. I know things a younger woman wouldn't." Her eyebrow ticked upward. "Especially things my daughter wouldn't know. She's by nature naïve. She can't help it. I do what I can to step in and protect her." The scent of roses surrounded Costello as if he were standing in the middle of the garden. "Sometimes, it requires some un-orth-o-dox"—Daphne tiptoed her fingers up his chest to the beat of the syllables—"methods."

Now Costello did step back. "What is it that you're trying to tell me, Ms. Summers?"

Her smile showed her perfect little white teeth. "I'm not paying you to date my daughter."

God, she knows. Costello played it cool. "You're not paying me at all. Jordan is."

"At *my* direction, or she'd have no idea how much danger she was in. She'd just blissfully dig away in her garden right up until Daniel found her and pushed her into the hole she'd just dug."

"You still think Daniel is a threat? It makes no sense for Daniel to attack Jordan, especially after all this time. He's got nothing to gain."

"You don't know my stepson. He's vengeful, out of control when he drinks, obviously."

"We've looked into records of his behavior while in prison. He entered an AA program on day one and never missed a meeting even if he had to make one up. No fights beyond a few little skirmishes, no time in solitary. He was a model prisoner, not a man who has deep anger issues."

Daphne waved him off. "He didn't have access to alcohol.

Now he does. He'll go right back to it."

Costello laughed. "You honestly think there's no alcohol or drugs in prison? That he wasn't targeted with it to have something over him?" He shook his head and watched her grow more irritated with every word. Okay, he enjoyed it. "No. Daniel resisted, showing great restraint. I have no reason to believe he'd suddenly go right back to drinking once he got out." He didn't bother telling her that Gina hadn't seen him purchase any alcohol and there were no beer cans or bottles in his trash.

Daphne sloughed off her usual smooth demeanor like a snakeskin. Her face suddenly looked its age. "I will repeat— you don't know him like I do. You weren't here for his evil stares and remarks. His insane jealousy of Jordan—a little baby girl, for Chrissakes. I wouldn't put it past him to find enough self-control to get him out of prison early just so he could get his revenge sooner." She hugged herself and glanced around the darkened room. "Do you think I wanted to leave Italy, cancel the next commission, and come back here? I *hate* this house. There, I've said it. I hate this place and all its memories. It's a tomb." Costello held back a flinch as she echoed Jordan's words. "Worse, it's a crime scene."

Daphne's face went from anger to honest grief. "I lost my husband here, and no matter what John Charles and Daniel think—what the *world* thinks—I loved that man. He saw more in me than anyone else ever did. *Ever* has, even before I had the money to hide behind. You know, I started here as a nobody, a kid practically, working the grounds under the head gardener. I was no one, but he saw someone. Someone special."

Her eyes glistened. "And I saw how lonely he was and my heart went out to him. It was rough at first, of course. The judgment, the idea his sons put into his head that I'd gotten pregnant with Jordan on purpose to trap him. And then that she wasn't even his baby. But she *was* his, the paternity test proved it. He married me after that, and we had a wonderful life together. He loved his daughter, and he loved me. *Me.* And I adored him, with or without his money. John Charles and Daniel will never understand that. You probably don't understand that. How could you? You didn't come up from nothing."

Costello's blood boiled as her words cut right to the heart of his shame. "You don't know anything about me and where I come from. Nothing." His palms hurt and he realized he was clenching his hands so hard his short nails were digging into the flesh. The pain brought him back to himself, saving him from blurting out his past and all its ugliness.

The memories were right there at the surface— rummaging through drawers in big houses almost as grand as this one while his mother distracted the owners using one scheme or another. Posing as a missionary looking for donations. Selling fake designer purses at a party. Cooking, cleaning, whatever it took to get herself and her son through the door.

But her favorite caper was pretending to be a psychic after she'd have him grill the kids on family history at school or at a park the day before. Costello suppressed a shudder at that one, the memories of tiptoeing around bedrooms, one ear listening for someone coming up the stairs, the other taking in the sobs downstairs as gullible people 'spoke' to their long lost loved ones through his mother, the fraud.

There are no psychics.

Daphne watched him, her eyes back to their coolly appraising nature. "Maybe I do know something about you after all," she murmured. "I hit a nerve, didn't I? Perhaps we aren't so different." She smiled softly, all the coolness gone from her eyes, a mirror reflection of Jordan's that startled him. "I hate to see a man in pain. Do you want to get a glass of wine and talk about it? You may not realize this, but among other things, I'm an excellent listener."

So was my mother when it suited her purposes. "No thank you. I never drink on the job."

"Never?" She turned coy. "But you must do this so often, spend time with a client twenty-four seven. You've never had a glass of wine or a beer with *any* of them?"

"No, ma'am. It's not professional." *Neither is sleeping with your principal but that didn't stop you* the voice in his head chided.

Daphne rolled her eyes and laughed musically. "*Enough* with the ma'am already, I told you." She laid her hand on his arm and started directing him across the room. "To the kitchen for a couple of glasses. I promise I won't turn you in over a teeny tiny glass of wine. Or anything else that might come up." Her smile heated. "Come on. A little wine with me might be *fun.*"

"I still have to decline."

Daphne cooled the heat. Costello practically watched the gears shifting in her head as she tried a different angle. "Well, I am *also* a mother with a mother's nurturing instincts, even if I don't look a day over thirty, and I sense that you need a sympathetic ear."

Costello stopped her. "No thank you. I think it's best that I say good night."

Something dark fluttered across Daphne's expression and was gone, replaced with an unmistakable look. "Maybe it isn't a mother you need." Her gaze traveled up and down his body again, then she sucked in her lower lip. "You know where I am if you change your mind." She turned and walked toward the kitchen. "Anytime, day or night. You know where I am."

"I won't be taking you up on that." *Dammit, Costello, just couldn't keep your fucking mouth shut, could you?*

Daphne stopped and turned and Costello knew he was in trouble. Her eyes could freeze lava. At that moment she didn't look a thing like her daughter. "It's not that I want you, you know. I could have anyone I want in the world. You're no one. Just another shiny toy for Jordan to play with. But I won't let her. I've seen the way you look at each other. I know you aren't as formal with her as you are with me. I won't let you try and seduce her. I thought I could do this the fun way, but apparently not. If I can't distract you from Jordan, I'll just report you if you get out of line with her." With that, she flashed those little white teeth and headed for the kitchen.

Fuck, what have I done?

Costello ran his hands through his hair. *Stupid, stupid. I should have just left it, kept my mouth shut.*

EIGHTEEN

For the next few days, Costello did everything he could not to get too close to Jordan whenever Daphne was around. At least John Charles was back to leaving Eden House and going in to work, insisting he didn't need a 'babysitter' to accompany him.

Costello smiled to himself. Gina made a great babysitter.

Daphne announced she had plans in town and had left that morning, taking with her the oppressive atmosphere that had grown since she'd attempted to seduce Costello. Jordan sat at her favorite table with her sketchbook and her phone. When Costello was sure Daphne was out of earshot, he approached her.

"Good morning," he said, unable to keep the smile off his face. She looked radiant in the morning sun streaming through the window behind her, the backlight limning her hair like a halo, the same way it had that first afternoon. She was hard at work on something in her sketchbook, writing instead of drawing, but she still looked up quickly and returned a smile full of happiness.

"Good morning, yourself." Her smile turned languid and

Costello had a hard time controlling himself. She lowered her voice. "Are we playing hide and seek again? From my mom?"

Hide and seek. It jolted him inside every time she said that. He was on the verge of mentioning it when she turned her sketchbook around and proudly displayed it. "Look what I've been doing."

He picked up the sketchbook and read down the list of names and organizations, some with check marks next to them. She'd listed the mayor of Malibu and a couple of council members, a woman in charge of a kids' day camp, the head of a nearby food pantry, and the local chapter of the veterans' association. And at the bottom of the list were two words: *Elliot's friends.*

"I've contacted the ones with checkmarks next to them already. But I could use a little help when it comes to inviting your friends."

"What about *your* friends? That's the one thing I don't see on here."

Jordan shrugged. "I don't...have that many. And the ones I do have are across the ocean."

Costello's heart clenched for her. She'd grown up as lonely as he did, but had yet to find her true family like he had. Well, he could help her with that. "In that case, get ready to make friends. I'll let them know at Watchdog that you would like to extend the invitation to your event to them, though most of the guys will actually be working security for the party already."

Jordan covered her mouth. "I hadn't thought of that."

"It's okay. It's what they do, what *we* do. Even off-duty we're still on-duty. Always on alert to protect our loved ones." He relished the color that rose in her cheeks. "Tell you what. I'll write my friends' names down here, but I'll do the contacting. Easier that way." He had an idea. "Have you arranged the food yet?"

"Um, no I haven't." She looked distressed. "I've never thrown a party before."

Costello grinned. "Eh, me neither. Guess we're winging it together."

"We've always seemed to do that."

That struck an odd chord. But, he was still learning Jordanspeak so he let it go. "When it comes to food and my crowd, there's only one way to go. My buddy Camden's fiancée is in charge of catering for a restaurant called Delia's and those ladies know how to cook. I'll see if they're available."

"Thank you!" There was that beaming smile again, the one he'd do anything for. "But, let me handle that. Give me her name and I'll call the restaurant. I need to learn to do these things if I'm going to be having parties."

"Sure thing. Hey. I'm proud of you."

Jordan shook her head. "Don't be. This is basic stuff. Socialization 101. I'm way behind."

Costello shook his head. "Important thing is, you're learning."

"It's funny. I woke up feeling overwhelmed just thinking about planning a party for people I don't know. But then I started thinking of it in terms of planning out a new garden and that changed everything." Her eyes got round. "Oh. But, you probably shouldn't tell your friends I think of them as plants."

That made Costello laugh hard. Yup, Jordanspeak was going to take a while. "Don't worry. Knowing how much you love and care for plants, it's a compliment. But, I'll keep that image between us for now." Though, now that the concept was in his head, he did think Gina would make a great amaryllis.

Jordan rolled in her lower lip. "It's all going to be okay, right?"

Costello lowered his voice. "You're talking about more than the party, aren't you?"

She nodded. "My birthday is coming up. My mother is talking more and more about how I have a hard time handling things. I keep doubting myself."

He held back an angry, frustrated growl. "Don't ever let me hear you doubting yourself. This party is going to prove you are capable to a lot of people. You're going to impress the hell out of everyone. Jordan, even if she tried to push for a conservatorship, no judge would believe her. Especially after this." He risked cupping her cheek. "I believe in you. And I'm here to protect you, body, mind, and soul." He decided to let her in a little on his plan. "My friends at Watchdog know the deal with your mother. They will be here as witnesses as well as friends."

"What if I say something weird or stupid, or I just go on about gardening and they think..." She squeezed her eyes shut.

"They're going to think you are smart, and funny, and talented, and capable of anything. Just like I do."

Costello's cell buzzed. He kept his expression neutral as he read the new message. Lachlan's text wasn't quite a call to heel—the command to stop whatever you were doing after receiving the message and come straight to the office because there was a universal attack against the company—but it was unusual. The one and only time Lachlan had issued a call to heel, Kyle had inadvertently ruined some big plans by the Capitoline Group. This was on a much smaller scale, but still concerning. Lach was calling a meeting and asking Costello and Nash both to come in for it. Substitute security personnel were already on their way to Eden House to cover.

"Everything all right?" Jordan asked.

"Yes, fine. My boss has decided to call a meeting and Nash and I need to be there. Two other men are on their way here to temporarily take our places. It's just for part of the day." He gave her what he hoped was a reassuring smile.

She rolled her bottom lip in again. Then she nodded. "My mom is out for the day. I'll be fine."

"Of course you will."

Nash went ahead to Watchdog while Costello oriented the new guys. They'd done 'second ring' work for this assignment when Jordan was directing the landscaping crew —staying on the perimeter and looking for threats before they could approach—so they were already familiar with the grounds but needed to be updated on security codes. Since Costello had discovered there was no immediate threat to Jordan's life, he'd dismissed the second ring, but he would use them again for her party. Once he'd oriented the subs, he headed for Watchdog, resigned to the fact that he was perpetually late to any and every meeting.

Costello dropped Anubis off at the kennels with Eric, the FNG who would be taking over for Kyle, and headed for the meeting. Voices grew louder as he got closer to the door— casual tones, conversational. This would be the first time he'd ever walked in before things had already started. When he heard his name, he stopped just outside the door and listened to the conversation between Nash and Jake.

"...I mean, Psychic's always been a little bit spooky, right? The way he knows shit before it goes down," Nash said.

"Spookier than Spooky at times, yeah."

"So, I'm just wondering if those two have hooked up."

Jake snorted. "Don't ever let Lach hear you say that."

"Wait, are you saying *Lach*—"

Oh for fuck's sake. Costello let his presence be known by coughing and walking into the room.

"...thinks that Dolly Parton is not the biggest country music star ever?" Nash covered. "Thems fightin' words. She's my cousin."

"Are you ladies done gossiping? Can we get started?" Costello took a seat, surprised that it was just the three of them.

Jake cleared his throat. "Hey, didn't see you there. Yeah, we can't get this party started until Lach and uh, Gina get here."

"And me," Kyle said as he walked in the door.

"Hey, short-timer," Jake lifted his coffee mug in a toast.

Kyle looked around the conference room. "Wait, are you telling me Psychic beat Lach to a meeting? Is Lach dead?"

"Funny," Costello said.

"And me?" Kyle patted his body all over. "Shit, am *I* dead? Psychic, can you see dead people?"

"Even funnier." Costello drummed his fingers on the table. "So, where *are* Lach and Gina?"

Nash and Jake side-eyed each other, eyebrows raised.

"What?" Kyle asked before he bit into the bagel he'd carried in along with his coffee. "Whud I miff?" he added as he chewed.

"The Watchdog Ladies' Coffee Klatch," Costello said. "In other words, not a damn thing worth hearing."

It was Kyle's turn to raise his eyebrows. "We'll talk later," he mock-whispered. Nash and Jake both gave him a thumbs-up.

Thank God Lachlan stomped in just then, chomping on his cut-down pen like it had insulted his mother twice. "Sorry I'm late." He looked at Costello as he took a seat. "Holy shit, I must be *really* late. Fuck, let's get started."

"Wait, where's Gina?" Costello said. He ignored the peanut gallery's ever-rising eyebrows.

"Gina will not be joining us and that's part of why I've called this meeting."

Okay, now Costello joined in with the eyebrow-raising. "What's up, boss?" His stomach sank. Gina hadn't reported in to him about Daphne and John Charles' whereabouts when they went to Los Angeles together, so he figured she wanted to do an in-person update. But now that she wasn't here, he hoped her absence had nothing to do with something bigger, like Marcus Porter. At least he knew she must not be missing, otherwise, Lachlan would have issued a call to heel, and half of L.A. would probably be burning.

Lachlan exhaled as he took the pen stump out of his mouth between his first and second fingers. "We might have fucked up with Daniel Summers."

"What do you mean?" Costello asked. "And with all due respect, I'm the lead on this assignment, so if anything's happened, I'm taking all the blame. There's no *we*."

"Really? So you were a goddamned one-man team with the SEALs, huh?" Lach started to raise the pen to his mouth but caught himself. "I thought you never forgot anything, so why'd you go and forget your BUD/S training? We're a team here, same as there, and when I say *we* I mean *we*."

"So what's happening, boss?" Jake asked.

"Gina was watching Daniel and she said it was the most boring assignment she'd ever been given. The man was like a monk—stayed in all day, only went out for food runs and to put in applications at one of those day laborer places and a couple construction sites. She said he looked like he was keeping in shape though, probably exercising all day, keeping up with his routine from prison. The man kept quiet and stayed damn near invisible. She agreed with your assessment, Costello, that he was harmless but still worth keeping some tabs on, so she decided to downgrade to checking on him every three days."

Lach shifted in his seat. "So she tailed Daphne and John Charles in Los Angeles like you asked—which we'll get to—and checked on Daniel after. Or at least she tried to, because when she got there, the man was gone."

"Gone completely?" Costello asked.

Lachlan nodded. "She waited thinking he was just out getting food. Then she tried his usual haunts—a couple convenience stores—then checked the day labor place and the construction sites thinking maybe he'd gotten hired, but no dice. So she went back to wait some more. Now, here's where it gets interesting. Gina's thinking she'll do more than just watch through the window; she'll go in and snoop around, see if our man left behind anything of interest, determine if he's left on his own or by force, and if it's something we need to look into or if he's just moving on. But before going in, Gina being Gina notices that at this point, she's not the only one watching Daniel's room."

"He's got a second tail?"

"Sure as shit does. And she's never seen these two assholes around there before. And we all know Gina—she wouldn't have missed that. She got photos of them which we're running through face recognition as we speak. She's out right now searching high and low for Daniel Summers and sends her regrets." Lachlan searched every man's face. "Thoughts?"

Jake spoke first. "These two moved in on Daniel once they knew we'd cut the surveillance."

"And while our man Daniel never saw Gina, he did pick up on the second tail and lit out would be my guess," Nash said.

Costello agreed one hundred percent. "Either those two got lucky with their timing, we have a mole at Watchdog, or Daphne and/or John Charles put a tail on him themselves once they knew we were standing down. I think we can all agree the first scenario is unlikely though it can't be ruled out entirely, the second is preposterous, so that leaves us the third option."

"And that brings me to what Gina saw when she tailed Daphne and John Charles." Lachlan started to raise his pen to his mouth, stopped halfway, then gave up and chomped down on it. "Costello, how would you characterize their relationship?"

"Hostile at the get-go but not so much now. They've gone from shooting freeze rays from their eyes at each other to huddling and talking from time to time. Which makes me worry even more. I'll almost catch them but I'm never quite able to pick up what they're saying, and they break apart the second I appear."

"Same," Nash added. "Like a coupla guilty kids fixing to steal the cookie jar."

Lachlan grunted and shifted the pen to the other side of his mouth. "Gina followed them both to Summers Shipping Company. Now, that would make sense for John Charles seeing as he's taking an interest in his own damn company again, but Daphne? By all accounts, she doesn't give a shit about SSC so long as the gravy train keeps pulling into the station. So what is she doing there, you may ask? Well, maybe someone else is pulling into her station, like her stepson." Lach opened the folder he brought in and shuffled through it.

"Gina took these from the building across the way." Lach tossed a pile of eight-by-ten photographs onto the table.

"Fuck, Lach, a warning please?" Kyle said.

"Well, now we know what Kyle doesn't watch online," Jake said. Kyle shot him the finger.

Costello leaned in to look at the top one. Taken through a window with a zoom lens, it was pretty clear that John Charles had Daphne in a serious liplock as she straddled his lap while he sat on his desk. "They get raunchier the further down the pile you go. Just a trigger warning for those of you with delicate sensibilities."

Costello's stomach churned. If he'd been foolish and morally bankrupt enough to take Daphne up on her offer, he would have been getting some serious sloppy seconds.

"This was a little celebration party, we're thinking," Lachlan continued. "Just before that, a serious meeting went down with a team of lawyers, both SSC's in-house and some we've identified thanks to Jake over here"—Jake dipped his head in acknowledgment—"from an outside firm specializing in estate planning."

Costello felt nauseous. "She's going to push for the conservatorship. Goddamn it."

"Take it from the son of an accountant," Kyle said. "Follow the money. It always comes down to the damn money."

"True, that. And there's a lot of money in this case." Costello stopped. "Or is there?"

"What? What are your Spidey senses telling you, Psychic?" Jake asked.

"Lach. I know you ran a check on Jordan's finances before taking the job. We don't work cheap and you took the assignment, so obviously, there is money there. But...did you only run it on Jordan's income, and not on her assets?"

"You thinking there's a mountain of debt?"

"Yes, I am. John Charles has been running their father's business, but he strikes me as an utter buffoon. A real shit-for-brains."

"Straight-up," Nash chimed in. "Bad with women, bad with money."

"What if he's run the company into the proverbial ground and he's using the house and everything in it as collateral?"

"We need to find out if the house is his," Kyle said.

"We have that intel but I sent the will straight on to Costello. Which, good call digging it up," Lach said. "So what does it say?"

"In a nutshell, Leo Summers set up trusts for everyone, with Jordan coming into her full inheritance later, her next birthday as a matter of fact. The old man favored her and gave her the biggest amount but knew she had some developmental issues—"

"Like what?" Kyle asked. "Sorry, late to the party here."

"Asperger's. High-functioning autism."

"I'm familiar. Arden has several clients like that. Cool people."

"Leo made Daphne Jordan's sole guardian if anything happened to him, up into her thirties. He named Daniel as the heir apparent for the business, which obviously was a mistake."

"Yeah, naming the son who has it in him to kill you in a blackout-drunk rage as your successor? Not wise," Jake said.

Costello shook his head. "But that's the thing. The old man was not stupid. Blind in some ways, maybe. Well, obviously, since he fell for Daphne."

"Or was he just trying to do the right thing and marry the mother of his child?" Kyle asked.

"Could be, of course, especially since he had a paternity

test done before the marriage. But Jordan says he and Daphne were close."

"She was a little kid. If her parents weren't out-and-out at each other's throats all the time, that could pass for close. Especially if she has trouble recognizing and labeling emotions," Kyle said.

"True. But back to the money. If Daphne and John Charles have burned through their inheritances and John Charles has fucked up the shipping business, they could be about to lose everything if they can't put up the house for collateral. The house and everything in it are part of Jordan's extra inheritance. Until then, they can't sell without everyone's signature and Jordan refuses to sign. Even though Daphne is her guardian it's baked into the will that she needs that signature."

"Shouldn't everything have gone to Jordan when she turned twenty-one?" Jake asked.

Kyle nodded. "That's pretty standard, but maybe Daphne convinced Leo that Jordan wouldn't be able to handle it that young because of her autism. But, hell, show me *any* twenty-one-year-old kid who has the sense to handle multi-multi millions. I didn't know my dick from my asshole at that age. Fuck, she probably woulda done better than most. So, I'd buy Daphne manipulating the old man so that she could maintain control for as long as possible. And if she declares Jordan incapable of taking care of herself and becomes her conservator—"

"She's got everything forever," Lach said.

Costello nodded. "And, even if the debt ate up all the assets, she'd have complete control over Jordan's continuing income, which is not insubstantial."

"Can you really make that much as a gardener?" Kyle asked.

Costello scoffed. "Calling Jordan a gardener is like calling

Da Vinci a housepainter. She's a genius and an artist. She commands millions upon millions for her work." He reached into his pocket for his phone and called up an article on her latest installation. "Take a look at this." He handed Kyle his phone.

Kyle studied the photos at the top of the article. "Wow, that's not like any garden I've ever seen. That could be on another planet. A really badass one."

"Scroll down to the article. The price tag is in the first line."

Kyle whistled. "Damn. Sixty-seven *million?* Is that a typo?"

"Nope. They're considered living works of art and you know how art's become a huge commodity. It's an investment for that family who commissioned her. She just doubled or tripled the value of their estate and that wasn't cheap to begin with."

"So, Jordan is loaded all on her own." Kyle handed Costello the phone.

Costello cringed. "It's not about the money with her. She'd do this for free. Actually, she's done things for free—landscaped fantastic play gardens for Ronald McDonald Houses, turned abandoned city lots into community food gardens, things like that. She'd do all of it for the sheer joy of planting, but Daphne prevents that. She stops Jordan from doing the free projects when she hits the tax write-off cap each year."

"And what I'm hearing is that it's in Daphne's—not Jordan's—best interests that Daphne take over Jordan's finances forever," Lachlan said.

"Sure looks like it, doesn't it? If Daphne is the conservator, she can force the sale of the house. But Daphne is also hedging her bets. If the company really is about to go belly-up and they're forced to sell everything to cover the debt, she'd still have Jordan's income coming in."

"She's the goose that lays the golden eggs," Jake said.

"More like the gardener who plants the golden beans," Costello answered.

"Affirmative." Kyle nodded. "So, what we gonna do about it?"

"The first step is to look deeper into SSC's finances," Lachlan said, leaning back in his chair, a sure signal the meeting was almost over. "Me and Gina have a friend who does that sort of work in his sleep." Costello watched Lach glance at Kyle who gave the slightest nod of recognition at the reference. "I have a feeling John Charles may have taken out some not-so-conventional loans and it would probably be good to see who the man owes his balls to."

"If at all," Costello said. "It's just a hunch."

"Fuck, Psychic. Your hunches are ninety-nine percent gospel truth."

"Thanks, boss. Speaking of, any word from Gina's friends on Marcus Porter?" That name drew groans from around the table.

Lachlan nodded. "Yeah. Motherfucker is back on his little Sick-Fantasy Island. Flight manifest says he flew his private jet straight there from Italy right after the Summers decamped for California. Not a peep out of him since. They're keeping an eye out though."

The knot in Costello's belly uncoiled—though not entirely—knowing that Porter was back at the center of his web and nowhere near Jordan. It still bothered him that Porter had left his island at all to meet her.

"I'll 'let' them continue to keep an eye on him. In the meantime, I need to continue building Jordan's confidence in herself away from her mother and brother without being accused of running my own psi-ops. You can cut the gaslighting with a knife in that house. The longer she's with them, the more she doubts herself."

"How can a woman who makes fucking sixty-seven million a pop have *any* doubts about herself?" Lach asked.

Costello grinned ruefully. "Self-doubt was spoon-fed to her since birth. Daphne uses Jordan's autism as a weapon against her at every turn. It's disgusting."

Jake sat up and tagged Costello on the shoulder. "Preach, brother. I saw that self-doubt in my own woman—still see it at times despite my best efforts—and look how fucking talented she is. She's just getting started with the music career and already she's halfway to the moon. But her piece-of-shit father kept her down all her life, did his best to teach her to doubt herself so that he could control her. Same storyline here, brother."

"Good thing she has you then, brother." Kyle tagged Costello's other arm.

For a moment, Costello hoped he hadn't given away his feelings for her. Of course, it would become apparent the moment they saw her through all this. He'd save her, and—

His head decided to stab him right then and he flashed back to his last nightmare. The fountain and the blood and the need to find Jordan. *There is no fountain. There is no blood.*

"Everything okay?" Kyle asked. The rest of the guys stared at him as he blinked away the pain.

"Yeah, fine. Not enough caffeine yet this morning."

"Saw y'all chug down a mug of it before I left," Nash said. He'd gone uncharacteristically quiet through most of the meeting.

"And that was my only one." Was Nash challenging him? *God, what if he saw something? Or suspected...what? Rein it in, Costello.*

Lach cracked his knuckles. "Best we wrap up anyhow. I wanna check in on Gina and get that financial deep dive started. Psychic, what're you planning on now?"

"Like I said, the objective has changed. Jordan has no interest in seeing her autonomy dry up but she's not sure how to manage that alone. Daphne already has a lot of financial and emotional control and Jordan isn't used to flexing her independence muscles. But, she's hit on this idea of hosting a party to open Eden House to the community. It'll be a way to show that she can handle big projects on her own and she'll have important witnesses to her competency. Also," he turned to Kyle, "She heard your fiancée is coming to town to meet everyone and would like her to be the guest of honor."

"Well, that's generous of her," Kyle said, though he looked puzzled.

"She's come to trust Watchdog and wants us as witnesses as well. And it's also her way of saying thank you." *And either I just covered my ass or I didn't.*

Lach chomped on his pen. "Not a bad idea. But it's gonna need extra security, not just for her, but for Rachael." He glanced at Jake, who nodded. "And depending on what other big names she's invited."

"Besides Jordan herself, Rachael's the biggest so far."

"Encourage her to keep it that way. We have Daniel in the wind for God knows why though, so the party might flush him out if he wants to make contact, though I have a feeling he's running *away* from his loving family. I just wanna know why and so does Gina." Lach nodded to himself. "But yeah, give her whatever encouragement she needs, keep an eye on Daphne and John Charles' reactions, and we'll handle the rest here." He turned to Nashville. "You got anything to add, Nash?"

"No, sir. Got my orders."

"If you want to take the rest of the day off, you can," Lach added. "Got Mitch and Jefferson watching at the house and they need more first ring experience anyway, Camden says."

Nash shook his head. "I'm good, boss. Got nothin' on the books today anyhow, so I'll head back up and keep an eye out, too."

"Suit yourself." Lach rolled his chair back from the table and stood. "Class dismissed."

Unexpected relief flooded through Costello. His head still hurt and he wasn't lying about getting more caffeine to combat the sudden migraine. He'd skip the office coffee pot because this time of day it was usually as good as burnt tar, grab Anubis from the kennel, and swing through the Dunkin' on his way back to Eden House instead.

"I'll walk with you to the kennels," Kyle said, catching up to him in the hall.

"Sure thing." They walked in silence until they got to the courtyard where Eric was running the in-house dogs including Anubis, Reggie, Toby, and Camo through an obstacle course. Costello was surprised to see Gina's dog Fleur there too. The two were almost inseparable—unless Gina felt she might endanger Fleur on a mission.

Damn. I made the wrong call pulling the surveillance off Daniel. Guilt rolled in. Was this a sign he was letting his feelings get in the way of his judgment?

Costello and Kyle stopped to watch the dogs, letting Eric finish up his training. Costello put on his sunglasses against the painful sunlight. "How's the FNG?" he asked.

"He's not me, but he's not bad." Kyle grinned. "Speaking of training, you were cool with letting me sit in today, right? Lach's showing me how it's done, running your own company and being the boss."

"Yeah. I appreciate your input. It won't be the same around here without you."

"And I appreciate that. Bud, I meant it when I asked if you're okay."

"Yeah. I'm just hoping I'm enough for Jordan."

Kyle paused before clapping him on the arm. "I know you are. You'll save her. We'll all help. Pisses me off how she's been treated by her family, especially with the Asperger's."

"Speaking of help, do you think I could talk to your fiancée?"

"Hell, yeah. I'm sure Arden would love to help with Jordan."

Costello rubbed the back of his neck. "I wouldn't just talk to her about Jordan, but about...some things I'm going through, too."

"Hey, no shame in that game, brother. She really helped me work through some of the shit I carried home from Afghanistan."

"Well, it's something else. Something even older than that. I think. I'm having some...dreams. Pretty much all my life."

"Say no more. Some had it rougher than others as kids. You want, I could give her the overall deets and you two could go for coffee or some shit while she's here. Or even Skype after the party if you don't want to leave Jordan alone at the house."

"Man, I'd hate to take Arden's time away from you."

Kyle's grin lit up the courtyard. "I got my whole life ahead with her. I miss her like hell but I think I can spare a couple hours for a brother. Besides, if she finds out I didn't tell her about something that she can help with, she'd never let it go."

Costello smiled. "Thanks, Pup. So, when are you going to make her an honest woman?"

Kyle belted out a laugh. "She'd *love* hearing that. We're thinking about Christmas, you know, since that's when we met."

"Do I get an invite?"

"Affirmative." Kyle side-eyed him. "So, Christmas. Think you'll have a woman on your arm by then?"

"Shit. Don't you start, too. There is *nothing* between Gina and me."

Kyle laughed. "What? You don't want little Spooky Psychics running around?"

"God save us from that horror show."

"No, man, they'd be like the superspy kids from those Nineties' movies, you know, where Jake's dad was one of the stuntmen."

Costello laughed. "Sorry to disappoint. Not happening."

Kyle laughed, too. Then he said, "So. No one else?"

Fuck. "I'm on the job right now. I shouldn't be thinking about romance." *That's close enough to the truth, right? Even though I can't stop thinking about the woman I made love to just last night. The woman of my dreams. Fuck, fuck, fuck. Does he suspect?*

Kyle nodded. "I'll give Arden a heads-up. About both you and Jordan. I think she can help."

"Your lips to God's ears, brother." *Because I think we're going to need all the help we can get.*

NINETEEN

A week after making her plans, Jordan clasped her hands together to keep them under control as she surveyed the little bistro tables set up in the garden courtyard. Soon there would be guests roaming the patio and taking in the gardens still under renovation. She wasn't sure which group made her more nervous—the community leaders she needed to convince to work with her, or Elliot's friends, who she wanted to impress even more.

Just pretend you're normal. She practically laughed at that. Normal people didn't choose clothing with pockets or think about all the things they could carry around just so they could keep their hand tics under control or at least hidden. They didn't script entire conversations in their heads for every possible scenario and practice the coordinating body language in the mirror.

Normal people made easy eye contact. They understood the nuances of facial expressions and body language without even trying. They knew when to speak and when not to, what to talk about and how much to say on the subject, and how to jump seamlessly into and out of conversations. All the things

Jordan was terrible at, things her mother simultaneously ridiculed and excused Jordan from learning and doing. Daphne stepped in and spoke for her daughter, smoothing out all the social wrinkles Jordan created and at the same time making Jordan feel somehow guilty and ashamed.

But not today. Today, Jordan was determined to speak for herself, to pay extra close attention to everyone around her. And to what her mother might be saying about her behind her back. Just because she didn't understand all the social dynamics didn't mean she was completely naïve to them, especially not since her eyes had been opened. She no longer blindly trusted her mother to have her best interests at heart. She knew Daphne would try and make Jordan look as socially awkward and incompetent as possible.

But she also knew she had Elliot, and Nash, and all of Elliot's friends on her side.

Anubis nudged her leg with his cold black nose. "*And you. You're on my side, too,*" she whispered to the dog as if he'd read her mind. And maybe he had—he always seemed to know when she was working herself up and then boom, he was right by her side. She knelt to pet him and give him a kiss on the top of the head. He wagged his tail and for the first time, licked the tip of her nose.

This will be okay. This will be fine. Think about it like a garden. You know gardens.

She'd prepped the soil by first researching what her community needed and how she could help, and by talking to Delia and Elena about catering and party planning. She planted seeds by reaching out to people in the community she could partner with and inviting them to the party. Through it all, Elliot provided the stakes and trellis and all the supports needed to make her plans and dreams grow up straight and tall. Then it was up to her to feed, water, and nurture what grew out of today, and part of that would be weeding out everything negative her mother said and did to stop her.

And Jordan was ready.

She spotted a couple of the men Elliot called the second ring walking the perimeter of the garden. More were hidden up by the angel gate. She tried not to think about the fact they were trained sharpshooters ready to defend her from a distance if need be. She wondered with all the dignitaries and billionaires she worked with how many times she'd been watched through a scope and had been blissfully unaware. She couldn't afford to be unaware now. Word of the party had gotten out, and that one of the guests would be Rachael Collins, a rising singer and songwriter with a brand new hit destined to become the upcoming summer's official song. With Rachael coming, half of Watchdog was on the job.

And if that wasn't stressful enough, another celebrity had at the last minute decided to crash the party and that pretty much brought in the rest of Watchdog.

Speaking of stress, Daphne joined Jordan on the patio, keeping to the side opposite Anubis. *Score one for having dogs around.*

After fighting so hard against the whole party, Daphne had gone and had a spa day complete with a new hairstyle and highlights, which Jordan hadn't noticed until Daphne pointed it out.

"Lovely day for a party, Jordan," her mother said.

Jordan said nothing back. She was saving her energy for her guests. Elena and Elissa would be here soon with their crew to set up the food but they were guests too. So the first thing Jordan would do would be to thank them and ask if there was anything she could do to help, as she'd practiced—

"I do hope you'll be all right."

Gardens. Think about gardens. God, her perfume is over-whelming today. She's standing too close on purpose. Back off.

Daphne tsked. "So quiet. Are you already feeling like it's too much before it's even started?"

Don't give her anything. Gardens. Roses. "There are approximately three-hundred and sixty species of roses, though experts differ on that number, as there are some that are so similar—"

"I hope you aren't expecting anyone to care about that." She touched Jordan's bare shoulder with her new nails. They felt like beetle shells scraping across her skin and she flinched.

"Oh, is this a no-contact day for you? That's inconvenient."

"I'm fine." Elliot should be coming back from checking on the men stationed at the angel gate. If she took a deep breath —*Ugh! Rose perfume*—and relaxed she could watch him in her mind's eye as he drove back up the road. He'd only be a minute and then she wouldn't be alone. She was already not alone. She hadn't been since the day they met.

"You don't *look* fine, sweetheart." Daphne brushed at a strand of Jordan's hair. *Beetle in my hair.* She flinched again. "You look like you're getting all wound up. See? Your hands are going."

Jordan glanced down and stuffed her hands in her pockets. She looked back over her shoulder. Maybe Elena and Elissa would be with Elliot. She knew exactly what to say to them. *Exactly what to say, exactly what to say, exactly what to say—*

"...Exactly what to say."

"What was that, Jordan?"

"I know exactly what to say. I am fine. Stop it."

"I doubt it. I'm already prepared to take over for you today. Like always. Even the wind's made your hair a mess."

Daphne reached out to touch Jordan's hair again and this time she ducked. She turned to see Nash making his way through the study to the French doors. He didn't look happy which was easy to tell because he always looked happy to Jordan. She started walking toward him.

"Sorry," he said as they met at the door. "I was—"

She pushed past him, desperate to get away from her mother and to find Elliot. He'd needed her once, and now she needed him, today, all day. She heard Anubis' clicking nails and Nash's footsteps behind her. *I should slow down and wait. He probably thinks I'm about to have a fit.* But she kept her pace up until Nash caught up with her as she headed for the kitchen. She would wait there.

And her instincts proved correct as Elliot and two women came in from the opposite entrance followed by several men and women pushing carts loaded with racks of glasses and plates, and insulated boxes of food.

Nash took in a quick breath beside her when he saw the younger of the two women. She glanced at him, smiled, but then turned and started directing the catering staff. The other woman who Jordan was pretty sure was Elena Martinez smiled at her and crossed the kitchen with Elliot. The younger woman stole another glance at Nash while she directed a man to place one of the insulated bags near the stove. Nash mumbled something about keeping an eye on Daphne and left the kitchen quickly.

"Hi, I'm Elena, nice to meet you," she said as she held out her hand for Jordan to shake.

Jordan took it and said, "Hi, Elena, Elliot has told me about you and that you have always wanted to run a restaurant and that you love cooking the way that I love gardening and I'm really excited to show you my new vegetable garden and eat your food today."

Damn. Way off-script. But she'd liked Elena's smile immediately and had gotten excited. "I mean, I'm really glad to meet you, too, Ms. Martinez. Oh! Is there anything I can help you with?" God, she was still shaking Elena's hand. She dropped it and glanced quickly at Elliot, who was grinning at her, but not in a mean, you-fucked-it-up way, but in his Elliot-way that always made her feel warm and protected. And now loved.

Elena didn't laugh at her the way people sometimes did. Or back off, which was always worse. She smiled wider and her brown eyes sparkled. "Costello has told me a lot about you, too. I can't wait to see your garden. There is nothing better than fresh produce."

"Well, there's no produce yet, but maybe you can use the herbs? I have rosemary, tarragon, thyme, oh, and the chives are just on the verge of blooming. And other herbs, lots of other herbs." At the last second, she stopped herself from naming them all.

"Perfect! Budding chives make such a pretty garnish." She turned to the younger woman. "Lissa, did you hear? We have permission to raid the herb garden."

Jordan laughed at that image. "Yes, yes. Raid away. Anytime. You can even come back. I'd like it if you came back when everything else is producing. Harvesting. Ready to harvest." *Okay, well, that should have permanently scared her off. Why can't I do this right?*

"Awesome! I will take you up on that. Thank you again, for giving Delia's the job, and for inviting my family. My daughter Tina is very excited. Her daddy is bringing her later, with Toby. If that's still all right?"

"Yes, of course. I love dogs. The more the merrier." *Ha!* She had anticipated a few variations of that question and had her answer queued up and ready. She bent again to pet

Anubis, who had not left her side all day. "But this boy is my favorite." He licked her hand and smiled—actually smiled—up at her.

"I've never seen him act so friendly," Elena remarked.

"He's obviously found the right person," Elliot said, making Jordan's heart flip.

The day only got better from there. The more of Elliot's friends Jordan met, the happier she felt. Luckily, they all arrived ahead of her more 'official guests' and she had a chance to talk to everyone individually, with Elliot at her side to boost her confidence. Elena's fiancé Camden was as funny as his nickname, Joker. Tina was an adorable little girl who fired off endless questions about gardening. She somehow managed to extract a promise from Jordan to help her plant sunflowers in Camden's garden so she could watch their faces turn as the sun moved across the sky. Tina was disappointed to learn that no one really knows how sunflowers can track the sun, but sat spellbound as Jordan explained the myth behind them—that it was a water nymph who fell in love with the sun god and watched him cross the sky until she turned into a sunflower.

Meeting Rachael Collins and her husband Jake thrilled Jordan. Rachael was nothing like how Jordan imagined her, though Elliot had told her that Rachael was pretty down-to-earth. Jordan had met her share of celebrities and they were a mixed-bag, some friendly and genuine, others completely shallow. But, Jordan ended up throwing out her script entirely when it came to Rachael. The woman was downright shy and humble. At one point, she described the first time she'd ever performed—in a little bar in Nebraska with Jake's encouragement—and how difficult it was to push through her initial stage fright, yet it was the best thing she'd ever done. "There's nothing like spreading your wings for the first time," Rachael said, "especially when you have someone there ready to catch you if you fall." Jordan knew exactly what she meant.

But the person Jordan liked meeting best was Arden Volker, Kyle McGuire's fiancée and the guest of honor as far as Jordan was concerned. The woman had a gentleness about her, and yet she was spunky too, teasing Kyle at every turn.

Jordan approached her before the other guests arrived. "I...Elliot said I could talk to you, that we have some things in common."

Arden smiled and her gray eyes shone like silver. "Of course. I guess we're both meeting the gang for the first time, aren't we?"

Jordan hadn't thought of that. "We are. Silly that I didn't even think of it, even though you're the one who partly inspired me to have this party."

"I appreciate you doing this. Your house is stunning. Costello said you were looking at opening this beautiful house to the public."

Jordan nodded. "Like what you do with your ranch. I'd like to help...well, I'd like to help *anyone*, but maybe people like me."

"With Asperger's. Yes. I think that would be a wonderful idea."

"I mean," Jordan studied the glass of wine in her hands, "I know not everyone is as into gardening as I am, but maybe there are other things. And, well, it really helped me figure out who I was. It kept me from being..." tears spring into her eyes, completely unexpected. *Why? Why would I feel like crying right now?*

"Is it okay if I touch your arm?" Arden asked. Jordan

nodded. Arden laid her hand on Jordan's upper arm and she noticed Arden's hands were callused like hers. She liked that. It made Arden feel like someone who Jordan could trust. They both worked with their hands and that meant something. She relaxed and the tears went away.

"Thank you," Jordan said. "For asking first. No one ever does that."

"You're welcome. Some people—with or without autism—don't like strangers to touch them and others do. I always ask."

"I don't mind usually. Unless it's someone I really don't like. Or, if it's my mother."

Arden nodded, listening.

"People sometimes think that if they touch me, I'll start screaming or something. Or that I wouldn't like sex. I like sex. I mean, oh boy." She laughed nervously. "TMI, right?"

Arden laughed too. "Hey, it's just girl-talk, right? You're fine." She leaned in. "Sex with the right person is the most amazing thing, I've found." Just then, Kyle walked by with their dog Camo trotting next to him. The look he gave Arden needed no interpretation, especially when Arden's cheeks flared red.

Jordan's mind immediately went back to her night with Elliot. "The most amazing thing." She felt warmth rise up her neck and into her face.

Arden smiled. "Yup, you know exactly what I'm talking about."

"Does he...make you feel protected?" Jordan asked.

"All the time."

"That's a good feeling too."

Arden nodded while studying her. "It sure is. So, I didn't mean to get us onto this topic, if there was something else you wanted to talk about?"

Relief. "Yes. I wanted to ask how you do it, how you use your home to help people. Does that sound...dumb?"

"Not one little bit." They talked some more, Arden answering every one of Jordan's questions until she felt like she'd known the woman forever. They exchanged cards with a promise to keep in touch.

Jordan was just beginning to think the party might go off without a hitch when her biggest guest arrived and changed everything. Elliot had given her some room to talk privately but after she spoke to Arden he came forward and whispered, "She's here," in Jordan's ear. He offered his arm as her heart sped up with butterflies dancing inside it.

Daphne had not bothered to come downstairs despite dressing up. But the moment Bette Collins arrived, her mother was at the door to greet the Oscar-winning movie star. Bette was Jake Collins' mother. Jordan would never have dreamed of inviting her, thinking that the woman probably had a million better things to do, but then Bette had more or less invited herself through Jake and Rachael.

Jordan had asked to be informed when Bette arrived, but leave it to her mother to have a sixth sense when it came to important, influential people coming within her sphere, and beating her to the door. She practically threw it open and then acted almost startled to see Bette there in her wheelchair, her husband standing tall and handsome beside her—the spitting image of an older, equally good-looking Jake.

"Bette Collins, as I live and breathe!" Daphne exclaimed, sounding as if they were long-lost friends, a voice she used with strangers all the time. "So glad you could make it today."

The woman whose career was built on her role as a brilliant psychopath eyed Daphne for a moment as if she were contemplating if Daphne would go better with a glass of red or white wine. "We haven't met. I'm looking for the artist Jordan Summers."

Bette looked past Daphne to Jordan and her entire expression changed to one Jordan liked much better. "Ah! Ms. Summers? I am a devoted fan of your social media." She pushed a button on her chair and rolled forward past Daphne. "I scroll through it whenever I need to remember how beautiful and inspirational and whimsical the world can be."

That floored Jordan. "I had no idea you liked my gardens."

"Like them?" She smiled wide, looking like the direct opposite of her villainous role. "I've been to visit most of them, at least the ones open to the public that I can access," she nodded behind her, "thanks for the ramp, incidentally. And I've also seen the gardens that either belong to friends or where I can safely crash the party." She winked and that made Jordan laugh. "Thank you so much for indulging me today. I have been dying to see this place for years. And now I get to meet the genius who will be bringing it back to life."

"She's already brought so much of it to life, just by being here," Elliot said beside her. Jordan couldn't have been happier or more filled with warmth. She had missed him so much, and now that she had him back, she would never let him go. Didn't he know that *he* was the one who brought her back here, who was ultimately responsible for giving new life to Eden House? She would tell him in no uncertain terms that night after everyone left. She only had two more weeks before her birthday and then she'd be free and they'd drop this farce and be together.

Bette reached out and offered her hand to Elliot. "So good to see you, Costello. You're looking handsomer than ever."

"Hey now," Bette's husband said, making Jordan nervous until she realized he was smiling and joking.

"I said handsome-*er*, not the handsome-*est*, my darling love," Bette said as she dropped Elliot's hand and took her husband's. Oh, I almost forgot." She opened her purse on her lap and took out a large manilla envelope. "This is for you, Ms. Summers, as a thank you and a hostess gift."

"Please, it's Jordan." She took the envelope as her mother came over to see what Bette had given her. Jordan looked inside. "What are..?" She reached in and pulled out eight smaller envelopes; some seemed empty while others bulged and rattled. "Oh, seeds! Thank you!" On each envelope was handwritten the species and the date the seeds were harvested. She glanced up at her mother, whose disappointed look was terribly familiar, and then at Elliot, who looked the opposite.

"Those are from my own flower garden, and I would be absolutely honored if you'd consider planting them," Bette said.

"Thank you. Thank you, I will." Jordan smiled at Bette.

"How sweet," Daphne said. "And I'm proud of you for remembering your manners and thanking Ms. Collins, Jordan." She used her sing-song voice, filling Jordan with shame, especially when she saw Bette looking like she'd just bitten down on something sour.

Before Jordan could reply, she heard someone squeal Bette's name behind her, and Bette's face went from sour to a bright, open smile.

"Now here's someone *else* one would *never* think of talking down to," Bette said as Tina came tearing into the foyer, followed by Toby. Daphne staggered backward as the little girl made a beeline for Bette's lap. Bette wrapped her arms around Tina and snuggled the girl close.

"Hello, Mermaid. Shall we *allons-y*?"

Tina nodded and at her command, Bette rolled farther

into the house, accompanied by her husband and no fewer than three dogs.

"Who invited that child?" Daphne mumbled as they followed, Jordan and Elliot walking behind her mother. Elliot took advantage of the situation to stroke her hair and Jordan drew in a deep breath of contentment.

The last bit of contentment she'd feel for the rest of the party.

TWENTY

Costello watched Jordan closely throughout the party. She was clearly nervous at first but his friends quickly set her at ease. He couldn't have been more proud of her or more thankful for his brothers. They didn't even know she was his (at least, he hoped no one suspected) they just knew she was a woman who needed their help and they were more than happy to give it, especially later when the other guests arrived and Daphne did everything she could to undermine and discredit her daughter.

It nearly killed Costello to keep his mouth shut whenever Daphne broke out her sing-song voice to 'correct' Jordan's behavior but his job was to stand silent guard. If he broke out of his role everyone would know something more was there, so he had to rely on his friends to defend Jordan for him.

And to the last man and woman, they came through.

When Daphne put down Jordan's 'sad little tomato patch' in front of the director of the local food pantry, Elena was there to praise Jordan's herb and vegetable garden and how she'd managed to create such a beautiful yet useful layout that would no doubt produce a bumper crop in a compact space—something the director could model in the community.

After Daphne told a couple of council members how she was concerned that Jordan was regressing and prone to uncontrollable fits, Rachael stepped up and praised Jordan's bravery for returning to such a personally tragic place, her creativity, and how much patience and focus she needed to restore Eden House and its gardens to a place of joy and service, one that would benefit the community.

Best of all, Arden kept a close eye on Jordan and was there to relieve her when she started to look overwhelmed, whether it was redirecting a conversation that was getting too personal or asking her if she'd mind showing Arden a different part of the garden or the house, just to get her a moment's peace to recharge and regroup. And she was a pro at blocking Daphne's attacks, often turning the barbs right back on the woman. Yeah, she'd definitely made an enemy but it didn't seem to bother Arden in the least, because she'd made friends for life with Jordan, Rachael, Elena, and Elissa. And she'd gained Costello's undying gratitude and admiration.

While Costello watched Jordan, he was in constant contact via earbud with the rest of his team, monitoring the comings and goings of every guest—and potential gatecrasher. Paparazzi buzzed around the gate like flies, hoping to photograph Bette or Rachael Collins coming and going, or to sneak in and get exclusive photos of the party at the "Murder Mansion" and its grounds. That was pretty routine stuff that his team could handle in their sleep. They'd already 'accidentally' disabled two illegal drones and detained a trespasser until the authorities arrived.

What Costello was really listening for was any sign of Daniel Summers, who remained in the wind. He had to give the man props for eluding Gina this long. He'd been gone at least five days, seven if he'd left or been taken immediately after she'd stopped surveilling him. If Daniel wasn't dead, then he had some mad hiding skills, or Daphne was right and he was well-connected and on the other side of the globe.

The other man who could stay on the far side of the globe was Porter. At least he had been staying put on his island according to Gina's friends. They had searched for a reason for him to be in Italy—Lord knew there was plenty of organized crime tied to human trafficking there, and a couple identified members of The Capitoline Group made their homes there—but Porter had only stayed for three days and reached out to no one so far as they could tell. By all appearances, he was there to hire Jordan and nothing else, and once she was gone, he scurried as fast as his plane could carry him back to the rock he lived under and hadn't moved since.

Which was fine by Costello, but he couldn't shake his unease about the bastard.

Then there was Summers Shipping Company's finances. They had been hit by strikes and slowdowns like every other shipping company, but those hits just seemed to be a little harder and a lot more damaging. John Charles had made some bad investments on top of that, compounding his losses and shaking the confidence of the board and SSC's investors. And yet there'd been a sudden influx of money the past month that even Lach and Gina's friend was having a hell of a time tracking down.

The man had solved one mystery though that Costello had yet to share with Jordan—Daphne was funneling a staggering amount of Jordan's income and trust fund payments into SSC through some accounting jiujitsu and several offshore banking accounts. But certainly not all of it—she'd tucked away thirty million for herself, a nice golden parachute if you could get it—and about two million for Jordan, how generous. Costello had learned of it this morning and decided to wait until after Jordan got through today's party to lay that bomb on her.

He turned his full attention back to Jordan, who was laughing along with Bette and Rachael at something the mayor of Malibu had said. Jordan appeared at ease but Costello noticed how tightly she clutched her glass with both hands. Daphne was part of the group too, and by the look of it, she was about to unleash her own bomb. Costello moved in closer.

Daphne placed her hand on Jordan's bare shoulder. She drummed the tips of her nails on her daughter's skin, a sensation Costello knew she hated. Jordan did her best not to jerk away, but Costello picked up on how she dropped her shoulder the slightest bit as if to shrink down and get away from the touch.

Daphne laughed, an utterly fake sound. "Well, Jordan's never worried about money because she's never *had* to, not the way I have. It's been my job to go gray over money worries. But it's not her fault—she's never really had the mental capacity for numbers—but she's lucky to have me to handle that for her or else we'd go broke if I let her control any project with a budget over ten dollars. So don't let her fool you—my daughter is spoiled and naïve, not selfless."

The other women looked stunned while Jordan withered like a seedling without water. But then she caught sight of Costello moving closer and she straightened up. She removed her mother's hand from her shoulder like she was plucking off a spider.

"You're wrong," she said. "You're completely wrong about me." Her eyes widened as if she realized she was stepping out of a cage. "I do know budgets, mine and others'. I know exactly how hard it is for the laborers I hire to make ends meet for their families. It's the same the world over. I've worked with women in India who knew the land better than I ever could and would have gratefully worked for less than the lost pennies and dimes we walk past on the sidewalk here every day if I had paid them that. I've worked with Roma in Italy who just wanted a day's honest pay without being spit on and called thieves." She glanced at Costello when she said that and he tried to swallow the lump in his throat.

"I just finished installing a brand new garden right here, working with men who do jobs all over our community but who could never dream of affording to live here. It doesn't matter where I go, I find people who are struggling just to get by while, yes, I am spoiled with what I have. But, I am acutely aware of it, Mother, and that's why I fight with you every... damned...time to raise the labor budget for a new installation, demanding that my team make enough money not just to get by but to get ahead for once."

As Jordan raised her voice, other conversations around her stopped as people stared. This was where Costello would normally step in and separate the principal from the source of aggravation. Nash stood at the ready just past the group directly across from Costello, with Reggie whining and agitated at his feet.

Nash's voice came over the comm. "Psychic, you fixing to break this up or you want me to? I can tell it's not gonna go in her favor if things get out of hand." He sounded almost confused, though he kept his expression professionally blank.

"Hold off, I'm making an exception because Jordan has it all under control," Costello answered. Daphne needed to be put in her place and Jordan needed to be the one to do it. She'd gotten louder but her voice stayed even and strong.

"I don't like it but it's your rodeo," Nash answered.

While Nash and Costello were talking, Jordan continued.

"When I start the major, long-term renovations on Eden House's gardens you'd better get ready for another fight because you'd better believe I'll be providing my team with healthcare, free lunches, and a 401K, right down to the last laborer. And that goes for any and all community projects I'm asked to do. Anywhere I can help, I will, whether I have your approval or not, Mother."

Daphne smiled and looked around as if to say *can you believe this?* "Indoor voice, Jordan. You're getting a little out of control, don't you think?"

"No, I *don't* think so, and I will *not* lower my voice. Not to you. Especially not after my next birthday. Things are going to change and I don't think you'll like them."

She turned her back on her mother and faced the mayor. "But you will." Jordan had lowered her voice back to a conversational level. "I want to work with you to make our community a better place to live for everyone. I'm learning that we all need each other. We're all connected, like in a garden. If one element is out of balance, the whole suffers. But when we help each other," She smiled at Rachael and Bette, "we can be brave and do the most amazing things." Then Jordan switched her gaze to Costello and there was no mistaking the love in her eyes. "Especially when we have the right people there to save us."

His heart filled to bursting and he struggled to keep his face neutral. This was killing him now, so he focused on later when he'd tell Jordan he loved her. Then he'd show her how much every single day—with every kiss, every touch, every orgasm he'd ring out of her body.

When Jordan turned away from her mother, Daphne's face had gone from her usual composed, haughty expression to a mask of rage. Or, maybe that wasn't the mask; maybe that was her true face revealed publicly at last. Costello snapped back to the present as he anticipated her next move. He signaled to Nash and started forward—*now* this needed to be broken up.

Daphne clamped down on Jordan's shoulder. Jordan's face contorted as Daphne dug her nails in and spun her around.

"You listen to me, young lady—" was all she got out before Costello had a hold of Jordan and was pulling her away.

Too late. Jordan was already scratched and hurt. She thrust her arm out to keep Daphne from advancing, but Nash had acted fast and was already turning Daphne away, pouring on the charm molasses-thick as he walked her inside.

"Are you all right, Ms. Summers?" Costello asked Jordan, furious with himself. Too distracted, too slow to react, too much deception for the sake of keeping her safe.

"I'm fine, El—Mr. Costello," she lied, rubbing her scratched shoulder and looking around, dazed.

Bette huffed. "That woman, that feral *bat*, ought to be caged." She rolled up to Jordan. "Jordan, honeybee, are you all right?" Nash wasn't the only one pouring on the sweetness.

Jordan smiled at Bette. "Yes." She noticed everyone looking at her, but where she might have crumbled, she held strong as Costello kept his arm around her.

She took a deep breath. And that's when she astounded Costello with her strength and grace. "Please excuse my mother's outburst. This place holds some bad memories for her as you can imagine, so your understanding is much appreciated."

Everyone was silent. Then the mayor spoke up. "Of course. It must be so difficult on both of you," she said. "I'm going to have my assistant call you next week to set up a meeting to discuss some of your proposals. Monday for sure. I think you're going to become very busy and I want to make sure I'm first in line." She smiled and walked toward one of the tables laden with desserts. The other guests went back to their conversations while Bette whispered something to Rachael who nodded and disappeared into the crowd.

Costello realized he was still holding Jordan. Just before he let her go he gave her arm a squeeze, making sure to angle away from the camera over the patio. She looked into his eyes and mouthed *thank you*.

"Can I get you something for your arm?" he asked, but Elissa was already jogging out of the house with a wet washcloth and a small first aid kit.

"Hi," Elissa said, her cheeks flushed and her voice bubbly, matching her California Surfer Girl looks. "Nashville sent me outside. I'm the medvac."

Jordan grinned. "Thanks, it hurts but I promise I'm okay, I —oh." She brushed her long hair off her shoulder and Jordan noticed what the others had already seen—two streaks of blood running down her arm from the deepest of the half-moon wounds. The woman hadn't just scratched her but punctured her arm. Jordan's face paled.

And then so did Costello's. It was there between two of the nail marks. A mole. Smaller now, easy to miss, but there in the same place. Exactly like the one the woman of his dreams had.

No. No. I'm imagining it. Misremembering. Transposing the real one onto my dreams.

Elissa leaned in and wiped the blood away. "Hmm. I've seen worse, but you might want a rabies shot anyway." Her other hand flew up to cover her mouth. "God, that was rude. I'm sorry."

Jordan laughed a little. "No, it's kind of appropriate. I've never seen her go off like that, at least not in front of other people."

"So I heard." Elissa rolled her eyes. "Nashville gave me the briefest of rundowns when he grabbed a bottle of water for your mom." And there was that blush again. She put a bandage on Jordan's arm. "There you go. Good as new."

"Thanks, Elissa. Sorry I haven't had a chance to talk to you until now."

"Eh, you've been busy, I've been busy. We'll get to it. Thanks for the delish herbs though." Elissa turned to walk away but stopped when she saw Nash coming out of the house. At the same time, Rachael came jogging back up, a concerned look on her face. Bette watched her, looking equally worried.

"What is it?" Costello asked Rachael.

"The photographer. Bette thought she saw him snapping pictures of the fight."

Goddamn it. I missed that detail. Costello berated himself. The wrong photo could undo all the good Jordan had worked so hard for and put her into a bad light—the way Daphne intended. In a way, that was worse than the injury.

"It's okay," Rachael held up her hand. "I got him to delete them in exchange for some shots of me that I gave him permission to sell."

Bette looked mortified. "Rachael, darling, that's not how we do things. We don't negotiate with terrorists."

Damn it. "Rachael," Costello said, keeping his voice as even as he could. "You should have told me immediately and I could have sent one of my men to handle it. You should not have approached him under any circumstances." He started to alert the front gate when Nash laid a hand on his arm. "I saw him too and already took care of it. He's at the gate right now and they just confiscated his memory card and looked his camera over. No pics of the fight." Nash looked at Rachael. "I can have them delete y'all's photos, too. Let us be the villains."

"Oh, no that's—" Rachael started to say.

"—Wonderful of you, thank you," Bette said.

"Will do." Nashville grinned and did his best Brad Pitt.

Bette smiled until her nose wrinkled. "*Legends of the Fall*, wonderful movie. You know," she added conspiratorially, "my husband was one of Brad's stunt doubles and taught him that little hat tip." She winked and gestured for Rachael to follow her as she rolled away.

"I'd...better get back to the kitchen and make sure the clean-up is going smoothly," Elissa said, taking one last look at Nashville as she took a few backward steps. And no wonder— as soon as Bette turned away and Nashville looked at Costello, all that Southern charm dried up like cracked red dirt.

Jordan looked back and forth between them. "I..." She stepped closer to Costello.

"Jordan, did you want to come with and check too?" Elissa asked, California smile in place but eyes pensive.

"Sure," Jordan answered. She glanced at Costello before walking away with Elissa.

Costello started. "Nash, thank—"

"Man, what is up with you? You don't miss a trick, and this afternoon you are way the hell and gone off your game. Those photos coulda been devastating. Can you tell me what's going on?"

Dammit, this is it. I'm caught. He suspects. If he confessed to falling in love with Jordan, he'd be pulled off the assignment and taken away when she still needed him to see her through her birthday and subsequent freedom. But he couldn't lie to his brother—everything disintegrated without trust and Costello had spent his life trying to prove he could be trusted. Never once lying, never once breaking a promise.

A life spent being perfect to make up for what his birth mother made him into.

Thief. Liar. Traitor.

This is the hardest needle I've ever had to thread. And to do it, he needed to dig into his oldest skills.

Here we go. Hide and seek.

"Nashville, you're making a good call. And you're absolutely right. I'm off my game." He rubbed his temples. "It's these damn migraines. I'm not sleeping. I'm having...nightmares."

Nash's expression softened and the concern in his eyes killed Costello. "I thought maybe it was something else. But no, of course not. Brother, you should have said something earlier. Or maybe I should have. You've been looking a little rough, I shoulda stepped up."

I'm such an asshole. "No, no. Thank you, but I'm fine. You stepped up today, and I'm grateful."

"You need to see a doctor. Migraines are nothing to fuck around with. I had a cousin who suffered migraines and it turned out to be a tumor."

Costello shook his head. "It's not a tumor. I've made an appointment to talk to someone about the...about it. Tomorrow." At least he wasn't outright lying about that. He'd talked to Arden earlier and she'd agreed to Skype with him the next day.

Nash clapped him on the arm. "Gonna hold you to that appointment. And you need some time off, brother. You work harder than any of us, 'cept maybe Gina."

Costello closed his eyes. "Maybe after this assignment." *Yeah, maybe after this assignment I won't have a job at all.*

"Good idea. Hey, I'll take the night shift tonight. You get you some sleep."

God, the sincerity in Nash's eyes was killing Costello.

Everything was killing him, including his head. As if summoned like the devil, the pain inside his skull roared up, bringing with it visions from his paradise-turned-hell.

Jordan as a little girl, running to hide. Stay hidden, Jordan.

No, that's not Jordan, that's my dream. Just a dream. Forget.

The angels at the gate pray for us, but they keep their eyes shut tightly.

"I've gotta find..."

"Brother? What? Find who?"

"The...the dogs. Where's Anubis and Reggie?"

"Inside with the ladies. It's all good. 'Cept I'm sure Reg is pissing off Daphne just by breathing."

Costello laughed and pain shot to his eyes. He squeezed them shut.

Nash's grip on his arm tightened and he steered Costello toward the house. "Tell you what, that little catfight was pretty much the finale to this party and folks are fixing to leave. You go on in and lie down. I got this."

He opened his eyes. "No, I'm the one in charge. It's my responsibility."

"Dammit, Psychic—"

There are no fucking psychics.

"—if you already didn't have an appointment, I'd be on the horn to the paramedics. I've half a mind to call them anyway."

"If I lie down right now, will you not?" They'd reached the house. The cool, dark interior soothed his head.

"Yeah, I'll make that deal," Nashville answered. They were climbing the stairs to the bedrooms.

A deal with a liar and a thief and a traitor and you don't even know it. "Thanks. I'll be better tomorrow, I promise."

"If you aren't, I'm calling someone. That's the other part of the deal."

"Sure. Yeah. But for now, don't let the team know. Or Lachlan. I got this, okay? I'm embracing the suck."

They'd reached Costello's bedroom. Nash looked unsure. Finally, he said, "My mama always told me pride goeth before the fall, but okay. Just for now though. You get any worse, all bets are off, y'hear?"

"Copy that." Costello smiled and opened the door. The bedroom's curtains were closed and the room was blessedly dark. "Feeling better already. I'm going to take my migraine meds and go to bed."

He closed the door and stumbled to the bed. In a daze, he took off his shoes first, then undressed and slid under the covers, guilt and shame and pain sending him into oblivion before his head even hit the pillow.

Night-blooming jasmine filled his senses, leading him up and out of the black pit he'd fallen into where he lay dreaming of the dark waters closing over his head one last time. Jordan must have refreshed the flowers in his vase again. He smelled the salt of the ocean and felt cool air brush across his face. His skin tingled—as much trouble as he was in, the mere thought of Jordan would always stir him. Faint blue light shone through his eyelids. He'd left the curtains closed and the window down.

Costello opened his eyes. The waning moon poured just enough light in through the tall narrow window to make it look like a door to another world. He turned to look at the bedside vase and yes, there was fresh jasmine. But that's not where the fragrance was coming from.

Jordan rose from a chair beyond the vase. She walked to the bed, her curves obvious under her sheer nightgown and robe. Or was he dreaming again? He thought of the other night, his fantasy of Jordan coming to him in his bedroom. His cock hardened to stone and a soft groan escaped his lips.

"Elliot, are you still in pain?" she whispered. "I can close the window if the light bothers you. I just wanted to see that you were all right."

God, she looked like an angel. "No. I'm not in pain, not anymore."

"Then I'll keep the window open. I want to keep looking at you."

And just like in his fantasy, she knelt on the mattress and the moonlight graced the swell of her breasts and the turn of her thighs. "I was worried when Nash told me you weren't well." She brought her hand to his cheek. "I don't want to lose you this time."

He didn't have a chance to think about that before she ran her hand straight down his chest and spread her fingers across his lower abdomen. His heart skipped and his cock jumped and he fought himself not to reach up and pull her down to him.

"You can't be here," he managed. "If they catch us..."

"They won't." Jordan shimmied out of her robe and let it slip to the floor. She ran her hand back up his chest and then swung her leg over his body, straddling his cock. She pressed herself against him the way he wanted and he groaned again. She leaned forward and brushed her lips against his. "And even if they did, it doesn't matter. You showed me today who I am. That I am strong enough to lead my own life and make my own decisions."

"Jordan—"

She pressed her fingers against his lips. "No, hear me

out. Tomorrow, we'll leave Eden House. We'll go straight to Watchdog and I'll tell them I no longer need their services. I'm safe. Because I have you, Elliot. And then being together will no longer get you in trouble. I would have done it tonight, but I didn't want to tip *her* off while you were ill." She kissed him. "From there, we'll go somewhere, anywhere, until my birthday next week. We'll lay low until then. And then everything will be fine. We can start over, together. I love you, Elliot. I won't live without you, not anymore."

Costello's head swam. *I love you, Elliot.* Could this be real? She loved him, even knowing who he'd been she still accepted, and trusted, and *loved* him. And she was all he'd ever wanted. No, she was better—she was real. She was no perfect fantasy that would never exist, but a living, breathing, loving, perfect-imperfect woman in his arms.

Her plan, with some modifications, could work. He'd still catch some heat, of course, but she was the client and she wouldn't file a complaint. They could say they never acted on their feelings, that they waited—

No.

He wasn't that person, not anymore, not ever again. He wouldn't lie to Lachlan tomorrow, and God forbid he make the love of his life lie for him to cover up his sins. That would make him no better than his manipulative mother. No, he'd come clean and let the chips fall where they may. He'd apologize to Nash for misleading him—which was bad enough—and hope he'd understand and that their brotherhood could be repaired.

He was done hiding the truth. He couldn't live without Jordan anymore. She was his life's breath. His destiny.

They'd found each other at last and nothing would keep them apart.

She watched his face, her pale green eyes so full of love and hope and everything good.

"I love you, Jordan. I always have. I'll do anything to keep you. But I won't make you lie. We're both done hiding. Tomorrow, we'll do what you've said; we'll go to Watchdog and explain and whatever happens, happens. Then, we'll go anywhere in the world you want. But one thing is for sure. We'll return once you're free and claim Eden House for you."

"And I'll still protect *you*, Elliot. I'll tell them I initiated everything, which is the God's honest truth." She looked deeply into his eyes. "I found you, and I wanted you, and when I had you close I took what *I* wanted for once." She licked her lips. "Just like I'm going to do right now."

TWENTY-ONE

Her Elliot lay under her, his warm body an unexplored landscape of plains and valleys, a fresh mineral smell rising off his skin like rain that's washed the rocks clean. His heart pounded a fast, steady beat and Jordan laid her head against his chest to savor the sound of life and desire there. She moved to his throat and tasted him—salty and slightly musky and delicious. He bucked beneath her, his cock a ready arch beneath the cotton sheets. His arms came around her, pulling her body to his and locking her in, making her already wet pussy gush harder. He tangled his fingers in her hair and grabbed a lock, then pulled her head back until they were face to face again.

"Mine, Jordan. You're mine. I'm going to make you remember that."

"I've never forgotten."

His eyes flashed just before he took her mouth roughly. He thrust his tongue into her mouth and explored at will, gripping the back of her head, leaving her no choice but to take him. She moaned against him as her senses melted together. He encircled her and she felt, smelled, and tasted him, listened to his groans as she gave her body over to him. She lost track of where she ended and he began, lost all sense of time. There was just her and Elliot, over and over.

Then he was turning until she lay under him like the earth beneath the arching sky, nothing but her nightgown between them. He'd gone to bed naked as she'd hoped, his clothes on the floor. Elliot covered her throat in kisses as she explored his bare back, every muscle perfectly defined as she slid her hands over them. She felt scars there, too, and wondered if he'd ever tell her their secret histories, which missions had given them to him.

Elliot lifted up and roughly pulled her nightgown up her body to her neck. She hadn't bothered with panties, they'd only get in the way, and now she regretted even bothering with a nightgown under her robe. She went up on her elbows so that he could take it off completely. When she started to sit up all the way, he gently gripped her upper arms and lowered her back to the pillows.

"I want to look at what's mine," he whispered. She smiled and stretched her arms over her head and arched her back, wanting him to cup her breasts and tug her nipples. She wanted him to see all of her and know she was his, body and soul. His eyes roamed over her first, his lips parted, his gaze rapt as he took her all in. She knew he was memorizing her and locking the sight away, never to be forgotten.

Jordan was doing the same—starting with the top of his head and his mussed hair, pale in the moonlight. His strong jaw, the slight cleft in his chin. His perfect lips and the mouth that had already given her so much pleasure. And those intense eyes—she wanted to see them unfocused, wanted to help him let go and just *feel*.

Her gaze followed the cords in his neck to his broad shoulders and the strong arms that held her so tightly. The capable hands that she could still feel gripping her wrists as he brought her to orgasm for the first time.

His chest was a marvel, broad like his shoulders, his pecs defined but not overly-large, golden hairs scattered here and there. She'd only seen abs like his on the ceiling of the Sistine Chapel and here she had them to touch and lick and play with in real life. They made him real. The same with his perfectly chiseled thighs clamped on either side of her hips. Though Michelangelo would never paint the puckers and scars that graced his body, Jordan delighted in them. Each told a story of survival. *But I saved him first.*

Finally, her gaze rested on his upturned cock, hard and dark-headed, glistening at the tip. She'd only felt it through cloth, but now the sight of it made her realize it was much bigger than she'd thought. She wanted to rub her entire body over it, squeeze it between her breasts, take it deep into her mouth until she made him cry out in ecstasy. She wanted him inside her, to make him hers as much as she was his.

"Jordan," he whispered. "Are you real? Are you mine?"

"Yes, Elliot. Always."

He licked his lips. "God, I'm going to come so hard inside you." He brushed his cock between her lips and against her clit and she pressed back against him, needing his hard, rough touch.

"Inside me." She reached for his cock to guide him. He caught her wrists in one huge hand and held them, making her stomach flutter with anticipation.

"Not yet, beloved. If I enter you now, I'll come immediately." A drop of precum slid down his shaft as if to emphasize the point. "I want to explore you first." He brought her hands up over her head and pressed them against the pillow so her body was stretched out under his. He lowered himself until they had full contact. Her nipples hardened against his skin.

He kissed her forehead, brushed his lips across each eyelid, kissed her cheeks, then sucked her lower lip into his mouth and pulled. The contrast between his gentleness and the rough tug unmoored her and she moaned into his mouth. He ran his tongue between her lips and teeth, exploring every last secret place.

He pulled back and then gave her nipples the attention they craved. He released her wrists so that he could play with them—brushing his fingertips across the tips, then rolling them between his thumbs and first fingers. He bent to take first one, then the other into his mouth. He rubbed his chin and cheeks across her cleavage and she was surprised to feel stubble, realizing it was blond and all but invisible. "So good," she whispered only loud enough for him and the moonlight to hear.

He hummed his approval against her skin. Then she was in his arms again as he rolled and reversed their positions so that she was on top. He kissed her as his hands roamed down her back to her ass. He lifted and turned her until his face was between her legs and his body was spread out before her. His tongue laved her lips and clit as she ground down on his face, biting back her moans. She leaned forward and hand-walked her way down his body.

"Where do you think you're going?" he said against her sensitive skin.

"To do the same for you." Head poised over his engorged cock, she admired it for a moment before slipping the wet head between her lips and sliding her tongue around the tip, coaxing out precum and eliciting a groan he attempted to muffle against her inner thigh. She positioned her head to take more of him in, her lips tightening around his shaft as she slid down its length. As he filled her mouth, his tongue brought her closer and closer to orgasm until she was bucking against him, willing him to come when she did.

Just as she went over the edge into pleasure, he pulled his cock out of her mouth, never slowing his tongue, his lips, his mouth, bringing her closer to orgasm. She ran her cheek back and forth across his tip until her whole body tensed. She sucked his cock back into her mouth as she came. The moment she finished, he turned her until she was lying under him again, face to face.

"I wasn't done," she protested. "I wanted you to come with me."

He grinned. "I will. Inside you during your second one."

She smiled back and kissed him, then reached down between them and wrapped her hand around his cock to guide him home.

He slowed her hand as she tried to understand his expression. It was serious now as his gaze roamed over her face. "I've wanted you for so long. Wanted this. I need to know if you want it too."

"I do. So much."

His smile returned. "I don't want to hurt you or push you."

"You won't. You aren't. I love you. I trust you."

"Beloved," he whispered and ran his thumb over her lips. He lined himself up and rubbed against her lips and over her clit, sending her back on her way toward ecstasy. He stretched her out as he pushed inside her. When he moaned into the hollow of her throat, she gripped his back and nuzzled into his hair. He pulled back, and with every thrust pushed deeper into her until she'd taken his entire length.

"Mine," he groaned.

He found her clit and rubbed it hard as he sped up his thrusts. She squeezed around him, matching his rhythm and climbing back up and up until he gasped and she felt him spasm on the deepest, fastest thrust. True to his word, they came together as they breathed each other's names.

Elliot slowed down then was still. He buried his face in her neck and breathed in her fragrance. "Real at last. I don't want this to end. I want to stay like this forever. Stay inside you forever."

"After tomorrow, you can." She ran her fingers lightly up and down his spine until goosebumps rose under them.

She felt him nod. "I want to keep you in my bed all night tonight. Make love with you until the moon and the sun change places. Then I want to see you naked by the light of day, laid out, sated, ready to finally sleep in my arms."

She sighed, perfectly happy at his words. "I want that too. So much." She started to drift off.

"I found you. I can't believe I found you."

"I was here all the time," she murmured, already half-asleep. "Why didn't you come for me? If you wanted me—"

"I didn't know, Jordan." She woke fully as he pushed up onto his elbow and looked deeply into her eyes. "How could I have known? You were only a dream to me."

His words puzzled her. "Only a dream," she echoed. She studied his face as if seeing him for the first time.

"What is it?"

"Sometimes, I think you're a different person." She stroked his hair. "But it is you. I know it is. I found you, too. I found you first."

She snuggled back into him and he stroked her hair. She tried not to drift off again but she was so content in the warmth and safety of his arms, his clean mineral scent surrounding her.

But after a while, he said, "It kills me to send you back to your room, you have to know that."

She nodded sleepily. "I know. It's not safe. I understand why it has to be this way."

"It won't be forever. You'll be back in my arms, in my bed, tomorrow night. And then you won't have to leave." He lifted his head and his gaze still intense despite his half-lidded eyes. "I love you, Jordan."

"I love you, too. I want to spend the rest of my life making up for the time we've lost."

He helped her back into her nightgown and then picked up his boxer briefs and pulled them on, then his pants. He slipped his shoes on and picked up her robe from the floor.

"You aren't going back to bed?" she asked as he slipped her robe over her shoulders.

"I'm too wired now. I'm going to walk you down the hall to your room like a proper gentleman and then I'll head downstairs, see where Nash is at and trade-off with him so he can get some shuteye." He put on his white button-down shirt and she buttoned it up for him. He grabbed his cell phone, then reached between the mattresses and pulled out a handgun, and grabbed its shoulder holster from where it hung on the bedpost.

He silently opened the bedroom door a crack and looked out into the hall before motioning for her to join him. The hallway was nearly pitch-black, lit only from the sliver of moonlight coming from Elliot's room. He opened the bedroom door and they walked down the dark hallway to her room and stopped in front of the door.

Elliot kissed her forehead, a soft, silent brush across her skin. Still looking up into his face, she turned the knob and slipped inside, then shut the door behind her. She closed her eyes and pressed her ear against the wood, listening to Elliot's receding footsteps.

So she didn't see the man's silhouette against her open

window until she opened her eyes, and by then he was covering her mouth before she could scream.

As he pulled her away from the door, she realized it was her brother and she stiffened with terror. "We'll see about that will now, little sister," he whispered in her ear. She felt a sharp little stab in her arm and then the world went sideways.

TWENTY-TWO

Costello was downstairs when he heard the scream. Nash and the dogs were behind him a moment later as he ran back up, taking the steps two at a time. A second scream tore through the house as he hit the landing. Daphne stood in the hallway, still screaming. She was backlit by the moon coming through Costello's open door.

"He's here! Daniel's *here!*"

The dogs ran past Costello at the top of the stairs. "Where?"

"Jordan's room!" Before he could stop her, she hit the hallway light switch.

"No, wait." The lights came on and he threw his hand up against the sudden brightness. Nash swore behind him. There went their sight. He blinked rapidly as Daphne dashed into Jordan's room.

His heart stopped. *Oh, God, Daniel took her right the fuck out from under me. He must have been waiting for her in her room.*

Costello's heart started again when he looked in the door. To his relief, Daphne sat on Jordan's bed cradling her daughter, Anubis at their feet while Reggie stood at the wide-open window, obviously Daniel's escape route. Both dogs turned their heads to the door and growled. Confused, Costello thought they were growling at him and Nash until he heard a noise behind him and turned.

"I heard screaming. What the fuck?" John Charles stood in the hallway rubbing his eyes against the light.

"Jordan was attacked by Daniel," Daphne shouted. "And these two are doing *nothing!*"

Nash was already entering the room and heading for the window. Costello started toward Jordan and Daphne but the feral look in Daphne's eyes gave him pause. "Tell me what happened," he said as he studied Jordan curled up into a ball, her face tucked into her mother's neck.

"I couldn't sleep. I heard footsteps in the hall and when I came out of my room it was empty, but then I heard a struggle in Jordan's room. I opened the door and saw him. He had Jordan, Daniel had my daughter—"

Jordan lifted her head and made a terrible little animal noise that tore his heart open.

"I screamed and he let her go and went out the window. I screamed again and then you two finally showed up." She stroked Jordan's hair as she rocked. "My daughter is in a *state*, thanks to your incompetence."

"We need to get down there and find him, now," Nash said.

"That's the first thing either of you has said that'll do any good." Daphne glared at Costello. All he wanted to do was tear the woman away from his Jordan and see to her. Jesus, she looked shocked, her eyes glassy.

"Get her some water and call 911," he told Daphne. "I'll see if they caught anything on the cameras," he said to Nashville as they signaled to the dogs to follow. He pulled out his cell.

"I know what my daughter needs and how to take care of her, *Mr. Costello.*" He ignored her and dialed Watchdog as he caught up with Nash.

"Mike, Costello. Any of the sensors tripped at the Eden job?" By now they were halfway through the house on their way out the back to the gardens.

"Nothing tripped, Cos. SITREP?"

"Intruder, principal's window."

"I'll check camera two."

Costello kept an eye on the dogs for any sign they'd picked up on Daniel. They went to the left along the back of the house and stopped under Jordan's window. Pea gravel and stepping stones covered the ground. Nash shined his flashlight around, looking for any tracks in the gravel. The dogs sniffed and Costello aimed his flashlight at the side of the house, looking for a way Daniel could have climbed up. There was the obvious trellis covered in roses and bougainvillea. Both plants had thorns and he searched for any snagged cloth or broken canes while he waited for Mike to report back—*what the hell was taking him so long?*—and wracked his brain for a way Daniel could have gotten onto the property unseen—

Oh, no. I know how. I'm a fucking, fucking idiot. He glanced at Nashville. His brother, who was about to realize just how horrible Costello really was.

Liar. Thief. Traitor.

Mike's voice came back over the phone. "Cos, that camera's been disabled. Happened three hours and twenty-two minutes ago."

"Fuck! I fucked up."

Nash looked up from the gravel. "What?"

"Thanks, Mike." He started to hang up but Mike stopped him.

"No, Cos, wait. Not physically disabled. It's been on a loop. I would've noticed if it'd gone out, but someone hacked in and looped the footage. I'm checking the rest of the feeds now."

Jesus. Daniel *did* have well-connected friends.

"I misjudged everything." He shook his head. "Mike, get Lach on it, STAT. He has a friend who'll find the hacker. Thanks, bud."

That really got Nash's attention. "Watchdog's been hacked?"

"The camera pointed at this window's been on a loop for over three hours. Mike's checking for others."

"Damn. And no motion detectors triggered. They hacked us good, brother. If I weren't here, I'd be on that like stink on shit." Nashville considered himself a decent white hat hacker. He swept his flashlight's beam across the ground. "I can't find hide nor hair of a trail."

Here it is. Here's where I lose my brother's trust. "I think I know how he got in. If we hurry, we might still catch him."

Costello ran toward the ocean side of the garden, toward the dark brick wall ringing them in.

"The...patio...gate?" Nash asked as they ran.

"No." He veered to the right, away from the other, known gate to the secret one.

They ran under the rhododendrons to the hidden rose garden, the white roses giving themselves away in the last light of the setting moon.

"Where...we going?"

Costello didn't have time to answer as he pushed through the roses, each scratch from their thorns a painful reproach. He found the wooden gate behind the ivy. It was closed but that didn't mean anything. He started pushing as Nash first watched, then joined in shoulder-to-shoulder. It was easier to open thanks to the broken ivy and Nash's help.

"Brother, how'd you know about this door?" Out of the corner of his eye, he saw Nash pause and turn his head, a look of disgust in his eyes. "Never mind. I get it now. Thought it was just the garden or my imagination, but it's unmistakable this close." His accent was practically non-existent, a sure sign of his anger.

They opened the door and went through. Sure enough, there in the grotto was a blanket that only could have come from a cheap hotel and some empty water bottles and protein bar wrappers. There was no other sign of Daniel.

Costello's dream garden, his paradise, torn apart and turned inside out into a nightmare.

"I think there's a path that goes down to the beach," Costello said. He crossed the grotto and found a path between the rocks. He signaled for the dogs to track and away they went down a narrow trail along the cliffside. Costello and Nash followed as quickly as the tricky path would allow.

"Thought you were the golden boy, Costello. Never fucked up, always knew shit before the rest of us. Always had your brothers' backs. Why the fuck did you have to go and seduce a principal?"

Seduce? Rage filled him. "It's not like that—"

"Bullshit it ain't like that." Nash plucked at Costello's shirt. "You think I can't smell jasmine all over you? Caught a whiff before, figured it was all the damn flowers. But man, standing up next to you, I can smell *her* on you. You think I'm just a dumb hick, but I had my suspicions even before tonight, but no, golden boy'd never do that. How long did you wait after lying about your damned migraine before fucking her?"

Liar. Thief. Traitor.

"I did not lie about the migraines! Fuck! It's not like you think at all." Costello maneuvered around an outcropping.

"Yeah, you just go on, keep lying. Daphne was sniffing around you; tell me, you fuck her, too?"

Costello stopped, turned, and drew back his fist. The last spark of rationality stopped him from throwing the punch. This was Nashville. His partner, his brother. He *had* lied to him, a lie of omission. Nash had every right to be pissed, to accuse him of terrible things. Costello had broken the rules, had been weak-willed and followed his oldest instincts, and stolen the shiny thing he wanted, even if Jordan wanted the same thing. And in the process, he'd betrayed his brothers, all of them.

Worst of all, he'd betrayed Jordan by getting distracted and sloppy and now she was paying the consequences for his greed.

Yeah. Nashville had it right.

Liar. Thief. Traitor.

Costello dropped his fist. "Nashville, I'm sorry. I...I did lie to you but not like that. And I have never, ever thought you were a dumb hick. Now, we've got a fugitive to catch." He started back down the path. "We're not done with this and I'll explain everything as soon as we've got Daniel in custody."

"Damn straight you will," Nashville muttered.

Reggie barked up ahead.

"Fuck, he's down there." They moved double-time until they saw a dark shape in the path.

Reggie. Chewing on a protein bar.

"Son of a bitch. Reggie!" Nash scolded the dog, who looked as shamed as Costello felt. "Biggest problem with Labs, they're stomach-driven."

They continued down the cliff hoping Anubis had managed to keep on Daniel's trail.

They found another protein bar on the path farther down. There was no sign of the dog until they got close to the beach and saw two more dark shapes in the sand near the base of the trail—Anubis circling something or someone curled up in a ball and lying still. The dog looked up and barked once.

"Good boy," Costello called. But as they got closer, he realized that the shape was too small to be a grown man, even one curled up tightly.

"It's just a big old backpack," Nash said. "Goddamn."

And it was. Nashville pulled out two pairs of gloves and they put them on while Costello looked up and down the beach. The moon was just setting, but by its last faint light, there was no trace of him. Even when Costello gave the command to track from the scent off the backpack, the dogs just raised their noses and sniffed the air as if Daniel Summers had disappeared into it.

"Fuck."

While Nashville went up and down the beach with his flashlight, even shining the beam out into the water, Costello opened the pack and rummaged through it. More protein bars and bottles of water, but not many. A toothbrush and tube of toothpaste. A roll of toilet paper. Deodorant. A couple pairs of jeans and some t-shirts. Underwear. Something jingled like spare change and Costello located a half-zipped pocket. Sobriety tokens. And a torn piece of paper stuck in the zipper's teeth. It looked like the bottom corner of a hand-written letter.

Costello squinted at the handwriting. Cursive. He could tell it was a woman's handwriting from the loops. He took out his phone and hit the flashlight app. Then nearly dropped both his phone and the paper.

The signature at the bottom was his mother's. Ellen Lewis.

Shocked, Costello stuffed the paper into his pants pocket just as Nashville came jogging back up the beach. "Find anything?"

Later. I'll show them later as soon as I know I'm not insane. Costello handed him the backpack. "The man traveled light. No wallet or phone, either."

Nashville fixed him with another suspicious look. *I'll have to get used to those from now on.* He rummaged through the bag. "If he did have anything in here, he took it with him."

"Agreed."

Nashville sighed and looked back at the path. "Nothing for it but to head on up and back to the house. Hope the police are there by now. Maybe they can throw out a dragnet, catch him."

They started back for the path, the dogs at their heels. "Nash—"

"Save it. I don't want to hear it. If you'd been transparent, we mighta found him hiding there when we were setting up security for the party."

"I know." Costello rubbed his temple. "But you've got to believe me when I say that there's more here than meets the eye. I can't even figure it out, but I'm working on it. I need to talk to Arden."

"Kyle's fiancée? Why the hell do you need to talk to her?"

"About the migraines. She's the one I'm seeing tomorrow. Today," he amended. The sky was lightening and the moon was gone. *If she'll still consent to see me.*

"Don't see how that's gonna help this, how your headaches are tied in." Nash stopped. "You think you do have a brain tumor? That'd explain y'all's fuck-ups." His accent crept back in.

"No. I'm making stupid mistakes all without the benefit of a brain tumor right now."

"The little head'll do that when you let it think for you." His voice turned thoughtful. "You haven't gotten laid in a coon's age up 'til now, have you? And long as I've known you, I don't think I've ever seen you with a woman. Even after we all go for a night out, you don't ever seem to leave with company."

"How would you know? You're always the first one out the door with the hottest woman in the place."

"Flattery ain't gonna get you out of this mess." He sighed and his voice turned serious. "I'm going to have to report this to the boss, Costello."

Costello's stomach fell. "I understand. And I know you must be pissed as hell at me right now—"

"Beyond pissed."

"And you have every reason to be. But, I'm asking you, if not for my sake, then for Jordan's, will you wait until I've had a chance to explain my side to Lachlan first?"

"I'm not gonna promise anything, Costello. It's my ass if I don't speak up, and it might hurt our chances at helping Jordan, too."

Fuck. "Copy that."

TWENTY-THREE

When they got back to the house, Daphne was waiting for them on the back patio.

"Did you call the police?" Costello asked. He'd never heard sirens and he didn't see anyone. "How is Jordan?"

"You slept with my daughter."

Costello's stomach dropped through the floor.

"You took advantage of my sweet, innocent daughter."

"Took advantage? Daphne, please. We're—"

"Both of you will find your things outside the mudroom door. You're leaving. You're leaving *now*," she shrieked.

Costello held his hands out. "I understand you're upset. This was not supposed to happen. But if we leave now, we're leaving Jordan in danger."

"You have *put* my daughter through enough danger already. You've, you've...*defiled* her."

Costello actually barked out a laugh. "Defiled her? Daphne, she's a consenting adult and of sound mind despite what you believe and how hard you try to force her to be otherwise. I know what you're up to and so does she. Jordan's guardianship is ending, she is coming into her inheritance and you want to control it." There, he'd said it. Cards on the table at last. "So let's see you drop the concerned mother act and let your daughter live her life the way she wants to."

"How dare you? How *fucking dare* you? I want what's best for my daughter and I always have. I've shielded her from a world that would have destroyed her otherwise. Because of me, she's been able to flourish in her art. Without me, she'd be literally banging her head against the goddammed wall—"

"How many of those episodes were brought on from having you as a mother? How often have you driven her into a state like that? Because that's not who she is. It's not who she ever was. She *never* did that."

Daphne went silent. Waves of cold hostility practically blew off her as she composed herself. "Oh, no? Really? You know she's not like that for sure, huh? You were here all her life to watch her melt down when she got overstimulated? You were here when she'd scream at the top of her lungs if a plant died? You felt her flinch every time you tried to touch her because she couldn't take it?" She sneered. "She doesn't like to be touched. It makes me wonder what you did to her to convince—"

Costello started forward, barely aware of Nash grabbing his arm and holding him back. "Don't. You. *Dare* accuse me of anything like that. The only reason why what we did was wrong is because she's my client and that should never have happened with a principal. But what we feel for each other is real and mutual. I will not touch her again while I'm working here. You can file as many complaints against me as you'd like. But I will not abandon her."

Daphne crossed her arms, the smug expression on her face telling Costello she knew she ultimately held the power. "Oh, I will be filing complaints, Mr. Costello, believe me. And as soon as the conservatorship goes through, I will also be filing criminal charges against you."

Fuck. "What I did was the height of unprofessional but I committed no crime. I would *never* hurt any woman like that, and I'd die before I'd take advantage of Jordan."

"You've really convinced yourself of that, haven't you?" She shook her head as if to shame him. "You've built yourself this little bubble of denial that you live in. You don't see things as they are and so you hurt the people around you. Tell me, have you done that all your life, or only now that you've seen how Jordan lives and you want a big piece of it?" Her eyes narrowed. "I know who you are now, Mr. *Lewis.* You're nothing but a criminal."

His gut turned to ice. "I don't care if Jordan lives in a shoebox in an alley. Her money, this," he waved his arm, "means zero to me. *She* means everything."

"If that were true, you'd already be walking around the house to collect your things and leaving because *that's* what's best for her."

"No. What's best for her is to get her away from you, to get her someplace truly safe. I want to see her."

"Costello," Nashville warned.

"Why? So you can manipulate her? Prime her to say what you want to get your ass out of trouble?"

His heart stuttered. "I would never...I *won't* use her like that. And she'd never *do* that."

Daphne laughed and shook her head. "You are such a manipulator." She pursed her lips. "You know what? I *will* let you see her. Maybe this will convince you of the harm you've done."

God, if they've done anything to her. If they could just talk, everything would be okay. He needed to get her out of here and away from her manipulators.

Daphne turned on her heel and marched to the patio door. Costello started to follow, eager to check on Jordan. Nashville kept his grip on Costello's arm.

"Let go, Nash."

"Do *not* go in there, man. It's what she wants. Can't y'all smell a trap?"

"I have to see her."

"Later. We can regroup at Watchdog. Explain everything. Lachlan will know what to do. I'll let you talk to him first like you wanted, okay?" That Southern charm was back in full-force.

Costello wrenched his arm away from Nashville. "Jordan doesn't *have* later. Come in with me or don't. But I'm going to see her." He jogged to catch up with Daphne, faintly aware of Nashville ordering the dogs to stay and then following him.

Upstairs, it was dark and quiet as death. Every door in the hallway was closed and only a couple of lamps on small tables at either end of the hall gave off any light. Daphne led him past Jordan's bedroom to the converted trunk room at the end of the hall, the bedroom with the smallest windows.

"Why isn't Jordan in her own room?"

"Oh, you'll see," Daphne said in a casual tone.

"Jordan!" Costello called.

Daphne glared at him. "Don't rile her any more than she already is."

They got to the farthest door and Daphne barely knocked on it. "John Charles?"

Her brother's in there with her?

The door opened and John Charles peeked out. His eyes widened when he saw Costello.

"It's all right, John. I want him to see what he's done to her and then he's leaving."

"We'll see about that," Costello said as he pushed the door open and shouldered John Charles out of the way. "Jordan?"

He stopped just inside the door and looked at the woman curled into a ball on the bed. Her hair was a mess and she was still dressed in her nightgown. There was something about her arms. She was rocking back and forth, her eyes staring out into nothing. All the curtains were drawn and the lights were low.

"Jordan, love, what's going on?"

She didn't acknowledge him but kept rocking. As his eyes adjusted to the gloom, he realized her arms were covered in long scratches.

"Jordan."

She looked his way without any sign of recognition. "Ell-i-ot. No. No."

He took a step toward her when John Charles grabbed him from behind.

"Don't get any closer to my sister," he snarled.

"What have you done to her?" Costello whipped his head around. "Let go of me!"

And then Nashville was there restraining him, his gaze fastened on Jordan.

Daphne leaned in close to Costello's ear, her rose perfume at a gagging level. "She's having one of her episodes, Mr. Costello. You know, the ones you said she never had?" She pushed past him, crossed the room to her daughter, and sat on the bed. Jordan kept rocking until Daphne touched her arm. Jordan flinched and scooted away with a whimper a little animal might make.

Daphne looked back at the men, her eyebrows arched, her expression imperious. "See what you've done?"

"No." Costello tried to jerk away from John Charles and Nashville. "Jordan, look at me."

She kept looking away, into an unknowable middle space. She mumbled, "Foun'. No. Foun'. Nooo."

Daphne quickly pulled Jordan to her and held her tightly while Jordan moaned.

"This isn't right." Costello broke away from Nash and John Charles and ran to Jordan as Daphne yelled. He knelt and touched Jordan's arm. "It's Elliot. Do you want to leave?"

When he made contact, she flinched. "No. No, go, go." She scooted away from him.

Costello's heart broke in two. He'd failed her. Lost her.

"You did this," Daphne hissed. "And now you're leaving before you hurt my daughter any more than you already have. Get out!"

Arms came around his shoulders and Nashville hauled him up. This time Costello didn't have the will to fight. "You need to get her to a doctor," he said as Nash pulled him away.

"I need to see the last of you and so does she!"

Then Nashville and John Charles were dragging him down the hall. "I need my phone, I'm calling a doctor for her." His own voice seemed to be coming from far away as the next migraine closed in while every other sound in the house turned sharp and close.

"Fucking do it, asshole," John Charles snarled. "Fucking do it, and we'll tell them the truth, that you're responsible. You'll just speed up your trip to jail for assault. My sister is fragile. She always has been. And you fucking pushed her until she broke."

"Costello," Nashville warned. "We just need to leave. We're off the job, partner. Let's not make things worse for these folks. You don't want that for her."

Then they were outside in the pale morning light. The door shutting behind them sounded to Costello like the sealing of a tomb.

TWENTY-FOUR

Costello walked to the SUVs in disgrace.

"Man, you're not listening to me," Nashville said as they gathered their things and loaded up the SUVs with the dogs. "We gotta get back to Watchdog and regroup."

But all Costello could focus on was Jordan's face, her vacant eyes, the self-inflicted scratches on her arms. He'd done that to her. He'd wanted to protect himself, his job, and he'd neglected to secure the secret gate to the grotto. Of course, Daniel would know about it—he grew up here. It was the perfect hiding place and the way in to attack Jordan and Costello hadn't added a camera or alerted Nashville to it. It was his and Jordan's secret and some secrets kill.

"Costello!"

He tried to blink away the guilty thoughts and the migraine sloshed in his head. Nashville was looking at him intently. "This ain't over, brother."

"You shouldn't call me brother. I don't deserve it."

"Fuck your pity party, golden boy. Look, you fucked up, not gonna let you off the hook for that. But something just ain't right here. So let's haul ass back to headquarters and figure it out."

Costello nodded and winced. His sunglasses were...somewhere...and the sunlight was getting stronger.

"You weren't lying about the migraines. You got one right now, don'cha?"

"Yeah, I do."

"You okay to drive, man?"

"I'll have to be. I think I have another pair of sunglasses in the SUV and the windows are tinted. Yeah, I'll be fine."

Nashville nodded, still studying Costello. Then he turned to his SUV and said, "Let's get the hell out of here."

Nashville was in the lead when they passed between the angels at the front gate of Eden House. To Costello, they seemed to have their heads down lower and their eyes shut tighter, but whether they were deeper in prayer or trying harder not to witness the day's events, he did not know.

Looking at them brought up what he was convinced were now memories and not dreams or fantasies like his mother had led him to believe when he was a child and in the hospital with pneumonia. In his dreams back then, he and the little girl—she *was* Jordan somehow; he was convinced of that now —talked about the angels and how Jordan's father told her they were there to watch over the family but that there were a lot of things they didn't see. God, why didn't he talk to her about it, about his dreams? Did she remember meeting a little boy when she was a little girl? But he was too busy worrying about what she'd think of him instead of trying to solve this mystery.

Golden boy is right. Always have to be the perfect one, the smartest one, the one who believes only in the rational and dismisses the unexplained.

He shook his head. *Get over yourself and fucking use your*

head, Costello. Jordan needs you and you can't afford to be wallowing.

The scrap of paper with his mother's signature was still in his pocket. Evidence right there that she at least knew Daniel Summers. Otherwise, why would she write a letter to a stranger in prison? But when did she write it? She'd been dead for over three months. And when did he receive it? *It must have been after he got out because prison mail is scanned heavily. If it had anything important in it, it would have been flagged.*

Had his mother targeted the Summers family with one of her schemes after all? Then why didn't he remember? Why the dreams instead?

Why did she lie to him?

His head pounded. Thank God there'd been an extra pair of sunglasses in the SUV.

When they got to the end of the driveway, Nashville pulled a Daphne from the day they first came to Eden House and tore out onto the highway, speeding away from Costello. He was under no illusion that Nashville was already on the horn to Lachlan, filling him in. God only knew what he was saying. *It doesn't matter if I lose my job, just so long as Watchdog doesn't abandon Jordan. I will do whatever it takes, inside or outside of the law, to make her safe.*

Costello needed to talk to Arden—to someone—about his dreams. But he really needed to talk to her about Jordan. The two had met the day before. He wanted Arden's take on the severity of Jordan's Asperger's and why she might be near-comatose now. Was that normal? The more he thought about it, the more he didn't think so.

Goddamn, I shouldn't have left! It took everything he had not to turn the car around and get her. *No. I'm clearly compro-*

mised. Until I talk to Lachlan and Arden, I can't trust myself to make any sound judgments.

He'd always relied on his perfect memory and his skills of observation to save him and his team, and now his mind had betrayed him. Had possibly been lying to him all these years.

That terrified him.

A call came over his speakers. Lachlan.

"Boss," he said.

"For now. Conference room one ASAP." Lach disconnected.

Costello hit the gas and caught up to Nashville.

"I'll meet you in con-one," Costello told Nashville in Watchdog's parking garage. "I'm dropping Anubis off with Kyle first."

"I'll tell Lach. Won't be the first meeting you're late to."

"Might be my last though."

Nashville shook his head and went in with Reggie at his heels.

Costello looked down at Anubis. The dog stared back up at him. Then he wagged his tail. Slowly, tentatively.

Costello reached down and scratched behind Anubis' ear. The tail-wagging increased. Then he knelt and took the dog's face in his hands. He moved his hands back, cupped the dog's ears, and gave him a good scratch. Anubis sat and his whole body relaxed while Costello rubbed and scratched his ears, head, and down his flanks.

"It was never personal, buddy. My mom taught me to mistrust dogs. A smart, alert dog means danger to a thief. And you're the smartest dog I've ever seen. Nothing ever gets past you, so you put me on edge. But you always had my back, didn't you, boy?" He scratched Anubis' chest. "I'm turning you back in to Watchdog now. I just want you to know that's not personal, either. This is my way of having *your* back."

He clicked a leash onto Anubis' collar and walked him to the courtyard and Kyle.

Camo ran to Anubis and the two dogs greeted each other like old friends. Kyle smiled and waved at Costello. "I'm just finishing up, then I'll catch up with this meeting. What's going on?" By his easy demeanor, Costello knew Kyle really had no idea. He could use that to his advantage, or he could come clean.

"What's going on is that I fucked up big."

"Oh, shit." Kyle's smile disappeared. "You never fuck up. How big?"

"Can I ask you something first?"

"Sure, yeah." Kyle knelt and unhooked Anubis' leash as he ran a hand over the dog's head. Costello expected the dog to take off with Camo, but he sat down instead.

"How did the dogs get assigned to us?"

Kyle grinned. "I tried to pair the dogs with human partners who'd be compatible. You seemed like you weren't overly crazy about dogs, and Anubis thinks he's a human anyway, so there you go. He's a perfectionist, like you." He stood up. "That's really what you're asking, isn't it? Why I gave you Anubis."

"Yeah." Costello shook his head. "No. I'm asking because I'm wondering where he'll go next."

Kyle's eyes widened. "Oh. *Shit.* You fucked up *that* bad?"

"I did. But look, I still need to talk to Arden. It's not for me, it's for Jordan. Please."

"Brother, you're talking like you're a fucking serial killer and I should protect her from you. Whatever it is you did, it can't be *that* bad." His eyes widened. "You slept with

Jordan, didn't you?" And then to Costello's astonishment, Kyle broke in to a wide grin. "You dawg. Shit." He tagged him on the arm. "We knew it. I mean, not that we were gossiping—"

"Are you kidding? Watchdog is a fucking gossip mill."

"Affirmative to that. But no, I mean me and Arden after the party. Man, she was right. She totally clued in on what was going on between you guys. And I said, no way. No way Psychic would ever do that on a job."

Costello cringed. "Well, I did. And I'm sure you'll be briefed on it in the meeting. But I really need to talk to Arden about this. Jordan was attacked last night and she's...not well."

"You're fucking kidding me. What the hell happened? Is she in the hospital?"

"No. He didn't hurt her, not physically at least. It was her brother Daniel, the one who was in prison. He managed to get into the house through her window. Nash and I went chasing after him, and by the time we got back, she was..." He paused. "She's.... I've never seen her like this. She's completely shut down, rocking. Her eyes are glassy. I tried talking to her and she looked right through me. I tried to touch her and she pulled away and said no, no, go."

Foun. She also said foun...or was it found? Fount? Fountain. Fuck.

Kyle knitted his brows together. "Arden's been working with people with autism for a long time, and since I've been with her, I've met some of her clients. Jordan didn't recognize you?"

"No, she didn't."

Kyle pulled out his cell. "That's not right. I'm calling Arden now and telling her to get down here. She can talk to you after the meeting." He motioned for them to head in while he dialed.

"If I'm still allowed on the property after fucking up so badly."

"Fuck, brother. That won't happen, or they woulda gotten rid of me a long time ago."

A lie can travel halfway around the world while the truth is still putting on its shoes Costello thought as he looked at the screen in the conference room. Gina was doing her usual standing and pacing while Lachlan, Nashville, and Camden sat at the conference table when Costello and Kyle walked in. Seeing Camden there did not bode well—he was in charge of training and personnel, including handing out the occasional walking papers. But it was the headline on the screen that stopped Costello cold.

It was a news article dated that morning. The headline read, "Breakdown at the Murder Mansion: Heiress Has Complete Meltdown in Front of Famous Guests" and it was trending online. The accompanying article was a complete and total character assassination of Jordan, calling her mentally unstable, a danger to herself and others around her, and accusing her of using her wealth and position to cover up her debauched lifestyle. Of course, the sources were all 'confidential' and 'unnamed but close to the family' which as far as Costello was concerned, were misspellings of the name Daphne Summers.

But more damning than the article were the accompanying photos.

One was taken straight off the security camera positioned over the patio and showed Jordan telling off Daphne. But from that distance and angle, the captured frame showed a woman who seemed to be yelling her head off while stunned guests looked on.

The other photo was far more damning—clear and close and taken by the photographer Rachael had run down, the lying, traitorous asshole. That photo captured the moment after Costello had grabbed Jordan when Daphne scratched her. The photo made it look like Jordan was not defending herself but lashing out at Daphne.

Before Costello could say a word, Lachlan pointed at an empty seat, mercifully at the opposite end of the table. "Sit."

Costello sat.

"Had a little chat with Daphne Summers this morning while I had Nashville on the other line, so he pretty much confirmed some of what she said." Lachlan took a deep, cleansing breath, put his chewed up-pen in his mouth, and smiled. Then he let loose.

"Swear to fucking God, I'm gonna put up a poster in my office of Whitney Houston and across it, I'm gonna scrawl: *You are not in a movie guarding this woman!* And you know what I'm gonna use for ink? The blood of the next asshole who pulls this unprofessional bullshit. Only, there's not gonna be a next time, so I guess I'll be using *your* blood, Costello."

Lachlan stood up and slammed his chair against the table. He started pacing back and forth. Camden looked ready to leap in and prevent him from pounding the shit out of Costello.

"Goddamn. What the fuck am I supposed to do with you in the meantime, Psychic? You're my second-best operative next to Gina, and Gina's a goddamned superhero. I can't just fucking let you go, but I can't let *this* go, either. *Fuck!*" A definitive snapping noise came from his chewed-down pen.

"Boss, did you sign off on upping the dental plan this year yet? Just askin'," Camden said.

Lachlan stopped and stared down his personnel manager. "Don't you fucking get smart."

"Wouldn't dream of getting smart because dumb's worked really well for me so far. Just looking out for your continued wellbeing, Boss."

Lachlan growled. He paced toward Costello. ""Look, man. You never fuck up. *Never*. All around me, I got people making all these daily little fuck-ups, but not you. You shoulda been named Perfection, not Psychic. Now it's like you took all the little fuck-ups and saved 'em up and baked them into one great, big, colossal fuck-up pie."

He shook his head. "There are half-a-dozen guys here I woulda expected to do this before you, and I would expect them to do this not at all."

"Lachlan," Costello said. "This isn't about me just wanting to get laid. That's not *me*."

"Fuck no, it isn't you. Ah, that's it. It's the woman. The problem's always a goddamned woman."

"I'm right here," Gina said.

Lachlan's gaze snapped to her. "You're not a woman, Gina. Didn't you just hear me say you're a goddamned superhero?"

She raised her eyebrows and crossed her arms. "Thanks?"

"So," Camden said, waving his hand. "Getting back to it, the vibe I'm getting here is that we're not firing Costner...I mean *Costello*, but that this cannot go unpunished."

"I'm willing to resign if I can just stay on long enough—"

"The fuck you preach, Costello," Lachlan said. "You're not going nowhere unless I personally escort you to hell. You got two things going for you right now and *only* two things. One, you saved the life of my best friend back on the teams, and two, you know more about this goddamned mission than anyone else. You fucking *know*—"

Costello cringed at the air quotes.

"—the principal better than anyone else right now. We were in no uncertain terms fired from this assignment, but there is still a woman in danger out there who you've helped put into *more* danger. And I'll be damned if we're gonna let that stand. So for now, you're with us."

Costello breathed a sigh of relief. Because nothing was going to stop him from saving Jordan and it was going to be a hell of a lot easier to do it with his team at his back.

Lachlan stomped back to his chair, yanked it out, and sat down. "Now that I've ventilated your ass, let's take a look at this shitshow and I want you to figure out how to fix it." He turned and pointed at the screen. "Two problems here. One, we've got a principal who is looking unstable, which is ammo for her family to push through that conservatorship."

"So we fight fire with fire," Costello said. "We have plenty of other photos of Jordan looking relaxed and happy and lots of witnesses to that. Get someone online searching the party-goers' social media and harness the positive feedback. Get that going on the web as well as building a file to present to any case managers or lawyers."

Lachlan nodded. "Done. Next—our camera feeds were compromised sometime yesterday obviously." He pointed at the first picture. "Now that just doesn't happen. And Mike told me about the looping footage, too. We're still tracking the source."

"Were all the cameras hit?"

"That's where it gets interesting," Lach said. "The back patio cam was hit for the photo, but the only ones with loops were the camera focused on the principal's window, the camera on the front gate, and the camera along the driveway." Lachlan let that sink in.

"Not the cameras in the garden that would have captured

Daniel Summers' route from his hiding place," Costello said. "The other cameras were blocked to cover someone coming in from the front. And something tells me there was no footage captured of Daniel at any point."

Lach nodded once.

"If the cameras were linked to Daniel's supposed well-connected friends, they would have blocked the others knowing he was coming in from the garden."

"That's my thinking, too."

"I don't think Daniel ever made it to Jordan's window. We spooked him from his hiding place only when we went looking for him. He never tried to nab her, at least not that night."

Lachlan considered that. "Yeah. So two possibilities. Either someone else came in from the front, got to her window, and Daphne interrupted like she said, or—"

"Daphne and John Charles set up the whole thing," Costello interrupted. "There was no break-in, no Daniel at the window."

"But how did they hack our feed?" Nashville asked. "Our cyber-security is some of the best in the world, and I should know because I helped build it. Hacking us would take some major resources."

Costello's head pounded with the possibility of who Daphne and John Charles aligned themselves with. He rubbed his temples. "Marcus Porter. Nobody else would have those resources or the balls to use them. He's thumbing his fucking nose at us. They already had the photo the photographer took and it's a more damning one anyway. They didn't need this one for the article. But *he* took it to show us he could."

Hide and seek.

Costello scrubbed his face with his hands.

"Costello?" Lachlan asked. "What's happening? Nash mentioned migraines on top of everything else."

Costello took a big breath and let it out. "First, do we have anything back on SSC's finances?"

"Our friend is still looking into that," Gina said. "He should have the results any time now." She pushed away from the wall. "But let me be the psychic for a minute. We're going to find ties to Marcus Porter." She knelt beside Costello. "What else are we going to find?"

Costello pinched the bridge of his nose. "I...this is impossible, but. I have these dreams. Only, now I don't think they're dreams. I've had them since I was a little kid, and I think they're tied in to all of this."

Gina tilted her head. "How is that possible?" The rest of the room was silent.

Costello tapped his head. "It's up here. It's all up here and I can't remember. Not clearly, but it's trying. The walls are crumbling." He shuddered at the fresh, stabbing pain.

Gina glanced at Lachlan, then back at Costello. She put her hand on his shoulder. "We need to get you to a hospital."

"Brain tumor," Nash murmured, nodding.

"No!" Costello winced. "I'm not crazy and it's not a tumor." He reached in his pants pocket. "But it's real. Here." He handed Gina the scrap of paper. "This was in Daniel's backpack."

She took it. "Why was it in your pocket, Costello? You aren't acting ration—"

"Because that's my mother's signature."

"Rhea Costello?" She unfolded the paper. "That's not what this...Oh. I see."

Costello nodded his head almost violently. "Ellen Lewis is my *birth* mother. But you already knew that, didn't you?" Of course, they'd done a thorough background check when they hired him. But they'd never brought up his childhood with him.

He looked at Kyle. "Is she here yet?"

Kyle's expression was as concerned as everyone else's. "ETA in five."

"She who? Someone fucking fill me in." Lachlan said, chomping on his pen.

"Arden. She's going to work some of her magic with Costello," Kyle answered.

"I hope," Costello said. "I hope there's such a thing as magic."

TWENTY-FIVE

Ten minutes later, Costello was in one of the safe rooms with Arden and his head was killing him.

Watchdog had two of these rooms and they were set up to protect principals who were under the biggest threats, who couldn't even be stashed in an outside safehouse. That was exceedingly rare, so the rooms were most often used by employees pulling extra-long shifts who needed a couple hours' sleep. They were set up like hotel rooms with an en suite bathroom, two beds, a television, couch, table, and chairs.

Costello lay on one of the beds, Arden in a chair beside him and a small recorder on the table. She'd turned on one of the lamps across the room and left everything else dark.

"How long will this take?" he asked.

"That's up to how receptive you are to hypnosis," Arden answered, her voice already low and comforting. "Try your best to relax. Go to your favorite place."

Costello smiled. "If that's the case, this should go quickly. My dreams are my favorite place."

"Good. Then go there and listen to my voice. Whatever

happens, whatever you see, remember that it's in the past and you're perfectly safe right here, right now. I'm going to count down..."

Arden's voice came from a long way away—somewhere in the future. But the five-year-old boy Elliot was busy helping his mom with a scheme.

"I'm in a garden. It's beautiful. But the best part is that I have a friend. She's really nice, even though she's a little younger than me. We've been playing all day. I'm not supposed to like the kids I play with during a scheme. They aren't friends, they're marks. But she's different. She doesn't have any friends either and her brothers are already grownups so she's lonely even though her dad is really nice to her. I met him earlier, and it's true. He is nice, but he also seems really sad. I met one of her brothers too, and her mom, but I don't like them as much. I really don't like her brother and later, I think he must be the one who makes her dad sad.

"But I like the little girl. We've played together all day while my mom is talking to hers. She says she'll be my friend forever and that I can always come here and play whenever I want. She doesn't care like the other kids—the other marks—about who I am, who my family is, where I come from. We're friends, she and I, friends forever. To prove it, she shows me the rose garden, the one with the secret door and the other secret garden behind it. The flowers smell good there and I can smell the salty ocean and I'll always remember this and think of her.

"But it's dark now. We've played too long. I'm supposed to be inside the house helping with the scheme. I don't want to. I don't want to steal things then meet up with Mom at the angel gate and never come back. I don't want to lose my friend."

"What's your friend's name, Elliot?" Arden's voice is soft and calming.

"It's Jordan. Her name is Jordan."

"And this place? Do you know it?"

"It's Eden House."

"Okay, Elliot. I want you to keep doing what you were doing that day. Go back there. What happens next?"

"I tell Jordan it's time to play hide and seek. She needs to hide far away and I'll find her. And then I think for a second and I tell her not to hide near the angels. And she laughs and says, 'They won't see me. Daddy says the angels at the gate pray for us, but they keep their eyes shut tightly.'

"I'll never see her again. My friend. So just before I start to count, I kiss her cheek and she laughs. Then I close my eyes, turn and face the fountain, and count."

"The fountain?" Arden sounds puzzled.

"There's a fountain in the garden, in the courtyard near the house."

A pause. "Tell me what happens next."

"I count until I'm sure she's gone. I'm supposed to sneak into the house now, but I'm afraid. I can hear an argument. It's Jordan's brother and her dad yelling at each other. They're in the room with the door open to the garden and I'm afraid they'll see me. But Mom is counting on me. She's somewhere in there too, keeping Jordan's mom distracted. She already played hide and seek and told me she found the jackpot room and now it's my turn. So I sneak into the house.

"I'm walking through the halls, but now I'm playing hide and seek the way my mom taught me. I'm looking for all the things she likes—jewelry, money, anything that looks gold or silver. In a house like this one, Mom says, 'if it looks gold, it is gold.' I duck into a room. It's dark and I hear a noise like a monster. I duck down behind a bed. Is it under the bed? No, it's not a monster, it's a man. He's snoring, asleep, but he's not in the bed. He's in a chair. There's a smell in the room, both sweet and sharp. It's coming from an empty bottle by his feet. I explore the room, glancing back at his face a bunch of times to make sure he doesn't wake up."

"Do you recognize the face?"

"I don't know who he is. I haven't seen him here before."

"Have you seen him since? Do you know who he is now?"

"He's Daniel Summers."

"Keep going, Elliot. He can't hurt you."

"I'm scared he'll wake up and be angry that I'm in his bedroom. Mom told me if a grownup catches me to always say I'm playing hide and seek. Act younger than I am. Adults don't pay attention to kids and they can get away with murder.

"I see a watch on the table beside him. I grab it and put it in my pocket. There's some loose change and a wad of bills so I grab those too. I start to leave the room, glad to be out of there, when I hear someone running down the hall. I duck behind the bed and get ready to crawl underneath. But there are boxes under the bed and I can only fit partway.

"A man comes in. He's breathing heavily. I smell copper, something metallic. He says, 'Daniel.' I recognize the voice from earlier. It's Jordan's brother, John Charles. He's trying to wake up Daniel. He swears. Now he's trying to pick Daniel up. I sneak a look. Oh, oh no."

"Remember you're safe, Elliot. This is all in the past and you're just observing. You're an adult now."

"I'm...okay. John Charles is covered in blood. His face... the expression on his face. I never want anyone to look at me like the way he's looking at Daniel. It's evil. Pure evil.

"I don't know why he's trying to move Daniel. Maybe he needs help. But I can't help or I'll get in trouble with Mom. Daniel wakes up but he's dead drunk. He's not making any sense. John Charles is stumbling too. I think he must be hurt. He flings Daniel's arm over his shoulder and tells him they're going for a short walk. They leave the room. I'm going to follow them. I don't want to get in trouble but I have to figure out how to help if someone is hurt.

"I hang back far enough that they don't know I'm there. They're going slow enough and talking so they're easy to follow."

"What are they saying?"

"I can't make out everything. But John Charles is saying that he can't believe how angry Daniel is. I don't understand what he means. Daniel was passed out. How can he be angry? John Charles keeps talking. He's asking Daniel how he could have hurt their father like that. Now I really don't understand what he's talking about.

"They go into the room where...no. I don't like that room. I don't want to go in there again."

"Elliot, you are in control. This all happened a long time ago. You can stop anytime you want. But the more you can remember, the more you can help Jordan. It's your decision."

"I have to protect Jordan. I have to remember everything. Okay. I'm okay. They go into the room where I heard John Charles arguing with Jordan's dad. It's the one with the doors to the garden, the important room Mom was talking about. The jackpot room.

"I want to see what's happening but I can't just walk up to the door. So I duck back outside. I can see in through the glass doors from the garden, but I have to be careful because I know Jordan is hiding somewhere out there. I don't want her to find me. She's never supposed to see me again now that I have my pockets full. I'm supposed to meet Mom where the angels are and we'll leave. But I can't leave yet. I have to know what's going on. If someone is hurt, I have to help. If Jordan is in danger, I have to save her.

"I'm outside now. The garden is dark. The crickets are chirping and the ocean waves are crashing hard. But I can still hear the fountain."

"Elliot? You're shaking. Do you need to go to your safe place?"

"No. No. I'm this close to remembering everything."

"Take your time. Remember that no matter what happens, you're safe now."

"I'm up next to the windows by the doors. I'm looking in. Oh my God, it's her dad. He's on the floor. There's so much blood...his head...it looks...it doesn't look like a person's head anymore. It's..."

"You're safe, Elliot."

"He's dead. The blood all over John Charles, it's his father's blood. John Charles killed him.

"He's taken a handkerchief out of his pocket and he's picking something up off the floor. It's the obelisk, the one I saw on the desk. It's cover in blood and...and hair. Skin. Other...no. No.

"John Charles is wiping off the base, trying not to touch it with his bare hands. Now he's giving it to Daniel. Daniel takes it and is looking it over. He can barely stand. John Charles is yelling at him. 'How could you kill our father?' He's taking off his shirt and telling Daniel to put the obelisk down and take off his. Daniel is crying. I hate watching men cry. They're switching clothes.

"John Charles is going to get away with this unless I tell. Mom will never let me tell, I know it. We don't ever get involved unless there's money in it. I'm worried about Jordan seeing this though. If her brother would do this to his dad and his brother, he'd kill Jordan too if she knew. I have to find her. We can hide in the secret garden.

"I turn to run but I trip and fall. As I'm trying to get back up, I hear footsteps. Oh, God, it's John Charles. He's seen me. He knows. I get up but it's too late. He's standing over me and he has that look on his face. The evil one. He's going to kill me too.

"I dodge past him and he chases me. I don't know where to run. What if I accidentally run right into Jordan?

"I'm running past the fountain. He's right behind me. He's grabbed my hoodie; he's got me. The gravel makes me slip and I'm falling backward. He's got me. I'm fighting him and he...he slams my head against the edge of the fountain. Oh, God, it hurts...no, I'm blacking out. I can't black out.

"Now I can't breathe. I'm underwater. Someone's holding me down. Just a shadow. I can't... It's him. John Charles is trying to drown me. I can see his shape over me, above the water. He's just a shadow. A shadow is drowning me. I'm blacking out again. My last thoughts are of Jordan. He's going to kill her if she sees. I have to fight to stay alive."

"Elliot?" Arden's voice sounds alarmed.

"The pressure holding me down is gone but I can't move. I can't see. I'm still underwater but it's peaceful now. I'm not breathing. Am I dead? Jordan. I can't be dead, I have to help Jordan.

"Someone's lifting me up. Is John Charles back? No. This person isn't as strong. Struggling. I'm being pulled out of the water by my legs. My head hits something again. God, it hurts. I try to speak but I can't. My lungs, my chest is heavy. I'm coughing. I'm throwing up. Jordan is here. She's saying my name, she's crying. I think she pulled me out of the fountain. I think...she saved my life. No! She can't be here, she needs to hide! He'll kill her. He'll—"

"Elliot, it's time to come back. You've done it. You've remembered everything you need to remember. You're safe, Jordan is safe. He didn't find her. Go to the safe place."

"Okay. Okay."

"Tell me when you're there...Elliot?"

"I'm there now. In the secret garden."

"Good. That's good. You're safe now. I'm going to count backward from ten and as I do, you're going to feel like you're waking up. You're going to feel well-rested and calm. Ten, nine, eight...slowly becoming more aware...seven, six...you're safe and relaxed, waking up...five, four...almost awake...three, two, one. Open your eyes, Elliot."

Costello was back in his adult body. He felt the bed under him and his head no longer hurt. He blinked at the soft light in the room. He touched his cheek and his fingers came away wet. He rubbed his face and realized his cheeks were slick with tears. They'd soaked into either side of the pillow. He quickly wiped his cheeks, totally embarrassed.

Arden handed him a tissue. "It's all right, don't feel bad. That was intense." She leaned forward. "Those tears belong to a scared little boy from a long time ago who was never allowed to cry. Never allowed to *be* a little boy."

"Not until the Costellos fostered and adopted me." Costello remembered this was being recorded and glanced at the recorder. Its red light was off.

Arden smiled. "I got it all, but turned it off when you wiped your face."

"Thank you." He blew his nose. Arden looked pale

despite her kind smile and no wonder. "Jesus! I need to tell them. I need to get Jordan to safety."

Arden laid her hand on his arm, stopping him from standing. "Yes, I get it, but she's not in immediate danger just because you've remembered. John Charles doesn't know that and he—they—need her alive. We need to get everything down first so you have a full case against him. If you remember anything else that you haven't mentioned, I can turn the recorder back on when you're ready."

Costello nodded. Arden was right. The immediacy he felt came from that little boy. Nothing had changed in the current situation to add to Jordan's danger. *Keep calm. Do this right so he can't slip through any cracks.* "Sure. Let's get the rest of it down. I'm ready."

Arden hit the button and identified herself and Costello, then stated the date and time. "Go ahead."

"I'm fully conscious now, not under hypnosis," Costello stated for the record. "My memories around this are coming back. It's *all* coming back. The next thing I remember I was in the hospital, alone. Something was in my mouth. I think now that it must have been a breathing tube. I must have had complications from nearly drowning. I was drugged up. I remember sleeping a lot and waking to nurses coming and going, taking my vitals. Everything was blurry because I didn't have my glasses. I didn't know where my mom was or if Jordan was okay and I couldn't ask."

The memories were filling in now like pavers in a path stretching ahead of him—still vague, but when seen through his adult eyes, he could puzzle things out. "I must have been there several days. It's hard to know for sure how long. I woke up one morning and the tube was gone and I was in a different room with fewer things humming and beeping around me."

Costello felt calm at the moment but the memories of being a scared little boy were right under the surface. "I wanted my mom. I wanted to ask about Jordan but I was also afraid to say anything. I didn't want to find out that John Charles got her. I asked one of the nurses but she didn't know who I was talking about. She said I must have had some scary nightmares while I was...in the coma." Costello shook his head in disbelief. *Jesus, a coma?* How could he have forgotten all of this?

"I still slept a lot. I don't know if I was just really sick, or if they had me on strong meds. Maybe both. When I was a kid, I remember being home and being really sick. Just exhausted. It's one of my first memories. *Was* one of my first memories, I should say. I didn't associate it with my hospital stay, but now I think it happened after this. *Right* after this. When I asked my mother about it she always told me I'd had the flu bad enough to go to the hospital. I always thought it happened when I was much younger, around two or three maybe."

"The mind can play tricks in order to make sense of events," Arden said. "Do you remember anything else about the hospital?"

"Yes. One of the nurses told me in this chipper tone that I had a visitor. I wanted it to be Jordan, to know she was alive. I wanted to see her so badly. I wanted to thank her for saving me and tell her we were friends always. But it wasn't. It was my mom. She finally showed up."

This memory was coming in clearer now. "My disappointment must have shown on my face because when she got close enough that I could be sure who it was, her smile disappeared and her face fell."

Costello drifted back into that memory of the hospital room. His mom had pulled up a chair and sat beside the bed. She'd taken his hand.

"How are you feeling, kiddo? 'Bout lost you there. You're not allowed to break up the act like that." She grinned and wiped a lock of sweat-dried hair off his forehead.

"Jordan," Elliot whispered.

"Who?" She pursed her lips. "Haven't the foggiest who you're talking about. You must've had some bad dreams. The nurses said you might—"

"Where's Jordan?" Elliot started to sit up. He barely lifted his head off the pillow when he felt woozy and let it fall again.

His mom smiled one of her here's-the-plan-for-our-next-scheme smiles. Only, there was something different about it. There was a little bit of the smile she gave a mark at the beginning of a con. The trust-me smile. "Honey, here's how it is. You've had the flu and it turned into pneumonia. That's why you're here—she waved her arm indicating the room—ask any of the nurses if you had pneumonia and they'll tell you that you did, okay? You had a lot of weird dreams that go along with a high fever."

"Jordan's not a dream," Elliot whispered, growing angry.

His mom shook her head and caressed his forehead again. "Don't know who that is, Baby Owl. Here's what I do know. We did a job like we always do," she gave him that customary wink whenever she talked about their work, "and you got sick while we were there. Good people that they are, they've offered to pay all your medical bills and then some. Which, thank the sweet baby Jesus, or else I'd have to hock you." She winked again, their little running joke. "And I'd sure miss you. You're all I've got in this world that I want to keep."

That wasn't right. Was his mom lying to him? "No, I remember. Jordan was there—"

She put her fingers over his lips and *tsked* to shush him. Her expression went serious. "This is the story, Baby Owl. I didn't realize how sick you were and how much danger," her voice cracked on that word, "you were in. The pneumonia filled your lungs with water. You were so sick, you fell and hit your head. You've been in a coma."

She blinked back tears and swallowed hard. "They treated you for a concussion and put you on all sorts of meds to clear up the infection in your lungs and keep you out of pain." She dropped her gaze and squeezed his hand. "I'm so sorry you've had to go through this. So sorry. I'm the worst mom in the world for not catching it." She clenched her jaw, going against her own rule of *stay cool as a cucumber and never let them see they've squeezed you like an orange.*

"But the upside is, you're okay now. You're better than okay. That job turned out to be a good one that's going to pay dividends." She tapped the end of his nose. "All you need to do, Baby Owl, is to put all of this behind you. I mean *all* of it, understand? No more talking about it. No asking about someone named Jordan."

"Mom, I need to know if she's okay. There was...there was..." Elliot closed his eyes against blood-soaked visions. He didn't want to remember that, not ever.

She put her arms around him. "There was you sick as a dog, and that's it. The rest was all a dream." She gently took his face in her hands and looked him in the eyes. "Dreams aren't real, Elliot. And sometimes they can become nightmares if..." She shook her head. "Put this behind you and move forward. For both our sakes."

Her conspiratorial smile returned. "You've got to stay grounded, stay sharp. We're a two-man team against the world, Baby Owl. Speaking of," she pulled back and reached into her purse, "I brought you your glasses. No more fuzzy world."

Elliot took his glasses from her palm. The wire frame was

MORE THAN PARADISE 263

slightly bent. He put them on and the world went from fuzzy to a little wonky. He blinked at his mom.

"Okay, so maybe the world isn't crystal clear. But you know what? We've got the funds now, so as soon as we can, we're gonna get your eyes fixed. You'll see the world through brand-new eyes, kiddo." She paused. "No more glasses at all. No more bullying." Her voice had gone soft, uncharacteristically, well, *motherly*. "I'll miss seeing my Baby Owl though."

***

Costello stopped talking. His throat was tight and he couldn't swallow. Arden waited patiently and wiped at her eyes quickly enough that Costello almost didn't catch it. She turned off the recorder.

"So she knew," Arden said at last.

"She knew. And she lied to me. All those years whenever I asked. She told me it was a dream. That Jordan wasn't real. And she *knew*. She fucking *conned me*." His hands shook and he clenched them.

"It sounds like she was trying to protect you." Arden held up her hand when he started to protest. "I'm not justifying her behavior. Please don't think that I'm doing that. Your mother had many, many flaws. They were right to take you away from her. But, Costello, she loved you. And she did her best and she fell far short of the mark. You're going to have to square that inside somehow."

Costello bent forward and ran his hands roughly through his hair. He wanted to yell—no, *bellow*—out his pain and frustration. But there was no time and he didn't want to lose his shit in front of Arden. *Pull it back in and hold it together.* He took a deep breath, held it, and blew it out. He did it again and felt nominally better. When he looked up, Arden was smiling at him.

"Reminds me of Kyle."

"It should. He's the one who taught me that."

"I knew he was a keeper. So, what's your next move?"

"My mom wrote a letter to Daniel. I have the bottom corner piece of it with her signature and a few other words, 'Have the original if you need it.' She took something big from the jackpot room and it might have gotten Leo Summers killed."

Arden covered her mouth. "Oh my God."

"I think I know what it is. I need to go to my mom's storage unit and see if it's there, or if there's anything at all that ties back to the Summers family." Costello stood and Arden followed. He smiled down at her and it hit him how tiny the woman actually was. She always seemed so much bigger. Arden opened her arms and he hugged her.

"Thank you, Arden."

"You are so welcome, Cos. Stay safe. And please, come out to visit us anytime. The ranch house is begging for guests."

He grinned. "I'll be there for the wedding for sure."

She beamed up at him. "Wonderful! I cannot wait to have everyone there for Christmas. That's when a house should be full of friends and family and those who are both."

"Thanks again. I've got to run."

"Understood. I'll get the audio of our session to Lachlan," Arden said.

"Perfect, thanks."

As soon as Costello opened the door, Lachlan came around the corner. "Perfect timing. We need to talk *now*, Costello."

TWENTY-SIX

L achlan studied Costello. "You look like a truck just hit you then ran over your best friend. We need an ambulance for you?"

"No. I'm better. And we got part of what we needed."

Arden handed Lachlan the recorder. "Costello already knew Jordan from when they were kids. His mother was involved, and the wrong man went to prison. It's all here."

"The fuck?" Lachlan looked from the recorder to Costello and back again.

"Just listen, Boss. In the meantime, I've got to run and confirm my suspicions. Do we still have the cameras going at Eden House? We need eyes on Jordan to make sure no one's coming out to evaluate her in the state she's in now." He started down the hall but Lachlan grabbed his arm and stopped him.

"Hold up, Costello. Some things you need to know first." He glanced at Arden.

"I know my cue to leave." She gave one last smile to Costello, then headed down the hall and around the corner.

As soon as she was out of sight, Lachlan started. "The

intel on SSC's finances came in. Looks like John Charles really fucked the pit bull. Jordan's money kept them partially afloat—pardon the pun—for a while, but we're talking about hundreds of millions of dollars they needed to bail them out. So it looks like he made a deal with Marcus Porter. Porter has dumped a shitload of money into SSC over the past month and he's added their stock to his portfolios which'll bring in more." Lachlan ran a hand through his dark, auburn hair. "I don't think he's looking to have that loan paid back in cash, but in services. And, we all know what the rumors are."

Costello's heart stopped for a beat. "Drugs and human trafficking. And now he's got a shipping company in his debt."

"Gina's other people are already on it and grateful for the intel."

Costello's heart raced at the thought of Jordan getting caught in the crossfire. "Boss, I need to hurry. I—"

"That's the other thing, Costello. That's really your mom's signature?"

"Yeah, that's hers."

"The finance intel goes all the way back to when Leo Summers was murdered. I just had my friend do a quick search on Ellen Lewis. SSC started making regular deposits into an account under her name a month after John Charles took over the family business. The payments went on for five years then stopped."

They've offered to pay all your medical bills and then some. The regular deposits to his mother's account must have been the *then some.* For five years, John Charles paid her off to keep her mouth shut about her son. Those payments ended when his mother was arrested and he was put into foster care. But why did John Charles pay her at all? What leverage did she have?

Whatever she found in the jackpot room. And I think I know what it was.

"Those payments were blackmail money, Boss. It's all on the recorder. I know who killed Leo Summers and it wasn't Daniel. It was John Charles. But I need more proof. His motive."

And was Daphne part of it? Was she the other half of *they* or was his mom just saying that to make it sound like the whole family was concerned, to normalize it? He couldn't imagine Daniel knowing about the attempted drowning. He'd been lied to about his father's murder, framed for it. An innocent man had gone to prison—both bodily and in his head—thinking he'd killed his father in a drunken blackout.

And now Daniel was back in the wind, gone from being the threat to the threatened. There was no doubt in Costello's mind that the other men watching Daniel had been hired by John Charles and possibly Daphne. Watchdog had to find him.

But for now, Costello needed to dig up the last of his mother's secrets to save Jordan.

"So do we still have eyes on Eden House?" Costello asked again.

"Yeah, and they don't know it. They think we powered down. Everyone's still there and no one else has driven up. Daphne never called the police last night either, and she *thinks* she's using that as leverage over us. If we get near the house, she's calling them."

"Keep an eye out for anyone coming or going. Their next move is to have Jordan evaluated and they'll do it soon. Something is seriously wrong with her. I'm worried now that they've drugged her. We need to find Daniel Summers and I need to get to my mom's storage unit. I think there's evidence there and we need it to free Jordan and put John Charles behind bars." He tapped the side of his head. "I'm back in the game. Just trust me on this, Lachlan." He grimaced. "If you still can."

"Son." Lachlan laid his hand on Costello's shoulder. "None of us is perfect. Just get what you need to save your woman and we'll worry about what comes next after that."

A drop of sweat rolled down Costello's neck and into his collar as he unlocked the storage unit and rolled up the door. Hot, stale air rolled out in waves. Another blistering day in Los Angeles.

The woman went soft in her old age was all he could think as he peered in at the shapes draped with tarps. They'd always traveled light but the unit was surprisingly full.

You're all I've got in this world that I want to keep.

He pushed the memory of his mother's words away as he pulled off the nearest tarp and uncovered a beat-up old recliner. He uncovered the rest of the old, worn furniture. True to form, there was nothing nice or valuable in the unit— she'd sold all the treasure as fast as she got it and hung on to the junk. Now she had several years' worth of it piled up, collected after she'd apparently settled down.

I should have brought someone to help look through all this.

He moved on to the boxes stacked at the back. That's where he needed to look. Ellen Lewis hadn't been greedy. She didn't live the way she did to make a lot of money or to have nice things, and God knows, some really nice things passed right through her hands. *She lived for the thrill of not getting caught* Costello thought. She liked to be the cleverest person in the room and was never happier than when she realized she'd pulled a fast one over on someone who could have outgunned her if they knew.

Costello opened the top box. The box held scrapbooks—his mom had definitely gone soft if she was keeping mementos. Well, he was positive she was hiding papers; maybe this was camouflage. He opened the first cover and what he saw shocked him.

Newspaper clippings—yellowed, faded, and about him as a kid.

There he was at eleven grinning out of a black and white photo of his Little League team, the one he'd begged Peter Costello, at that point still his foster father, to let him join with his foster brother, Patrick. Then came the football photos. When he saw the honor rolls, he realized she'd collected his school newspapers and the bulletins from the church that the school was attached to.

As he flipped through the pages, the newspapers turned to computer printouts, but they all documented Costello's life from the moment he was taken away from her, through his military career, and even some photos pulled from the tabloids showing him in the background guarding one celebrity or another.

He didn't find what he was looking for, but he'd found what he'd never suspected. His mom had kept track of her son long after he'd stopped being her Baby Owl.

And there was more.

The next scrapbook was all about Jordan.

Page after page covered with photos of her installations, a couple of bios, gossip about her private life, even a few photos of her smiling at the camera, standing beside overjoyed clients. But none with any friends or boyfriends that he could tell. Either she didn't have any, or she was careful to hide them from the public eye.

Hide and seek.

Jordan was still playing that game. With him.

She remembered him from their childhood. She *knew* him. She'd hired *him* specifically, not Watchdog.

'I found you. I nudged her into hiring Watchdog over another company. She thinks she picked you guys out but it was me. Don't tell her.'

The day she was arranging the vases of flowers.

'I could only guess how you felt when I read the stories about you. I mean, you weren't mentioned by name in any of the military ones of course, but I was assured they were about you and your team.'

'You must have hired the best to look into me.'

He'd thought she'd done some fast but thorough research on the trip home from Italy. But he was wrong. Jordan had kept track of him through the years, too.

Friends forever.

'I understand why you don't want to talk about it. Please, we can go back to pretending that I don't know a thing about your mother...I'll keep your secret. We won't talk about it anymore, I promise.'

"Hide and seek. You're still trying to protect me, Jordan, to save *me* when I should have been saving *you*. And I was too stupid to know it, trying to deny that my dreams were real. Because there are no psychics."

No, there weren't. But there were people like his mother who pretended to be. People who snuck around houses, snuck around people, gathering their secrets and taking advantage of them.

At the bottom of the box was a manilla envelope. He lifted it out and turned it over. It was addressed to him in his mother's handwriting.

Inside he found what he was looking for. What his mother

had stolen and held onto all those years ago. He was sure its disappearance led to Leo Summers' death. And Costello's near-death if an angel hadn't opened her eyes, gone looking for her only friend, and pulled him out of the fountain.

Costello was convinced Jordan didn't know John Charles was the murderer. She hadn't seen that much.

But did John Charles know that?

Hurry.

He thumbed through the pages just to be sure of what he had and that it was all there. At the back of the sheaf was a copy of the letter his mother had sent Daniel. And a letter addressed to Elliot.

His cell buzzed with a text from Lachlan that made him dash out of the unit, barely taking time to lock it behind him. A car had been spotted passing through Eden House's gates and they researched the license plates. Jordan was about to be evaluated and Daphne was one step closer to controlling her life forever.

Why the fuck did he have to be all the way across the city?

As Costello sped back to Watchdog, more bad news came in—the car had left after only fifteen minutes.

TWENTY-SEVEN

Jordan's thoughts swam like koi in a murky fountain. Every time she tried to reach for one, it slipped through her fingers and disappeared back into the dark. *Where am I? Where did Elliot go?*

Why was John Charles waiting in my room and what has he done to me?

It was pitch dark. She was lying down on a bed, that much she could tell. She tried hard to remember everything that happened after she felt the sting of a needle in her arm. She'd figured that much out, at least...

Jordan startled out of sleep again. She knew she'd been dreaming because she'd been in the garden with Elliot and now she was alone again in the dark and he wouldn't leave her like that.

No, he is gone. I told him to go. He'll end up in the fountain otherwise, just like before.

That wasn't right either. The fountain had been gone for years, taken out after Jordan pulled him from it. Poor Elliot had seen Daniel murder her father. He didn't want to remember, so she didn't want to make him remember, even now. Her mother had told her the little boy had jumped into the fountain to clean the memories out of his head and that they should never, ever talk about him again. That it was their way of protecting him, by keeping his secret. She had the fountain demolished after that so Jordan would forget, too.

But of course, she didn't forget. She *never* forgot the fountain or the boy she saved from drowning in it. Her Elliot. Her only friend. She remembered him until she was old enough to find him. She'd needed help with that—Elliot Lewis had seemingly disappeared off the face of the earth—but eventually, with the help of a private investigator, she'd found him.

Elliot Costello. He was a year into his career as a SEAL, and even though what he did was classified, she paid the investigator enough to dig a little deeper and provide her with regular updates through the years, updates she kept well-hidden from her family.

He may have changed his name to Costello, but he was still brave and good, and she'd hoped he was still kind. He'd grown up to be the most gorgeous man she'd ever seen. She started dreading whenever she saw an email with the next update. Would there be a wedding photo in this one, Elliot in a tux beside a beautiful woman? One who wasn't her.

So many times she resisted contacting him. He wanted to stay hidden, or he would have contacted her, right? She was easy enough to find, all he had to do was look her up on social media.

But he never did. He drifted out to sea, away from her.

Jordan woke again not even realizing she'd drifted off. *Stay awake. Remember what happened. You need to get out of here.*

But she could barely move. God, she was thirsty. How long had she been lying here?

John Charles. The needle. Then...Elliot. *Go away, Elliot.*

After that, she'd slept until her mother woke her and told her it was time to talk to some people about her life.

Jordan had done her best but she could barely keep her head up so she stared at her lap instead. She kept plucking at her nightgown—she shouldn't be wearing that if she had guests. They were asking questions and her mother was answering for her when she couldn't. They were all talking so fast she couldn't keep up. She'd gotten a couple of words out, she was sure of it, but what she'd said was lost to her.

She hoped the meeting wasn't anything important.

At some point, her mother helped her drink a glass of water, then there was another needle. Jordan had tried to fight John Charles when he jabbed her—why was her mother letting him do this?

"Because you're leaving the country and you need your shots first."

Jordan must have managed to ask her question out loud.

She remembered John Charles laughing and asking her mother, "Did you really just say th—"

And she was out again before she heard the answer.

A tear slid down her face as her head cleared just enough to realize she was in big danger. She tried to lift her head but it was the size of a boulder. She moved her arm and dropped her hand on her stomach. She was no longer wearing her nightgown, that much she could tell. She felt a zipper and soft cotton. A hoodie? She really was going somewhere. But where?

No place good. And someplace far away from Elliot.

She'd finally given in and contacted him when Marcus Porter scared her. Elliot was the only friend she could trust, her forever friend. He was a former SEAL. He could protect her.

He loved her. They were going away together.

Get up! Get up! Get away from here.

Light tore through the darkness and Jordan closed her eyes against it. But she'd seen enough to know she was still in Eden House, in the back bedroom. The trunk room, where all the luggage was stored in the olden days, as her dad called them.

"Time to go, Jordan." John Charles stood in the doorway, a shadowy silhouette blocking the light coming from the hall.

"No."

"Oh, yes. He's taken a liking to you, little sister." John Charles lifted her like a garment bag draped over his arms and carried her through the door. "Ever since meeting you in Italy especially. He's admired your work for a long time and he's been obsessed with the idea of having you design him a labyrinth to play with. Something to chase the little boys and girls around in. He calls them his sacrifices."

Jordan struggled to get out of John Charles' arms. She slid down and her feet touched the floor. He slapped her and scooped her up again.

"You're a couple decades too old to be one of his sacrifices, so calm the fuck down. Besides, he needs you to build him his toy." John Charles carried her down the hall to the stairs. "And I need you for collateral against the loan while I'm still getting the infrastructure set up so he can use our shipping services. It's a win-win."

Jordan tried to fight him again going down the stairs. So he set her down and dragged her.

"You...wouldn't fight me...if you saw...where you'll be living." He picked her up again at the bottom of the steps. "It's...a paradise, sis. I should know, because I've been his guest there a few times. You can have anything you want.

Anything." He laughed. "I was going to say that you wouldn't be interested in the hot and cold running sex, that all your frigid little heart wants is the chance to dig your little holes and plant your little seedlings, but you proved me wrong with your damn bodyguard, didn't you? Your mom told me she was very surprised to see the two of you walking back to your room from his. She thought you just kept things to the garden."

They were outside now. Late afternoon sunlight, but what day was this?

"We also thought he was just a bodyguard. But we did a little digging on him. Naughty Jordan. You had this all planned, didn't you?"

John Charles was carrying her to the garage. She thought of her little blue convertible—her father's favorite, the one she'd learned finally to drive. But now she'd miss her appointment to get her license.

Oh, God, and there was her luggage.

She struggled against him until her feet touched the driveway. He slapped her again. She wasn't in pain but figured she'd be in for a world of it after the stairs, once the drugs wore off. The slap stung though, so she used it to keep herself alert. When they were in the car, she just needed to stay awake enough to alert another driver to her situation.

If Costello didn't come for her first. He'd see her on the cameras, wouldn't he? The angels might have their eyes closed, but he wouldn't. He would see her and save her.

"You waking up a little, princess?" He had something in his hand.

"No." Jordan struggled to get away but he grabbed her wrists and zip-tied them together. She tried kicking him, even biting the top of his head, but it did no good. And then a sound in the distance growing louder distracted her.

Oh, God, no. Please. Elliot, please find me.

John Charles leaned in and whispered in her ear. "I drowned him once, Jordan. Your 'bodyguard'. Your *friend*, Elliot. If he comes after you, I'll drown him again. But this time, he'll stay dead."

TWENTY-EIGHT

C ostello spread the papers out on the conference table for Lachlan, Gina, and Nashville to see. They were back in con-one. The screen at the front of the room was now divided up into several smaller feeds, each from one of the active cameras around Eden House. Costello's attention swung back and forth between the shots of the garage and the angel gate—he wanted to know the second anyone came or went to the house—and presenting what he'd found to the others.

"Here's John Charles' motive for killing his father and endangering Jordan. This is the updated will. Leo Summers changed his will to leave everything to Jordan after he learned she wasn't his daughter."

"What?" Nashville leaned forward to read the paper. "But I thought the paternity test matched."

"Why would he leave everything to her after finding that out?" Lachlan asked.

"It matched because they were looking for it to match, and back then, the tests weren't as accurate as they are today. Leo left everything to Jordan because she's his *grand*-daughter."

Costello smacked one of the pages of the will with the back of his fist. "It's right there. Leo discovered that one of his *sons* was actually Jordan's father."

Nashville whistled.

"Leo was disgusted by Daphne and his sons so he quietly changed the will to exclude them. It's signed by a notary public, but it never made it to the lawyer's office. Why? Because my mother—my birth-mother—found it while she was snooping and stole the will. That's all outlined here," he angrily tapped another sheet of paper, "in this letter she wrote. I never would have thought my mother was one for a deathbed confessional, but she always was full of surprises."

Lachlan and Gina both stared at the pages, shocked.

Costello went on. "She heard the argument. Leo discovered the theft and thought either Daphne or one of his sons discovered the will and stole it. When he confronted John Charles, they fought and Leo was murdered. My mother saw the murder and later, I saw John Charles try to frame Daniel."

"This is unbelievable," Lachlan said. "Your mother tried to make you forget?"

Gina shook her head. "She would have made a phenomenal psy-ops agent."

Costello smiled ruefully. "Well, she made a decent black-mailer, as you can see from SSC's finances. My mother threatened to expose John Charles unless he paid her. That went on for five years, up until she was arrested. Then, nothing, no contact, until she somehow got a letter and a copy of the second will to Daniel."

Gina paced. "Daniel must have gotten it after he was released, then laid low until he disappeared."

"Any sign of him?" Costello asked.

"No. He's still in the wind. The two of you scared him off," Gina answered. "But we have enough here to go to the authorities, get John Charles arrested, and get Jordan out of there."

"What about Daphne?" Nash asked. "You think she knows?"

"I don't know and I don't care so long as Jordan is safe," Costello said.

The phone in the middle of the conference table beeped and Lachlan hit the button. "Gladys?" he answered the receptionist.

"There's a man here who would like to see you, sir."

"Tell him to relax, have a seat, I think y'all will wait a minute," Lach said, standing and pulling his sidearm.

The other three were already up and headed for the door, weapons drawn. Gladys used 'man' instead of 'gentleman' if she thought the 'guest' was a threat, and Lach had just told her that he, Gina, Costello, and Nashville were on their way, respectively. Gladys would silently lock the doors, secure the area, and get herself to safety as trained.

Costello came around the corner first into the lobby and stopped. He pointed his gun at their guest as the others caught up.

Daniel Summers stood alone at the receptionist's desk.

He looked even rougher than he did in the photos Gina had taken of him at the hotel. His hair was stringy, his beard grown out and scraggly, and his jeans and t-shirt were wrinkled and stained from sleeping on the ground in them.

Daniel put his hands up and locked his fingers behind his head. He turned slowly to show he wasn't carrying. He had the shuffle of a long-time prisoner going through a familiar routine.

It never should have been him Costello thought *An innocent man ruined by secrets and greed.*

"I'm unarmed," Daniel said. "I'm here for your help. Or to help you."

After they patted him down and made sure he was harmless, they escorted Daniel to the conference room. As soon as he saw the papers on the table, he sighed.

"There goes my biggest bargaining chip."

"Sit," Lachlan ordered Daniel. Everyone else stayed standing. "What do you want?"

"I'm here for your protection and to help Jordan if I can." He ran a hand through his greasy hair. The smell of his sweat was already filling the room.

"Talk," Lach said. "Let's start with, why do you need our protection?"

Daniel smirked. "It isn't obvious?" He gestured to the will, the copy of the letter. "My brother wants to kill me like he did our father." He eyed Costello. "Like he will Jordan."

"Not going to happen," Costello growled. "You laid low for quite a while. What made you think he was going to kill you all of a sudden? Unless he knows you have the will?"

"He might suspect I was the one who took it. I was shocked to get it, to find out about you or your mother. At first, I figured that John had no idea what had happened to the will. He'd left me alone, both in prison and once I got out. I'd kept track of Jordan the best I could and she seemed safe. So I thought I'd just go on with my life, pretend like I never saw that damn thing." He gestured at the table.

"Then I caught sight of those two thugs and knew I was being watched. I assumed it was John Charles keeping an eye on me, either making sure I wasn't going to approach Jordan, or waiting for the best opportunity to kill me. I couldn't take that chance so I paid up the room for the next week and sneaked away. I had to warn her if they were watching me; I thought the noose must be tightening around her neck, too. I hid out on the streets and crashed with a couple friends who got out before I did and owed me a favor. When I heard about the party, I knew I had a brief window to get in to talk to Jordan. Security would be tight, but I knew a way in that, with any luck, you'd all overlooked."

"The secret door in the wall behind the white rose garden. You took the path up from the beach and camped out in the grotto. You knew about it."

"I was Dad's favorite once. He didn't make that place for her, but for me when I was small. Not that I care. I'm glad she knew about it. I'm glad Jordan had something nice from my father, something for herself." Daniel swallowed hard.

Movement on the screen caught Costello's eye seconds before anyone else saw it. He lunged for the phone and hit Mike's extension in Surveillance. "Camera four, Mike, please."

"Whoa. You got it, Cos," Mike said over the phone. The screen changed; the other shots disappeared and Mike enlarged the feed from the garage camera.

"Shit. What's John Charles up to?" Costello asked as they watched the bastard carrying luggage to the wide bib of a driveway in front of the garage.

"Think he's made up with his fiancée and is moving back home?" Nashville said. "Me neither."

He disappeared out of the frame and Mike readjusted the camera to follow him. The next set of bags looked way too feminine with their flower design to belong to him. He dropped them beside the first set and disappeared back into the house.

"Those are Jordan's bags. I recognize them from when they arrived from Italy," Costello said. "He's taking her some-where. And wherever it is, he's going along."

"Damn. It could be anywhere," Gina said. She turned to

Daniel. "Does your family have any safehouses, other properties besides John Charles' place and the corporation?"

"No, unless they bought other properties while I was incarcerated."

Costello's gaze was glued to the screen as he said, "I want eyes on his place, I want eyes along the highway. I want LAX security, Van Nuys security, hell, every airport within a hundred-mile radius needs to be contacted and told to be on the lookout for John Charles and Jordan Summers." He glanced away just long enough to add. "Marcus Porter wants her on his island, and if the conservatorship goes through she's never coming back."

Lachlan nodded, grabbed the phone, and relayed the orders to Gladys.

"Jesus," Daniel said. "My brother's involved with *that* guy?" He stood up as his eyes darted around the room.

"Who do you think was watching you?" Gina asked. "We ID'ed them and traced their payments to one of Porter's accounts."

"You're not going anywhere," Nash added as he stood and walked to the door to block it.

"Then help me." Daniel implored as he looked at every face. "Help me save her."

"You're her real father, aren't you?" Costello asked.

Daniel nodded. "I'm pretty sure I am. Could be my fucking brother, but Jesus, I hope not. Daphne slept with all three of us. My father didn't know. If I'd known for sure Jordan was mine, I would have done the right thing and married her, too. You gotta believe me."

"I do believe you," Costello said.

"Dad took the paternity test. It looked like Jordan was his. My guess is Daphne slept with my father the moment she knew she was already pregnant, or maybe she already was sleeping with him but wasn't getting knocked up. So she slept with both of us just in case Dad was shooting blanks."

He shook his head. "Doesn't matter, does it? Not in the end. He loved Jordan like she was his daughter. She married my father to secure her own place at the top of the food chain. Nothing else would have been good enough."

"So your father discovered the lie, thought you all knew, changed the will, then confronted John Charles when it was stolen and your brother killed him."

"Before your mother wrote me that letter with the truth in it, I spent years thinking I was the one who killed Dad in a blackout. I've been consumed with guilt wondering how I could be such a monster." He looked Costello dead in the eye. "But I'm no monster, just a man with an addiction that was used against him. The monsters are my brother. And Daphne. And your mother. She saw the murder, then ran and hid. But worse, she kept hiding the truth later."

"I'm sorry."

"It wasn't you. Jesus Christ, you were as much a victim as I was, as Jordan is. They lied to all of us. But as angry as I am at Ellen Lewis for not coming forward and leaving me to rot in prison, I can understand her motives. I think I would've done the same damn thing. She was protecting her boy. In a fucked-up way for sure, make no mistake. But John Charles would have killed you if you'd ever slipped up or decided to talk."

Costello nodded. "I know. Because he didn't hesitate to try the first time. He thought he'd killed me and he walked away with no remorse."

"And that night if Jordan had come out of hiding just a few minutes earlier, he would have drowned her in the fountain right next to you."

"And if she'd come out one minute later than she did, I'd

be dead." Costello shuddered. "The angels watch over children, drunks, and fools."

"All right," Lachlan said. "LAX and Van Nuys have been alerted. Santa Barbara, too. Gladys is on the line with Airport in the Sky on Catalina and has Bob Hope Airport on hold." He fixed his hard stare on Costello, who was ready to burst out of his skin. "I know what you're thinking and the answer is no, you are *not* driving out there."

"Boss—"

"Costello." Gina laid her hand on his arm. Her eyes looked pained. "This has gotten way bigger than what you can handle, what Watchdog can handle. My friends are involved. They haven't been able to touch Porter and they see this as a way in."

"Dammit, I am *not* sacrificing her to him!" He shook her hand off his arm.

"That's not what I'm saying!" Gina shouted. The room went silent. No one had ever heard Gina raise her voice at one of the team. "They will handle it now. They'll have the airports covered. The highway, too, okay? But you need to stay out of the way." She'd gone back to her normal tone. "They'll want John Charles in one piece for questioning and I don't think you can guarantee that right now, can you?"

Costello started to answer when John Charles came back into view on the screen. Carrying a half-conscious Jordan. She struggled until she wiggled out of his arms and he slapped her.

Costello roared.

She slumped down on the cobblestones, next to the luggage. John Charles reached into his pocket and pulled something out. He grabbed her wrists.

"Fuck!" Costello shouted and Gina's hand was back on his arm. He was aware that Nashville had stepped closer to him. Lachlan stood and came around the table.

"Easy," Lach said like he was calming a spooked horse. "We've got eyes on the highway. Whichever direction they take, we'll alert that airport up the road they have incoming. And if he's got a hidey-hole here instead, we'll cover that, too."

But Lach's words faded into the background as Costello watched the screen. Something else was wrong. They weren't going into the garage. John Charles left Jordan on the ground and turned around.

"He's not taking his car. They're waiting for a ride," Costello said.

"We still have the feed on the gate," Lachlan said. "We'll see the car, ID the plate, alert Gina's friends, they'll be on it."

But Costello's blood turned to ice water. "No, they won't. There's no car coming for them."

No sound feed was attached to the cameras but if there had been, Costello knew that as John Charles looked up and shielded his eyes they would hear the *whump whump whump* of rotors turning.

The black helicopter landed on the wide cobblestone driveway a moment later.

Lachlan was back on the phone in an instant. "Get me the numbers on that fucking thing."

"There won't be any," Costello said. The camera zoomed out as John Charles picked up Jordan and carried her to the helicopter as another man got out and grabbed the bags. Every fiber of Costello's being wanted him to run to the parking garage, jump in his SUV, drive to Eden House, and rip John Charles' fucking head off. The helicopter lifted and the camera angle changed to follow, not a number to be seen on its shiny black carapace.

"Lach—"

"I'm already on it, Psychic." Lachlan barked more orders

into the phone, demanding all helicopter flight itineraries starting with LAX.

"Me, too." Then Gina did something she'd never done before—contacted her friends directly in front of the Watchdog team. "Orchid's airborne, traveling—" she looked at the screen but Costello was quicker with the answer.

"South by southeast," he said as he watched the helicopter shrink down to a black dot.

"Okay," Lach said. "Nailed down LAX, Santa Monica, and Cata—"

"They won't stop at any of those." Costello's voice was deadly calm. "That's an ACH135. They can make it to Mexico in an hour. From there..." *From there, she's gone* he thought then pushed it away. "...from there, they can load her onto a jet bound for the cays." He turned to Gina. "Unless you have someone in Tijuana."

Gina sighed and shook her head. "I'll see what I can do, but..."

Costello clenched his jaw. "I'm going to his island. I don't fucking care how I get there. I'll swim if I have to."

"Costello. We will get her back." Gina fixed him with determination in her golden eyes.

"That's a promise," Lachlan added.

Nashville clapped his hand on Costello's shoulder. "I'm here too, golden boy. We all are."

TWENTY-NINE

Mexico was a bust. Jordan was off the helicopter in Tijuana and onto Porter's Gulfstream before anyone could stop them. And the flight plan was straight for the Bahamas followed by another helicopter to Porter's island, Little Edward Cay. Photos from the airport showed that Jordan was at least able to walk under her own power between the airplane and the second helicopter and that John Charles was still with her, his hand gripping her arm and pulling her along.

It killed Costello to see her hands were still bound.

Costello shook the image from his mind and shut down his emotions—this time he really couldn't afford to let them cloud his thinking. He looked out the airplane window into the darkness. He couldn't discern the water from the night sky—stars and the lights from distant ships dotted both—and went over the plan in his mind. The Watchdog team followed a day and a half behind, but it felt like a hundred years to Costello. Gina had come through with intel about the island, Porter's compound, the movements of his guards. But it was limited—Marcus

Porter was so well-connected he was damn near a phantom.

Costello's team flew in a borrowed Gulfstream curtesy of Gina's friends. They had the toys for sure, but what they lacked was the authority to conduct the missions, or so they claimed. That's why they played so well with Watchdog—everything was off the books.

After landing, Watchdog would be rendezvousing with another team that had a similar arrangement. No names exchanged, just nicknames. No locations, no histories, no shoe sizes, or favorite sports teams. This was a first—they'd never teamed up with another group before. The other team would provide backup and support, but Watchdog was the tip of the spearhead.

Besides the crew, on board the Gulfstream were Costello, Nashville, Camden, and Kyle. Gina was there too after fighting with Lachlan about the mission.

"I'm going along," She'd told Lach at the planning stage when they were all in the 'war room' at Watchdog.

"You're needed here," Lach said without even looking up from his monitor.

"I said I'm going along, Lachlan."

He finally looked up at her resolute tone. "And I said, you're..." Lachlan's face changed to the softest expression any of them had even seen him make as realization dawned. He and Gina shared a look that held an entire conversation, one they'd probably had in private a hundred times. Finally, he nodded. "You're going along. I get it. Pardon my denseness."

"I always do." She grinned back.

"I'm glad to have you onboard," Costello said, and he meant it. He started rearranging the plan in his head to accommodate Gina and felt a hundred times more confident that Jordan would come home safely and quickly.

He still believed that as he looked around the cabin at his team. He could ask for no better teammates or friends.

They had all quieted down from their typical bantering about two hours into the flight. Even though she'd joked with them, Gina looked as tensed up as a coiled snake the entire time. Her expression was blank now but her eyes looked haunted. Times like these, Costello was reminded that Spooky originally got her nickname because none of them was sure if she was retired from the alphabets or if she was still an active CIA plant pretending to run a security company. She would neither confirm nor deny *any* status, but they'd all come to suspect the latter was the truth. This mission convinced Costello she must still be in it.

Or maybe something like it, something off the books.

"You okay, Gina?" he asked. She came back from whatever place she was at in her head and nodded.

"Just going over the mission," she answered. "Running through what little we know of the compound in my head." She gave him a thin smile. "Your plan is a good one and I agree with it one-hundred percent. But now that we're almost there, I have to tell you that I need to take a detour when we get there."

"A detour?"

She held up a hand. "It has nothing to do with your plan and I'm not trying to subvert it. I'll give you a heads up when it's time for me to break away and I'll report back in to help you finish your mission and get Jordan to safety."

Oh. Costello nodded. "Thank you for telling me. I trust you." He grinned ruefully. "I won't make you confirm or deny that you might have another...team leader."

Her smile widened but her eyes reflected sadness. "I appreciate that, Costello. You're a good friend. I appreciate that, too. I haven't had many. Not ones I could trust completely."

That touched him deeply. "Thank you. So are you." On impulse, he reached out and squeezed her hand. It was freezing cold. "Are you sure you're all right?"

"I'll have to be." Gina swallowed and her eyes flicked briefly to that dreaded thousand-yard stare, leaving him to wonder what her true mission was. Was she being sent in on a suicide mission to kill Porter?

No. She wouldn't have looked this haunted. A weapon like her never did.

Costello tried not to think of the alternatives.

"If you ever need someone to talk to, I'm pretty damn good at keeping secrets." He squeezed her hand before letting go.

She took a deep breath and pressed her lips together. She gave him a tight nod and that was enough.

The next night found the team waiting chin-deep in blood-warm water for the patrol boat to pass. The team they'd rendezvoused with flew them by seaplane to an uninhabited cay about five miles from their target. After swimming from sandbar to tiny island to sandbar in water that ranged from twenty feet deep to waist-deep, they were finally within sight of Little Edward Cay, Porter's nightmarish paradise. Thank God the moon was no more than a crescent that wouldn't give away their shapes in the mercifully calm water. They ducked underwater as the wake from the boat washed over them; all in a day's work for the former SEALs. They'd had to go slower than Costello wanted for Gina to keep up since she wasn't a former SEAL, but not by as much as he'd anticipated. She'd performed admirably and took her cues from them.

As the boat moved out of sight, Costello gave the signal and they moved forward. The beach was only a few hundred yards away. The water would get deeper before it got shallow again, but the tide was coming in. As the sand sank beneath them, Costello felt something big bump against his body and swim away. He hoped that at worst it was a curious black-tipped shark and not a hungry bull.

The narrow beach looked deserted. They were north and west of the compound in a section that had not been developed and landscaped yet so they had plenty of scrub for cover. Once they hit the beach, they scrambled across the sand and got under cover as soon as possible before anyone could see their dark suits against the light sand. They opened their dry bags and removed their weapons and comms. A quick gear check and they were ready to go.

They moved as a group about an eighth of a mile in. The island was quiet except for the sound of insects and the ever-present susurrus of waves and wind. Their intel had been good for once—no party at the compound tonight. Porter had pulled back on inviting guests over the last month according to flight itineraries, but that didn't mean he was here alone or that guests who wanted to remain discreet weren't enjoying a dark bit of paradise.

Once the compound came into view, Costello addressed Kyle and Camden over the comm.

"Pup and Joker, you good?"

"Affirmative," Kyle answered. "Meet at the rendezvous at oh-four-hundred." Then the two of them split off and headed toward the boathouse and docks to the north of the main house.

That left Costello, Nashville, and Gina to breach the

house, locate Jordan, and get the hell out. Gina was already playing with one of her toys—a thermal camera. She scanned the closest of three guest cottages and came up empty.

"We couldn't luck out and have the hostage in one of the cottages, could we?" Nashville said.

Gina scanned the second cottage. "Negative for two. Doesn't look like it, Nash."

For the third cottage, they needed to move in closer. They made it twenty feet before stopping and ducking into the brush as two guards passed, talking and joking—obviously unconcerned and completely unaware of their presence. Costello tried to tune out their conversation about how the latest 'shipment' needing to be cleaned up before the next party. Their jokes about the young girls sickened him.

Focus on the mission.

The thermal camera indicated the third cottage was occupied by three people. As they moved closer, voices coming from the screened door indicated one older man and two teenaged girls. Their drunken laughter spilled out followed by slaps and shrieks and more laughter.

Costello recognized one voice. John Charles.

Disgusted but hardly surprised, they moved past the cottage toward the main house, on the lookout for more roaming guards. Costello spotted the pair first. They were standing near the edge of a veranda in the shadows, quieter than the other two on patrol. Nash and Costello took them out quickly and silently while Gina scanned the house. There was no one in the first-floor room but someone was definitely up on the second. The person was lying down, probably in bed, making it impossible to determine their size.

They rounded the veranda. No other guards outside.

Porter must feel cocky when he's at home.

Kyle's voice came over the comm. "In position. Rendezvous secured."

"Copy," Costello said, followed by Gina and Nashville.

"Here's where I leave you for a bit," Gina said.

"Godspeed, Spooky," Costello answered and was met with silence. She was already gone into the shadows.

He jerked his chin and he and Nash silently climbed the steps and entered the house. They quickly swept the dimly lit foyer despite the reassurance that no one was there. The house had interior cameras and they had to move fast. They climbed the wide front staircase and split up at the top, Nashville going left and Costello moving along the hall to the right. He prayed the person lying in the bed was Jordan. He went all the way down the hall to the last room.

The door was closed and padlocked—from the outside. If she wasn't in there, then he had another hostage to deal with. His heart pounded as he busted the lock and threw the door open.

The small figure in the bed drew in a sharp breath and sat up.

"Jor—"

Before he could get out her name, she flew at him, her arm outstretched. He caught her wrist first before she could stab him with what looked like a mirror shard wrapped in cloth. Then he pulled her into him.

"Beloved, it's Elliot."

"Elliot?" She whispered, searching his face. "I knew you'd come." Then she buried her face in his chest. She was fully dressed and apparently ready to go.

Costello spoke into the comm. "Hostage secured." He received four 'copies' in return. "Nashville, to me."

"Copy."

Costello lifted her chin. "Can you run?"

Jordan nodded. "They drugged me but not today. I can run." She let go of him and crouched. He bent to pick her up thinking she'd collapsed but she was only retrieving her makeshift weapon.

"No time," he said, scooping her up and carrying her to the door. "You want a knife, I've got knives, but you won't need one."

"But I made mine out of the mirror from my eye shadow palette and I'm proud of it, dammit."

Costello couldn't hold back a shocked laugh. His woman amazed him.

Nashville was already at the top of the stairs. He smiled when he saw Jordan then his gaze flicked to Costello's. "Swear I was right outside Porter's door. We could take him—"

Costello felt more than heard a rhythmic sound downstairs. "No time!" he said, turning and setting Jordan down behind them as two men raced into the house through the front door. "Stay down," he told her.

Nashville was already firing when Costello turned back around and added to the assault. The guards got off two shots before Nashville and Costello took them out.

Costello pulled Jordan to her feet and the three raced downstairs. When they got to the front door, he maneuvered her against the wall, then he and Nashville flanked the door.

"Down," he told her again, and she dropped just as guns fired and bullets blew holes in the wall right above her head.

More racing footsteps. More gunfire. Two more dead guards.

Costello grabbed Jordan's hand and they ran across the veranda, down the steps, and into the night. They needed to backtrack past the cottages and into the brush, back toward the boathouse. As they approached the cottages, they heard the girls' hysterical crying.

"Someone's shooting!" One of them yelled.

"Shut the fuck up, do you want whoever's out there to find us?" John Charles shouted even louder.

Running past the cottage, Jordan barely slowed at her brother's voice. But it was enough to distract her and she stumbled.

As Costello swooped her up into his arms, John Charles came to the door in time to see them running.

"Jordan! Fuck!" he called out behind them. "Fuck, you can't leave, he'll fucking skin me!" Costello heard his clumsy, drunken footsteps following behind them.

"Elliot," Jordan said.

He read her tone. *Jesus.* The man had sold her into slavery and she still had the heart to try and save him. He shook his head.

"No. The girls," she said softly, crushing his heart.

John Charles' footsteps faded behind them.

The comm crackled. "I'm...coming back...Psychic," Gina said. Dread filled him at the cold and haunted tone of her voice.

"We're nearing the rendezvous, Spooky."

"Copy. I've got you in my sights. Coming at five o'clock."

And suddenly she was there just over his left shoulder, her face ten shades paler and seeming to float in the darkness over her black clothing. Jordan startled in his arms and he gave her a reassuring squeeze.

"Mission accomplished?" he asked Gina as they moved quickly through the brush.

He thought maybe she hadn't heard him when she didn't answer right away. Then she said, "Yes. But not to *my* satisfaction." Her voice held a tremor he'd never heard there before. For the first time, Costello thought he might not want to know what she'd seen and done.

Or, maybe *not* done. A sick feeling crept over him. *Oh, God. God, no. Oh, Gina.*

Spooky spied. That's what she did best. And sometimes spies could only watch instead of act on the atrocities they were sent to document.

Costello's mission was to save only one captive. But there were others on the island who needed saving, too. Lost little girls. They'd heard two of them but Gina had *seen* the rest. Recorded them. Was returning with proof of their captivity.

But not *with* them. That wasn't part of her other commander's orders.

All of this speculation flashed through his mind as they were running toward the boathouse.

"Spooky?"

"Cages, Costello. The...filth."

He resolved to let her debrief with him as much as she could allow herself. And he would tell her how much Arden had helped him dig some of the darkness out of his soul.

"Pup. Joker. Coming in. Ready?" Costello asked.

"Affirmative."

A bullet whizzed past Costello's head.

"Incoming hostiles."

Kyle and Camden flanked the door as Costello and Nash had earlier. Gina and Nashville joined them. They returned gunfire as Costello loaded Jordan into one of the speedboats. "Let's go, let's go!" he shouted before starting the engine. Still shooting, the rest of the team backed up and then got in. Costello piloted the boat out as guards filled the boathouse. They'd be sorely disappointed to find the other two engines sabotaged.

They sped over the dark waters on their way to the cay where the seaplane and the other team waited. Camden searched the boat for anything useful in case the patrol boat caught up with them.

"Oh, now this is fun."

"What have you got?" Costello asked, still speaking over the comm.

"LG 440 grenade launcher. Hmm. Wonder if these are exploding rounds."

Costello grinned. "Looks like you'll have a chance to find out. Three o'clock."

"Goddamn, Psychic. How the fuck did you see—"

The patrol boat speeding toward them had its own toys. Something flew at them and splashed into the water about ten feet away, sending up a wall of spray and rocking the boat.

"Give it here," Nashville said to Camden. "I'm the better shot." He grabbed the launcher, stood at the back of the boat, and fired.

Camden had his answer about the rounds when the patrol boat disappeared in a ball of fire and fiberglass.

They had no trouble the rest of the way to the waiting seaplane.

THIRTY

One week later

Costello walked from Lachlan's office to the courtyard and then into the kennel area. It was late in the day, obedience classes were over, and the younger resident dogs were barking excitedly, waiting for their turn to be fed. He was not surprised to see Kyle putzing around the kennels, giving every dog a head-scratch as he filled their food bowls, Camo right at his heels like he was second-in-command.

"What are you doing here, Pup? Don't you have your own agency to run?"

Kyle filled the last bowl, set it down, and looked up with a grin. "I'm already feeling nostalgic for the good old days." The two clapped each other on the shoulder. "We'll be heading back to Colorado tomorrow. There's a music festival coming up we'll need to cover. Rachael will be there and I want to make sure everything is solid."

"You've got this, Pup."

Kyle's expression turned serious. "Heard you had a meeting. So. How'd it go?"

Costello grinned. "I'm here to get my dog out of hock."

Kyle's smile practically reached ear-to-ear. "That's great." Then it disappeared and his brows turned down. "I mean, that sucks."

"Sucks?"

"Well, yeah. Because if Lach was letting you go, I was going to offer you a job. I've got an agency to build."

That went straight to Costello's gut. "Even after all this?"

"Man, the heart wants what it wants and it don't listen to reason. All those years ago, wow, you two made that connection and Jordan held on to it. Called you when she needed you and you were there for her because you'd held on to it too. Your heart remembered, even if your head let you down. But you listened to your heart even if you couldn't believe. If you'd gone with your head and not your heart, I think Jordan would've gone to that island sooner and she'd sure as hell would still be there. So yeah, I need guys like you on my team, men who know what's important."

"Damn, brother. Thank you. That means a lot." Costello squeezed the bridge of his nose. "I was worried about betraying everyone's trust and never getting it back."

"You've been here for us so many times, man, and you will be again. We knew that. Lachlan knows it. That's why you're still here, right?"

"Yeah. Even if it's the second ring now, I'm still here."

"No shame in that game, brother. You can spot danger from a mile away and a week before it happens. You're still gonna save lives."

He nodded. Yeah, he would. But he couldn't quite shake the shame of being knocked down a peg.

"Dude, I can see that shame you're hanging on to and I'm telling you to fucking drop it. Voice of experience here— they forced me out of the service and gave me an other than honorable discharge. I carried that motherfucker on my back for years. Even though I'd done the right thing, the world told me I'd fucked up and I believed it. I *acted* like it. It wasn't until I met Arden and she set me straight that I was able to drop that bullshit and rise above it. You've got Jordan now, and I think she's gonna help you sort your shit, too."

Costello nodded. "She already is."

"Then *let* her, man. In her eyes, you're always gonna be perfect, even when you aren't."

Costello chuckled. "Thanks, brother." At least he had Kyle's trust back. It was still going to take some time before he and Nashville were completely square and that bothered him. Nash was taking some time off. He'd told everyone he'd been planning on it anyway, but Costello couldn't help thinking that he'd instigated the leave.

"So, let's get your dog outta hock." Kyle started walking to the far end of the row of kennels and Costello followed. "See, that's another good sign. No way Lach would let you have Anubis back if he wasn't planning on keeping you long-term. He loves these dogs way the hell more than he gives a shit about us." He chuckled.

"You're the only person I know who loves dogs more than Lach does, Pup."

"Damn straight I do, but don't tell him that unless you feel like fighting." They reached the farthest kennel. Anubis waited patiently inside, posing like his namesake Egyptian statue with his legs straight out in front of him and his head up, nose pointed forward.

But as soon as he saw Costello, he broke his pose, stood up, and ran to the front of the kennel, tail wagging hard enough to put Reggie's to shame.

"Hey, buddy. I missed you," Costello said as he knelt down while Kyle opened the door. Anubis went straight to him, tail wagging and tongue licking. Costello ran his hands over the dog's head and down his flanks. "Who's a good boy? You're a good boy. And Jordan's beside herself missing you, too."

Kyle shook his head and grinned. "Yeah, I knew that pairing would work out."

Costello couldn't agree more. He clipped the leash Kyle handed him onto Anubis' collar. "All right, partner, We have a very important mission."

An hour later, Costello, Anubis, and Jordan were almost to Eden House.

Costello reached across to the passenger's side and took Jordan's hand. "How are you doing?"

Jordan squeezed his hand. She looked at him and smiled "I'm going home, finally. With the man I've loved all my life. You promised me this day, and here it is."

God, could I love her any more than I already do? His heart squeezed at what she'd gone through—the drugging, the kidnapping, the heartbreak of discovering the man she thought was her father was probably her grandfather instead. Now she was facing one last challenge, in some ways the hardest, most necessary one, but she was facing it with a smile and an open heart looking toward the future. And this amazing woman loved him and wanted him at her side. Trusted him. Believed he was a good man.

Kyle was right. Jordan was healing him. He would do everything in his power to give her all the happiness, love, and devotion she deserved in return.

He glanced at the fading scratch marks on her arms—not self-inflicted it turned out, but from her mother's nails. Anything to make Jordan look unstable.

"I don't know where you're finding the strength to face this day," he said quietly.

"He's sitting next to me."

Straight to the heart.

"I love you." He made the turn onto the drive that led to Eden House. "And I'll do anything and everything to protect you. You can wait in the truck until it's over."

"No. I have you and Nubie with me. I will be fine, and it will be over, and we won't lose a minute more of living our lives together where we belong."

She sounded so strong and so sure of herself. A woman in charge of her life and looking forward to nothing but happiness.

Tonight, he would add to her happiness. But first, they had to take out the trash.

The three of them walked up the steps to the front entrance, only the second time Costello had ever walked through those doors. The first time, he'd been a boy made to feel like an adult too soon. On the other side of the door had waited a girl who would always be made to feel like a child.

Together, they would create a bond to last their lifetimes.

"Cycles," Costello heard Jordan whisper to herself. He didn't need to be psychic to know exactly what she was thinking.

He reached into his pocket, took out the key, and handed it to her. Anubis waited on guard as she unlocked the double doors and threw them open wide, letting the sun pour in across the floor.

They found Daphne in Leo's old study. She sat behind his

desk, hands folded on its surface, nails painted bright red. The smell of roses permeated the shut-up room.

Her eyes glittered like cold diamonds up at them. Her smile was a colder scythe.

"Happy birthday, darling. Come to gloat? To kick me out?"

"The truth is, I'm surprised you're still here," Jordan said. "The eviction notice has been on the front door for days, and today is your last one."

"Well, I can see you haven't gotten any wiser about money. It's impossible to go anywhere or do anything if you don't have any. Which, thanks to you, I don't. All my accounts are now empty."

"Oh, well, I was just taking back what was mine to begin with. Thirty million you managed to siphon off for yourself. But hey, thanks for the two million you put aside for me, though I honestly think you were just hiding that from the tax collector."

Daphne tilted her head and shrugged. "Maybe you have wizened up a bit." She looked at Costello. "But only when it comes to money, which I'm sure this criminal will take from you as quickly as he can."

Jordan beamed up at Costello, her face full of beauty. "I don't think so. He's done nothing but save me, from the moment we met."

"We save each other," he whispered back, then kissed her forehead. He tore his gaze away to look at Daphne. "But speaking of criminals, I have some bad news for you."

Daphne waved him off with a bitter laugh. "I already heard. How much of John Charles did they actually find washed up on the shore?"

"Enough to know he was probably still alive when the

sharks got to him. Though, not all in one piece even at that point. Blood does draw them." He watched for any sign that the news that her lover was dead affected her and got nothing back. "But that's not what we were going to talk about."

Jordan placed her hand on Costello's arm, quieting him. She couldn't meet her mother's eyes as she said, "I'm only going to ask you one question today. If you respect me, if you *love* me, you'll tell me the truth, whatever it is, so that I can decide how to feel about you."

"And what's the question?"

Jordan took a deep breath. "How could you?"

"How could I what, darling?"

Jesus. The woman had nerve.

"How could you let me...no. How could you *sell me* to the devil?"

Daphne looked affronted. "I never *sold* you to anyone. It was in your best interests that you take that commission. You needed a break, like you said. It was obvious from your behavior in Italy and at the party. Even at your evaluation, they said they wouldn't trust you to tie your own shoes let alone run your financial empire. So, instead of letting you stay in this place that made you so much worse," she glared at Costello, "and to get you away from *that* horrible man, Mr. Porter agreed to give you a second chance with the commission and I took him up on it." Her voice turned self-righteous. "It was for your own good, Jordan, and one day, I hope you'll understand how I've always tried to protect you, and how much you have hurt me by not trusting me."

Not that Costello had expected anything but denial from Daphne, but to actually witness the level of it shocked him. Jordan too, by the way she started shaking. He put his arm around her and pulled her against his side. He would never,

ever let her suffer again. Even now he hated what she was doing, but knew she needed to do this hard thing. The best he could do was be present as a witness and to put her back together if she needed it afterward.

Then Jordan stopped shaking. She straightened up and said, "John Charles *drugged* me. You let him—"

Daphne shook her head. "This is why you need me. You have no idea...we gave you a mild sedative to calm you down."

Jordan's mouth dropped open. "Marcus Porter keeps little girls in cages. He does terrible things to them. You *drugged* me, tried to make me helpless, and then you sent me straight to him."

Daphne shrugged. "That's all rumor and hearsay."

Now Costello was shaking with fury.

Jordan's voice got louder but stayed firm. "It's not just rumors, it's true."

"Well, if it is true, like you said, he keeps *little* girls in cages, Jordan, and you are no little girl, obviously." Her gaze flicked again to Costello. "Besides, he needed you for other things. You were his *guest* and he treats his guests very well. So you were perfectly safe. Much safer than you are now that you've ruined everything."

Costello looked at Jordan. Her expression was unreadable, but she stood perfectly still. "I can't tell if you believe everything that just came out of your mouth. If you do, then I pity you. If you don't, if you really expect me to believe this twisted lie you've made up..." She shook her head. "Then, I don't think I can love you anymore."

Any mother with a heart would have been devastated by that Costello thought.

Daphne looked down at her hands and sucked in her cheeks. She looked back up and said, "Well, I don't need your pity. And if your love is going to be that conditional, then I don't need your love, either."

So she's proven she doesn't have a heart. Costello tightened his arm around Jordan and gave her a reassuring squeeze.

Anubis turned his head at the same time Costello heard sure and steady footsteps coming up behind them.

Daphne smirked. "Are those the bouncers coming to drag me out of my house? Some more of your thug-friends?"

"It's *my* house, Mother," Jordan said, her eyes not quite meeting Daphne's. "It's always been mine, all of it has. But I'm turning SSC over to Daniel, who should have had it long ago. I wish him well; he's got a hard time ahead of him." Jordan met her mother's gaze. "You have a hard time ahead of you, too, but I don't think I'm going to wish you well."

Two uniformed policemen walked into the study. One looked at Costello and said, "You were right, Mr. Costello, all we had to do was follow the smell of roses." The officers approached her to the left, handcuffs out.

Daphne stood up quickly enough to send the office chair rolling into the curtained window behind it. "What is this? What is happening?" She tried to escape from the other side of the desk but Anubis was already waiting for her, teeth bared.

"Daphne Summers, you are under arrest for being an accomplice to the kidnapping of your daughter, Jordan Summers. You have the right to remain silent—"

"She's lying! I want my *lawyer*," Daphne shrieked as they cuffed her. "I will sue!" She whipped her head around to stare down Jordan one last time. "I will disown you, and I will sue for what's mine! You are not my daughter. *You are not my daughter.*"

She shouted that and worse as they dragged her through

the house and out the door. Costello wrapped Jordan in his arms and held her. They swayed for a while as he wordlessly nuzzled in her hair. Then she smiled up at him, kissed his lips, and pulled away. She walked around her father's desk and pulled the curtains back, then opened the doors out onto the garden. A clean, salty ocean breeze blew in.

The reek of rose perfume faded from the room.

THIRTY-ONE

After Jordan opened the door to let the fresh air in, she turned to see Elliot watching her the way he sometimes did as if she were a rare flower suddenly and unexpectedly in bloom.

"What?" she asked.

"Standing there with the light behind you, you look like an angel. Don't move." He walked toward her, Anubis on his heels. When he stood inches from her, Elliot cupped her cheek. He ran his thumb across her lips. "Are you all right?"

Jordan thought she would feel devastated watching her mother arrested. She also thought there would be tears, maybe an apology from her mother once the truth was laid out. Watching Daphne in the midst of denial instead, Jordan realized she'd lost her mother a long time ago, if she'd ever had her in the first place. Her time of mourning was long over.

She nodded. "Yes. I'm all right. Finally."

Elliot breathed a sigh of relief. "Good." He kissed her gently, reverently. She leaned into him and he held her tightly. Then he said, "Let's go outside."

She knew exactly where they were going as they crossed

the courtyard and headed for the wilder part of the garden. He opened the wooden gate and let her pass through ahead of him.

The grotto had been cleared of Daniel's things. It was strange to think of him as her father and Leo as her grandfather. So she decided not to. Not everything had to change. Only the things she wanted to prune out of her life so that other things could grow there instead.

Friendships. Community. Love.

When she turned, Elliot was down on one knee, a small box in his hand. Anubis sat beside him looking especially serious; so much so, it made her laugh. She covered her mouth, realizing how inappropriate it probably was to laugh at a man who was about to propose marriage. *Oh, God, I've ruined it* she thought. But as that thought raced through her head, Elliot glanced at Anubis, and wonder of wonders, he started laughing too.

He ran a hand over the dog's head. "Thanks, buddy. I was incredibly nervous."

Jordan tilted her head. "Why would you be nervous?"

"Why? Because what if you say no?"

Jordan laughed again. "I don't understand. Why would I say no?" She clasped his hand holding the box between hers. "My whole life has been leading me back to you. The boy in the fountain has become the most amazing man I've ever met. He's brave and intelligent. He's selfless and caring. He's protective and yet helps me grow in ways I never imagined. *And* he's drop-dead sexy." Heat blossomed in her cheeks. "I love you so of course I'm going to marry you."

Elliot closed his eyes and swallowed. When he opened his eyes again, they shined up at her with all the love in the world. "Now I'm the one who can't think of what to say, and I'd even scripted and practiced my proposal. But you've wiped it clear out of my head except for the most important part—I love you, Jordan. You have always been my guide, even when I didn't know it. You saved my life in more ways than one. I want to spend the rest of my life with you, making you happy, watching you grow and thrive. I want us to have a family someday, to bring life and love back into this house."

Sudden tears welled up from someplace deep in her heart. A family—a real, loving family. "I want that, too. But I want it sooner rather than later. So, you'd better go ahead and propose even though you already know the answer."

Elliot laughed again. "Jordan Summers, will you marry me?"

"Yes, Elliot Costello, I will marry you."

Jordan awoke as the first light of dawn stole through the sheer curtains. Elliot was still asleep, his arm curled protectively around her. He'd slept deeply every night since getting back to California. He told her his migraines were gone and his dreams were all good now that he was living in his best dream.

She had to agree. She watched the light hit her diamond engagement ring as she spread her fingers across his bare chest.

Elliot stirred and blinked as he awoke. His hand covered hers and he looked into her eyes. "Good morning, beloved." She loved his growly, first-thing-in-the-morning voice.

"Good morning to you." She arched her neck and back. He kissed her throat mid-stretch and she sighed. She could have spent all day in bed with him like they had a couple of times now, but today was another big day.

The day he would introduce her to his family.

She was nervous meeting them. "Tell me three things about each of your parents and your brothers and sister," she'd asked him over dinner on the patio the night before.

"Why do you want me to do that?"

"So that I know what to talk about ahead of time. I mean, I know Pat played Little League so I already did some research on baseball."

Elliot laughed. "That was quite a few years ago, love."

"Okay, so update me. What does he like to talk about now? I need to practice what I'm going to say."

Elliot reached out and stroked her cheek. "You don't need to practice a thing, beloved. They're going to love you as much as I do." He took her hand and kissed it, and together they'd walked through the garden to the secret door and made love in their grotto.

Now he kissed her hand again. "You're still worried about meeting my family, aren't you?"

Jordan nodded. "Just a little. I hope they understand, oh, everything." She shook her head. "Starting with not celebrating my birthday with them."

He kissed her hand. "Next year you will. Mom will insist."

"And I will say yes. I would rather have been with them for this one."

"They understand this birthday was a little...different."

The clicking of toenails on wood let them know Anubis was on his way in to the bedroom. "And there's our alarm clock," Elliot said. "Time to get up."

They showered together, got dressed—with a little detour that led them straight back to bed and hopefully the start of their new family—then had breakfast. Jordan looked over the garden and made plans in anticipation of the next crew coming in.

Elliot appeared next to her. "Jordan, time to get ready." She'd lost track of time again. She stood, brushed off the dirt from her hands onto her overalls, then went inside to change, carrying the flowers she'd use to make bouquets.

———

Before they arrived at the Costellos' house, they took one detour Jordan had suggested, then insisted on when he told her he wanted her to meet his family. Elliot had balked at first, then agreed. "You're right," he finally conceded. "Of course you're right."

Now they stood in a quiet spot before a headstone. Elliot had not visited his mother's grave before. Jordan handed him the bouquet she'd made, which included a branch of cedar for loss.

Elliot knelt at the grave. "Hey, Mom. It's been a while." He blew out a breath. "I'm just going to get to the point. I was angry at you for a long time. I thought I needed to be perfect in order to cover up who I was, who I thought you made me. I thought you'd abandoned me because I couldn't be useful to you, that I wasn't the only thing you thought worth keeping anymore. Not long ago, I had to give up my partner, and I did it to protect him." He glanced at Anubis standing guard beside him. "I did it because I didn't think I was good enough for him and that he would be better off with someone else. And that made me realize you did the same thing for me when you found out the Costellos wanted to adopt me. You didn't abandon me; you gave me a chance at a better life. You did your best to try and redeem yourself at the end, Mama Owl. You were so far from perfect, but you did your best. And I forgive you."

He laid the bouquet over his mother's grave. Then he

kissed his fingers and touched the stone. Jordan took his hand as he stood, and together, they went to meet the rest of his family.

R hea Costello opened the front door before they'd even gotten halfway across the front porch. Elliot's mom took one look at Jordan, smiled, and opened her arms without a word. Jordan smiled back, mentally threw away her practiced, opening lines, and walked into the woman's embrace. Getting a hug from Rhea made Jordan feel like a flower opening to the sun for the first time. Jordan wondered at the tears that suddenly sprang to her eyes but welcomed the woman's warmth into her heart.

Even better, Jordan felt another pair of arms go around her from behind as Elliot hugged her and his mother both.

"This is her, Mom. The woman of my dreams. Feels good to finally introduce the two most important women in my life to each other."

Jordan's heart pounded at those words. Now her tears fell in earnest.

Elliot gave them a squeeze then stepped back. Rhea looked Jordan in the face. She was crying, too. Both women smiled through their tears. It was funny how even though Elliot was not related to this woman by blood, she swore he had Rhea's eyes. Jordan decided it was the identical loving light that shone in them.

"Welcome to our family, Jordan," Rhea said.

Yup, every scripted word was gone. "Thank you. I feel like I already know you through Elliot's goodness, and bravery, and love."

Jordan heard Elliot suck in a breath behind her. Then his

hand was at the small of her back, supporting her. Anubis walked beside her after receiving a good head scratch from Rhea.

Rhea smiled and said, "Come on in and meet the rest of your family. They're as excited and happy as I am."

And they were, as they stood around the kitchen table, a birthday cake decorated with flowers and lit candles in the center.

"Happy birthday, beloved," he whispered in her ear.

Jordan turned her head, kissed his cheek, and said, "Thanks to you, I feel reborn."

THIRTY-TWO

N*ashville Jones*
Three Weeks Later

G *reat.* Nashville Jones was driving along the highway headed back to the last place he wanted to be right now.

Eden House. For *another* party.

It wasn't that he didn't like Jordan—he did, a lot, actually. She was one strong, sweet lady and he was happy for her now that she was out from under her mother's shadow. And it wasn't that he didn't want to hang out with his friends—he was always up for a good time.

It was that Camden and Elena would be there. And that meant Elena's friend Elissa would be, too.

The last time he'd seen her was also at Eden House. He was following Jordan Summers straight to the room he'd hoped to avoid during that fancy-schmancy party and that was the kitchen. Sure enough, he was coming in one door and

Elissa was coming in the other, and boom, their eyes met. She had the bluest eyes he'd ever seen under a fringe of hair the color of hot, sunny sand, light against her tanned skin. Yes sir, she fit the bill for the quintessential California girl. Which meant the quintessential *Nashville* girl as far as he was concerned.

Too bad she was always dating one loser or another.

Judging by the ones he'd seen, Nash did not fit her bill. These guys all ran to a type and that type was slick. Gelled hair; bodies sculpted, not built; and a wardrobe that rivaled any woman's. What the hell did a grown man need seventy-five pairs of tennis shoes for?

"Sneakerhead," Nash muttered under his breath. He turned up the SUV radio and shook his head. That was how Elissa had described her latest boyfriend.

"His entire spare room is like a shrine to his shoes," Elissa had told Elena while they were setting up for the party. Unseen, Nashville had listened in while he waited for Daphne to come downstairs after her second wardrobe change. "He pretty much turned the whole thing into a giant closet with shelves and an air purifier so they won't get dusty. Not that they ever come out of their boxes unless he's showing them to me."

Now isn't that a fine way to show a lady a good time, hanging out in your closet with all your damn shoes? Nash could think of a thousand places he'd rather be with Elissa given half a chance, and there was no way he'd be showing her his *shoes.*

"And he won't even let me touch them in case my hands are dirty, can you believe that?"

He continued his imaginary conversation with her. *You can touch anything of mine you want, sugar, and just so's we're clear, I'm a big ol' fan of ladies with dirty hands.* Nash blew out a breath. If he kept those thoughts up, he'd be making his own hand dirty the minute he was alone.

"Lis, why do you date these guys?" Elena asked. "He sounds like an uptight prick."

Fist bump, Elena! Remind me to buy you flowers or kitchen utensils or some damn thing like that.

Elissa laughed, but it didn't sound like a particularly happy one. "Oh, I don't know. It's fine. It's not like I'm looking for anything permanent, you know? He's good enough."

"Good enough?" Elena sounded incredulous. Nash could just see her standing there with one flour-covered hand on her hip. "You deserve better than *good enough*, chica."

Damn straight you do, sugar. Damn straight.

"What? He fulfills my two requirements right now: he has a degree from Stanford so my parentals aren't getting on my case, and he's athletic. He promised to come with me to Hawaii for the race."

Hawaii? That sent a painful jolt to Nash's heart. *Why does it have to be Hawaii?*

High-heeled footsteps and rose perfume alerted Nash to Daphne's imminent presence. "I'm *almost* ready to meet our star guest, Nash," she said as she strutted down the hall. The two women in the kitchen immediately hushed up when they heard her. *Well, shit.* Now they probably knew he'd heard everything.

Daphne stopped in front of him and turned around. Her dress had a zipper in the back that was open down to the crack of her ass and the top of her lacy red thong. She wasn't wearing a bra. "A little help, big guy? I just can't seem to reach."

Jesus wept. Really? He sighed again. No use trying to fight her or she'd come up with something nasty to do or say at the worst possible time and place. He grabbed the zipper and tried to pull it up as quickly as he could.

Not quickly enough. Elissa stuck her head around the corner just in time to see him.

"Mmmm, you've done this before," Daphne purred as she looked over her shoulder. When she spotted Elissa, she added, "Sorry the zipper was going up, not down, this time."

Elissa's eyes went round. Nash stepped back like Daphne had just caught fire. Daphne laughed and headed down the hall toward the foyer to lie in wait for Bette.

He turned toward Elissa, hoping to clear things up. "I—" But she was already back in the kitchen.

Things only looked worse later as he escorted Daphne away from the party after she attacked Jordan. The woman draped herself on his arm like a dead possum. He was half-carrying her through the house, laying the sugar on thick just to get her away without another scene. Elissa had been coming out at that moment with a fresh tray of food. She couldn't look away fast enough.

After he'd deposited Daphne in her room with a glass of vodka and his wingman, Reggie on guard, he came down to the kitchen for the bottle of water she'd requested. And there was Elissa again. He wanted to tell her that everything she'd seen was just not the God's honest truth. The woman was a skank and there was nothing at all going on.

What came out was, "I'm getting a bottle of water for Daphne in her room."

Well, shit.

"Don't let me stop you." She stepped away from the refrigerator, her eyes downcast and her cheeks blazing.

"Jordan's outside, bleeding. I need to see to her too."

She looked up, shocked, then immediately composed herself and dashed across the kitchen. She opened a box on the counter. "First-aid kit right here. And I've had some para-medic training." She rummaged through until she came up with bandages and ointment. "Go on upstairs, I got this."

So, the woman was a grade-A programmer, she went to culinary school, she surfed and was going to be in some sort of race, *and* she had paramedic skills? Not to mention she was kind, sweet, and funny. All wrapped up in a smokin' hot body.

"Elissa?" he said before she left the kitchen.

She looked up. "Really, I promise, I got this." She turned and started toward the door.

"I know that, sugar."

That stopped her in her tracks.

"Just wanted you to know you deserve more than good *enough*."

He heard her take in a breath but she didn't turn around. She hurried out the door instead.

She only moved faster to get away from him a few minutes later when he came back outside to check on the situation. And she was long gone before he could talk to her again.

Nash hadn't seen hide nor hair of her since and that was fine. He didn't need the reminder that he'd blown it with Elissa. Not that he'd had a real chance.

Good enough.

Hell, he wasn't even that. Not for her. She was obviously not interested.

Now he had to face her again. Would she pretend he hadn't said anything? Would he? Nash groaned—what if she brought along ol' Sneakerhead? He wouldn't be able to resist; he'd grab Jake and Camden and fill them in—hell, Camden probably already knew the sitch—and then pummel the shit out of him.

Verbally. Only verbally. Just because everyone thought Nashville was a hick from the holler didn't mean he was. But Sneakerhead wouldn't know his ass from a pickle barrel once the three of them got out a few one-liners at his expense.

Nash parked alongside the other vehicles, let Reggie out, waved at the cameras, and walked through the open house to the gardens.

And there she was. Elissa was in a sky-blue slip dress that matched her eyes, sipping a glass of white wine and talking to Elena and Rachael. Her hair was down in the back and pinned up on the sides and she looked so good he could have eaten her up with a spoon. Then he noticed her usual smile was gone. She looked devastated.

Nash looked around for any strange assholes wearing tennis shoes that could lift a mortgage. Fuck pummeling him verbally; if that son of a bitch hurt her...

No one there fit that description. Nothing but friendlies as far as the eye could see.

"Hey, Nash." Camden walked up next to him, two beers in his hands. He handed one to him.

"Thanks, friend." He popped the top and took a swig. Now all three women looked upset—Elena and Rachael looked fit to be tied and Elissa was even sadder. Nash tipped the neck of his beer bottle toward the trio. "What gives?"

Camden grunted and shook his head like a bear with a hornet buzzing around it. "Elena's been in a mood all day because Elissa's latest douchebag went and dumped her right before they were supposed to go on this big trip."

Nash's heart sank. By the looks of it, she really did care about the guy. "So she's heartbroken."

"Oh, hell no." Camden took a swing. "Well, heartbroken

because now that she might not be going to Hawaii. She's been planning this..."

Camden's words faded into Nash's peripheral. Hawaii. Shit.

Before he realized what he was doing, Nash marched over to Elissa. She looked up, surprised, and her eyes locked on to his as her cheeks turned pink.

"Howdy, Elissa. Heard you might need someone to accompany you to Hawaii. I'm on leave right now and would love to take you."

Read about Nashville and Elissa in More Than Thrills, Watchdog Security Book 5

Want to read more about Pup's new life with Arden in Colorado? Pick up the first book in the Watchdog Protectors Series, Protecting Harper http://bitly.ws/e2wJ

Olivia's Lovelies

Never miss a release from Olivia Michaels by signing up for the Olivia Michaels Romance Newsletter. Be the first to read advance excerpts, see cover previews, and enter giveaways at https://oliviamichaelsromance.com/

Follow Olivia on BookBub at https://www.bookbub.com/authors/olivia-michaels
Want more? Come be one of Olivia's Lovelies on Facebook. I can always use another ARC reader or two...
https://www.facebook.com/groups/639545290309740/

AFTERWORD

Hi there! So, here's the part where I get to peek out from behind the story and talk to you.

More Than Paradise is the most complicated book I've ever written, plot-wise and, I think, character-wise as well. I've wanted to write about a person on the autism spectrum for a long time now because I'm an Aspie myself. There are so many misconceptions about people with autism, especially when it comes to emotions (yes, we have them!) and romance (yes, many of us like it a lot!).

I love the saying, "If you've met one person with autism, you've met...one person with autism." It's true to the point that I had a surprisingly hard time getting into Jordan's head at times because I didn't want to make her a carbon copy of me and because it required me to stop and look at how my own brain works, and then reverse-engineer it and compare it to how 'normal' brains work (is anyone really normal?). At times, it was a little like watching my feet while riding a bicycle. But in the end, I'm happy with who she became—someone who is not me, who has her own identity, her own struggles and strengths. Just like anyone else.

I hope you love her.

And I hope you love Elliot, who did a lot of growing in this book. I like a tortured hero (they're so much fun to poke at and then fix) and boy, did he fit the bill. He's perfectly imperfect. He surprised me with Anubis—I kept wondering why at the beginning I would write a scene and then when I got done, realize that I forgot to put Anubis in...again. It finally dawned on me that Costello was uncomfortable around his canine partner, which sent me off to wondering why. The more I thought about how he was raised, the more it became obvious—if he'd continued down the path he was going, one day Costello might have found himself being chased down by a guard dog Anubis.

I can't wait to see where Jordan and Costello go in the rest of the series, though I suspect they'll be raising a family here pretty soon.

So, here's the part where I say that all locations are fictional even if they share the names of real places. Same deal with any persons depicted—everyone is a product of my overworked imagination and not meant to represent any real-life people (or dogs).

I've tried to depict as accurately as possible military working dogs and service dogs—their training, their challenges, and their devotion to their people. There is an amazing program called Puppies Behind Bars (PBB) that trains prison inmates to work with dogs who become service animals that can do anything from detect explosives to helping wounded veterans and first-responders with PTSD. This is a win for everyone! I've known a couple of dogs trained in the program and they are simply amazing. So are the people who make PBB happen. For more information, check them out at https://www.puppiesbehindbars.com/

ALSO BY OLIVIA MICHAELS

Romantic Suspense

Watchdog Security Series

More Than Love

More Than Family

More Than Puppy Love

More Than Paradise

More Than Thrills

More Than Words Can Say (Coming Soon)

More Than Beauty (Coming Soon)

More Than Secrets (Coming Soon)

More Than Life (Coming Soon)

Watchdog Protectors Series

Protecting Harper

Protecting Brianna (Coming Soon)

Protecting Grace (Coming Soon)

And more...

ACKNOWLEDGMENTS

As always, thank you, Reader, for giving me a chance. I hope you enjoy reading both the Watchdog Security and Watchdog Protectors series and that I can give you a fun little escape from reality for a while. My goal is to create a world that you would love to live in, because those are *my* favorite kinds of books. I hope to see you around on Facebook, or join the newsletter at https://oliviamichaelsromance.com/ so I can thank you personally!

Undying gratitude to my mentors and friends Caitlyn O'Leary and Riley Edwards who have kept me sane and made me laugh—I hope I've been as much help to you as you've been to me. My Soul Sisters Michelle Jonjak and Sara Judson Brown. More undying gratitude to my writing sprint/brainstorming loves: Trinity Wilde, Ophelia Bell, Godiva Glenn, and Emily (What time is it where y'all are? You're kidding, right?) Becca Jameson, who is all of the above (Book's done and I'm heading your way! First round of margaritas and fajitas are on me!) My amazing assistant Amber Hamilton, who always goes above and beyond. Beta Reader Extraordinaire Marsha McDaniel and Kim Ruiz of the Eagle Eyes. Last but not least, fellow noob, Rayne Lewis. Special thank you to Susan Stoker for letting me play in your world!

Love and gratitude to you all!

ABOUT THE AUTHOR

Olivia Michaels is a life-long reader, dog-lover, gardener, and a certified beachaholic. When she's not throwing a Frisbee for her fur-baby, harvesting tomatoes, or writing, you can find her playing in the surf, kayaking, or kicking back on the sand and cracking open a hot and steamy beach read.

Made in the USA
Las Vegas, NV
24 July 2022

52086556R00184